THE HIGHLANDER'S ENGLISH BRIDE

"You are truly an awful man," Sabrina said to Graeme.

For the last few minutes, his instincts had been telling him to get her back to the house as soon as possible. Now, they were all but blowing trumpets in his ear.

"You love me anyway," he replied as he scanned their surroundings.

"In your dreams," she muttered.

That was exactly his dream, that Sabrina would love him. But he'd have to keep her alive first.

"Mr. Brown is incredibly well-mannered and kind, which is more than I can say for you." Sabrina gave a haughty little sniff. "In fact, I like him very much."

"Oh, do ye, now? And what, exactly, does that involve? More secret visits to the parsonage? More pints of ale in the local pub?"

"I will visit whomever I please." She jabbed Graeme in the chest again. By now, his cravat was likely demolished. "And you have nothing to say about it."

He leaned in so close that her peacock-blue eyes practically crossed. "Oh, I'll have something to say about it, lass. Count on it."

She blinked, then a slow smile curved up [...] mouth. "Well, I do believe you're jealous, Mr. [...]

THE
Highlander's English Bride

VANESSA KELLY

ZEBRA BOOKS
KENSINGTON PUBLISHING CORP.
www.kensingtonbooks.com

ZEBRA BOOKS are published by

Kensington Publishing Corp.
119 West 40th Street
New York, NY 10018

First Printing: June 2020
ISBN-13: 978-1-4201-4705-6
ISBN-10: 1-4201-4705-6

ISBN-13: 978-1-4201-4706-3 (eBook)
ISBN-10: 1-4201-4706-4 (eBook)

10 9 8 7 6 5 4 3 2 1

Printed in the United States of America

Chapter One

London, England
June 1822

Graeme Kendrick lurked beneath the giant elm, keeping his prey within sight. After losing the slippery *Sassenach* a few hours ago, he'd spotted the bastard climbing over the wall that separated Kensington Gardens from Hyde Park.

He'd surely earned that bit of luck. Graeme had spent the last month stalking the wiliest criminal gang to hit London in years. The thieves were ripping through the *ton* like marauding Norsemen, lifting expensive jewels, fine art, and precious antiques. Normally, this was a job for Bow Street, but when the Duke of York's gold pocket watch—a royal family heirloom—was filched at a ball, the situation had changed. King George was outraged, Bow Street was embarrassed, and Captain Aden St. George, England's chief spymaster, was summoned.

Much to Graeme's surprise, Aden had placed him in charge of the case.

While Graeme had come closer to finding the thieves than the Runners had, success continued to elude him. Each time, they'd dodged his grasp. Yesterday, Aden had made it clear how displeased he was with Graeme's lack of progress.

Very displeased.

It was even worse when the chief riding up one's backside was family. Aden was half brother to Victoria, Countess of Arnprior, who happened to be Graeme's sister-in-law. To make things even jollier, both Aden and Victoria were illegitimate offspring of the king himself, making old Georgie part of Graeme's extended family, too.

When it came to the Kendrick clan, familial relations were ridiculously complicated. If Graeme failed to crack this case, he would disappoint every member of his family, including the blasted *Sassenach* king.

Of course, in Graeme's world, disappointing family was baked into the oatcakes.

Keep your mind on the job, idiot.

He tugged off his rain-soaked cap and pushed back his damp hair with an even damper glove before shoving the cap back on. For some reason, his target had paused behind a tree near the Serpentine, the small lake that wound through the park.

Given the dreary weather and the early hour, Hyde Park was deserted. Locals would often frequent the area on a warm summer's morning, the more adventurous taking a dip in the Serpentine, but today the park was curtained in a steady drizzle, and a cool morning mist curled up from the wet earth.

"What the hell are you up to?" he muttered.

"Maybe he's hoping to snaffle a rich nob on his way home, just to round out the night."

Sighing, Graeme glanced over his shoulder. A sturdy lad of fifteen, clothed like an errand boy, hunkered down behind him.

"Got the jump on you, didn't I?" Tommy said with a cheeky grin.

"Lad, I haven't slept in twenty-four hours. I might be a bit off my game."

Tommy jerked his head in the direction of their quarry. "Good thing you spotted him coming over the wall. The captain would be right frosty if you lost the bastard again."

"And the captain's wife would be right frosty to hear you swearing. It's barely dawn. Does Lady Vivien know you're wandering about so early?"

"The captain does. He sent me to see if you needed help."

"Check on me, more like," Graeme scoffed. "It'll go down like a treat when Lady Vivien discovers he's sending you out on missions in the middle of the night. She's doing her best to make you a proper fellow, you know."

Tommy rolled his eyes. "I'm plenty proper, guv, and I do my lessons with her ladyship every day. But that don't mean I can't help the captain, when needs be. Besides, it ain't the middle of the night."

"*Doesn't* mean, and *isn't* the middle of the night," Graeme corrected before refocusing on the thief.

The man was waiting patiently for . . . something.

Graeme also forced himself to wait. But it had been a long night, tailing his prey from one gaming establishment to the next, all over the bloody town. The thief had obviously managed to befriend two wealthy but dim-witted noblemen. Briefly, Graeme had considered finding a way to warn the men they'd been marked. But he knew them, and they were mean-spirited bounders of the first order. If the fools had their pockets rifled by the end of the night, one could argue that Lady Justice had been served, albeit in a roundabout fashion.

Besides, Graeme had a bigger game to play—running the leader of the ring to the ground. To do that, he had to discover where the crime lord holed up. Somewhere in Covent Garden or the rookeries of St. Giles, he and Aden suspected. This morning's events might answer that question, since it seemed reasonable that the thief would soon be returning to the gang's lair with his ill-gotten gains.

Graeme would be on his tail.

"Come on, ye son of a whore," he whispered. "Get yer arse movin'."

"You're talking funny again," Tommy muttered.

"It's called a brogue, as ye well know."

"Still sounds funny, if you ask me."

Graeme snorted. When Tommy was excited or upset, his cant grew as thick as the brogue that emerged from Graeme when he was frustrated or angry. These days, that brogue surfaced more than he liked.

Then again, anger and frustration were better than rampant boredom. Better to be up to his eyeballs in danger and mayhem than sitting about like a useless ninny, bored out of his skull.

Or, worse, getting dragged to *ton* parties by Lady Vivien, who said he needed a *social life* to cheer him up.

"Nothing to be cheery about, anyway," he muttered.

Tommy threw him an odd look, which Graeme ignored, too tired to explain. It had been weeks since he'd had a good night's rest. Maybe Vivien was right. Maybe he *was* working too hard.

His companion jabbed him. "He's on the move."

Graeme unbent from his crouch. "Looks like he's heading straight along the footpath to Piccadilly. See if you can get ahead of him, in case he changes course and cuts up to one of the other gates."

Tommy nodded, but before he could dart off, Graeme clamped a hand on his shoulder. "Do *not* get close to him. He'll be armed, and Aden will skin me alive if anything happens to you."

The lad huffed with derision. "I ain't a flat, guv. I've been doing this longer than you have."

"I'm *not* a flat," Graeme absently corrected as the boy ghosted off into the mist and drizzle.

But Tommy was correct. He'd been a trusted part of the St. George household for four years now, running errands and delivering important messages. Still, he was more a member of the family than an errand boy or even an agent in training, and Graeme would cut off his own arm before he saw the lad placed in danger.

Before he saw *any* child placed in danger. He'd been stupid enough to allow that to happen once before, and . . .

He impatiently shook the gruesome image from his mind and slipped out from behind the tree. Following the path, he kept a respectable distance from the thief while doing his best to adopt the attitude of a local out for a leisurely morning stroll. Ridiculous, given the weather, but since the barmy bastard was all but creeping along the path, Graeme couldn't exactly set a brisk pace. The fellow was either up to something or suspected he was being followed.

If the latter, then Graeme had to be ready for the man to bolt.

When the thief slipped behind yet another bush and froze, Graeme realized his quarry was behaving like one of the barn cats at Castle Kinglas stalking a mouse. Moving deliberately closer to his target, exercising care not to be seen.

But who—

Graeme had his answer a moment later, when the man darted across a narrow strip of lawn that ran along the bank of the Serpentine. A figure was lingering by the water, a woman swathed in a dark cloak, a deep-brimmed bonnet serving as protection against the rain. Her back to them, she peered toward the footpath that led up to Grosvenor Gate, oblivious to her surroundings and absently swinging a plump-looking reticule. It didn't take a genius to realize what would happen next.

Mentally cursing, Graeme took off at a run. He'd be

damned if he let a woman be robbed, even if it meant blowing his cover. And why the *hell* hadn't he noticed her before? What in God's name was she doing here, anyway?

He closed the distance, but his thief was too far ahead.

"Lass, behind you," Graeme yelled at the top of his lungs.

The woman spun around, only to be seized by the thief.

Graeme spotted Tommy running in from the other direction. He threw out an arm to warn him off, but the lad ignored him, veering around a stand of oaks as he neared the couple.

The lady wasn't giving up without a fight, struggling mightily to keep ahold of her reticule.

"Let go of 'er, you stinkin' napper," Tommy yelled.

When the thief threw a startled glance at the boy, the woman kicked her assailant in the shin.

It only encouraged the bastard to redouble his efforts. He yanked the reticule from her grip, then tossed a glance over his shoulder at Graeme before grabbing the woman by the arms and dragging her to the very lip of the embankment. Then he shoved her over the edge.

The woman desperately windmilled her arms before toppling into the Serpentine with a resounding splash.

With Graeme closing in, the thief took off toward the closest gate to the park, directly into Tommy's path. The man slipped a hand into his jacket and pulled out a knife.

"Tommy, duck," roared Graeme.

The boy dove for the grass and rolled before coming up in a defensive crouch. The man kept running, heading for Piccadilly.

Graeme abandoned his pursuit. The woman was flailing about, obviously panicking as she struggled to keep her head above water, her sodden bonnet half covering her face.

"Hang on, lass," he called as he stripped off his coat.

The Serpentine, while a piddling excuse for a lake, was certainly deep enough to drown someone dressed in layers of clothing, including a heavy cloak. Water was a killer, as he knew all too well.

He leapt in, sending a huge splash over the woman, all but submerging her. By the time he reached her, she was sputtering some surprisingly salty oaths.

"I've got ye," he said, grabbing her shoulders.

She blindly swatted at him, the brim of her soaked bonnet now almost down to her chin. Still, she managed a good clout to his ear.

"Get away, you bounder," she gasped.

"You need help, guv?" Tommy called from the shore as Graeme struggled to keep himself and the woman from going under. She was a slender thing, but no weakling.

"I've got this," Graeme barked as he clamped his hands around the woman's ribcage and pulled her against his chest. "Get after the bastard, but do *not* get too close. Just follow and report back. I'll paddle your arse if ye do otherwise."

The lad nodded and took off. Probably a lost cause, but if anyone could catch up, Tommy could. Hopefully, he'd obey orders and keep his distance. This mission was now officially a cock-up, but Tommy was a bright one, and Graeme had to trust him to be smart now.

Right now, Graeme had to focus on keeping the woman in his arms from drowning them both, which she seemed determined to do.

"Stop strugglin', ye barmy lass." He managed to drag her toward the embankment. "I'm not tryin' to rob ye. That idiot's long gone, no thanks to ye."

The woman finally stopped swatting long enough to yank her bonnet away from her face. Graeme encountered a gorgeous—and furious—peacock-blue glare. That fury in no way detracted from the rest of her attractive face. Stunning, in fact, if one ignored the tangle of hair plastered to her forehead or the glob of mud across her perfectly straight nose and sharply delicate cheekbone.

"Release me, sir. Right *now*."

She gave him a surprisingly strong shove, which unfortunately caused her to lose her balance and go under again.

Sighing, Graeme hauled her back to the surface. "If you would hold still for a minute and let me get this bonnet off, you would see that I am not your assailant."

She stopped flopping about. He yanked the blasted hat back so it dangled from her neck instead of covering her face.

"I'm trying to rescue you," he added.

She glared at him. "You're making a hash of it, then. And I'm perfectly capable of rescuing myself."

"I don't think the man who attacked you would agree." Graeme pulled her to the edge of the greensward that surrounded the water.

"I was doing quite well on my own, thank you very much."

"Yes, I noticed that when you were tumbled into the water."

"Which only happened *after* you rushed up at us."

Graeme stared at her in disbelief. "He was attacking you, lass. What in God's name was I supposed to do? Stroll on by and let you two thrash it out?"

For a moment, it seemed she would continue her fiery tirade. Then she reached up and rubbed her nose, as if trying to prevent a sneeze. When she dropped her hand, Graeme saw her mouth curve up in a rueful smile. She had beautiful lips as plump and pink as a budding rose.

Which, of course, had nothing to do with anything.

"I sound awfully ungrateful, don't I?" she said. "It was very kind of you to jump in after me, although quite unnecessary. I'm a very good swimmer."

"No bogged down by that rig. That cloak must weigh twenty pounds by now."

"Perhaps you haven't noticed that we're both standing on the bottom. The Serpentine's not very deep at this end of the park."

Graeme looked down. He was only submerged to his waist, while the water reached her chest.

"It's deeper further out, but I only went under because he pushed me so hard," she said. "I was quite safe at all times."

Graeme couldn't help feeling annoyed. "To me, it looked like you were drowning. Anyone would have assumed that you *were* drowning."

"I was just surprised, that's all. But of course there was no way for you to know that," she hastily added.

He was beginning to get the sense that she thought him rather dim-witted. "It's not as if genteel ladies make a habit of paddling around in the Serpentine."

She nodded. "Correct. Having said that, do you think we could get on with the rescue?"

Apparently, he *was* a dimwit. "My apologies."

The lass shoved the wreck of her coiffure out of her eyes. "I'd like to get out of here before anyone sees us."

"Little chance of being seen with this weather."

A quick glance around the park confirmed it remained deserted. Even the men of the Royal Humane Society had failed to put in an appearance, despite all the watery flailing about. The small building on the opposite side of the Serpentine was staffed at all hours in the event a hapless Londoner needed rescuing. In this case, it probably hadn't occurred to the staff that anyone would be larking about on so dismal a morning.

Why *this* particular woman was larking about was the question. Because of her, Graeme had lost his thief. Again. And that was *incredibly* annoying.

"Thank goodness," she said. "Naturally, I'm grateful for

your help, but it might have been better if you hadn't come along at all."

Unbelievable.

He planted one hand on the embankment, keeping hold on her with the other. "How awkward of me. Thoughtless, really."

She crinkled her nose. "I just sounded rude again, didn't I?"

"Oh, not a bit."

"I will need your help climbing out of the water," she replied in an encouraging tone. "I'm positively waterlogged, and my fingers are rather chilled. Who knew the water would be this cold in the summer?"

It felt more like bath water to him, but he was a Highlander. He was used to mountain streams and lochs that could freeze the balls off a bull in August.

"Then let's get you out. Are you sure you've got your footing?"

She shoved her sodden cloak back over her shoulders. "Since I am now standing barely chest-deep, I believe I can manage to stay upright."

The mention of her chest naturally brought his gaze to that part of her anatomy. Her pale yellow dress was a sagging mess that exposed the tops of her stays. It also clung to what appeared to be a grand set of breasts—perfectly round and full. And she obviously *was* chilly, because even through the various layers of fabric, he could see the jutting of her pert nip—

"*Ahem.*"

Graeme jerked his head up to once again meet an irate peacock stare.

"Right," he said briskly. "Let's get to it."

He vaulted up onto the embankment, inadvertently splashing her with yet more water. She spluttered indignantly as he reached down a hand.

"Sorry," he apologized.

She wrapped her gloved fingers around his wrist. "I suppose you can't help it, since you *are* exceedingly large."

"Aye, that."

He hauled her out and set her on the grass, keeping a hand on her waist to steady her.

"And strong," she said, a trifle breathless. "And Scottish, obviously."

"Guessed that, did ye?"

She made a game attempt to shake out her dripping cloak. "I'm not a moron, sir, despite certain indications to the contrary."

"Never said you were. And you'll catch your death if you keep that stupid cloak on."

He swiped up his coat from the grass. While damp, it would be warm compared to her soaked garments.

The poor girl was shivering, and her pink lips held a tinge of blue around the edges. Graeme's worry spiked. If he didn't get her dry and warm, she could catch a fever. He'd seen it happen in his own family, and results had been dire.

"Let me help," he said, as she struggled with the ribbons of her cloak.

They were hopelessly knotted, so he just snapped them and tossed the cloak to the ground.

She grimaced. "That was new and *quite* expensive."

"Lass, you're safe. That's what matters. Now, let's get that bonnet off, too."

"Also new and expensive." She pulled off the offending headgear and tossed it onto the cloak.

He tucked his coat around her shoulders, then tapped one of her delicate gold earrings. Graeme had never found ears enticing before, but hers just might be the first.

"At least you didn't lose your earrings."

She pulled his coat tight around her body. "Thank you for this. It's so—"

Breaking off, she reached inside the jacket and gingerly extracted his knife.

"Sorry about that." He slipped the knife into his right boot.

"There seem to be a few other, er, implements in your pockets."

"Right. Sorry."

Feeling like ten times an idiot, Graeme extracted his pistol from one of the coat pockets, shoving it into the back of his breeches, then pulled a pair of knuckledusters from the other pocket. Those he tossed on top of her cloak before tucking the jacket back around her body.

She eyed him. "Are you by any chance a Bow Street Runner?"

"No, just the sort that likes to be prepared. Never know whom you'll run into, as you just discovered," he added with a wink.

His answer got the response it deserved. She shuffled back, which brought her dangerously close to the edge of the embankment.

"Watch it, miss. You don't want another dunking."

She studied him for a few moments longer before apparently making a decision. "I suppose if you wanted to murder me, you would have done it before now. But it is rather odd to be carrying so many weapons on one's person."

"No odder than a genteel young lady wandering alone in Hyde Park at the crack of dawn, in the rain."

Her eyes popped comically wide. "Oh, my goodness. Hannah!"

"Hannah?"

"My maid. I didn't want her to get wet, so I sent her off. . . . Oh, dear!"

She darted around him and headed toward a clump of oaks at the end of the lake. Graeme followed and saw that there *was* another person in the park—a girl who lay in a heap on the ground.

The woman crouched next to the slender girl, who looked to be a few years younger than her mistress. "Hannah must have fainted when I was attacked."

"How helpful of her."

"The poor thing obviously suffered a terrible shock."

"You're the one who suffered the shock. This one didn't even scream or try to help," Graeme said.

She started to pat the girl's cheek. "That is disappointing, but Hannah just came up from one of our country estates a few weeks ago. She finds London intimidating."

"Maybe you should give her a good shake. That might wake her up."

"I don't suppose you have any smelling salts?"

"I normally carry them right next to my pistol, but I seem to have forgotten them just this once."

She flashed him a scowl. "There's no need to be sarcastic."

"Really? I would disagree."

The whole situation was now officially beyond ridiculous. They were as wet as drowned hens, he'd lost his man, and he was beginning to grow concerned about Tommy. If the lad had taken any foolish risks, he'd never forgive himself—and Aden would probably kill him and be done with him once and for all.

"I do generally carry smelling salts, but they were in my reticule," she said.

"Perhaps the thief will find them useful," Graeme acerbically replied.

"Instead of making such unhelpful comments, perhaps you might do something useful instead."

"Such as?"

"You could drip on Hannah's face. That might do the trick."

When he laughed, it pulled a rueful smile to her lips. "There I am being rude again," she said.

"I canna blame you one bit," he replied. "But fortunately your girl seems to be recovering."

Hannah let out a moan as her eyelids fluttered open.

"Oh, my lady," she said faintly. "I was sure you were dead."

Ah. Not simply genteel. The drenched lassie was a member of the Quality.

"I'm fine, although quite wet," her mistress replied. "Why don't you try to sit up?"

When Graeme reached down to help, the maid let out a faint shriek. "He's still here, my lady. He'll kill us both!"

"Hannah, this gentleman *saved* me from my attacker. Now do please try to sit up."

They helped the maid to a sitting position and propped her against a tree.

"Are you sure he won't hurt us, my lady?" Hannah quavered, peering up at Graeme. "He looks a dodgy sort."

"Calling him a dodgy sort is hardly going to endear him to us."

"But who is he?" the maid asked.

Her mistress glanced over her shoulder, lifting an eyebrow at Graeme.

He sketched a brief bow. "I'm Graeme Kendrick, at your service."

"That don't tell us if you're respectable or not," the maid suspiciously answered.

"He's perfectly harmless, Hannah," her mistress said. "I assure you."

Perversely, Graeme found himself irritated by that description.

"What is now important," continued the young woman, "is returning home without anyone seeing us."

"But the other servants will be up by now, and you look

like something the cat drug in." Hannah grimaced. "I knew this were a bad idea, sneaking off to meet his lordship like—"

"We'll discuss that later," the young woman hastily interjected. "Besides, lamenting the situation will not solve anything."

"Might I make a suggestion? Lady . . ." Graeme pointedly trailed off.

She briefly pressed her lips into a flat line. "I'd rather not tell you."

Understandable, under the circumstances. Secretive meetings between members of the opposite sex rarely ended well, as he knew from painful experience.

"Are you acquainted with Lady Vivien St. George?" he asked.

She brightened immediately. "I am. Do you know her?"

"I'm well acquainted with both Lady Vivien and her husband. Their townhouse is only a few blocks from the park, as you probably know. You could get dry there, and Vivien could find you suitable clothing that should make it easier for you to return home."

"That is an excellent idea, sir," she said.

"Oh, miss, are you really going off with him?" Hannah cried in dismay.

"Mr. Kendrick has proven himself trustworthy," her mistress crisply replied. "Besides, if I don't get out of these clothes, I will turn into a block of ice."

A sudden and massively inconvenient image flashed through Graeme's mind. He was stripping off her clothes, and then warming her body with *his* body.

His naked body, naturally, since that was how his brain worked.

"But how will I explain where you are?" Hannah protested.

"You are to say that I'm still in bed with a headache,

and that you stepped out to the apothecary to fetch some headache powders."

"But Lady Sabrina, you never get a headache."

Graeme caught her flinch at the use of her name. He began flicking through his mental files to place it.

"I've certainly got one now," the lady muttered.

"Hannah, since the rain has finally let up," he said, "I suggest you be on your way. I'll see to your mistress."

"But—"

"Please do as he says, Hannah," Lady Sabrina said firmly.

"But how will you get back into the house?"

"I'll think of something. Just remember what I told you."

"Well, if you're sure," Hannah doubtfully replied.

"I am." Her mistress pointed a finger in the direction of the Stanhope Gate. "Now, please."

Casting Graeme a final, suspicious glance, Hannah bobbed a curtsy and hurried off in the direction of Mayfair.

"Can you trust her to do as instructed?" Graeme asked as he led Lady Sabrina back to retrieve her discarded garments.

"I hope so, or my goose is cooked. My father will go into hysterics if he finds out about this."

"Sneaking out to meet strange men rarely meets with parental approval, oddly enough."

She made an impatient sound. "There's nothing strange about this gentleman. He's perfectly respectable."

"Not if he's meeting young ladies at this time of day."

"Nonsense. Couples stroll in Hyde Park all the time."

Graeme snorted. "This early, and in the rain? Try again, lass."

"I *was* chaperoned, you know."

"Aye. Hannah seems quite the dependable sort."

Lady Sabrina muttered something under her breath while he bent down and quickly wrapped her cloak and bonnet into a neat bundle, after stashing his knuckledusters inside his waistcoat.

"Do you find you need those on a regular basis?" she politely asked.

"Only when I'm attending balls in Mayfair. Those affairs are cutthroat."

That elicited a reluctant smile. "After today, I'm thinking of getting a pair myself. Perhaps you might give me advice in that regard."

"They generally don't come in ladies' sizes."

She swiped a lock of bedraggled hair out of her eyes. Lady Sabrina had quite a lot of hair, thick and wavy, it seemed. Graeme suspected it would glow like the palest of wheat under a summer sun when dry.

"Ladies could use them, and more often than you think," she said in a serious tone.

Graeme had no doubt of that. Several of the women in his family had been forced to protect themselves under fairly dire circumstances.

He took her elbow to encourage her to pick up the pace. Now that the rain had eased off, traffic would soon pick up. In fact, someone had turned into the footpath and was trotting—

Tommy.

"Finally," he muttered.

"Someone you know?"

"Aye, he's a good lad. He works with me."

She shot him a curious look. "Mr. Kendrick, what exactly do you do? Besides rescuing damsels in distress."

"That's actually one of my prescribed duties."

Graeme was spared what was obviously going to be a tart reply when Tommy rushed up.

"Everything all right, guv? Is miss hurt?"

"We're fine," he replied. "Have any luck?"

Tommy's mouth twisted sideways. "Caught up with the blighter on Curzon Street, but he gave me the slip past Regent."

Dammit to hell.

"You can show me exactly where you lost him, later. I might get some ideas from that."

"Please do not trouble yourself on my account," Lady Sabrina said. "I'm sure he was just a common cutpurse."

When Tommy shot him a look, Graeme gave a slight shake of the head.

"As you wish," he said to her. "Tommy, could you run ahead and fetch a hackney? I'm taking the lady to the captain's house. She and Lady Vivien are friends."

"Really? 'Cause ladies ain't usually hanging around the park by themselves, 'specially not this time of day," the boy replied with his usual and fatal candor.

When Lady Sabrina bristled, Graeme cuffed him on the shoulder. "No cheek from you, lad."

Tommy let out a dramatic sigh. "I didn't mean no offense, miss. My name's Tommy, by the way. Pleased to meet you."

"And I'm happy to meet you. My name is . . ."

When she hesitated, Graeme finished for her. "Lady Sabrina Bell."

She flashed him a startled look "How did you know that?"

Graeme led her toward Knightsbridge, as Tommy jogged ahead. "I think you'll discover I know quite a lot, my lady."

Her silence suggested she wasn't best pleased with his answer.

Chapter Two

Sabrina rarely set a foot wrong when it came to dealing with gentlemen, but she'd made a capital blunder with the blasted marquess. Now she had to hope that Mr. Kendrick could shield her from the consequences of her error.

"Serves you right," she muttered to herself. She'd ignored her instincts when it came to this morning's assignation.

She couldn't be blamed for falling afoul of a cutpurse, though. And who in his right mind would shove a person into the Serpentine?

Kendrick peered down at her. "What was that?"

Even when sitting he loomed over her, and also quite squished her into the panels of the hackney coach. Scottish people did seem to run on the brawny side, perhaps an effect of the clean Highland air.

"Nothing of any note, sir."

She shifted, but there wasn't an inch between them from their shoulders to their knees. And given how damp they both were, and how Kendrick's wet buckskins clung to his muscled thighs and to . . . well, the rest of him, Sabrina couldn't help feeling unnerved.

Drat the blasted marquess. It was most disappointing that his lordship had proved so unreliable.

Then again, men generally disappointed her.

"We're both dripping wet, which is no fun," Kendrick said. "I had to pay the coachman half a guinea before he let us into this confounded thing."

"I'm happy to pay for the coach, sir."

He flashed her a ridiculously charming grin, one that no doubt had susceptible ladies swooning on a regular basis. Thank goodness she was impervious to such masculine charms.

Mostly.

"Och, don't fash yourself, my lady. I'm good for it."

He had an interesting voice, a rough sort of purr laced with a brogue. His eyes were an arresting shade of forest green, and his forceful jaw paired with a firm mouth that seemed more inclined to scowl than smile.

When he did manage to smile, it made one's heart skip a beat, which Sabrina found *quite* annoying.

As for the rest of him, his wet hair appeared to be a dark red, and his lean cheeks sported bristle. He seemed an odd combination of rough and refined, and it was the rough part that had initially panicked her.

That he was both kind and a gentleman was not in doubt. What sort of gentleman was he, though? Sabrina had a finely honed sense of social distinctions. Not that she judged one's character by such a standard, but it did help in deciding how to respond to people in various situations.

That this was a social setting she'd never before encountered went without saying.

"Are you cold?" he asked.

The husky note to his voice sent a little thrill coursing through her body. She firmly quashed it, as she did the memory of him gazing at her chest while they were in the water. He'd seemed quite appreciative, and she'd been forced to communicate her disapproval.

"Indeed, no. Your coat is very warm and comfortable."

Especially once she'd divested a hidden inner pocket of

yet another knife, one she'd discovered when she sat down on it in the carriage. Fortunately, it was encased in a sturdy sheath.

Although quite certain Mr. Kendrick was not a member of the criminal classes, Sabrina wondered what he did for a living.

It's none of your business.

"You must be chilled, though," she added.

"Och, no. Anyway, we're almost there."

"It might have been faster if we'd walked to Captain St. George's house."

Their destination was a townhouse off Cadogan Square, normally a short drive from the park. But the rain had made for slow going.

Kendrick chuckled. "Yes, I'm sure Lord Musgrave would have been thrilled to hear of us strolling about town, looking like a pair of mud larks. Let's hope that maid of yours is trustworthy, by the way."

She winced. If Father ever found out about this little expedition, she was sunk. "If Hannah does bungle the story, I'll simply say I needed some fresh air and stepped out for a stroll."

"Yes, nothing sets one up like a toddle in the pouring rain, I always say."

"One problem at a time, Mr. Kendrick," Sabrina firmly replied. "Right now, I am simply desperate to get out of these wet clothes."

He looked blankly down at her for a moment before shifting uncomfortably on the seat. Clearly, he wasn't the only one feeling rather squished.

"I told the driver to take us around to the mews." His voice sounded oddly strained. "We'll use the kitchen entrance to avoid being seen."

"I imagine it'll be quite the surprise when we appear like this."

"No worries, lass. Tommy ran ahead to warn St. George."
Kendrick pulled a slight grimace. "Sorry. I should be calling
you Lady Sabrina. I'm much too informal."

Sabrina rather liked it when he called her lass, which was
absurd. "You must admit that our introduction has been
decidedly less than formal."

"That's one way of putting it."

He'd gone back to sounding grim. Once again, she got
the feeling he was immensely frustrated about something—
not her, per se, or her idiotic accident. It was obvious that
he hadn't simply been taking a morning constitutional. He'd
been in the park for a reason, and her topple into the Serpentine had knocked him off course.

Still, there was nothing she could do but apologize,
which she'd already done. Right now, her primary objective
was avoiding the incineration of her life from a horrendous scandal of her own making. Even though the marquess
was a handsome and charming man, he certainly wasn't
worth *this* much trouble. At the end of the day, what man
truly was?

The hackney took a sharp turn, all but tumbling her into
Kendrick's lap. She once more became sharply aware of
his muscled thighs and imposing body—aware in a way she
found shocking. Especially since the front of his wet
breeches perfectly outlined—

Sabrina righted herself. "I beg your pardon."

"We're here," he brusquely replied.

He was already opening the door and swinging out before
the carriage came to a complete halt.

Trying to ignore the heat rushing to her face, she took his
hand and stepped down with as much dignity as she could
muster.

"You're very flushed," Kendrick said with a frown. "I
hope you're not catching a fever."

She mentally winced. "I'm sure I'm not. I rarely fall ill."

There was an awkward pause.

"Oh, well, that's splendid," he replied.

This had to count as the most embarrassing day of her life, and the clock had yet to strike nine.

He steered her to a sturdy iron gate in the garden wall. Extracting a key from his waistcoat, he unlocked the gate and ushered her through, pausing to lock it behind him. His caution seemed excessive, but more to the point—why did *he* have a key to St. George's garden?

Kendrick led her along a gravel path through a small but pretty enclosure. A tidy kitchen garden was tucked into one corner, while a wrought-iron gazebo, surrounded by beds of roses, took up the rest of the space. Even in the rain it was a charming retreat, and a great deal more welcoming than the formal Italianate gardens behind Musgrave House.

At the end of the walk stood a modern-looking brick townhouse. The St. Georges had moved to Cadogan Square shortly after their marriage, and now led a life of quiet domesticity. Since Lady Vivien, a vivacious and charming social butterfly, had once been one of the most popular beauties of the *ton*, Sabrina still found the change in her friend rather mind-boggling.

"There you are," cried the lady herself as Sabrina stepped down into a low-ceiled and blessedly warm kitchen.

Vivien, in a frivolous dressing gown and an even more frivolous nightcap, dodged around the cook, the kitchen maid, and a footman, all of whom seemed unsurprised by either their mistress's unconventional appearance or by a pair of bedraggled guests muddying up the clean stone floor.

Ignoring Sabrina's bedraggled state, Vivien gave her a hug before turning to a neatly dressed, middle-aged man who appeared from the pantry with a stack of clean towels. "Ah, Simpson, thank you."

She removed the damp coat from Sabrina's shoulders

and replaced it with a wonderfully thick towel. Then she turned to Kendrick.

"Graeme, I do hope you're not responsible for Lady Sabrina's condition. I'll be most annoyed if you are."

Kendrick, who'd taken a towel to dry his head, regarded her with disbelief. "I'm the one who pulled her pretty arse out of the Serpentine. She'd have been in quite the fix if I hadn't come along."

After recovering from the shock of his outré language, Sabrina bristled. "I would have been perfectly fine. The water wasn't even over my head."

"Yes, and I'm sure you could have then strolled right home through Mayfair. And let's not even mention your idiotic maid."

"What happened to your maid?" Vivien asked.

"She fainted when the cutpurse pushed me into the water," Sabrina replied.

"How dreadfully unhelpful of her. Perhaps you might think about hiring a new maid, my dear."

Sabrina blinked, nonplussed by her friend's casual attitude toward the morning's events. "Er . . ."

"And what," Vivien interrupted, leveling a glare at Kendrick, "were you doing while all this pushing and fainting was going on? Aden will be most displeased to hear that you allowed this to happen, Graeme."

"That'll be a change of pace," Graeme sarcastically replied. "The fact is, I wasn't close enough to stop the blighter from attacking the silly girl, or I obviously would have."

Silly? Sabrina was *never* silly.

You were this morning.

"I was simply minding my own business when that dreadful man decided to rob me," she said, adopting a tone of offended dignity.

"Minding your own business?" he said. "What young

lady in her right mind goes larking around the park at that hour of the morning?"

Vivien scrunched up her nose. "Graeme does make rather a good point, my dear. Fashionable persons rarely stroll in the park before noon, and certainly not in a downpour."

Sabrina's cheeks heated again. This was not a conversation she wanted to have in front of the servants, although, to be fair, none of them seemed the slightest bit interested. Simpson stood with a patiently resigned attitude, as if these sorts of events happened on a regular basis.

"Vivien, I'm absolutely desperate to get out of these wet things," she said. "Do you think we could hold off further explanations until I do so?"

Her friend was instantly diverted. "Goodness, we're all brutes to keep you standing here. And I'm sure Cook is beside herself at the mess Graeme is making of her kitchen."

"I'm not doing anything," Kendrick protested.

"You're dripping," Vivien replied. "Drips make Cook positively demented."

The cook, a tall, lanky woman with an impressively competent manner, rolled her eyes as she assembled a lavish tea service that Sabrina devoutly hoped was for her, since she was positively famished.

"Not to worry, my lady," Cook said in brisk Yorkshire accent. "I've sent up hot water and a maid to assist her ladyship, and the tea tray will be up in a twinkle."

Vivien beamed. "You're a gem, Evans. What would we do without you?"

"Starve to death, most likely," the woman responded.

Sabrina blinked at their familiar exchange. Clearly, the household was more than slightly unconventional. That wasn't surprising, since Vivien had always been somewhat eccentric herself. There'd been quite the scandal over her marriage—something about a Russian prince, whom she'd thrown over in a very exciting fashion for the mysterious Aden St. George. Sabrina was some years younger than her friend and had barely emerged from the schoolroom at the time, so she'd never known the full details.

Vivien took her arm. "Let's get you dry and into something warm." She shot Kendrick a warning look. "Once *you* change, you're to report to Aden."

"Lucky me."

"And whatever happened to the maid?" Vivien asked. "Surely you didn't leave her lying under a bush in the park?"

Kendrick looked up at the low ceiling, as if searching for patience. "We sent her home with instructions to say that Lady Sabrina was still in bed, nursing a headache."

"Quick thinking on your part," Vivien said.

"It was Lady Sabrina's idea," he replied.

Vivien let out a delicate snort before leading Sabrina to the stairs.

Glancing over her shoulder, Sabrina threw Kendrick an apologetic smile. He simply shrugged and went back to drying his hair. It was now a beautiful russet shade, as vibrant as an autumn leaf.

"I do owe poor Mr. Kendrick a debt of gratitude," she said as she followed Vivien up the back staircase. "He was quite helpful in such unpleasant circumstances."

"Graeme knows I'm teasing. Mostly. He can be reckless, so the occasional reprimand does him good."

"I never thought of you as the managing sort, Vivien, but you seem quite good at it."

"Not as good as you, dear. Your ability to manage gentlemen of all sorts is legendary."

Sabrina sighed. "I seem to have slipped a jot this morning."

"Ah, so you *were* meeting someone in the park."

"Why else would I do something so stupid?"

Vivien steered her down the second floor hall. "You can tell me all about it once you're warm and dry."

"And I'd better be quick. If I don't get home . . ."

"Graeme and Aden will come up with a plausible story. They're quite good at that sort of thing."

From the end of the hall, a long-case clock bonged out the hour.

"Drat," Sabrina muttered. "Already eight o'clock."

Vivien cocked her head. "Yes, the children are certainly awake," she said with a smile.

"I'm so sorry to drag you out of bed for something this ridiculous."

"Nonsense. Aden and I are both early risers. That man is up at the crack of dawn most mornings." She cut Sabrina a sly smile. "Which means I am, too."

Sabrina huffed out a laugh as Vivien ushered her into a cozy bedroom. Decorated in shades of cream and primrose, it had comfortably modern furnishings piled high with cushions covered in lovely floral fabric.

Even more appealing were the roaring fire in the grate and the bowl of hot water on the Sheraton-style dressing table. A maid bustled about, laying out a flannel wrapper and a fresh set of underclothes. Sabrina slipped behind a wooden screen to strip off her clammy garments. A minute or so later, she heard the tea tray arrive. After it was set up, Vivien dismissed the servants.

Attired in the wrapper, Sabrina came out to find a steaming cup of tea and a plate of pastries on a small table by the fire.

"Wash your hands and face, and then let me comb your hair," Vivien said. "You look like someone dragged you through a thorn bush."

Sabrina meekly washed up before gratefully sinking into

a low chair. "You shouldn't be waiting on me, Vivien. I'm sure you have other things to do."

"Nonsense. Besides, I'm simply dying of curiosity. Tell all, darling."

Sabrina took a sip of tea. "That's what I'm afraid to do."

"I won't breathe a word, I promise."

"I believe you, but it's too late. Your servants have seen me."

Vivien carefully began to detangle Sabrina's locks with a silver comb. "Our staff never gossip. Aden wouldn't allow it."

"But—"

"My husband's duties at Court require the utmost discretion from this household. There will be no gossip as a result of your visit this morning."

"Not even from Mr. Kendrick? Or Tommy?"

"Tommy is completely reliable, as is Graeme."

"I thought you said he was reckless."

"Certainly not with a lady's reputation."

They were silent for a few moments as Sabrina ate a pastry and Vivien worked the comb through a particularly bad snarl.

"Who *were* you meeting in the park?" Vivien finally prompted.

"Tell me about Mr. Kendrick first," Sabrina stalled. "He seems like a gentleman, although he's rather gruff. He works for your husband, I take it."

Vivien laughed. "That was a commendable dodge, pet."

Sabrina sighed. "I'd like to know more, since I got the sense that my stupid accident was more than a simple inconvenience to him."

Vivien's hand paused. "What do you mean?"

"He seemed . . . well, frustrated. As if I'd interrupted some important task."

"Like a mysterious assignation in the park, for instance?"

Sabrina twisted around to look at her. "You think he was meeting a lady? He gave no indication of such a thing."

Vivien's mouth twitched. "You don't know Graeme Kendrick."

Sabrina repressed a scowl as she turned back around. "He certainly didn't seem the sort to engage in . . ."

Drat. Secret assignations. Like she'd been doing.

"As I said, Graeme can be reckless, but he *is* a gentleman," Vivien replied.

"So was the man I was meeting. In fact, he's a wealthy aristocrat."

Vivien came round to settle in the chair on the other side of the hearth. "Why doesn't this aristocrat simply take you for a proper stroll at a proper hour?"

"You know how hard it is to have a decent conversation with a man. Everyone is *always* watching."

"There's a reason for that, dearest."

"I'm not a chit just out of the schoolroom, Vivien. I've been running my father's household for years."

Vivien wriggled her feet, encased in frivolous feathered mules, closer to the fire. "Why not invite him to Musgrave House and take a quiet stroll in the gardens? I'm sure you could easily find a private corner to chat."

Sabrina waved an impatient hand. "Father would hate that. He fusses when it comes to potential suitors."

"Your dearest papa is afraid you'll marry and leave him."

"Honestly, I haven't been that keen on the idea either. I've yet to meet one blasted man who could tempt me to . . ." She twirled a hand. "Rather the opposite, actually."

"That's because you haven't met the right one."

"Well, they can't all be like Captain St. George. He's the very definition of dashing."

Vivien breathed out a happy sigh. "He is at that. But how about Graeme? He's certainly not your average gentleman of the *ton*. He's a Highlander, for one thing." She flapped a hand in front of her face. "My dear, that brogue. *So* delicious."

"Vivien St. George, and you a married woman with children!"

"Very happily married, which means I have an excellent eye—and ear—for the right sort of man."

"Surely you cannot be serious. Mr. Kendrick was exceedingly . . ."

Attractive.

". . . Bossy," she concluded.

"He's a man, Sabrina. And a wise woman bosses right back. I suspect you could manage Graeme Kendrick quite well."

"I literally just met the man," Sabrina replied, exasperation setting in. "While I was waiting to meet *another* man, I might add."

"And he didn't bother to make an appearance."

Sabrina grabbed the comb from Vivien's hand and began to unsnarl the last of her tangles. "This is a ridiculous conversation. Besides, if my father wouldn't approve of a lord with a large estate, he certainly wouldn't countenance a mister. Especially not a Scottish mister."

"But your mother was Scottish, and you were born a stone's throw from the border. How can Lord Musgrave not approve of Scotland?"

"We were residing at our Northumberland estate at the time of Mamma's illness. Father is convinced she'd still be alive if we'd been in London, where we could have accessed the best physicians."

Her mother had died of an infectious fever before Sabrina was even three years old, carried off in less than a week. Since the poor lady had always been in delicate health according to Father, it seemed unlikely that any doctor could have saved her.

Vivien's blue gaze softened with sympathy. "I'm so sorry, dearest."

Sabrina shrugged. It always felt awkward speaking of her mother, since she had so few memories of her.

"Thank you. It affected Father dreadfully, of course. He loathes the country now, especially the north. He'd fall into hysterics if I so much as gave a single thought to marrying a plain old mister from Scotland."

"There's nothing plain about Graeme Kendrick. He's the brother of the Earl of Arnprior, which means he's the brother-in-law of—"

Sabrina almost dropped the comb. "No!"

"Yes. Brother-in-law of Victoria, Lady Arnprior, the illegitimate daughter of the king himself."

"Lady Arnprior is your husband's half sister."

It was one of the worst kept secrets of the *ton* that Aden St. George was the natural son of King George IV. Sabrina had forgotten about Lady Arnprior—not surprising, since the king and his royal brothers had quite a shocking number of children born on the wrong side of the sheets.

"And that means Graeme is part of our family, too." Vivien ruefully smiled. "Although it does get rather complicated when one isn't supposed to publicly acknowledge such relationships."

When the bracket clock on the mantel chimed out the hour, Sabrina grimaced.

"I wish Mr. Kendrick the best, and I'm grateful to him," she said. "But I simply must be on my way. If you would let me borrow your carriage, I would be desperately grateful."

Vivien rose. "Of course. But won't you tell me who you were meeting in the park?" She pointed a finger. "I do think you owe me."

"Blackmail, in other words," Sabrina wryly replied as she crossed to the bed to begin dressing.

Her friend's gaze sparkled with mischief. "I'm quite good at that sort of thing."

"I suppose it doesn't matter, since the wretch never showed up. It was the Marquess of Cringlewood."

Chapter Three

Aden St. George reached for a decanter tucked into the inset bookshelves of his study and poured a splash of brandy into a glass. "It's barely nine in the morning, Graeme, but I think you need this."

"Since I've been up all night, let's call it a last drink before I get to bed."

Graeme had learned to appreciate a good brandy almost as much as a good Highland whisky, like the one he'd brewed in his illegal still on Kendrick land. He and his twin had caught holy hell for that adventure once Nick had discovered their secret.

As he propped his booted feet against a cast-iron firedog, Graeme relished the fact that he was once more warm and dry. While he had a set of rooms at Albany House, he maintained a spare bedroom here at Aden's that was stocked with clothing for emergencies, which now included dragging damsels out of the Serpentine.

Aden settled into the other club chair and poured a cup of coffee from the breakfast service on the table between them.

Nothing in the generous spread tempted Graeme. He hadn't much of an appetite these days. Meals often consisted of a pasty from a stall in Covent Garden or a hastily bolted plate of beef and a pint of heavy wet in a tavern before heading back out on the thieves' elusive tails. This morning had been the closest he'd ever gotten to the bastards.

"Thank you for not raking me over the coals," he said.

"I'm reserving that right," his chief replied with a wry smile. "Although there wasn't much you could do, given the circumstances."

"Silly chit," Graeme muttered into his glass.

"On the contrary. Lady Sabrina is an extremely sensible young woman."

"Lurking about Hyde Park at dawn, in the rain, is an extremely sensible activity for young ladies?"

"It's odd, I admit."

"She was meeting a bloke. That was clear enough."

"Suitors have been lining up for years to woo her. Lady Sabrina has no need to lurk in parks."

Graeme ignored the irritated twinge in his gut. "She's no deb just out on the marriage mart, obviously."

Aden put down his cup. "Sabrina has been running her father's household for years. Lord Musgrave is quite dependent on her, and he leaves the ordering of his domestic affairs in her capable hands. Given how much freedom and wealth she has, I suppose there's not much incentive to marry."

"Why tie yourself down to some rakehell who will likely ignore you, while spending every last shilling of your fortune on gambling, horses, or mistresses."

Aden flashed a sardonic smile. "Says the former rakehell."

"With the emphasis on *former*. Can't say as I blame the lass for wanting to avoid the marital state. If she's wealthy, what does she have to gain by marrying some toff who'll have the controlling of her?"

"I suspect that no one controls Lady Sabrina."

"I suspect you're right. She actually had the nerve to reprimand me for rescuing her."

Aden laughed. "That sounds just like her. But the point remains—what was she doing meeting someone in the park at that hour of the morning?"

"Maybe she's changed her mind about marriage," Graeme said. "Women do tend to be fickle in that regard."

"Perhaps you're simply spending time with the wrong women."

"Or the right ones."

Aden ignored the lame jest. "I find your view of the married state unnecessarily jaded, Graeme. I wonder where it comes from?"

Graeme tried not to shift under his chief's uncomfortably penetrating perusal. It reminded him too much of his oldest brother Nick's gaze. The Laird of Arnprior possessed an uncanny ability to read his mind, as if Graeme's skull was made of glass.

"Shouldn't we be focusing on my assignment instead of on that blasted girl? Tommy and I would have run the blighter to ground, if not for that stupid escapade."

Graeme shot down the rest of his brandy in one gulp before rising to refill his glass. When he returned and sank back into his seat, the leather and wood loudly creaked, causing Aden to wince.

Graeme shot him a weak smile. "Sorry."

"Vivien was forced to replace two chairs in the dining room. If you break another one, it's coming out of your wages."

For no reason that anyone could deduce, Graeme and his twin had always possessed an unerring capacity to destroy furniture. It was a running joke in the Kendrick family, although he was beginning to find it tiresome.

"Best just dock me now, since it's bound to happen again."

Exhaustion from the long night tugged at his bones.

Something else also tugged at him, a sense of failure, or even shame.

"Are you all right, Graeme?"

He forced a smile. "Och, of course. Why wouldn't I be?"

Aden cocked his head. "I don't know. That's why I'm asking."

"I'm frustrated. This mission has turned into a royal cock-up, and I'm not sure why. It's not the hardest assignment I've ever had from you. Not by a long shot."

In working for Aden these last two years, Graeme had undertaken some truly dangerous missions. Initially, his chief had been cautious, pairing Graeme with experienced agents—partly to blunt the fussing from Graeme's blasted family, especially his sister-in-law, Victoria. But he'd soon proved himself especially adept at undercover work. Almost single-handedly, he'd disrupted a dangerous smuggling ring off the coast of Kent within his first six months on the job.

Despite his family's misgivings, Graeme didn't give a hang about the danger or the difficulties. He'd never been much good at anything, but he was good at running criminals to ground. His work gave him a sense of satisfaction he'd never felt before.

Until this case.

Aden put down his coffee cup. "Frankly, in recent days you seem restless and lacking in focus. That might be having an impact on this mission."

Graeme mentally winced at his chief's too-accurate assessment. He *was* restless these days. To his surprise, he was missing Scotland, especially the windswept peaks and rolling glens of Kinglas, the family estate. As a lad, he'd never been able to imagine living anywhere but within that awe-inspiring and challenging landscape of mountain, loch, and sky.

But eventually both Kinglas and the family mansion in

Glasgow had grown confining. As much as he loved his brothers and their growing broods, Scotland had begun to seem quaint and provincial.

So Graeme had leapt at the chance Aden had offered him. For those first months, Graeme had loved everything about London and his new life, the whole sprawling, glorious, and gritty mess of it. He'd finally found something that mattered, something he was good at.

Now, though, his sense of purpose was slipping away, and he'd be damned if he knew how to stop the slide.

Aden sighed. "I should have sent you back home after that last job. You needed time to rest and be with your family. It was a mistake to reassign you so quickly."

"Bollocks," Graeme quickly answered. "That was my mistake, not yours. Besides, it turned out all right in the end. That bastard will never hurt another child, or anyone else. I saw to that, didn't I?"

Sadly, the little girl he'd rescued that day might never get over the shock of the gruesome scene. The poor, wee lass had seen everything, including what Graeme had been forced to do to protect her from her own father.

Aden pinned him with a stern eye. "You did the right thing, but you were almost killed. It was a near thing, Graeme. Too near."

The memories of that day still made him queasy. "I'm fine, ye ken."

"Another inch to the left, and you would have been dead," Aden said, shaking his head.

"It was just a flesh wound, man. Nothing to get fashed about."

Actually, it had been a nasty flesh wound that had laid him up for three weeks. If Graeme hadn't twisted aside at the last moment, that knife would have sliced through his kidney and God only knew what else.

Still, there was now one less monster prowling the streets of London.

"My sister was quite fashed as I recall," Aden tartly replied. "I thought she and your grandfather were going to flay me alive for that incident."

"My family knows I'm exactly where I want to be, doing exactly what I want to do."

Aden's dark gaze turned hawk-like. "But are you? Really?"

Graeme was spared an uncomfortable reply when Vivien sailed into the room, holding the hand of Maggie, her six-year-old daughter. When the bairn saw him, she screeched with joy and threw herself into his arms.

"Hullo, lassie," he said, hoisting her onto his lap. "How are ye this grand mornin'? Yer lookin' as pretty as the May queen."

She giggled at his brogue, which he always adopted to tease her.

Margaret Edwina St. George was a miniature of her mother. Blond and blue-eyed, she had a sweet, snub-nosed countenance. Thankfully, she was also good-natured, since everyone, especially her papa, spoiled her rotten.

Right now, however, Papa was regarding her with a mixture of fondness and exasperation as Maggie patted Graeme's cheeks.

"Uncle Graeme, you're whiskery."

"That's because I've been up all night, hard at work."

Maggie twisted in his lap to frown at her father. "Uncle Graeme was sick. You shouldn't make him work so hard, Papa. It's mean."

Aden threw his wife an incredulous look. "Really?"

Vivien came over to lean against her husband's chair. "She has a point."

"I'm in capital shape, Vivi," Graeme replied. "You know that better than anyone."

When he'd recuperated in the St. George household, Vivien had cared for him with terrifying competence, shoving noxious potions down his throat and threatening him with dire consequences if he dared to get out of bed too soon. Much to his surprise, Graeme had enjoyed the fussing—not that he'd had much choice, given his condition.

Once he'd gotten over the worst of it, Maggie had been allowed into his room. There, she'd spent hours reading to him from her schoolroom primers, until Graeme had grown so desperate he'd begun teaching her to play piquet. Aden had been rather stormy about that, but Vivien had approved. Vivien was a terror at cards and was thrilled that her daughter had inherited her mathematical skills.

Maggie returned her little hand to Graeme's cheek, turning his face back to hers. "Mamma and I have to take care of you. We promised Aunt Vicky and Uncle Nick."

The child's earnest gaze made Graeme's chest go tight.

"I'm fine, sweet lass," he said gruffly. "I promise."

But when he caught the glance between Aden and Vivien, he swallowed an oath.

"I'm *fine*," he said.

"No need to get testy, laddie boy," Vivien replied.

"Laddie boy? I'm twenty-nine years old, Vivi."

"Not too old for me to scold, and I certainly will if you need it."

Graeme threw Aden a speaking glance.

His chief came to his rescue. "My love, as delightful as it is to see you and Maggie, Graeme and I are working."

His wife heaved a sigh. "Maggie wanted to see her uncle. I couldn't possibly say no."

The little girl nodded. "I haven't seen Uncle Graeme in days and days."

"Sweetheart, you saw me three days ago," Graeme replied. "Besides, your da is right. We're having a right serious conversation about work."

Maggie brightened up. "Oh, did you have to give someone a drubbing or haul them off to the clink?"

Graeme managed to choke down a laugh. It was no mystery how Maggie picked up her colorful vocabulary. The household servants were either retired spies or still on active service. They protected the St. George household and acted as Aden's eyes and ears throughout London. While they doted on Vivien and the children and would give their lives for them, more than a few could be described as rough about the edges.

Aden tried to establish a normal atmosphere in the house for the sake of his wife and children. Normal, however, would never apply to the seemingly quiet townhouse off Cadogan Square.

"Darling, you mustn't use cant," Vivien said. "Papa doesn't like it."

Aden directed a paternally stern look at his daughter. "Young ladies mustn't use rough language, sweetheart. It's not proper."

Maggie looked perplexed. "But Papa, you say words like that all the time, and you're a gentleman. Why do gentlemen get to say fun things and ladies don't?"

"I say," said Graeme, "I'd like to know the answer to that one, too."

Vivien cut off her husband's impending lecture. "It's because Papa is a spy, Maggie. Spies say all sorts of odd things."

Aden stared at his wife in disbelief. "Vivien St. George, spy is *not* a term we use in this household."

"Oh, pish. Maggie would have to be very dim not to notice all the clandestine activities, and my daughter is very far from dim."

"That is not a reassuring answer," Aden replied.

"I'm very good at keeping secrets, Papa," Maggie said in a solemn tone. "I want to be a spy just like you some day, so I practice very hard to keep *all* the secrets."

Aden covered his eyes.

"You're certainly very good at making up stories, which is a useful attribute in a spy," Vivien said. "Just this morning, you told me that Justin broke your rocking horse."

The little girl's chin stubbornly tilted. "But he did, Mamma."

"Hmm, I wonder how your little brother managed to do that, since he was sleeping, and you were actually *on* the rocking horse at the time."

Maggie crinkled her nose. "Did Nurse tell you that? Maybe she needs new spectacles."

Graeme couldn't help it. He had to laugh. "Aye, you'll make a grand spy, lass. You already know how to tell a whopper with a straight face."

Her chubby cheeks split into a happy grin. "Thank you, Uncle Graeme."

Aden's glare threatened dire consequences.

"Do not encourage her, you idiot." Then Aden switched his irate gaze to his wife. "Vivien . . ."

She took pity on her beleaguered husband. "Maggie, say good-bye to Uncle Graeme, and then you can have breakfast with Nurse and your brother."

Maggie breathed out a gusty sigh. "Do I have to? Justin always makes a mess."

"He's only three, darling, and he's a boy. Messes are what they do."

Graeme dropped a kiss on top of Maggie's bright curls.

"Your mam is right, lass. I'm a grown man, and I still make messes."

"That is certainly true," Aden sarcastically replied. "Speaking of the latest one, I assume Lady Sabrina is now safely on her way home?"

"Maggie and I sent her off in the carriage just before we came to see you," Vivien said. "She extended her regards and thanks to both you and Graeme."

"I'm the one who did all the work," Graeme said. "You'd think she could at least make a proper good-bye."

Vivien wriggled a hand. "She was embarrassed, and so preferred to slip out. I know she's very grateful."

He affected a casual shrug. "Doesn't matter. I'm sure I'll never see her again."

Maggie craned around to study his face. "But Uncle Graeme, when Papa first met Mamma, he rescued her, and then they went and got married. Maybe you're supposed to marry a lady when you rescue her."

Graeme almost choked. "I barely know Lady Sabrina, pet. Besides, I'm waiting for you to grow up so we can be spies together, remember?"

Aden almost levitated with outrage. "What?"

His daughter ignored him to give Graeme another cheek-splitting grin. "I remember. That'll be such fun."

"Oh, my God," her father muttered.

"Come along, darling," Vivien said, "before you give your father an apoplectic fit."

Maggie slid off Graeme's lap and joined her mother. "What's an ap . . . popectic fit?"

"It's what you give Papa on a regular basis."

"She's not the only one," Aden grumbled.

His wife ignored him, ushering Maggie out into the care of a waiting maid. When she returned to perch on the leather ottoman at her husband's feet, Aden sighed.

"Now, what?" he asked with resignation.

Vivien flashed a smile. "You're awfully good, you know. I *swear* you can read my mind."

Aden leaned down to press a lingering kiss to her forehead. Vivien's eyes fluttered shut, and she rested a hand on her husband's knee.

Envy flashed through Graeme like a bolt of lightning— envy for what Aden and Vivien shared, good and bad. They had a lively and sometimes contentious relationship, but there was no doubt they loved and guarded each other and their children with fierce devotion.

"I've had plenty of practice in doing so," Aden said. "Especially since you're as good at keeping secrets as your daughter."

Vivien grimaced. "This is one secret I wish I could keep."

"Is it about who Lady Sabrina was waiting for in the park?" Graeme asked.

"Yes, and neither of you is going to be happy with the answer." She threw Graeme a troubled look. "Especially not you."

"I've just met the lass. Why would I care?"

"Because she was meeting the Marquess of Cringlewood."

For several moments, ominous thunder seemed to rumble around in Graeme's head, even as a fraught silence weighed heavily on the room. The mental noise inside him built to a crescendo, pushing him up out of his chair.

"Right, I'm off," he said.

Aden pointed a finger at him. "Sit down, Graeme."

"Bugger that."

"Sit. Down."

Graeme grimaced, but sat. When Aden employed that

tone of voice, everyone—even stubborn Highlanders—obeyed without question.

Still, he couldn't help glaring at his chief. "Did you know the bastard was back in town?"

"Of course not. I would have told you about it—and done something about it, too."

"I don't know that you can do anything," Vivien said.

"Nonsense. I'll go straight to my father," Aden replied.

"I'm afraid that won't work. Not this time."

"Why the hell not?" Graeme demanded.

Aden's eyes narrowed to obsidian slits. "Watch your tone with my wife, lad."

Vivien patted her husband's knee. "No, Graeme has every right to be upset."

Graeme forced down the choking anger. Now was not the time to lose control. He'd do that later, when he had the bastard in his sights.

"I'm sorry, Vivien. I'm just . . . surprised," he said in a softer voice.

"I was, too. I almost fell out of my chair when Sabrina told me."

"I thought we'd driven him right out of England," Graeme said.

"He returned seven weeks ago," Aden replied, "and has been living in seclusion in the country. Sir Dominic and I made it clear that he risked a great deal of trouble if he returned to town, but our warning obviously didn't sink in firmly enough."

"And you never thought to tell me he was back?" Graeme asked.

"Since you would have run off half-cocked, I did not. I wrote to Lord Arnprior, as well as to Royal and Ainsley, and assured them I would deal with it. At the time, I deemed that to be enough."

Graeme covered his eyes, fatigue warring with fury in

every muscle. He couldn't believe his family was again faced with the nightmare that was the Marquess of Cringlewood.

The man had once been a force to reckon with. From a distinguished family and with deep connections in the aristocracy, the marquess had been a prime catch on the marriage mart.

Cringlewood was also a rapist. He'd assaulted his fiancée, the beautiful and very wealthy Ainsley Matthews. Impregnated by her attacker, Lady Ainsley had fled to Scotland to bear her child in secret. She'd then turned to the only man she trusted to care for her daughter and to keep her secrets safe.

That man was Graeme's brother, Royal.

As befitted the finest man who'd ever walked the planet, Royal had claimed little Tira as his own daughter, and eventually married Ainsley. The pair had been building a new life in Glasgow until Cringlewood ferreted out Ainsley's secret. With a band of hired thugs, the marquess had traveled north and kidnapped mother and daughter. Since Cringlewood had been massively in debt from bad investments and in need of Ainsley's fortune, he'd intended to blackmail her into using Scotland's more lenient marriage laws to obtain a divorce and marry him.

The Kendricks had rescued the lassies, but Ainsley had shot and wounded Cringlewood in the process. Angus, Graeme's grandfather, had also killed one of the thugs in the ensuing mayhem. That had put them all in legal jeopardy. Cringlewood was a monster, but he was also Tira's father *and* a nobleman. Royal and Ainsley had been forced to flee to Canada, taking Tira and Angus with them.

In the ensuing months, Nick and Victoria, along with Aden and other influential friends, had exerted pressure to keep a lid on the scandal and convince Cringlewood to draw in his horns. The threat of even more dire financial consequences had done the trick, and they'd finally wrung an agreement from him. The marquess had departed for the Continent to lick his wounds and escape his creditors.

In the meantime, Graeme had made it his personal mission to track down all the remaining kidnappers and bring them to justice. His success in that regard had attracted Aden's notice and the invitation to work for him.

Just this past spring, Royal and Ainsley had finally returned home, secure in the knowledge that Cringlewood, ostensibly still in exile on the Continent, was no longer a threat.

Now, though, the bastard was back and likely to cause trouble.

Graeme lifted his head to look at Aden. "We have to contain the situation, before Royal gets wind of it."

"Of course we do." Aden turned to his wife. "I haven't spoken to the king in a few weeks. Why do you think I won't be able to get him to boot the scum out of town?"

"Sabrina mentioned that Cringlewood and Lady Conyngham are close, and you know what that means. I suspect her ladyship is running interference for him."

"Dammit to hell," Graeme muttered. Lady Conyngham was the king's latest mistress.

"My father is an idiot," Aden said with a sigh.

Although not particularly fond of his royal parent, Aden maintained a cordial relationship with the king, who generally took the advice of his spymaster son. But His Majesty was also greatly influenced by whomever his current mistress happened to be, so this was not a good development.

"We can assume that Cringlewood is after Lady Sabrina's fortune," Graeme said, "which he needs to repair his pathetic finances."

"No doubt," Vivien said. "But he's been canny enough to keep a modest profile, and avoid those who would snub him or gossip to Lady Sabrina. He's a monster, but he's not stupid."

"Bastard," Graeme snarled.

Vivien nodded. "Indeed. I wasn't sure what to say to Sabrina, other than to warn her about Cringlewood's bad character. Since we need to protect Ainsley and Tira, I thought it best to avoid details until I spoke with you."

"I wouldn't put it past Cringlewood to lure her into a compromising situation," Aden said. "Why else persuade her to meet him in Hyde Park at so early an hour?"

Rage flickered like sparks at the edges of Graeme's vision. His sister-in-law had already suffered agonies at Cringlewood's hands. He would *not* allow that to happen to another woman.

"If that bloody *Sassenach* king won't deal with this, I will."

When Graeme stood, Aden rose and clapped a hand on his shoulder. "If you try to charge out like an enraged bull, I swear I'll lock you in the wine cellar."

Graeme had no intention of brawling in front of Vivien or breaking any more of her furniture. But once he got out of this house . . .

"I know exactly what you're thinking," Aden said, "and it's not on. *I* will take care of Cringlewood."

"Like ye did last time?" Graeme retorted. "Because that worked so well."

"Oh, dear," Vivien sighed. "My poor furniture."

While Aden didn't back down, his expression held more sympathy than reprimand. "I know how grim this is for you, lad. But if Cringlewood has friends at Court, anything you do to him wouldn't help."

"Tossing the blighter off a cliff would do the trick."

"Graeme, you know Aden will take care of this," Vivien said firmly as she came to join them.

"I'll enlist Dominic," Aden said. "Between the two of us, we'll set it to right."

Sir Dominic Hunter, England's former spymaster and one of the most powerful men in the *ton*, still exerted considerable influence within the royal family. It made sense to turn the matter over to him.

Graeme mentally balked. "I can't sit around and do nothing."

Aden lifted an eyebrow. "You still have a mission to complete, do you not?"

"But—"

"The sooner you arrest the thieves, the happier the king will be. And a happy king means a pliant king."

Graeme sighed. "If you put it that way, what choice do I have?"

"None," Aden said, taking a step back. "Now go home, get some sleep, and then get back at it."

Graeme shot his chief a hard look. "You'll keep me apprised of the situation with Cringlewood?"

"You have my word."

"You best, or I promise there will be hell to pay."

Aden simply rolled his eyes.

Vivien snapped her fingers. "Oh, I do have a bit of good news, dearest. I received a letter from Mamma this morning. She's coming to town for a visit, and she intends to stay with us."

Graeme took advantage of the ensuing argument to slip from the room.

Chapter Four

Tucked behind the marble column, Graeme tried to fade into the background. It was something he achieved with far greater success among the criminal classes than in aristocratic ballrooms.

The initial plan had been to stake out this blasted affair disguised as a footman. But the silly livery and powdered wig probably wouldn't do the trick of disguising him, not after that unfortunate incident at the Duchess of Leverton's assembly a few months back where an expensive Chinese screen had ended up in pieces on the floor. The *Sassenach* who'd picked the fight with him held the blame for that. The slimy toad had tried to fleece a sweet but slightly dotty dowager at cards, and Graeme had spotted the cheat. As discretely as possible, he'd dropped a warning whisper in the old gal's ear.

The dowager, who'd possessed more spirit than anticipated, had promptly tossed her champagne punch into the cheat's face. Face dripping, the cheat had jumped up and accused Graeme of lying. Since that was not the sort of insult any Kendrick could allow to stand, events had quickly escalated.

The end result had seen the cheat sprawled on the floor amid the remains of Her Grace's Chinese screen.

Fortunately, the Duchess of Leverton—who happened to be Victoria's cousin and a bit of a hellion, herself—had simply told Graeme that his actions were perfectly understandable.

The Duke of Leverton, however, had been decidedly less impressed. Graeme had generally made a point of steering clear of His Grace ever since.

Fortunately, the duke and his duchess had left town for the summer months. Most of the nobility, wishing to escape the heat, had followed suit. Still, there were enough left in the city to make Lady Peregrim's ball sufficiently crowded.

That was why Graeme now lurked behind a pillar like an idiotic character from a melodrama as he watched the guests laden with jewels, gold watches, and gem-encrusted snuffboxes. The Peregrims were hosting one of the largest events of the summer and, in both Aden's and Graeme's opinions, it would be too tempting a target for the gang of thieves to resist.

Unfortunately, he'd yet to see any hint of a thief in the ballroom, so it was time to investigate other parts of the house, including the library. There, Lord Peregrim kept a priceless collection of snuffboxes in a glass case, under lock and key.

As Graeme well knew from his youthful escapades, a lock never stopped a determined thief.

He slipped out to the hall. Aden was hanging about somewhere, and there were guards posted on the grounds. Aden's coachman and grooms were also out front, keeping their eyes on arrivals and exits. They were finally well positioned to catch the thieves in an inescapable net.

As Graeme passed the main drawing room, he stuck his head in for a quick look for Aden and almost collided with the doorframe.

Lady Sabrina Bell was seated on a velvet chaise under a massive pier glass, surrounded by a small group of fawning suitors. And seated next to *her* on the bloody chaise was the bloody Marquess of Cringlewood.

Disturbingly, the lass seemed receptive to his attentions, with her head tilted politely in his direction as she listened to what were no-doubt smarmy lies. Clearly, Vivien's warning had failed to take. Since Cringlewood was both handsome and a marquess, Graeme told himself he shouldn't be surprised.

True evil lurked beneath Cringlewood's polished exterior, an evil that destroyed lives without hesitation. The thought of an innocent young woman like Sabrina falling into his clutches . . .

Graeme forced himself to punch through the fury clouding his mind. A public confrontation with Cringlewood would reignite all the ugly gossip about Ainsley. Graeme's best course was to find Aden and send him to deal with the situation. After all, the girl was sitting in a drawing room, surrounded by friends. She wouldn't come to harm in the few minutes it would take Graeme to hunt down his chief.

Bollocks to that.

As he crossed the spacious but crowded room, Graeme's brain issued a stern directive to march back in the other direction. That also failed to take, and he came to a halt in front of the chaise. Lady Sabrina had just turned her attention to a clearly smitten lad with bad skin and a worse cravat across from her. She glanced up at Graeme and her peacock gaze popped wide, her pink mouth rounding in a surprised oval.

"Oh . . . ah, Mr. Kendrick," she stuttered. "How are—"

"Lady Sabrina, I regret the interruption, but this is our dance," Graeme said firmly.

She blinked, politely nonplussed, as was her little group of suitors.

But not Cringlewood. The marquess glared up at him with an unconcealed hatred that even a blind man could have sensed.

Graeme half turned his back on Cringlewood to focus on

the other men. "Forgive the intrusion, gentlemen, but I'm sure you can understand my desire to claim my dance."

Out of the corner of his eye, Graeme saw Cringlewood flush at the deliberate cut. Sabrina's other suitors looked vaguely horrified.

Sabrina regarded Graeme with a slightly quizzical smile, as if waiting to see what would happen next.

The lad with the blemished skin spoke first. "Oh, absolutely. Devastated to lose her ladyship's company, naturally, but none of us can blame you one bit." He stood and gave Graeme a carefully correct nod. "I'm Reggie Park, by the way. My parents are Lord and Lady Peregrim."

"Our gracious hosts," Graeme said with a smile. "They throw a splendid party."

"Reggie, this is Mr. Graeme Kendrick," Sabrina said. "I believe your parents know his brother, Lord—"

"Arnprior. Quite a barbarian, even for a Scot," Cringlewood interrupted in an elegant drawl. "I confess to some surprise that Lady Peregrim has lowered her excellent standards by inviting riffraff like a Kendrick to her affairs." He flashed Reggie a smile. "Surely that was an oversight on your dear mamma's part."

Reggie blinked, and Sabrina's two other suitors went rather pale. One, a sober, middle-aged gentleman, mumbled something about meeting his mother and all but scuttled backward in his haste to escape. The other, a genial looking fellow about Graeme's age, also stuttered an excuse and made his exit.

Sabrina barely gave them a glance before turning to narrow her gaze on the marquess. Despite the fact that she was a dab little lass, at least by Graeme's measurements, she did an excellent job of staring haughtily down her nose at Cringlewood.

Graeme had to swallow a chuckle. The idiot was so consumed with his hatred for all things Kendrick that he'd failed to notice how he'd offended the woman he was trying to woo.

Reggie was also leveling a glare at Cringlewood. "If my mother invited Mr. Kendrick, I'm sure he's perfectly up to scratch, sir."

Cringlewood flipped open his snuffbox and extracted a pinch with a bored air. "One of your tender years cannot be expected to sort through the niceties of polite society, dear boy. I'd be happy to tell you and your parents all about the Kendricks." He leaned closer, as if sharing a confidence. "Highlanders. Barely civilized." His gaze suddenly darted toward Graeme, gleaming with malice. "And I've got the scars to prove it."

Graeme considered living up to that barely civilized accusation by tossing the moronic marquess out the nearest window. But Cringlewood was obviously hoping to cause a scene, and seek the only kind of revenge he could at the moment—social revenge—against Royal and Ainsley.

Graeme wouldn't play that game.

"I'm half-Scottish, my lord," Sabrina said, coolly polite. "My beloved mother was born in the Highlands."

Cringlewood momentarily froze, but quickly regrouped. "Fortunately, your dear mother had the excellent sense to marry an Englishman, Lady Sabrina. And your esteemed father, I believe, is not fond of Scotland. A man of excellent sense, Lord Musgrave."

Sabrina gave a shrug, her shoulders as silky and smooth as her shimmering ivory gown. "My godfather—that would be the king—would not agree. He's quite mad for Scotland. He's considering a visit to Edinburgh in the near future."

The marquess lost his smarmy smile when he realized he was losing the battle.

"Careful, old man," Graeme said. "Your irritation is showing."

Reggie covered his mouth, as if to smother a laugh.

"Visiting Edinburgh would be sadly unwise of His Majesty, since the Scots are hardly loyal subjects of the Crown. Always dreaming of rebellion and their glorious past." Cringlewood sneered with contempt.

Graeme laughed. "It's the nineteenth century. We've been loyal to king and country for decades."

Mostly. His grandfather, for one, wouldn't be averse to giving old King Georgie a shove into a cold loch.

"Any talk of rebellion is spoken only by fools," Graeme added.

"Did you just call me a fool, Kendrick?" the marquess demanded.

Sabrina tapped Graeme's arm with her fan. "I do believe our waltz is beginning, sir."

She rose, forcing Cringlewood to do the same. The marquess loomed over her, radiating repressed rage as Graeme took her hand.

Reggie cast a troubled glance at Sabrina.

"Is something amiss, my lord?" she asked Cringlewood with chilly courtesy.

He quickly gathered his manners and flashed an artificial smile. "I'm simply disappointed to lose your company, dear lady. Perhaps you'll save me a dance?"

Her fingers gripped Graeme's hand.

"I'm afraid all my dances are spoken for, my lord."

"With me, for one," Reggie said with a shy smile. "Don't forget we're doing the country dances. If you're not tired by then, that is."

She rewarded the young man with a brilliant smile. "I would never be too tired to dance with you, Reggie. And perhaps you can take me down to supper afterward."

The lad beamed. "Of course. Mamma would be ever so pleased if I escorted you."

"Of course your mamma will be pleased," Cringlewood drawled. "Quite the coup for you to secure the most charming guest for supper. You leave the rest of us in the dust, dear boy."

Reggie's uneven complexion mottled red in response to the bastard's sarcastic tone.

"Her ladyship has snagged an excellent supper partner," Graeme said, winking at Reggie. "Certainly the nicest, which I intend to tell his excellent mother as soon as I see her."

When the young man flashed a grateful smile, Sabrina squeezed Graeme's hand before letting go and taking his arm.

"I'll see you later, Reggie." She gave Cringlewood a brief nod. "My lord."

Resisting the impulse to flash his teeth at the fuming marquess, Graeme escorted Sabrina toward the door. Curious gazes and whisperings accompanied them.

"Sorry about all that," he quietly said.

"It couldn't be helped, given his lordship's behavior." She darted Graeme a sideways glance. "But that dreadful little scene would not have occurred if you hadn't decided to come to my rescue. I assume that's what you were doing, wasn't it?"

"I suppose."

As far as rescues went, it wasn't one of his better ones, since it had drawn a fat lot of attention. Aden would not approve, nor would Graeme's family.

Jumped before you looked, as usual.

"What made you think I needed rescuing?" Sabrina inquired as they crossed into the hall. "After all, I was simply sitting in a drawing room, surrounded by other guests. It's hardly the middle of a battlefield, or even Hyde Park in a rainstorm."

For a moment, Graeme had the gruesome sensation that he'd made a capital blunder. "Oh. Well, you see—"

She huffed out an infectious chuckle. "I'm teasing, sir. As it happens, I was very happy to be rescued."

He smiled with relief. "I suppose I earned a teasing, after the way I ordered you about in the park."

"Nonsense. You were exceedingly kind and patient with me there."

"I was?"

"Well, most of the time. You must admit, however, that it was a very embarrassing situation. I was not at my best."

Graeme had a sudden mental flash of sodden clothing clinging to plump breasts. "Oh, I wouldn't say that."

Her smile turned quizzical. "Then you are a very kind man, Mr. Kendrick, since I cannot be counted as anything but a nuisance to you. And I'm sorry you were forced to put up with Lord Cringlewood's rudeness." She shook her head. "Honestly, what a dreadful man."

"Och, lass, don't worry about me. It was the poor lad I truly felt for."

"Yes, I was angry about how he treated Reggie. His lordship was fortunate I didn't throw a drink in his face." She exhaled a sigh. "Now you know how rude *I* can be, as well as how poor a judge of character I am. You must be *quite* shocked."

"Utterly appalled. I feel faint with horror, if you must know."

"I'm sure," she replied, amused. "But you must also see that I'm perfectly capable of managing dreary Lord Cringlewood. The only true danger from him is being pestered to death. I suspect I shall have to speak strongly to him, at some point."

Graeme held his peace until they entered the ballroom. Then he drew her behind the marginal shelter of a marble column.

She frowned. "Are we dancing, or was that simply a ruse?"

"We'll dance in a moment. But first you must promise not to speak to Cringlewood again. In fact, avoid him completely, if possible."

The lingering humor in her pretty gaze faded. "So, Vivien's rather vague warning was not strong enough, I take it. What aren't you telling me, Mr. Kendrick?"

"What did Vivien say?"

"Just that Lord Cringlewood was not a nice man, and that he was in financial straits. In fact, I'd already deduced that he was not a nice man—"

"Because he stood you up?"

A blush pinked up her elegant cheekbones. "It . . . it was partly that. But he never should have asked me in the first place, and I should never have agreed. I'm quite ashamed to have made such a blunder."

"We all make mistakes." That one, however, could have ruined her life.

"I don't," she said firmly.

Graeme bit back a grin. The lass had a full measure of confidence, and then some.

He waved a hand toward the dance floor, where the guests were taking their places for the second waltz of the evening.

She shook her head. "Not yet. I want to know why I should avoid Lord Cringlewood. Obviously, I will not be accepting his suit—"

"I should bloody well hope not."

He'd kill Cringlewood before that happened. But he also realized he didn't like the idea of her accepting *anyone's* suit.

Idiot. You just met the woman.

"What are you and Vivien so concerned about?" Sabrina pressed.

"Best to just leave it at that, lass."

Her mouth twitched with irritation. "I have a right to know, Mr. Kendrick. If Lord Cringlewood is more than just s typical fortune hunter, he shouldn't be allowed to swan about the *ton*, courting unsuspecting women."

Graeme couldn't disagree with that, but how much to tell her?

"Let me think about it, then."

He gently pulled her from behind the column and swept her into a gap in the colorful throng. Sabrina let out a delicate snort but gracefully came into his arms.

For a few minutes, Graeme let himself relish the mundane yet now somehow profound act of dancing with a pretty girl. He couldn't recall the last time he'd drifted away on the music and motion, letting all his thoughts and cares drift away, too. How long it had been since he'd just . . . felt. Now he relished the sensation of Sabrina's trim figure held lightly but securely in his embrace, the swish of her bright yellow skirts skirling around his legs. She was lithe and light-footed, and followed his steps with easy assurance.

Even better than his enjoyment was *her* enjoyment, shining through in her bright gaze and in the upward tilt of her rosebud mouth. That Lady Sabrina Bell was a canny lass and nobody's fool was evident enough. But there was also an innocent verve about her, so fresh and appealing that it stirred a visceral response deep within him—something that seemed perilously close to happiness.

It was such a wee frippery, this dance, and yet Graeme found himself wanting this feeling again and again. Wanting *her*.

That was the perilous part. It was stupid and impossible and all the things that made such emotion the height of idiocy.

Sabrina Bell came from a world that was no longer his, a comfortable, peaceful world inhabited by comfortable, peaceful people. Graeme had strayed beyond that world some time ago and could never go back.

Nor did he *want* to go back, knowing what he did about the dangers lurking at the edge of that peace and comfort.

That other world needed men like him, willing to do the ugly, dirty work necessary to protect it.

Protect her.

As the music rose to a flourishing conclusion, Graeme skimmed his partner to the edge of the crowd, turning one more circle before halting. His gaze locked with Sabrina's in a disconcerting and intimate understanding, as if they'd both gone into the Serpentine that day as strangers but had emerged from that chilly water as something much more.

Sabrina blinked and stepped out of his arms with a self-conscious laugh. "Goodness, Mr. Kendrick, you are certainly an energetic dancer."

It took him a moment to answer. "I'm a Highlander, ye ken. We're barely civilized, remember?"

"You seem quite civilized to me. On the surface, at least," she added, as if to herself.

That was a bit too close to the mark. "May I fetch you a cup of punch? Or take you back to your . . ."

He frowned. Who was she with tonight? There hadn't been even the slightest hint of a chaperone, something which fit with her independent attitude.

"Your party," he finished.

"No, thank you. What I'd like to do is finish our discussion about Lord Cringlewood."

Hell and damnation.

He flashed his best rueful smile. "Must we?"

"You know, I much prefer it when you're not trying to be charming."

"But I'm famous for my Highland charm, ye ken."

"I've never heard that. In fact, I'd never heard about you at all until the other day." She frowned. "How is that possible? You've obviously been in town for quite some time. Do you not socialize?"

He was rather surprised she hadn't gotten wind of the incident with the Chinese screen. "Not much at all, I admit."

Again she studied him as if he were an exotic species. "I see. Then perhaps you could take a moment to tell me what I need to know about the marquess before you fade back into obscurity."

Then she flashed a dazzling and utterly knowing smile, one guaranteed to knock the sharpest fellow off his pins. She was a vision in her pretty yellow gown, sunny from the bouncy curls at the top of her head to the tips of her fancy gold slippers. But what had emerged from her lips was more command than request. Graeme suspected she was a lassie to whom very few said no.

"You owe me, Mr. Kendrick," she added.

That was debatable. Still, Sabrina seemed the sort who'd go digging, and that would not be good for her or the Kendricks. Especially Ainsley.

"It's a bit tricky, I'm afraid."

She glanced past him. "I see two empty chairs waiting just for us. Shall we sit quietly and discuss it?"

"I have the feeling you'd chase me down if I refused," he said dryly.

As he led her to the chairs, he didn't miss her smug little smile. She was insanely adorable, and he had to repress the urge to kiss that smile right off her lips.

Sheltered by large potted palms, a shallow window bay afforded a semblance of privacy while maintaining propriety. He handed her into one of the chairs, then carefully sat in the other. A spindly, fashionable thing, it creaked under his weight. Graeme hoped he would not find himself sitting on the floor in yet another pile of expensive wood.

The lady neatly folded her hands and gave him a nod, as if giving him permission to start.

Easier said than done.

"Mr. Kendrick," she said after he remained silent, "aside from his rude behavior—which his lordship was adept at concealing until now—how bad can it be? Is Cringlewood completely in dun territory? While that would be an unpleasant revelation, the marquess would not be the first man intent on gaining my fortune through the wedded state."

He grimaced. "I'm sorry to hear that."

"Don't be. The positives generally outweigh the negatives."

She was refreshingly blunt for a society miss.

"It's true that Cringlewood's pockets are severely let. He's been forced to rusticate and sell off whatever wasn't entailed to the estate."

"Is that the real reason he went to the Continent? He told me he was buying art."

"He was fleeing his debts." And fleeing Aden St. George and the Kendricks, but she didn't need to know that.

She frowned. "It seems rather foolish to have come back, then."

"As you mentioned to Vivien, he has friends at Court."

"I see." She crinkled her nose. "Thank you for the warning, sir. I will keep the marquess at arm's length, and there will certainly be no more assignations in the park."

"No assignations, anywhere," he sharply replied. "He's completely untrustworthy."

She looked startled for a moment, but then gently rested her gloved hand on his arm. Graeme had a mad urge to gather her up and keep her safe from anything that could ever harm her.

Och, yer a bloody fool.

"You can tell me everything, you know," she quietly said. "You have my solemn word that I will keep our conversation in the strictest confidence."

Trust was a hard thing for him. But her gaze, so open and earnest, convinced him.

"Very well, then. Are you acquainted with my sister-in-law, Lady Ainsley Kendrick?"

"Lady Ainsley is a few years older than I, but our families know each other." She flashed that brief, sunny smile, the one Graeme was beginning to like quite a lot. "She's so lovely and witty, and had a legion of suitors, as I recall."

Lovely was certainly accurate, as was sharp-tongued and rather terrifying. Graeme had a great deal of admiration for Ainsley, and even more admiration for his brother for having the courage to marry her.

"You're just as pretty as she is, lass."

Sabrina scoffed. "Don't be silly. I couldn't hold a candle to her. None of us could."

"If you believed that, did it bother you?" he asked with genuine interest. In his experience, the marriage mart was more competitive than a prizefight.

"Of course not. I have an absolutely lovely life. And it's not been easy for Lady Ainsley, I understand. If I recall correctly, her parents cut her off when she married . . ." She trailed off.

Graeme raised an eyebrow.

"Heavens, I'd forgotten she was all but betrothed to Cringlewood." Sabrina frowned. "There was something of a scandal, wasn't there? We were in Bath at the time so my father could take the waters, so I don't remember much."

"A bit more than something of a scandal," Graeme replied.

"One can certainly understand why Lady Ainsley would throw over Cringlewood. But to suffer a permanent breach with her family *and* lose her inheritance?" Sabrina shook her head. "She must have been *quite* in love with your brother to risk so much."

From her rather mystified tone, Graeme could only deduce the lass had never been in love.

"She was indeed going to marry Cringlewood, at least initially. But he was . . . abusive to her."

Sabrina stared blankly at Graeme.

"Physically abusive," he tersely added.

She gasped. "Did her parents know?"

He nodded.

"And they still encouraged the marriage? If so, how utterly appalling of them," she said, disgusted.

"The marriage settlements had already been signed. Cringlewood threatened to sue for breach of promise, as a means to pressure Ainsley's parents."

Her earnest gaze went wide. "He tried to *force* Ainsley to marry him?"

"Yes."

"But—"

He briefly squeezed her hand. "Please understand that I can't say more. The details are not mine to share, and my family needs to protect Ainsley's privacy as much as possible."

She drew in a wavering breath. "I can appreciate that, sir. But if his lordship is as ugly a customer as you say he is—"

"Trust me that he is."

"Then he shouldn't be allowed to go about preying on unsuspecting women and their families."

"I agree. But it is not up to us to correct the situation."

"Then who *will* correct it?" she demanded.

"St. George will be addressing the matter in every way possible."

Her gaze narrowed to frosty blue slits. "That's not a very satisfactory answer."

"We must trust him to handle the situation."

"But—"

"No, my lady." He sympathized with the lass, but Ainsley needed to be protected, and Aden could be trusted to do that. "You must leave it alone. I promise Cringlewood will be dealt with."

Her expression suggested a desire to whack Graeme on the nose with her fan.

"Sir, I *cannot* believe—"

"There you are, Sabrina," interrupted a querulous voice. "I've been looking *everywhere* for you, my dear."

A few feet away, an elderly gentleman leaned on a cane, regarding them with disfavor. A slight, balding fellow, he was dressed as a tulip of the *ton*, with pink waistcoat, enormous cravat, and other furbelows better suited to a younger man.

Actually, better suited to no one. The poor fellow looked ridiculous.

Sabrina breathed out a sigh and rose. Graeme followed suit.

"Forgive me, dearest," she said. "I thought you were playing cards with the Duke of York."

"He complained of the heat and departed. Lady Peregrim's affairs are *always* such a crush. I'm sure the air is dreadfully unwholesome."

As if to prove the point, he dramatically flapped a kerchief. It wafted the scent of perfume up Graeme's nose, making him bite his tongue to keep from sneezing.

The old gent scowled at him before turning to Sabrina. "Who is this person? You shouldn't hide in corners with strange men, Sabrina. People will talk."

"Father, we're in the ballroom. Everyone can see us."

"Still—"

"Let me introduce you," she cheerfully interrupted. "Mr. Graeme Kendrick, I have the honor of introducing you to my father, Lord Musgrave."

Graeme gave his best bow. "It's an honor to meet you, my lord."

A decidedly unhappy silence ensued.

"Sabrina, he's Scottish," Lord Musgrave eventually said.

"Yes, dear," Sabrina replied. "As was Mamma."

"The insalubrious Highland climate was the cause of your mother's infirmities, as you well know. Scotland ruined her health."

The Highlands might currently be all the rage, thanks to Walter Scott and his silly novels—but apparently not with Lord Musgrave.

"It can be a wee bit damp in the winter," Graeme said, smiling. "But my brothers and I are healthy as oxen."

"How many brothers do you have?" Musgrave asked.

"We are seven, my lord."

"I take it you are not the eldest?"

"I am not, sir."

That information was met with a disapproving sniff, a typical response from aristocrats with marriageable daughters. Impecunious younger sons best not lurk about their precious darlings.

"Mr. Kendrick's brother is the Earl of Arnprior," Sabrina explained. "Surely you remember that Lady Arnprior is well known to the king."

As in, Vicky was old Georgie's by-blow.

Musgrave eyed Graeme for a few more moments before adopting a doleful expression. "We must return home, Sabrina. I'm feeling most unwell."

"Of course, dearest." She threw Graeme an apologetic grimace. "Excuse me, sir."

He gave her a slight bow. "Of course, my lady. Please think about what we discussed."

Lord Musgrave let out an outraged huff, but Sabrina simply nodded.

As she led her father toward the ballroom exit, the old poop was clearly delivering her a scold. Good thing Graeme *wasn't* courting the lass, because her dear old da would no doubt pitch a heinous fit. But Graeme had gotten through to Sabrina about Cringlewood, and that's what counted— not fruitless imaginings of time spent with a woman he'd likely never see again.

Back to work, old boy.

His work was the only thing that mattered.

Chapter Five

Graeme's sweep of the upper floors had included a visit to Lord Peregrim's study to check on his lordship's snuffbox collection. A burly footman was guarding the priceless trinkets, and the fellow had reacted quite poorly when Graeme snuck into the room. To escape a dustup, he'd acted like a drunken sot who'd lost his way to the water closet. He'd also crossed paths with Aden, who'd reported that he'd found nothing amiss.

He was beginning to think the entire evening was a wild goose chase, and although Aden wasn't holding the lack of progress against him, it was still hard not to feel like a failure.

Again.

He mentally shook his head, impatient with that thought.

Taking the servants' stairs down to the main floor, he'd just rounded the corner of the mostly deserted hall when a door that led to the terrace creaked slowly open. Graeme retreated back to the corner, easing out only far enough to keep an eye on the door.

A powdered head cautiously appeared and did a furtive check of the hall. Then the man, dressed as a footman, slipped through. He tugged his liveried coat into place and headed toward the front of the house.

Perhaps he was indeed a footman on legitimate business, and the furtive attitude was the result of an illicit encounter with a lusty matron out in the gardens. But Graeme had made a point of registering the faces of all the household staff, and he'd not seen this one. So unless the fellow had spent the entire evening servicing a string of ladies, it looked like the thieves had finally taken the bait.

The fake footman calmly paused to accept empty glasses from a pair of cup-shot dandies. Once the idiots wandered off, he dumped the glasses into a nearby potted plant and proceeded to the front of the mansion. Luckily for him, the entrance hall was busy with early departures, and the other servants too distracted to recognize an imposter.

The man slipped up the central staircase unnoticed, and Graeme slipped up after him. It was clear he was heading to the family bedrooms for a spot of productive pilfering.

Got ye, ye bastard.

Graeme retrieved the knife stowed in the specially designed pocket of his tailcoat. He usually carried additional knives in his boots, but these affairs demanded breeches and stockings and bloody awful dancing shoes, which meant few places to hide weaponry.

The footman reached the second floor, then ghosted down the hall toward the family suites. Graeme was taking the rest of the stairs two at a time when he heard a rush of footsteps behind him.

"Graeme!" hissed a familiar voice.

Cursing, he turned to see Vivien pelting up the stairs, with her silky skirts bunched in her hands and the large plumes on her head bouncing wildly.

"Not now," he hissed back. "I'm working."

"Never mind that. We've got bigger problems."

"I just spotted one of the thieves. I've got to go."

When he started up, Vivien yanked on his arm, almost tumbling them both down the stairs.

He made a grab for her. "You daft woman, what are you doing?"

"It's Sabrina. She's in trouble."

"But she left with her father a half hour ago."

"No, I just saw her leave the ballroom with Cringlewood, and I was too far away to intervene. I've checked the drawing room and the supper room, and she's not in either."

Graeme's heart felt like it had slammed into a brick wall. "Where's Aden?"

"I can't find him. I just happened to spot you going up the stairs."

Graeme cast a frustrated glance down the hall.

"I'm afraid Cringlewood will try to get her alone out on the terrace," Vivien urgently added, "or even the gardens."

"Dammit, I told her why she had to avoid him. She couldn't possibly be that daft."

Vivien's eyes popped wide. "You told her about Ainsley?"

"Only in general terms."

She slapped a frustrated hand to the top of her head, dislodging one of her feathers. "Sabrina would be infuriated by that, you idiot. She probably felt compelled to confront Cringlewood herself." Vivien grimaced. "She wouldn't even recognize the danger, she's so self-confident."

Like Ainsley had been, before her assault.

Graeme took Vivien's arm and hurried her down the stairs. She glanced over her shoulder. "I could sneak up and see where the thief went, if you like."

"Absolutely not. You need to find Aden, tell him I've gone after Sabrina, and say that one of the thieves is upstairs. He'll know what to do."

"I'm quite capable of . . . Oh, hello, Lord Fotherby," she

said as they all but ran over a portly gentleman huffing up the stairs.

The old fellow plastered himself against the banister. "Lady Vivien, goodness gracious!"

"Sorry," she called back. "Graeme, dear, we're attracting attention."

"As usual." He pulled her over to the butler, who regarded them with genteel alarm. "Lady Vivien needs to find her husband immediately. Help her do so."

"Of course, sir."

Graeme spun on his heel and strode toward the back hall, ignoring the splutters of the outraged guests he pushed out of his way.

Sabrina ignored the thumping of her heart as she allowed Cringlewood to escort her from the ballroom. His lordship was famous for his handsome face and charming smiles, but now all she could see was the snake lurking beneath the polished façade.

If she had anything to say about it—and she had quite *a lot* to say about it—the snake would soon be slithering its way out of London, never to return. Sabrina intended to make it abundantly clear to the disgusting marquess that his days in the *ton* were over.

"How delightful that you decided to stay a little longer, my dear," Cringlewood purred, pressing her hand. "I had assumed you had departed with your dear papa. Imagine my joy to discover that such was not the case."

Sabrina resisted the impulse to yank her hand away. "As I mentioned a few moments ago, I believe we should have a little chat."

His gaze turned wary, but then he graciously inclined his head. "How delightful. Shall we stroll to the drawing room?"

"I thought perhaps the terrace. It's quite stuffy in the house, and I noticed some of the guests availing themselves of the cooler air."

Interest sparked in his eyes, which made her grind her back molars. Now he looked positively smug.

Though Sabrina needed a quiet spot to say what she needed to say, she wasn't fool enough to go off alone with the brute. Lady Peregrim's terrace was always popular during her summer parties, especially with the younger guests. There, they could chat with their chaperones close by, yet still have a bit of privacy.

"A little fresh air will be just the thing," the marquess agreed in an oily tone.

The spacious terrace could be reached from the hallway, and they came out at the far end, where shallow steps led down to the gardens below. It was a little more private, but well within sight of the ballroom and its open French doors.

The terrace was illuminated only by light streaming from the ballroom and a few lanterns placed on wrought-iron tables. Sabrina blinked to clear her vision. When it cleared, she had to swallow an oath.

There were only two other people there—a couple who quickly scampered down another set of stairs into the darkness of the garden.

Drat and double drat.

Cringlewood chuckled. "A stroll in the garden under the moonlight. Perhaps we should do the same."

"What an inappropriate suggestion," Sabrina said in a clipped tone.

"Really? You agreed to meet me in the park the other morning. By yourself."

"I brought my maid, in fact. And might I add that *you* never showed up."

Immediately, she wished she could recall her stupid

words. Because of course he would assume she was annoyed that he'd stood her up.

The flash of his white smile confirmed that.

After spinning on her heel, she marched along the balustrade until she was near the first set of open doors. Then she turned to face him and practically jumped out of her dancing slippers. He loomed so close he was virtually on top of her.

Snapping open her fan, Sabrina inserted it between them.

"That's why you've been so cool to me," he said. "You're annoyed that I failed to meet you. I simply assumed you wouldn't show, given the dreary weather that morning. Clearly an error on my part."

When he leaned in closer, she slid sideways. "Not true at all, sir."

He let out a dramatic sigh while eyeing her breasts. "What a fool I was not to anticipate such innocent eagerness."

"It was not eagerness but stupidity. And please cease looming over me in that annoying fashion."

The marquess studied her for a moment before stepping back. "It seems I have behaved unforgivably on two counts. First, by suggesting that we meet privately. And then, even worse, by failing to appear."

"I am most grateful that you failed to show."

"Of course, you're concerned about rumors of scandal," he said. "Your father would be quite shocked. He might even think you have designs on me." His smile turned lewd. "Lucky me."

"That is a disgusting suggestion," she indignantly replied.

Cringlewood suddenly plucked the fan from her hand. "You're growing rather heated, darling. Why don't you let me fan you?"

Sabrina yanked the fan back. The conversation was *not* proceeding as anticipated.

"Sir, if you do not step away, I will scream."

He seemed genuinely surprised for a moment. Then his gaze turned chilly. "I do not take kindly to foolish games, my dear. One wonders why you invited me out here in the first place."

"Not to flirt or encourage unwelcome attentions, I assure you."

"I see. Then you'll forgive me if I excuse myself. But do not think I will forget your shabby treatment, my lady." He flicked her a contemptuous glance before turning to leave.

"I know what sort of man you are, Lord Cringlewood," she flung after him. "Now, you will leave town, or I will make sure others know, too."

He spun around. "What the bloody hell are you talking about?"

"You abuse women and take advantage of them. I intend to stop that."

He stared blankly at her for a moment before barking out a harsh laugh. "Ah, Kendrick was gabble-mongering, I see. Well, my girl, I was the injured party in that affair. Ainsley Kendrick is little better than a whore, and her husband is a grub who was only after her fortune."

She shook her head. "You are positively delusional, Lord Cringlewood."

"No, you're delusional if you think anyone will believe such nonsense. Although *you* accepted the tale readily enough." His lips curled into a sneer. "I begin to wonder about your relationship with that Highland moron. Perhaps Lady Sabrina is not so innocent as she would like the world to believe."

Sabrina had to swallow her anger before she could reply.

"You are a vile man, and I will do whatever I must to make sure everyone knows it."

"I think not. I can ruin your reputation in an instant, just like I can ruin Lady Ainsley's. In fact, I will enjoy doing exactly that."

"And *I* will be having a chat with the king about your disgusting conduct. Perhaps you have forgotten that His Majesty is my godparent, and that my father is one of his oldest friends? You will no longer be welcome at Court or anywhere else once I am finished with you."

The marquess stood like a block of marble, as if fused to the flagstones. But his eyes blazed with hatred.

Sabrina snapped her fan shut. "Therefore, I suggest you leave town as soon as possible, sir. Now, if you'll excuse me—"

When he suddenly lunged, Sabrina reacted instinctively and leapt to the side. Cringlewood fell heavily against the stone balustrade, almost toppling over the rail.

"You bitch!" He righted himself and reached for her.

"Don't touch her, ye bastard!" Graeme Kendrick, in all his Highland glory, charged toward them.

When Cringlewood jerked round to face Graeme, Sabrina made an instantaneous decision. She rammed into Cringlewood, shoulder-first, knocking him over the balustrade.

"Ouch," she yelped, surprised by pain that shot down her arm.

Graeme reached her, a broad-shouldered giant radiating masculine ire. Sabrina had to resist the urge to throw herself into his arms.

Don't be a ninny.

He briefly cupped her cheek. "Sabrina, are ye all right?"

She flexed her arm and then shook it. "I gave myself quite a jolt."

His calloused fingertips brushed over her shoulder with

a surprisingly gentle touch. "Och, ye daft girl. There was no need to hurt yerself."

She managed a smile. "Your brogue becomes quite marked on occasion, I've noticed."

He let out a snort. "Aye, you're fine. Yon idiot, however, may not be."

They both peered over the considerable drop into the rosebushes below. The groans drifting up became curses, suggesting a decidedly hard landing.

Graeme's expression turned rather stern. "Sabrina, what were you thinking, coming out here with him? And knocking him over the railing? Not helpful, lass."

"But you were going to mill him down, were you not? Surely brawling on the terrace would have been even less helpful, for my reputation and yours."

His mouth twitched sideways. "Point taken, I suppose."

The noises from below suggested Cringlewood was attempting to free himself from his thorny prison. Graeme peered again over the balustrade.

"Stay here while I go check on the bastard," he said. "Better yet, go back inside."

Sabrina had no intention of complying with that instruction. For one thing, she suspected Graeme might take the opportunity to exact further punishment. While she sympathized, it was best not to draw any more attention to the scene. A quick glance around showed her that they'd been lucky so far. She'd like to keep it that way.

She picked up her skirts and followed him down the curving, shallow steps into the night-shrouded garden. Graeme came to a quick stop, and Sabrina almost collided with his brawny form.

"Do you never listen to anyone?" he asked.

"When I decide it makes sense, I do."

"Going back inside would make a great deal of sense."

"If I do, you'll no doubt commence brawling with his lordship, and that will cause more unwanted attention."

Graeme muttered something under his breath.

"Or you might even kill him," she added, remembering Graeme's apparent fondness for stowing knives on his person.

"Killing's too good for that bas—that bounder."

"It would not be good for you, however. Or for Lady Ainsley, I suspect."

"Good of you to remember that now," he sarcastically replied.

He headed down the steps, Sabrina in his wake.

A wide grass path ran parallel to the bushes. It was easy enough to locate Cringlewood, since he was still making an unholy amount of noise as he thrashed his way out of the dense shrubbery.

"A little less commotion might be appropriate, Lord Cringlewood," Sabrina said in a disapproving voice. "If anyone comes outside, they're bound to hear you."

The marquess finally tore free of the thorny rosebushes and staggered out. His clothes were a disaster, and even as dark as it was, Sabrina could see numerous scratches on his face and hands.

Graeme glanced at her with a reluctant smile. "I admit you did roll him up."

"I do try."

"You're insane," Cringlewood hissed at her. "How dare you attack me?"

"My sister-in-law would ask you the same question." Graeme's tone carried a hard warning.

"Your sister-in-law is a whoring bitch." Cringlewood then jabbed a finger at Sabrina. "As for this little piece, I'm guessing you already got under her skirts. Kendrick men have a—"

Graeme's massive fist shot out like Thor's hammer and

connected squarely with Cringlewood's jaw. The man collapsed without a sound.

Sabrina blinked. "Goodness, that was impressive."

"I do try."

"What in the bloody blazes is going on out here?"

Graeme sighed. "And the hounds of hell have been unleashed."

Aden St. George stalked up to them, with Vivien scampering to keep up with her husband's long strides.

Sabrina held up a hand. "No need to worry, sir. Everything is under control."

St. George came to a halt, fists propped on his hips as he inspected the wreck of both Lord Cringlewood and Lady Peregrim's prize rosebushes.

"You must have an unusual definition of *under control*, Lady Sabrina." Then he shot an irate glance at Graeme. "Really?"

Graeme shrugged. "Not sure what else I was supposed to do."

"You were supposed to let me handle it."

Vivien elbowed her husband aside and laid a hand on Sabrina's arm. "My dear, are you all right? Did Cringlewood hurt you?"

"The hurting went the other way, actually," Graeme said.

"I may have given his lordship a nudge in the direction of the balustrade," Sabrina admitted.

"Lass, you went at him like a battering ram, knocking him over."

"Yes, but after he got out of the bushes, *you* hit him."

"Only because the bastard was insulting you."

"Language, dear boy," Vivien said. "There are ladies present."

St. George covered his eyes. "You're all insane."

"Insanely effective, if you ask me." Vivien nudged the

marquess with her daintily shod foot. "I fear his lordship may not be waking up anytime soon."

"Well, I've got to get the blighter out of here before anyone sees him." St. George scowled at Graeme. "But don't think we won't be having a further discussion about this."

"In all fairness, this was mostly my fault," Sabrina said.

"That's true," Graeme said. "I told you to steer clear of him."

Well, that was annoying, when she *was* trying to defend the man.

"May we please focus on the issue at hand?" St. George asked in a long-suffering tone. "We need some muscle to carry this moron out through the garden to his carriage."

"Do you want me to fetch Lady Peregrim's footmen, my love?" Vivien asked.

"I'd prefer my own men, so as to keep this as quiet as possible. If you could—"

"Sir, I realize the need for discretion," Sabrina interrupted. "But I hope you're not intending to entirely cover up this matter. While I understand you wish to preserve my reputation and Lady Ainsley's dignity, Cringlewood must be stopped."

St. George shot Graeme an irritated look. "You told her about Ainsley?"

"Och, the lass wouldn't stop badgering me."

"How I came by the information is immaterial," Sabrina said with offended dignity. "What is not immaterial is the need for justice."

"The marquess will face justice," St. George replied. "I promise you that."

"But—"

"Lady Sabrina, I will go to the king myself."

"You can trust Aden, dearest," Vivien said. "He's just the one to take care of this nasty situation."

"I *was* taking care of it until you lot bolloxed it up," St. George said.

"Just ignore him," Vivien said to Sabrina in a loud stage whisper.

Graeme flashed St. George a meaningful look. "So, we're done here? I have that other business to attend to."

"I already sent Cooper up, but you'd best check on him," St. George cryptically replied.

Sabrina couldn't help wondering what that *other business* was. Some murky political affair was the likeliest explanation, given St. George's rather mysterious duties with the Home Office. But what did Graeme Kendrick have to do with any of that?

"No need for any checking," said another voice from behind them.

Vivien sighed. "This is rather turning into a garden party."

"A bit dark for that," Sabrina said.

"We can start a new fashion," Vivien wryly replied. "A moonlit al fresco party."

"Cooper, if you're waiting for this absurd discussion to conclude, you'll be waiting all night," St. George said.

The fellow was broad-shouldered and stocky, dressed in the plain garb of a servant. When he cast Sabrina a cautious glance, she crossed her arms and lifted a defiant chin. She had no intention of leaving.

St. George waved an exasperated hand. "Just report."

"I was too late, sir. Lady Peregrim's room had been tossed, and her maid had already raised the alarm. Shrieking her fool head off, she was. The butler wasn't much better. I had to shove 'em both back in the room and tell them to keep their blabbers shut. The butler had already sent for Lord Peregrim, though, so the cat's out of the bag."

"Was anything taken?" Graeme asked.

"Her ladyship's jewelry box was smashed open. A set of

pearls and a few diamond bracelets were gone. Probably more."

Graeme muttered a quite shocking and inventive oath.

"Well put," St. George said in a dry tone. "Where is Lord Peregrim now?"

"Waiting for you in his study, sir."

"Does Lady Peregrim know what happened?" Vivien asked.

Cooper grimaced. "She and her maid were just having a nice bit of hysterics together."

"Oh, drat," sighed Vivien.

Her husband cast her a look.

She flapped a hand. "All right. I'll go up and deal with Lady Peregrim."

"Do your best to keep her and the maid under wraps."

Vivien gave Sabrina a hug. "I'll talk to you later, my dear. Do go home and get some rest," she said before hurrying off.

Graeme nudged the now faintly moaning Lord Cringlewood. "Want me to take care of this idiot?"

"Cooper will see to it. You're not to go near the marquess again," St. George ordered.

"I wasn't looking for a fight, you know."

"And yet one found you, anyway," St. George replied. "As usual."

"Then what *do* you want me to do," Graeme said, his frustration evident.

"Get Lady Sabrina home, quickly and quietly. Take my carriage."

"That won't be necessary. . . . Oh, bother." Sabrina sighed at St. George's retreating back.

"Sure you don't need my help?" Graeme asked Cooper, who'd crouched down to inspect Cringlewood.

"Nay, sir. Best get the lady home, like the captain said."

"I don't need anyone to *get* me home," Sabrina protested.

Graeme took her arm. "Come along, you."

He marched her to the terrace steps. She had to scramble to keep up with him.

"Sir, I am not a racehorse."

"Oh, sorry. I keep forgetting you're such a dab little thing."

"I am not," she indignantly replied.

He led her up the stairs and across the terrace.

"I expect most everyone seems small to you," she added as he ushered her into the thankfully deserted corridor. "You're a giant."

"Not really. My brother Logan is taller than I am."

"I do hope he has better manners."

"Worse. We're a fairly blunt lot."

Sabrina was starting to develop a stitch in her side from all the rushing about. "Then I shall hope never to meet any of them."

He cast her an obscure glance. "No fear of that, lass. We're not Mayfair sort of folk."

His tone made her wince. "Forgive me. I'm sure your family is perfectly lovely."

That elicited a quick smile. "Lovely doesn't exactly suit, but we rub along just fine. Did you bring a wrap?"

"No, it's very mild out."

They made their way to the entrance hall, where two footmen and a maid stood in a huddle, excitedly whispering. Word of the theft had obviously filtered out.

The only guests there were an elderly couple that the head footman was escorting out the door. Thank goodness the couple were leaving. Although Graeme was obviously a gentleman, it would be considered scandalous for Sabrina to leave alone with him.

She and Graeme had almost reached the front door when she pulled up short. "Oh, I forgot that I'm supposed to go home with Lady Farnsworth. I promised my father."

He looked irritated. "Bad idea. Besides, I have my orders."

The head footman stepped forward, looking concerned. "May I be of assistance, my lady?"

"Yes," Graeme said. "Inform Lady Farnsworth that Lady Sabrina is unwell and is going directly home in Captain St. George's carriage."

Then Graeme marched her out the door and down the steps to the line of carriages.

"That was *very* rude," she huffed. "Whatever will the servants think?"

"I don't give a damn. Besides, once the news gets out about the robbery, no one will think twice about us."

His mood was grim, but his logic was sound. "I suppose that's true."

"Which is a lucky break for you, but not so lucky for the Peregrims."

"It's very unfortunate, but you can hardly blame *me* for the robbery."

When he shot her an immensely frustrated look, she blinked. If she didn't know better, she might almost have thought he *did* blame her for the theft.

That was silly, of course.

A dark-coated groom came around from the back of the St. George carriage and opened the door. "Any luck, sir?"

"Only bad luck, unfortunately."

"The captain won't like that."

"As I am painfully aware."

The groom's wince was sympathetic, which proved that this mysterious affair did have something to do with Graeme.

Sabrina adjusted her skirts as Graeme settled opposite, canting his long legs sideways to give her room. As the carriage pulled out of line, he crossed his arms over his chest and scowled out the window. Sabrina was positively bursting with questions, but tact seemed the wiser course at the moment.

After a few minutes, he cut her a sardonic glance. "You're uncommonly quiet."

She tried not to bristle. "I don't think you know me well enough to ascertain when I'm being *uncommonly* quiet."

"I know you well enough, lass."

While his tone was neither complimentary nor encouraging, she decided to take the opening. "I can't help thinking that tonight's events were rather curious."

"Which ones? There were quite a lot of *events*."

She resisted the urge to kick him, which showed how off balance she was. Ladies never kicked gentlemen, unless absolutely necessary.

"I'm referring specifically to the theft of Lady Peregrim's jewels. Both you and Captain St. George seemed to be uncommonly knowledgeable about those proceedings. Almost as if you anticipated them."

He studied her for a few moments. "Sorry, my lady. Don't know what you're talking about."

"That is patently untrue. That mysterious Cooper person, for instance, was sent to investigate the theft. He obviously takes orders from St. George, which means he works for him."

Then it hit her like a spiky pinecone bouncing off her head. How *had* she missed it? "As do you, since you were also intending to investigate the *other business*."

"Nonsense. St. George is family, that's all."

Graeme turned his gaze to the window, apparently to end the conversation.

As if a little thing like that would stop her.

"This has something to do with those dreadful robberies taking place within the *ton*, doesn't it? I'm going to assume that St. George is leading the investigation." After a long pause, she tapped Graeme on the knee with her fan. "Feel free to continue to pretend I don't exist."

Graeme scowled. "You really are the most annoying girl."

"Ha. That means I'm right. It makes perfect sense. St. George works for the Home Office *and* is the king's son. His Majesty is quite disturbed by the situation. He told my father so just the other day."

Graeme shrugged. "As I said, I wouldn't know."

"Nonsense. It's clear you're helping the captain. Are you an inquiry agent of some sort, Mr. Kendrick?"

For a few moments, Sabrina thought he'd simply refuse to answer her admittedly blunt question.

"I occasionally help St. George. Very informally," he admitted.

She snapped her fingers. "I knew it. You were at the Peregrims to help catch the thief." Unsuccessfully. No wonder St. George was cross. "I'm sorry he got away."

His green gaze turned sardonic. "Thanks to you."

That made no sense, unless . . .

"Oh, dear," she weakly said as realization dawned.

"Yes, I was following the blasted thief when I found out you'd gone haring off with Cringlewood. Of all the idiotic—"

She put up a hand. "I understand your frustration, but you needn't have interrupted your investigation. I would have screamed the entire house down before I let Cringlewood touch me."

"That is unbelievably naïve. The situation could have gone to hell in an instant. And I *did* save you from a bloody great scandal, by the way."

That part was true, so it wouldn't hurt to be charitable. "Then I am truly sorry for any inconvenience I caused. My sincere apologies, my dear sir."

He shook his head. "You *are* daft."

If her fan hadn't already suffered enough abuse for one

evening, she might have whacked him with it. "There is no need for insults, Mr. Kendrick."

"If you'd gone home like a good girl, none of this would have happened."

"Like a good girl?" she echoed in disbelief. "What a ridiculous thing to say to a grown woman."

"If ye'd gone with yer da, I would have caught the thief. And St. George was already dealing with Cringlewood, ye ken."

The brogue had returned, signaling his immense irritation.

He's not the only irritated one.

"One cannot rely upon others to solve one's problems, sir." Years of experience had taught her that men were generally unreliable. Sabrina had learned quite early to rely on herself. "Since Lord Cringlewood was pursuing *me*, it made sense to deal with the situation forthwith."

Graeme briefly covered his eyes. "Did I say daft? Deranged, more like."

Thankfully, she was spared the destruction of her fan by their arrival at her house. "On that happy note, I will bid you good night, Mr. Kendrick."

"Och, we're not finished, lass," he growled.

She threw open the door, almost clocking the poor groom who'd come around to set the carriage step. "We are *more* than finished, sir. Good night."

As she took the groom's hand, Sabrina ignored the brogue-heavy oath that followed her into the night.

Chapter Six

From their elegant box, Sabrina's father peered with concern around the theater. "I have never been to the Pan, nor has the king. Why would we? Those persons in the pit look quite dangerous to me."

The patrons were a perfectly normal mix of aristocrats, shopkeepers and their families, and boisterous but good-humored young men. But since Sabrina's father rarely went to public performances, fearing exposure to both infection and the *lower orders*, as he called them, his attitude wasn't surprising.

"You are perfectly safe, Lord Musgrave," said Chloe, Lady Hunter, who was seated behind them in the box. "My husband would never put any of us in harm's way."

"Indeed," said Sir Dominic Hunter. "Bow Street Runners are on the premises, providing security. There is also a decided lack of riffraff tonight, due to the cost of the tickets."

Tonight's gala performance was a charitable affair for an orphanage in St. Giles, as well as a home for unwed mothers and their babies. Lady Hunter ran the latter establishment herself.

Sabrina's father had known Sir Dominic for years, since the dignified magistrate had a close relationship with the king. But since the Hunters spent much of their time at their manor house just outside London, Sabrina knew them only as nodding acquaintances. Their invitation, although flattering, had certainly been unexpected.

"Father and I were very happy to make a contribution to your charity," Sabrina said, smiling at their hostess.

"Thank you, my dear. You were most generous."

Father looked vaguely alarmed. "We were? Did you—"

"I've never attended a theatrical event at the Pan," Sabrina brightly interjected. "I'm looking forward to it."

Lady Hunter's gaze twinkled with understanding. "It's usually a great deal of fun. Dominic and I always enjoy ourselves here."

"Yes, *great* fun," her husband replied with sardonic emphasis.

"I do hope there will be no bawdy or ridiculous romps," Father said fretfully. "The Pan is known for that sort of thing."

"I picked the program myself," her ladyship assured him. "Everything will be in the best of taste."

Drat. Sabrina could use a bit of fun after the debacle at Lady Peregrim's ball last week, followed by that humiliating scene in the carriage with Graeme Kendrick. She'd not seen him since, and was absolutely burning to apologize for her rude behavior. Not that Graeme had covered himself in glory either, but he'd had a very trying night, so she couldn't truly fault him.

"I *certainly* hope we will not be troubled by those dreadful thieves," her father added. "I asked Sabrina to wear her simplest jewelry, but she paid me no heed."

"Father, no self-respecting thief would look twice at these pearls. They're as plain as plain can be."

He flapped his handkerchief with agitation. "There is no such thing as a self-respecting thief, Sabrina. Goodness, me."

"It's a figure of speech, dearest. Of course, I'm dreadfully concerned, too."

Especially since her lamentable conduct at the Peregrims'
ball had been responsible for allowing at least one of the
thieves to escape.

"Bow Street will provide ample protection, Lord Musgrave," Sir Dominic said. "You have nothing to fear."

A subtle note in the magistrate's voice prompted Sabrina
to turn and catch his eye. She'd always found Sir Dominic's
craggy, impassive features difficult to read. Now, he met her
perusal with a bland smile.

"Oh, look. The orchestra is coming out to start the performance," said Lady Hunter.

"How splendid," Sir Dominic said dryly.

"My love, do try to have fun, for once," his wife said
with mock exasperation.

He flashed a wicked grin. "As you know, I frequently
have fun, my dear. I just prefer to do it at home."

When her ladyship's cheeks turned pink, Sabrina turned
to the front, stifling a grin. While not in the first blush of
youth, the Hunters were devoted to each other, and didn't
hide it. That sort of devotion made her feel . . . wistful.

"I agree, Sir Dominic," Father said. "A quiet evening at
home is more pleasant than anything."

"Indeed it is," the magistrate replied.

Fortunately, the mildly risqué riposte sailed over her
father's head.

After the anthem to the king, the performance began with
a classical recitation set to music. While Sabrina's father
clearly enjoyed it, she found it as dull as reading sermons on
a rainy afternoon in January.

"Dominic, would you change seats with Lady Sabrina,
so I can chat with her?" Lady Hunter quietly asked.

Thank God.

Sabrina all but jumped to her feet. "You'll get a *much*
better view of the stage from here, Sir Dominic."

"This bit is quite good," said her father. "You won't wish to miss it, my dear sir."

Sir Dominic rolled his eyes, forcing Sabrina to stifle a giggle.

"How did you know I was bored?" she whispered to Lady Hunter.

"I had to pick *all* the most boring pieces in the company's repertoire, so as to avoid scandalous chitchat." Lady Hunter flashed a wry smile. "Vivien and I expended considerable energy convincing the company manager to clothe the dancers in, shall we say, slightly more decorous styles."

The dancers were incredibly popular at establishments like the Pan, since they were invariably young, pretty, and scantily clad.

"What a disappointment for the men," Sabrina joked.

Lady Hunter winked. "True. It's a good thing the wives make the donations."

Her ladyship possessed a down-to-earth quality that was unusual in the *ton*. Sabrina found it enormously appealing.

"I'm so glad you asked us tonight," she impulsively said. "I'm not sure why you did, but please accept my thanks."

"Vivien suggested it. After hearing about your assorted adventures, I couldn't resist the opportunity to get to know you better."

Sabrina winced. "Oh, yes, you're Vivien's aunt. I suppose she told you about . . ."

"She told me what I needed to know." Lady Hunter glanced at Sabrina's father. "And I will keep those adventures private, be assured. Well done with Cringlewood, by the way. I cheered when Vivien told me what you did."

"Is . . . is that matter being dealt with?" Sabrina murmured.

"He has already departed London, with a stern warning from both Aden and my husband that he will be carefully watched. The marquess will not bother you or any other woman again."

Sabrina frowned. "But how—"

"My husband will see to it," her ladyship firmly replied.

Looking at Sir Dominic's stern profile, Sabrina believed it.

"Thank you," she said.

"You're welcome. And please don't waste another thought on that horrid man. He will get his comeuppance soon enough."

It was clear from her ladyship's tone that the subject was closed, and that more than suited Sabrina.

"Where is Lady Vivien this evening? I thought she would be here."

Lady Hunter inclined her head toward the other side of the theater. "Vivien has family visiting. She's sitting with her mamma and her younger brother, Kit."

"Oh, and I suppose the captain is also . . ."

Sabrina trailed off when she saw exactly who was sitting with Vivien and her family, and it wasn't Aden St. George. It was Graeme Kendrick, and he was staring straight at her with a disconcerting intensity.

She ignored the sudden, mad thumping of her heart and gave him a friendly smile. After all, theaters were so brightly lit that one couldn't pretend not to notice when someone stared. Still, it was hard to read his expression. She'd never met anyone who could adopt a stoneface better than Graeme Kendrick.

But when Graeme smiled at her, it was like enjoying the blaze of a bonfire when chilled to the bone.

Sadly, he wasn't smiling now.

Just when *her* smile was beginning to feel permanently fixed to her face, Graeme finally gave her a brusque nod. He then rose from his chair and slipped from the box.

Lady Hunter leaned close. "Don't worry. Graeme will get over it."

Sabrina waggled a hand. "I can't blame him for being annoyed. But it's not as if I knew about his role in catching the—"

Her ladyship held up a warning finger.

"Sorry," Sabrina whispered. "It's just that I'd like to apologize to him for making a mess of things."

"No apology necessary, although I'm sure Graeme would be delighted to speak to you again."

Sabrina doubted that. Still, if she did see him again, she would apologize, no matter how mortifying the experience might prove to be.

"Is Mr. Kendrick here tonight because of the . . ." She tapped one of her earrings. "You know."

"You're not to worry," Lady Hunter firmly said. "Please just relax and enjoy the show."

Discussion closed, again.

But Sabrina felt too scattered to concentrate on the musical interludes and the entirely absurd adaptation of Spenser's *The Faerie Queene*. When the interval came, she was grateful to stand and shake the fidgets from her arms.

"Would you like to go down to the saloon for a refreshment?" she asked her father.

He gave a little moue of distaste. "It's sure to be an awful crush, my love, and think of the risk of infection from such riffraff. We should remain in the box."

Sabrina pressed a gloved hand to the base of her skull, where a headache began to niggle. She desperately needed to stretch her legs and find something cold to drink.

"There are no riffraff tonight," Lady Hunter said, "and we have excellent champagne and lovely ices, as well."

Father wavered for a few moments, obviously not wishing to be rude, before shaking his head. "Thank you, ma'am, but Sabrina and I will remain in the box. Perhaps you might have a waiter bring us each a glass of ratafia."

Argh. Sabrina hated ratafia.

Sir Dominic winked at her. "I find myself equally loath to mingle with the crowd, Lord Musgrave, no matter how distinguished. The ladies should go to the saloon, while the men stay here and have a comfortable chat."

"Are you sure it's perfectly safe for the ladies?" Father anxiously asked.

"My word of honor. Besides, I've been meaning to quiz you about your renowned coin collection. I'm thinking of starting one, and who better to ask for advice than Lord Musgrave?"

Sabrina's father brightened. "I should be delighted to give you the benefit of my knowledge, dear sir. Mind, it's quite a complicated subject, so we will barely be able to touch on it."

"I'm ready to learn at the feet of the master," Sir Dominic replied with an entirely straight face.

"Do you have any experience with collecting?"

"None at all, I'm afraid."

"That will never do," Father sternly replied. "You must have a focus, or you will simply flounder."

While her father commenced peppering Sir Dominic with questions, Sabrina followed Lady Hunter into the hall behind the private boxes.

"Your husband is a prince among men," Sabrina said.

Lady Hunter laughed. "In more ways than you know."

They joined the line of chattering theatergoers heading down to the saloon.

"Well, thank you again for asking us. I know Father can be a bit of a trial. His health is indifferent, and that makes him fretful."

"The honor is ours. As I mentioned, Vivien has a great deal of respect for you, as does Graeme."

Sabrina wrinkled her nose. "I suspect Mr. Kendrick finds me a nuisance."

"I doubt that."

"He was quite annoyed when last I saw him."

"As I mentioned, he'll get over it."

Sabrina didn't understand why she hoped that he did quite so much. They weren't likely to see very much of each other. She lived a lovely but conventional life within the confines of Mayfair, while he obviously lived another kind of life entirely.

"I take it that Mr. Kendrick's family rarely travels to London," she commented as she and Lady Hunter slowly followed a pair of bombazine-clad matrons down the stairs.

"Lord and Lady Arnprior prefer to spend most of their time at Castle Kinglas or at their mansion in Glasgow."

"A castle in Scotland sounds so romantic," Sabrina wistfully replied. "I would love to visit someday."

"Then you should certainly make the trip. The Kendricks would love to meet you, I have no doubt."

Sabrina mentally blinked. "But I don't even know them."

"You know Graeme, and Aden is Lady Arnprior's brother. The Kendricks would be delighted to have you visit with them."

It seemed an odd thing to say, but perhaps Lady Hunter was simply being polite. "My father rarely travels outside London anymore, and then only to our estate near Oxford."

"You never go north to Bellwood Manor?"

"Father now finds the journey too taxing, unfortunately."

She loved the old northern manor, and perhaps someday she would travel there by herself, despite her father's objections.

"Your mother's family is from Scotland, I believe?" Lady Hunter said.

"Yes, she was a member of Clan Chattan. She left our family a small estate just south of Inverness. I hope to see that someday, too."

Her ladyship cast Sabrina a thoughtful glance. "We must

see what we can do about that. You would love Scotland, I'm sure of it."

Sabrina was spared a reply by the bustle in the saloon, especially around the refreshments table, where liveried footmen handed out beverages and ices. An acquaintance snagged Lady Hunter, so Sabrina squeezed by a portly old gentleman to snag a glass of champagne. Two friends across the room waved for her to join them, but she wasn't in the mood for chitchat. She preferred to amuse herself by watching the crowd.

Silly, you're looking for him.

But she wasn't seeing him, which was annoying.

Lady Hunter joined her with a glass of punch. "I'm absolutely parched, and Lady Purcell always rattles me. I'm terribly bad at socializing."

"Oh, Lady Purcell can be a bit of a trial. She never stops talking about her various ailments, especially her bunions. She and my father are fast friends."

Lady Hunter laughed. "Thankfully, she's making a generous donation to my charity, so I'm grateful for that."

Sabrina was about to reply when she spotted Graeme. He slipped quietly into the room, attracting little attention. It was quite the feat given his impressive size and the shock of gorgeous red hair her fingers simply itched to stroke.

As she watched him, it seemed as if no one but her *did* notice him. His actions weren't exactly furtive, but . . .

"What is he doing?" she muttered.

Lady Hunter glanced across the room. "Ah, I wondered when Graeme would appear."

"He's acting quite mysteriously."

Her ladyship lowered her voice. "It's his job to act mysteriously, as you know. I was surprised to hear that he confided in you."

"He didn't. I guessed it."

Lady Hunter's delicate eyebrows shot up. "You did?"

"He tried to deny it at first."

"One tends not to advertise such things."

"I won't say a word, I promise," Sabrina earnestly replied.

"I'm sure Graeme trusts you. He would have refused to admit to anything if he didn't."

"Do you think he's, um, working tonight?"

"Just as a precaution. There is no need to worry."

Sabrina's gaze once more returned to the handsome Scot, who was discretely but thoroughly patrolling the saloon. She marveled at how he managed to do it without drawing any attention.

"I never see him at social events," she said.

"Aden keeps him busy."

"That's quite a shame." Sabrina grimaced, mortified by the admission. "What I mean, is—"

Lady Hunter smiled. "Graeme is handsome and very charming when he's not being so serious. He *should* socialize more, especially with a lovely young woman such as yourself."

"Oh, I don't think—"

Vivien St. George suddenly appeared out of the crowd. "Ah, there you are. It's such a mad crush, isn't it?" She gave Sabrina a quick, verbena-scented hug. "You look splendid, dearest. Quite the prettiest girl here."

Sabrina smiled. "No, that would be you."

Vivien scoffed. "Flatterer. Would you mind if I stole Chloe for a moment? We have a minor crisis with the program that simply must be sorted before the interval ends."

Lady Hunter frowned. "I don't wish to leave Sabrina alone. Lord Musgrave would never forgive me."

"I'll be fine," Sabrina quickly said. "Several of my friends are right over there. I can go up with them."

Lady Hunter looked doubtful but acquiesced. "Go right back to the box, all right?"

"I promise."

"Chloe, disaster looms," prompted Vivien.

Lady Hunter allowed herself to be hurried off.

Sabrina watched them go before switching her attention to a broad set of Scottish shoulders disappearing up the staircase to a group of private boxes.

Discarding her glass on a sideboard and ignoring the determined waves of her friends, she slipped across the room.

The thieves would undoubtedly find tonight's gala too alluring a target to ignore.

Graeme checked the hallway behind the private boxes, his senses tuned for anything out of the ordinary. Guards were posted backstage, theater staff had been alerted, and Runners patrolled the premises. Finally, they had a real chance to bring the criminal ring tumbling to the ground.

He couldn't afford to fail again. If he did, Aden would be forced to pull additional agents off other, more vital missions. To Graeme's way of thinking, that would count as nothing less than abject failure.

He was bloody well tired of failing.

Graeme was also bloody well tired of the distraction posed by Lady Sabrina Bell. He had been hoping she wouldn't be here tonight, but then he'd seen her with the Hunters. She looked like a damn angel in a sunny dress that rippled like a river of silk, highlighting every beautiful curve of her body. A crown of bright, golden curls topped her head. Her smile was even brighter, a beam of sunshine that bathed him in unfamiliar warmth.

But she's not for you, laddie boy.

Besides, she was a royal pain in the arse, with a disapproving ninny for a father, who obviously thought Graeme not good enough for his daughter.

Spotting a door to one of the boxes that was half-open,

he interrupted a gossip between two elderly ladies dripping with diamonds and pearls.

The perfect mark.

"Young man, is there something you want?" one of the women frostily asked.

Graeme adopted his bumbling routine. "Oh, I say, I have the wrong box. Sorry to bother, dear ladies."

"Impertinent fellow," huffed the other woman as he backed out.

He firmly closed the door, then continued along the hall, hoping to check all the boxes before the patrons returned. Aden and his men were handling the pit and galleries, and Sir Dominic was no doubt directing his hawk-like gaze over all the proceedings from his well-placed box.

As loath as Graeme was to encounter Lord Musgrave again, he needed to check in with Sir Dominic. The thieves were most likely to strike after the interval, when most of the audience would be tipsy if not downright cup-shot.

A quick patter of feet sounded behind him. "Mr. Kendrick, please wait."

Well, that's just damn splendid.

Reluctantly, he turned to find Sabrina poised at the top of the staircase. Her cheeks were flushed and her breasts were . . . yes, the word was heaving. Lovely breasts they were, too—a creamy swell over the frilly lace of her trim bodice. Despite his massive irritation, Graeme felt something else threaten to grow massive, and he had an instant, insane urge to pull the lass into one of the empty boxes, take her down to the carpeted floor, and rip that frilly bodice right down.

You're a ninny.

"Lady Sabrina, you should not be wandering about—"

"But I wanted to—"

She was interrupted by a man's appearance at the top of the stairs, behind her. When she squeaked and almost jumped out of her shoes, Graeme cursed and started forward.

"I wouldn't, mate," the man said. "I've got a nice little popper on her."

Graeme froze, his gut congealing with fear.

Her captor was tall, with a hard, confident gaze, and was dressed in elegant evening clothes. One could easily take him for a banker or a wealthy merchant and not give him a second thought.

Sabrina, who'd gone dead white, cleared her throat. "I assume that *popper* refers to the pistol shoved against my spine."

Graeme took a cautious step closer. She was only ten feet away, but it might as well have been a mile. While he was very fast, he wasn't faster than a goddamned bullet. Sweat prickled under his collar. If anything happened to her . . .

"You'll be fine as soon as you hand over them pearls," the thief said. When he shot a quick glance down the stairs, Graeme shuffled another step forward.

"But these were my mother's," Sabrina protested. "They're not worth much at all, but they have sentimental value."

"As much as your bloody life?" the bastard snapped. "Now take 'em off before I throttle you with 'em."

"Harm a hair on her head, and you're a dead man," Graeme gritted out.

When Sabrina jumped again, the man grinned. "I'm shaking in me boots, I am. Now take them off, silly bitch, or I *will* hurt you."

Her gaze latched desperately onto Graeme's. He locked his gaze onto hers, trying to radiate calm. "Do as he says, lass. Please."

Her elegant jaw clenched, she reached up to unhook her necklace. Then she grimly stripped off matching bracelets from her wrist.

"Hand 'em over your shoulder," the thief ordered.

After she complied, he jerked his chin at Graeme. "Come closer. Slow like."

Frowning, Graeme took a few cautious steps forward.

"Closer."

What the hell?

The thief gave Sabrina a mighty shove, pitching her straight into Graeme. Her foot tangled around his ankle, and they went down to the floor. He landed hard on his back, with Sabrina on his chest. Her hip connected forcefully with his groin.

Pain sucked the air from his lungs. His brain shrieked at him to get up and go after the thief, who was pelting down the stairs. His body, however, refused to comply.

Sabrina pushed up, her hipbone pressing harder into his beleaguered cock.

"Argh. Stop moving," he yelped.

"That villain stole my pearls." She started to scramble up, as if prepared to chase after the thief.

Graeme shot out a hand to grab her. "He's got a gun, you henwit."

She glared at him through her coiffure, now listing over one eye. Impatiently, she shoved the bedraggled knot to the side.

"I remember. It was pressed into *my* spine."

He sat up, fighting the pain. "Och, lass. You're worth more than any jewels."

Her outraged expression suddenly crumpled. "But those were my mother's pearls. Father gave them to her," she said in a forlorn voice.

"I'm sorry—"

Aden strode round the bend in the corridor. "Graeme, what the hell is Lady Sabrina doing on the floor?"

"We were accosted by a thief," she said. "He just absconded with my pearls."

"He went down the stairs," Graeme said.

Aden cursed. "Get Sabrina back to the box, and stay with her." Then he disappeared down the stairs.

Sabrina, now on her feet, peered down at Graeme. "Are you hurt?"

"Do you recall when your hip connected with my body, perchance?"

She grimaced. "I suppose I did fall rather hard. I'm so sorry."

He breathed out, willing the pain to fade. "Not your fault. Just give me a few more seconds, all right?"

"Perhaps we should send for a doctor?"

"Lass, there's nothing a sawbones can do about this particular problem."

She blinked, then turned a bright pink. "I'm *exceptionally* sorry."

"Not to worry."

As he carefully hoisted himself up, Chloe and Vivien came rushing up the staircase.

"Aden said you needed help," Vivien said. "What's wrong?"

"I was robbed," Sabrina dolefully replied. "A terrible man took my mother's pearls."

Chloe folded her into a comforting hug. "That's awful. Are you all right?"

"I'm unharmed."

Vivien leveled a stern look at Graeme. "And you just let this person run off with Sabrina's jewels?"

He glared right back. "He had a bloody pistol on her, Vivien."

"There was really nothing Mr. Kendrick could do," Sabrina explained. "The villain came right up behind me out of the blue, with his awful pistol."

"And I was a good ten feet away, unfortunately." He grimaced but finally managed to straighten up.

"Graeme, are you injured?" Chloe asked.

"Mr. Kendrick hurt himself when he fell on the floor," Sabrina explained.

Vivien frowned. "That sounds quite unhelpful of you, Graeme."

"I didn't just *happen* to fall. Lady Sabrina tripped me."

"Not on purpose," she protested.

"You should *not* have been wandering about unescorted." Now that she was safe, his frustration—and the remnants of his gut-wrenching fear for her—had resurfaced.

"He has a point, dearest," Vivien said. "Theaters can be a trifle dodgy."

"I wasn't wandering. I was following Mr. Kendrick."

Chloe, who was trying to repair Sabrina's hair, raised her eyebrows. "Also not very appropriate. Dear girl, please stand still while I fix your coiffure."

"Why were you following me?" Graeme couldn't help asking.

She wrinkled her nose. "Because I wanted to apologize for the other night, when I was rather beastly to you."

"Oh. Well, no harm done, lass." Then he mentally grimaced at his idiotic response.

Vivien looked ready to laugh, but a swell of voices had her glancing toward the stairwell. "The interval is over."

Chloe started to usher Sabrina toward their box. "Coming, Graeme?"

Sabrina glanced over her shoulder. "Aden did say you were to stay with me, Mr. Kendrick."

"For all the damn good it will do," he muttered. The thief was probably long gone by now.

He stalked behind them down the corridor to their box.

Sabrina hesitated before going in. "I don't know what I'm going to say to my father."

"Don't say anything. Maybe he won't notice," Graeme said.

She shot him an incredulous look.

"I'll explain," Chloe said. "We don't want to worry poor Lord Musgrave any more than we have to."

Dominic suddenly opened the door from the inside. His gaze flickered over their little group, snagging momentarily on Sabrina's bare throat. He let out an exasperated sigh.

"Really?" he said to Graeme.

"It's rather complicated, dear," Chloe said.

"It always is when a Kendrick is involved."

Dominic waved them into the box, reserving a stern look for Graeme.

Graeme didn't blame him. Dominic, the former chief of the spy service, and Aden had specifically entrusted this case to Graeme, and he'd made a cock-up of it from the beginning.

Lord Musgrave starched up when he saw Graeme. "Sabrina, I do hope you haven't been dallying in the saloon with strangers."

"Indeed, no," Chloe said. "Sabrina was with me."

"I simply happened to, um, run into Mr. Kendrick on the way back to the box," Sabrina explained.

"That's right," Graeme said. "I thought I'd stop in to pay my regards to you and Sir Dominic. I hope you're well, my lord. It's a pleasure to see you again."

Lord Musgrave sniffed and made a point of ignoring him. Staring at his daughter, he blinked, and his pursed lips sagged open. "Sabrina, where is your necklace?"

She flushed. "Oh, ah, the clasp was catching in my hair, so I took it off."

Her father's gaze trailed down to her gloved wrists, now stripped of their matching bracelets. His eyes widened in horror. "Your bracelets are gone!"

She sat next to him and took his hand. "There was a little incident, Father, but I'm fine. There's no need to be concerned."

"Sabrina, where are your mother's pearls?" Lord Musgrave asked rather loudly.

His daughter winced. "Well, you see . . ."

"Lady Sabrina had a regrettable encounter with a thief," Sir Dominic calmly interjected. "Distressing, of course, but she is entirely unharmed, which is obviously the most important thing."

Musgrave looked ready to topple into a dramatic swoon. "Those were your dear mother's pearls, Sabrina. How could you lose them like that?"

When the poor lass bit her lip, looking ashamed, Graeme's barely restrained patience evaporated. "She didn't do anything wrong, my lord. She was robbed."

Lord Musgrave rounded on him. "And did you witness this robbery, sir?"

Sabrina gave Graeme a frantic little shake of the head.

Och, she was trying to protect him, but the hell with that. Her father was a querulous old ninny, and he had no business biting her nose off.

"I did, sir. There was nothing your daughter could have done to prevent it."

Musgrave practically vibrated with aristocratic outrage. "And there was nothing *you* could do?"

"He tried, Father. It was an impossible situation," Sabrina quickly said.

Tut-tutting, Musgrave reached for his cane. "I will never recover from this, Sabrina. We must return home, immediately."

She winced. "Father, I'm so—"

"I knew we should never have come tonight." Musgrave threw an angry glance at Graeme. "Full of riffraff, did I not say?"

Chloe gave Sabrina a gentle embrace. "Perhaps it's best if you take your father home, my dear."

"I'm so very sorry," Sabrina forlornly said to Graeme when Chloe released her.

He had to repress the instinct to fold her into his arms

and cuddle her. "Don't fash yourself, my lady. It wasn't your fault."

"Indeed not," Dominic said. "And please know that I will do everything possible to recover your pearls."

"I should hope so, Sir Dominic," Lord Musgrave said as he took his daughter's arm. "You can be sure the king will hear about this. He will be *most* displeased."

Dominic tactfully ignored the annoying comment. "Let me escort you downstairs."

"I would hardly be surprised if we were murdered on the way out to the carriage," Musgrave fussed.

"You needn't worry." Dominic threw Graeme a sardonic glance. "The situation is now well in hand."

No thanks to you was what that glance silently conveyed.

Dominic solicitously escorted Lord Musgrave out of the box, Sabrina trailing behind. Before she disappeared, she looked over her shoulder at Graeme and mouthed *I'm sorry.* Regret darkened her peacock-blue gaze, probably for once more cocking up his mission.

But he thought he saw something more, too, and it mirrored the emotion bumping around in his chest. It was an odd kind of sadness, because he was damn sure he would never see Lady Sabrina Bell again. After tonight's debacle, her father wouldn't let her anywhere near him.

Not that it mattered, he supposed.

Chloe sank into her chair. "That went well."

"Ugh, dreadful." Vivien flopped dramatically into an empty seat. "Poor Sabrina. I don't mean to be rude, but her father is an unbelievable fusspot."

"He's a complete chucklehead, if you ask me," Graeme said.

"No one asked you," Dominic said as he stalked into the box. He took the seat next to his wife and eyed Graeme with disfavor. "While Lord Musgrave can sometimes be a difficult man, his concerns were quite justified. His daughter was placed in harm's way, and that was our failure."

There were few people who could intimidate Graeme. His brother, Nick, was certainly one, as was Aden. But neither had a patch on Dominic Hunter in that regard. Dominic's disapproval made Graeme want to slink out of the box and disappear into a deep hole, preferably on the other side of the world.

Suddenly weary from too many nights prowling about London trying to solve this bloody case, Graeme dropped into the chair next to Vivien. It creaked ominously under his weight.

"Try not to break the chair, dear," Vivien said, almost automatically.

"He'll be lucky if Aden doesn't break it over his head," Dominic said. "This was not how either of us expected the evening to conclude."

"Nor did I," Graeme muttered.

He'd fully expected the evening to end in victory. The opposite had occurred, thanks once again, to Sabrina's inadvertent and disastrous timing. Fortunately, the lass had kept her head, responding with courage and even a bit of defiance. Sabrina frustrated the hell out of him, but she was brave, funny, and kind, and he should have done a better job of protecting her.

"Graeme feels bad enough," Chloe said, reaching forward to pat him on the shoulder. "And I'm certain Sabrina doesn't blame you at all, dear boy."

"I should hope not, since she's the one who was wandering about alone." He shook his head. "That was daft."

Vivien winced. "My fault, I'm afraid. I distracted Chloe and left Sabrina on her own. I do wish she'd waited for us."

"Yes, that was quite odd of her," Dominic said.

"I have an idea why she wandered off," Chloe remarked in an amused tone.

"It doesn't matter," Graeme firmly replied, "except to say she has a knack for stumbling into unfortunate situations. Needs a damn keeper, she does."

Vivien flashed him a cheeky grin. "Any ideas on who might like to take on the position, laddie boy?"

"No."

Aden joined them, interrupting the embarrassing discussion. He hooked an empty chair from the corner and pulled it over to sit next to Vivien.

"Anything?" Dominic asked.

"I almost caught the bounder out front before he dodged between two carriages." Aden snorted. "One all but knocked me flat on my arse."

Vivien squeaked and clutched his sleeve. "Are you all right?"

"I'm fine, love. Just annoyed."

"Better annoyed than dead," she scolded. "You're not supposed to take risks like that anymore. That's why you have Graeme."

"Exactly," Graeme said. "Unfortunately, I was ordered to escort Lady Sabrina back to her box."

"Aden probably wished to avoid Lord Musgrave's wrath," Chloe said with a twinkle.

"Lucky bastard," Graeme muttered.

Aden actually grimaced in sympathy. "That bad?"

"Worse, and he all but tore a strip off his daughter. The poor girl was already upset. She didn't need that old pinhead barking at her."

"Lord Musgrave is devoted to Sabrina," Vivien said, "but he is a trial, one must admit. I've always admired her patience with him."

"Too much patience, I'd say," Graeme replied. "She needs to stand up to him, or he'll run her ragged."

Chloe smiled at him. "That is a very astute observation, dear boy."

"I believe we are wandering away from the point," Dominic observed. "Which is that we have another failure on our hands."

"And still not a clue how to correct it." Graeme was ready to snarl with frustration.

Aden shook his head. "Not true, actually. I recognized the lout."

Graeme jerked upright. "Who is he?"

"He goes by the name of Russell. I first encountered him when he was with the Neale gang, out of Bethnal Green. They were running a similar rig back then, but on a smaller scale."

Graeme frowned. "The Neale gang? Everything up to this point suggested Covent Garden, not Bethnal Green."

"They've obviously expanded their territory." Dominic arched an eyebrow at Aden. "Anything else?"

"Russell had a partner working with him. Cooper was stationed in the lobby, and apparently saw Russell hand something off to a young woman who slipped out to the street."

"Sabrina's pearls," Graeme said.

"One imagines. Cooper told one of the Runners that he would follow the young woman. Since he has yet to return, I'm fairly confident he'll be able to track her to wherever she's headed."

Graeme felt a new energy surge through his muscles. If he could recover Sabrina's pearls . . .

"So, once Cooper gets back, we'll need to start organizing a raid," he said.

"I will organize the raid," Aden said. "You're taking on a new assignment."

Graeme glared at his superior. "The bloody hell I will."

"Language, dear," Chloe said.

Graeme barely registered the reprimand. "Aden, I've been on this since the beginning, and I want to be there at the end. I know I've not done the best job of it—"

Aden held up a hand. "You've done excellent work on a

difficult case, but we've now got it. I'll organize with Bow Street to wrap it up."

"But—"

"As Aden said, we've got another mission for you," Dominic cut in. "One that is significantly more important than recovering some jewels."

"Tell that to Lady Sabrina," Graeme retorted.

Dominic's gaze turned as cold as the North Sea in January. Graeme mentally cursed. He knew that look. The argument was over.

"All right," he conceded. "What's so bloody important about this new mission?"

Aden shot a quick glance around at the neighboring boxes. The performance had resumed a few minutes ago, with a dramatic presentation of the battle of Troy. It was ridiculous and noisy, and would certainly make it impossible for anyone to overhear the discussion.

"I think it's safe to talk," Graeme dryly commented.

Dominic huffed out a laugh, finally unbending. "Indeed. But this situation requires a great deal of care. It involves the king."

Ah. Now, that was interesting. Graeme liked interesting.

"You may or may not be aware," Aden said, "that my esteemed parent has become quite obsessed with your beloved Highlands."

Graeme snorted. "He's not the only one, thanks to Walter Scott and his blasted poetry."

And to Scott's novels, with their entertaining but—from Graeme's point of view—sometimes silly depictions of Highland history. While Sir Walter published the novels anonymously, anyone with a brain knew who the author of *Waverley* was.

"Yes," Aden replied. "As you also know, Sir Walter and my father are quite close. In fact, Scott has been instrumental in convincing the king that he is . . ." Aden paused, as if trying not to laugh. "The new Bonnie Prince Charlie, so to speak. True heir to the Stuart Dynasty."

Graeme snorted. "You do realize how ridiculous that sounds."

"Trust me, I do. My father has always had a colorful imagination, but that is hardly the point."

"Then what *is* the point?" Graeme asked.

"The king is going to Scotland, and so are you."

Chapter Seven

With its four bays, the elegant mansion on Heriot Row was the largest townhouse on the terrace. This was Graeme's first visit to his family's Edinburgh establishment, acquired after two Kendrick brothers had set up offices here—Braden for his new medical practice, and Logan for the expansion of his trading company. The house, in a prime location in New Town, a well-heeled, modern neighborhood above the old city, provided a home base for any family member with business in Edinburgh.

The true heart of the family and clan would always be Castle Kinglas. Then there was Kendrick House in Glasgow, always lively, especially now that Royal and Ainsley had recently returned from Canada. No matter how far each of them roamed, a Kendrick always returned home—and sooner rather than later, if the rest of the family had their way.

That tradition meant Graeme was in for a verbal drubbing now, since he'd only made one short visit to Scotland in the last two years. He had yet to even see Royal and Ainsley. While his work for Aden and the Home Office kept him busy, he doubted his family would see that as an acceptable excuse for his prolonged absence.

"Mister, ye takin' yer bag or not?" The grizzled, stoop-shouldered driver stood patiently by his hackney coach, waiting to be paid.

"Oh, sorry," Graeme said, shaking free from his reverie.

He retrieved his carpetbag and then fished coins from an inside pocket, handing them to the driver.

The man cast a shrewd look up at the house. "From the way yer hangin' aboot in the street, I'm thinkin' it's been a while since ye've been home."

"Two years in England." Two years of avoiding his loving but meddlesome family.

"Och, that's nae good, spending so much time with the *Sassenachs*. Families are a pain in the arse, but we canna live without them. It's nae our way, no matter how much trouble they make."

Graeme smiled. "Sounds about right."

Suddenly, the front door opened, and a young woman appeared in the doorway. "Graeme Alexander Kendrick, why are you lurking about in the street? And why didn't you tell us you would be arriving this afternoon? We would have sent the coach, you silly boy."

The driver flashed a wry grin. "Trouble has found ye, I reckon."

"You have no idea."

The Countess of Arnprior, in keeping with her former role as a governess, made a point of schooling every Kendrick male in proper behavior, starting with her husband and working down the long line. When it came to Graeme and his twin, Grant, she'd had her hands particularly full. But they'd met their match in Victoria. She might look like a delicate English beauty, but she had an iron will and a loving heart that had combined to whip them into line.

The driver climbed into his coach. "Good luck to ye, lad."

Graeme turned to greet his sister-in-law. Victoria stood, arms crossed, one foot impatiently tapping the step.

"Honestly, one would think you didn't even wish to come in," she said.

He picked up his bag and took the steps two at a time. "How could I not wish to see ye, bonny lass? Although I'm nae sure aboot the rest of that troublesome lot."

"Not the brogue, Graeme. Please."

When any of the family wished to tease her, they adopted the heaviest, most ridiculous brogue they could muster. He'd tried that on her the first time they'd met, and she'd all but bashed him over the head with the tea service.

With a wry smile, Vicky stretched up on tiptoes to give him a fierce hug.

Graeme gingerly hugged her back, since his sister-in-law was six months pregnant. With her tall, willowy figure, her belly seemed already huge, sticking out like a perfectly round ball. He adored her, but pregnant women made him nervous. They seemed so fragile, as if something could go wrong at any moment.

As she broke the embrace, she frowned. "You're too thin, and there are circles under your eyes. Has Aden been working you too hard?"

"Not at all. I'm perfectly fine. Let me look at *you*. Are you well?"

"Fit as a fiddle. You know I'm stronger than I look."

"Aye, strong as an ox, as your grandfather used to say," came a familiar voice from the entrance hall. "Still, I'd prefer you come inside rather than loiter on the step with my reprobate of a brother."

Graeme couldn't hold back a wince when his brother, Nicholas, Laird of Arnprior, loomed up behind his wife.

"Sorry, Nick. I shouldn't keep her standing about in the wind."

"Nonsense. It's a perfectly pleasant day," Victoria said. "But *we* shouldn't keep Graeme standing about. I'm sure he's exhausted from his trip."

Nick stepped aside as Victoria ushered Graeme into the lofty entrance hall, a grand affair with a molded and gilt-painted ceiling above a black-and-white marble floor. Will, the family's senior footman, closed the door and waited to take Graeme's things.

"Quite the place you've got here," Graeme commented as he shrugged out of his traveling coat.

Instead of answering, Nick subjected him to a silent inspection, his sharp gaze as always not missing a thing.

"He does seem pale," his brother finally said to Vicky, "and I do not like those circles under his eyes."

Repressing a sigh, Graeme handed his coat and bag to Will.

"Welcome home, sir," the footman said with a genuine smile. "It's grand to see ye after all this time."

"Yes, it has been a rather long time, hasn't it?" Nick pointedly added.

Will cast Graeme a brief sympathetic look before discretely retiring. The footman, who had been with the family forever, recognized the signs of an impending sermon from Lord Arnprior.

All done in Graeme's best interest, of course, but what Graeme thought in his best interest often conflicted with Nick's definition of the term.

"Nicholas, you are not to lecture your brother in the hall," Victoria said. "He just arrived."

"I thought I'd wait until we got to the drawing room. Although I'd like to point out that you already delivered the first lecture."

"True," Graeme said. "So perhaps we could skip any subsequent ones."

"It's my duty as laird to let you know when you stray," Nick said, his expression wry.

"Something you do quite splendidly," Victoria noted.

"And with alarming regularity," Graeme added.

"Hardly, since you're rarely around," Nick retorted. "Now, come here, ye cheeky lad."

His brother pulled him into an enveloping hug. While Nick was tall and brawny, he didn't match up with Graeme's size.

Still, Graeme's throat went tight. It was almost as if he were once more a small boy, running for comfort to the one person who'd always been there for him. More than their father, Nick had soothed his hurts, solved his problems, and knocked sense into him when he'd needed it.

For the first time in months, Graeme felt the twisted threads of his complicated life begin to unspool a wee bit.

Nick tightened his grip for a moment, then released Graeme and took a step back. Once more, that uncanny gaze swept over him. Big brother's frown again signaled he wasn't happy with little brother's apparent condition.

"I could use a drink," Graeme said. "Then you can proceed with the appropriate lectures."

Nick snorted. "My lectures are usually more effective after a wee dram, anyway."

"They're certainly easier to listen to," Vicky said.

"None of your cheek, *Sassenach*, or you'll find yourself on the receiving end of one of your own. In private, if you're not careful."

She gave an exaggerated sigh and rested her hands on her round stomach. "I do believe that's how I arrived in this condition, dear sir."

Nick waggled his eyebrows at her. "Practice makes perfect, my darling."

Graeme held up his hands. "Och, you're both making me queasy."

In truth, he found their relationship incredibly touching. Nick and Victoria's steadfast love for each other had greatly helped to heal the deep sorrows that had scarred the Kendrick family.

Vicky laughed. "We are rather nauseating, especially for such a fusty old couple."

"Speak for yourself," Nick said. "I'm in my prime, as I will be happy to demonstrate."

Graeme shook his head. "It never ends, does it?"

His brother grinned. "All right, I'll stop. Come upstairs and have a drink before you're inundated by the rest of us."

"How's she holding up?" Graeme murmured to Nick as they followed Vicky. "Well, I hope?"

"You're not to worry, lad. The doctor is very pleased with the state of her health."

How could he not worry? Childbirth could be incredibly dangerous. His mother had died of the fever, only a few days after Kade was born.

"What does Braden have to say? Does he agree Vicky's all right?"

"You do realize Vicky can hear you," she said over her shoulder. "And she is in fine fettle, despite the fact that she looks like she swallowed a cannonball."

She waited for them at the top of the stairs. "And if you think I'm going to let my brother-in-law deliver my baby, you are deranged. Family togetherness can only go so far."

Graeme frowned. "Braden is the best doctor we know. You've said it yourself, many a time."

"True, but he only just received his medical degree last year," she replied. "A fact you would remember if you'd been here for the ceremony."

"Sorry," Graeme muttered. He'd wanted to be there for the lad's convocation. Unfortunately, he'd been in Paris, dealing with a Russian spy who'd been causing a spot of trouble for the British ambassador.

"Victoria has an excellent physician *and* a midwife," Nick said. "The best doctors in the country are in Edinburgh."

"Still—"

"Victoria is strong," Nick said firmly. "Trust me."

"Yes, sir," Graeme replied. "Sorry to cause trouble, sir."

"Causing trouble is a Kendrick specialty," Vicky said with a twinkle. "Go in and get a drink. I'll round up the rest of the family."

Graeme followed his brother into a lofty room with elegant plasterwork and a gleaming parquet floor partially covered by a woolen carpet in muted plaid. A white marble fireplace held pride of place, topped by a dramatic landscape of Castle Kinglas and Loch Long. Two red sofas sat opposite each other, and several well-padded armchairs, trimmed in green velvet, were grouped casually around the sofas. Polished round tables were laden with books and fresh flowers, but still had room for teacups or glasses. Everything was bang-up to the mark, including the wall sconces with Wedgwood medallions that matched the green of the chairs.

Naturally, a large pianoforte was featured near one of the window bays. With two accomplished musicians in the family, no Kendrick household was complete without one.

"What do you think?" Nick asked as he headed to a large sideboard and its collection of decanters.

"It's splendid." Graeme strolled over to look out the window at the expansive green space across the street. "And a damn sight better than anything in Old Town."

Although there were many fine buildings in the historic parts of the city, much of Old Town was a crowded warren of sadness and decay. New Town, with its elegant townhouses, mansions, and green squares, had been built in the hope of attracting investment and revitalizing the city's fortunes.

Nick handed him a crystal glass with a generous tot of whisky. "Your sister-in-law has enjoyed spending our money to kit the place out."

"She's earned the right, putting up with us."

"Aye. Though to be fair, it was more Logan's money than mine." Nick shook his head with fond exasperation. "The bloody idiot wouldn't take no for an answer."

"Och, Logan is rich as Midas. Besides, he likes to spend money on the family. It's his way of—"

Graeme caught himself. He'd been about to say that spending money was Logan's way of making up for the mistakes of the past and his former estrangement from Nick.

"I know," Nick said, "but it's not necessary."

"It probably is for Logan. We all carry around our past, and some parts you can never truly put to rest. All you can do is try to make things better, both for yourself and for the people you love."

When his brother tilted his head in a thoughtful inspection, Graeme wished he'd kept his bloody mouth shut.

"When did you turn into such a wise old soul?" Nick finally asked.

"Never is the answer. I'm the same reckless idiot I've always been."

"You were never an idiot, although you and Grant worked hard to convince me otherwise."

"Grant has the brains between the two of us. You know that."

"I'll agree he's doing very well working for Logan. Lad's got a head for numbers, which was a surprise to all of us, I think."

"Not to me."

Graeme had always known his twin had both a sharp mind and a kind soul. Grant's unstinting loyalty had been the true gift of Graeme's life. Even in the worst of times, when their family had cracked under too many tragedies, Grant had been a steady and faithful presence.

When they'd finally struck out on their separate paths, it had been wrenching for both of them. He suspected Grant had managed it better than he had. There'd been many a difficult day—and darker night—when Graeme had wished desperately to see his twin. Grant understood him as no one ever had, and probably more than Graeme understood himself.

"Grant's worth twice of me," he said softly.

Nick lightly punched his shoulder. "Fah. You're equally fine men, and we're all proud of you."

"I was nothing but trouble for you, Nick. You didn't deserve what I put you through."

"Laddie, is there something you wish to tell me?" his brother quietly asked.

A million things, but he hadn't the words to express them. "No, but maybe someday."

"I'm here for you, Graeme. Always."

His blasted throat went tight again. "I know."

"And you can have a good chat with Grant. He should be rolling in from Glasgow in the next day or so."

Graeme propped a shoulder against the corner of the window bay. "Where's everyone else? Seems too quiet for a Kendrick household."

"I'm here," said Royal as he strode through the door. A broad smile lit up his lean features and made his green eyes glitter like emeralds. "Damn, it's grand to see you, laddie boy."

Graeme met him halfway and enveloped his brother in a bear hug. "I missed ye more than I can say. Thank God yer finally home."

Royal and Ainsley's return was a great, unalloyed blessing. Still, Graeme would eventually have to tell them about his encounter with Cringlewood, and about Sabrina's troubles with the bastard, too. He hated the notion of calling up such ugly ghosts from the past.

As for Sabrina, he'd been doing his best *not* to think about the lass at all.

"What's wrong?" Royal asked sharply.

Graeme refocused. "Nothing at all."

When he once more found himself under a narrow-eyed inspection, he grimaced.

"Victoria's right," Royal said. "You've been working too hard."

Graeme gave him a halfhearted shove. "Are you all going to treat me like a child? If so, I'll be on the next mail coach out of town."

"Let's talk about that," Nick said. "You know I would have been happy to pay for a private chaise. There was no need for such austerity, Graeme."

True, but Graeme had gotten used to a simpler life. In fact, he liked being mostly anonymous, taking on different roles for his work and spending most of his days on the fringes of society. It was easier to pretend to be someone other than who he truly was—a Kendrick, with all the complications that came with so distinguished a name.

He shrugged. "I like the mail coach."

"No one likes the mail coach," Royal said.

Vicky reentered the room. "I expect he wanted to sneak up on us. Now that he works for my brother, he's gotten very secretive."

"We're supposed to be secretive. It's part of the job."

She settled onto one of the sofas. "Don't think we won't be having a chat about your job, Graeme Kendrick."

Vicky, the overprotective lass, had never approved of his work.

He pretended to inspect the large medallion encircling

the chandelier. "And this is exactly why I don't come home very often."

"You *never* come home anymore," Nick said.

"I did last year, before Logan and Donella left for Halifax."

"And barely stayed a week," Nick replied with brotherly disapproval.

"Well, he's here now," said Royal, taking pity on Graeme. "Everyone will be thrilled, especially the children. They're out for a drive with Angus, but should be home any minute."

"Grand. By the way, where are Kade and Braden?" Graeme was eager to see his youngest brothers.

When Vicky and Nick exchanged a quick glance, Graeme's heart jerked painfully against his ribs. Kade had suffered from ill health when he was younger. Had he fallen sick again?

"What's wrong? Is Kade all right?"

"He's splendid," Vicky reassured him. "He and Braden are in Hanover for a few months, where Kade is studying with a violin master in Göttingen. Braden went along to take additional studies at the medical school. I wrote to you about that last month, remember?"

Graeme winced. "Vaguely."

Royal made an exasperated sound. "You clearly are working too hard."

"I'm just busy. And disappointed that I've missed them."

Nick was right. Graeme had stayed away too long. His family loved him and worried about him, which was not surprising after all the losses the Kendricks had suffered over the years. He made a silent vow to do better by them, once he found the time.

"I'm here," Ainsley said as she sailed through the door. "And that surely more than makes up for any lack of Kendricks."

"Does not," Graeme muttered as he dutifully bent to receive her embrace.

She gave him a jab before hugging him. "None of your

nonsense, Graeme Kendrick. As your grandfather would say, yer nae too big for me to paddle yer bum."

"I'm still not sure why you ever married this woman," Graeme said to Royal.

Ainsley raised a dramatic black eyebrow. "Really?"

Graeme waggled a hand, although he couldn't help smiling.

His sister-in-law was an extravagantly beautiful woman, with a figure guaranteed to stun any man not half-dead into speechless admiration. She'd certainly stunned Royal, who'd fallen into a fierce, though initially unrequited love within days of meeting her.

Ainsley also possessed a mind as sharp as a finely honed blade and a tongue to match. Her family nickname was *Sassenach saucebox*, and the description fit. Graeme wasn't too proud to admit she'd once intimidated the hell out of him. On two occasions, he and Grant had climbed out a window to escape a scold from her. It was hilarious and ridiculous, now that he thought about it.

"You look like hell," she said. "What's wrong?"

"I just got off the mail coach. Everyone looks like hell then."

"No, it's more than that," she countered. "I can always tell, so don't deny it."

She could, too, which was incredibly annoying.

"Leave the poor lad alone, sweetheart," Royal said. "Although it *is* annoying that he felt obliged to travel on the cheap. Doesn't St. George pay you enough?"

"No one ever got rich being a spy," Graeme quipped.

"You're *not* a spy," Vicky said with a scowl. "You're an inquiry agent contracted to the Home Office on a temporary basis. My brother specifically promised there would be *no* spying."

Ainsley steered Graeme toward one of the chairs. "Sit down and finish your drink. The countess can give you a proper scold later."

"Graeme, do sit on one of the sofas. They're quite sturdy," Vicky hastily said.

Argh.

"I haven't broken any furniture in months."

"Of course not." Nick guided him toward the sofa.

"I am hardly the largest Kendrick, you know," Graeme grumbled.

"You are in this room," Vicky said.

"Grant is just as big, and he sits wherever he wants."

"Because he doesn't break furniture," Ainsley replied.

"Please kill me now," Graeme sighed.

Royal smothered a laugh. "Just sit and tell us what you've been doing with yourself."

"And why the sudden visit to Edinburgh," Nick added.

"I just wrapped up a case and had time to come north," he said as he gingerly settled on the sofa.

He had no intention of discussing his mission with the ladies. Aden had been crystal clear that Graeme was to keep the women away from trouble, especially Vicky.

Graeme launched into a colorful version of his exploits with the jewel thieves. He left out Sabrina's dunking in Hyde Park—and her nasty encounter with Cringlewood— but her name did pop up. Overall, though, Graeme thought he did an excellent job of minimizing her involvement.

"Aden has rolled most of the gang up, and if he hasn't already—"

Ainsley ruthlessly interrupted. "So, you met Sabrina. What did you think of her?"

He mentally ground his teeth. "She seems nice enough."

His annoying sister-in-law scoffed. "Oh, so you completely failed to notice how lovely she is, or how sweet—"

He tried to continue. "As I was saying—"

"Or that she's a considerable heiress," Ainsley continued. "Surely you can do better than *nice enough.*"

"Very well, she's nice enough for a *Sassenach.*"

"The men in this family have a marked inclination for *Sassenachs*," Royal said.

"Not Logan. He married a proper Scottish lass," Graeme joked.

"And just how considerable is Lady Sabrina's fortune?" Nick asked.

Leave it to his oldest brother to focus on that part of the picture. Nick was determined to see all his brothers well married. That's why he'd hired Vicky in the first place—to teach the Kendricks how to be proper gentlemen, fit for proper wives.

In Graeme's case, however, she'd barely made a dent.

"Stupendous, actually," Ainsley said. "Musgrave is disgustingly rich, and much of the estate is not entailed. Sabrina will inherit everything not tied directly to the title."

Vicky perked up. "And you say she's both pretty and nice?"

"Oh, she's more than pretty," replied Ainsley. "She's been a huge catch on the marriage mart ever since she stepped out of the schoolroom. She's no flighty miss, either. Sabrina is very intelligent."

Nick lifted an eyebrow at Graeme. "That sounds very promising."

Graeme pointedly ignored him. "How do you know so much about the lass?" he said to Ainsley. "You didn't go to school together. You're much older than she is."

Royal winced. "Good God."

"Only a few years older, you jinglebrains," Ainsley replied. "And now that I think about it, Sabrina's much too good for you."

"And I think this is a ridiculous conversation," Graeme said.

"Hmm," Nick murmured. "What does Lady Sabrina think of you, Graeme?"

"I suspect she thinks him a dunderhead," Ainsley said.

Probably true. "I have no idea."

"Perhaps you could try to find out," Nick said with an encouraging smile.

And they wondered why Graeme never came home. "I repeat—"

"Uncle Graeme!" Tira cried.

Thank God.

When his little niece belted across the room, Graeme swept her up in his arms. "You're looking grand. Almost as tall as your da, I'm thinking."

Tira giggled as she hugged him tight. "You're silly, Uncle Graeme."

"Your uncle specializes in silly," Ainsley said to her daughter. "Now, sit next to him on the sofa like a good girl, before you strangle him."

"Yes, Mamma."

"You could sit on my knee," Graeme suggested.

Tira gave him a kind smile. "I don't want to wrinkle my dress, but I'll be happy to hold your hand, Uncle Graeme."

He swallowed a smile as she sat beside him and arranged her skirts. She'd clearly developed her mother's regard for fashion, and was endearingly dignified for a bairn. Tira was also the sunniest, sweetest little lass he'd ever known.

"Where's your brother?" he asked.

"He fell asleep in the carriage, so he had to go to bed. He's such a baby."

"And what about Rowena?"

"Here I am, Unca Gwaeme!"

Clutching her great-grandfather's hand, Nick's pride and joy and toddled across the room. Nick had lost the only child of his first marriage in a tragic drowning accident years ago, leaving his spirit horribly scarred. But his marriage to Vicky and Rowena's birth had given him true peace and joy. The tragedies that had plagued the Kendricks for so many years seemed finally consigned to the past.

Graeme reached for Rowena. "Give your uncle a hug, little imp."

"I mithed you," she said with her sweet toddler's lisp as she snuggled close. "Why don't you come thee us any-more?"

Graeme rolled his eyes at a grinning Nick. "You're teach-ing her well, I see. Here, love, go sit on Papa's knee while I say hello to Grandda."

Angus MacDonald was the Highland version of an Old Testament patriarch—ancient, but spry and indomitable. Today, instead of his usual tatty kilt and leather vest, he was kitted out in a respectable tailcoat and breeches, and his boots for once were polished. His hair, as usual, looked like an exploding dandelion, but at least he wasn't wearing his beloved, ratty old tam.

"You look almost normal," Graeme said to his grand-father. "Has Vicky been dosing you with laudanum to keep you compliant?"

Angus jabbed him in the shoulder with a gnarled finger. "None of yer cheek, laddie boy. Yer still nae too old for me to paddle yer bum."

"Graeme's already been warned," Ainsley said.

"He'll need more than one." Then the old man's face split into a grin. "Give yer grandda a hug. I've missed ye some-thin' fierce."

Smiling, Graeme complied. Grandda had always been his ardent champion, through thick and thin. Of course, the crazy old fellow had often instigated the thick, but he had always stuck up for Graeme, no matter what.

After heartily slapping Graeme's back, his grandfather gave him a sharp eye. "Yer lookin' fashed, son. What's amiss?"

Ignoring the question, Graeme gave Angus a gentle push toward the sofa. "Sit with Tira while I get you a dram."

"Can I have a dram, too?" Tira piped up.

Rowena, snuggled on her father's lap, pulled her thumb out of her mouth. "Me too."

"No drams for little girls," Ainsley said. "Graeme, will you pull the bell for tea?"

He complied and then went to fetch a whisky for his grandfather. By the time he returned, the girls were already chattering like magpies, describing all they'd seen on their drive through town.

Graeme settled in to listen to several overlapping conversations. As always, Kendricks were a noisy lot, but the lively scene felt surprisingly peaceful to him. He realized that he'd not had peace in a long time.

Not that he was truly looking for it, not with his life. His life was exactly as he wished.

After the tea things had appeared and everyone had been served, Angus turned his attention back to Graeme. The rest of the adults fell silent, also placing their focus on him.

"Now, lad," his grandfather said in a shrewd tone, "why don't ye tell us why ye *really* popped up on our doorstep like a bolt out of the blue?"

Chapter Eight

The royal yacht was due in three days. The wet, blustery weather was already complicating security plans, as was the complete lack of credible information regarding potential threats to the king. Graeme didn't feel close to being prepared.

For now, all he could do was focus on overseeing the arrival of the steam packet transporting most of the king's luggage from London. It made sense to keep a close eye on the arriving supplies, which included dozens of crates of ceremonial silver and plate, and even food. If someone *was* trying to assassinate the old fellow, tampering with the specially chosen food supply could do the trick.

Royal joined Graeme on the landing as the steam packet approached the Leith docks.

"I sent the coachman into the shelter of the warehouses," his brother said. "No need to have the horses standing about in this wind."

Graeme glanced up at the angry gray clouds scudding overhead, the reason they'd traveled here by carriage. "Bloody inconvenient, this weather."

"Not as inconvenient as the bloody crowds," Angus said as he stomped up. "Idiots, the lot of them, prancing aboot in silly outfits, pretendin' to be true Highlanders."

The throngs pouring into Edinburgh did worry Graeme. But Sir Walter Scott, the chief architect of the king's visit, was actively encouraging a large turnout for the festivities, as were the Edinburgh authorities. That was exactly why Graeme needed his family's help. The local constabulary would be too challenged with managing the massive event to investigate any nefarious activity.

Of course, family assistance also meant having Angus in the mix, with the usual unpredictable results. Grandda had insisted that his number one job was to help Graeme and keep him from *falling into the shite*.

"I'm as wily as an old fox, ye ken," he'd said. "If there's anything afoot, I'll be sure to hear aboot it first."

The notion of Angus conducting *spy work*, as he liked to call it, was alarming. Still, it was less problematic to bring him along than to let him wander about on his own.

Royal watched the steam packet fight the heavy chop as it neared the pier.

"So," he said to Graeme, "we're to be on the lookout for evil assassins, but we really have no idea who they might be or why they wish to kill the king. And we're to stop any potential plots, even though we have zero information to guide us."

"I'm aware that it's ridiculous and frustrating," Graeme said, "but annoying commentary will not make the task any easier."

Royal laughed. "Laddie, maybe there *is* no actual plot. Vague rumors are hardly unusual, given George's lack of popularity."

King George had been roundly disliked both during his time as Prince Regent and now as monarch. His profligate ways, numerous mistresses, and selfish behavior were strong black marks against him. The recent debacle of the queen's trial had only increased the general animosity and heightened the fraught political climate. All sorts of people thoroughly hated the king, including more than a few Highlanders.

"Aye, we could be in for trouble when old King Fathead arrives," Angus said. "After all, what self-respecting Scot wouldna want to pop off that *Sassenach* twiddlepoop?"

That trenchant comment did nothing to improve Graeme's mood. "Please keep your voice down, Grandda. I would prefer you not be arrested for sedition."

"And don't forget that King Fathead *is* Vicky's father," Royal added. "Your arrest would embarrass the family."

"That old ninny never did a bloody thing for the puir lass," Angus protested. "And ye ken as well as I do that the *Sassenach* royals are nae but trouble for true Highlanders."

"May I remind you that His Majesty—whom you will be meeting in a few days—is your king, too," Graeme said. "And if you embarrass Vicky by spouting off about evil *Sassenachs*, I will be forced to murder you."

Angus bristled. "I subscribe to a higher power than any *Sassenach* king."

"Really? Who?" Royal asked.

Their grandfather's dramatic pose, right hand soulfully pressed to his chest, was diminished when a gust snatched his ratty tam from his head. Graeme barely managed to catch it before it flew into the water.

He handed it back. "You were saying?"

Angus crammed it on and resumed his pose. "Our laird, chief of Clan Kendrick, is the only power I need hear and obey."

Royal practically doubled over with laughter, while Graeme shook his head in disbelief. "Grandda, you hardly *ever* do anything Nick asks. Usually you do the opposite."

"Ye exaggerate, lad. And sometimes I do ken what's best, whether Nick kens it or not."

"Like you did this morning, when you tried to get him to boycott the Regalia Ceremony?" Royal choked out.

The Regalia Ceremony was the first major event to mark the king's visit. The Scottish crown, scepter, and sword of state, which had been tucked away in an old trunk and essentially forgotten since the Act of Union, were being moved in procession from Edinburgh Castle to Holyrood Palace. Sir Walter Scott had instructed the clan chiefs to provide regiments of "well-dressed Highlanders" to march in the parade. In some cases, that garb consisted of highly inaccurate versions of Highland attire.

"Fah," Angus said. "That bloody Walter Scott deserves to be shot, along with the rest of those no-nothing ninnies running aboot in fancy dress. Silly poofs."

Graeme yanked his outraged grandfather out of the way of two dockhands, who were rushing to prepare for the ship's arrival.

"Fortunately, you were neither forced to attend nor forced to dress like a silly poof," he said. "And also, fortunately, the packet is about to dock. I want to see that cargo unloaded and stowed as quickly as possible."

"At least that jinglebrains of a parade will be over by then," Angus said. "I well nigh shot that idiot Glengarry when I spotted him in the procession from the castle. If I see him again, I just might."

The chief of Glengarry, who fancied himself an exemplar of Highland tradition, had all but forced himself to the front of Scott's carefully planned procession, wearing a highly colorful interpretation of clan garb. Angus had practically climbed out the carriage window, ready to challenge the man for his mockery of the old traditions. Graeme had hauled Angus back in, while Royal had patiently explained that since almost *everything* about the king's visit would make an unintentional mockery of the old traditions, there was little point in getting fashed about it.

"Glengarry's a disgrace in more ways than one," Royal

said. "Acting like a bloody throwback to Robert the Bruce, all while clearing the tenants off his lands."

"Hypocrite." Angus leaned over to spit in the water.

"He's not the only one engaging in Clearances," Graeme said as he watched the packet slip into its berth. Dockhands deftly untied the massive ropes from the bollards, waiting to tie the boat off.

An alarming number of landowners were emptying out the glens, driving tenant farmers from their homes. The appalling practice upended a social order based on clan ties and traditions that had stood for centuries. After all the English had done over the years to degrade the Highland way of life, some Scottish lords and ladies were now doing the rest, essentially destroying the old ways. Money drove their decisions, since sheep and cattle were now more profitable than people. Left with nowhere to go, many crofters and tenants had moved to the cities or departed for America, hoping for a fresh start.

It made Graeme ashamed to call himself a Scotsman.

"If yer lookin' for reasons to knock off King Fathead, the Clearances would be it," Angus said in a thoughtful tone.

"Yes, it's an excellent motive for assassination," Graeme replied. "But of the king? The Clearances don't really have anything to do with George."

Royal thoughtfully stroked a gloved hand under his chin. "Is Aden truly sure the king is the target?"

Graeme threw Royal a startled glance. "Why would you doubt that?"

"If the Clearances are a motive, it stands to reason the target might be a Scottish lord who is close to the king, or in his retinue for these events. After all, the rumors are about an attempt in Scotland, not England."

Graeme scowled down at the wooden planks under his feet. That there were rumors of a plot involving the visit here was certain. But even Aden had admitted the rumors were frustratingly vague. That was why Graeme had been sent to Scotland in the first place.

Maybe they'd gotten the wrong end of the stick, after all.

"I don't know nearly enough," he finally replied, "despite practically living in the stews this last week and shaking down every damn criminal in Edinburgh. All I can do is keep searching, and make sure the king and his entourage are protected."

"Then best keep yer mind on the task and forget the folderol." Angus pointed at the boat. "Looks like they're startin' to unload."

"Thank God," Graeme muttered. He was sick of standing around, playing nursemaid.

They moved down the pier to keep an eye on the astounding amount of cargo coming off the boat.

"Good God," Royal said as the dockhands lugged crates and trunks off the boat and loaded them onto waiting carriages. "Is the king intending to take up permanent residence here?"

"King Fat—er, King George is bringing his own household goods, along with a considerable amount of special clothing for each occasion," Graeme replied.

"I suppose all the expense and trouble will be worth it if it buries the grudge between the Crown and the Scottish people," Royal said. "It's time to move on."

"Not for me, laddie," Angus retorted.

Graeme ignored his grandfather. "You're right, Royal. That's why this little jaunt needs to go off without a hitch. If anything goes wrong, the political consequences could be dire."

"The consequences for you, too, I imagine," said Royal with a wry smile.

"Don't worry. If I go down, I'm taking the rest of you lot with me."

"What . . . what in the name of all that's holy . . ." Angus jabbed a finger at dockhands unloading crates of live poultry. "Does the daft *Sassenach* not think we have chickens in Scotland?"

"Yes, but we have Scottish chickens, Grandda," Graeme sardonically replied. "Not nearly as tasty as British chickens."

"I'll nae be havin' ye insultin' our chickens," Angus blustered.

The idiocy of it all was giving Graeme a headache.

"There's a young woman on the boat," Royal said, elbowing Graeme. "And she seems to know you."

Graeme moved out of the way of two dockhands struggling with an enormous trunk. "Where? I can't see anything with all these bloody crates."

Royal pointed toward the front of the boat. "There she is, ordering those poor cargo fellows about. Don't you see her?"

Oh, now Graeme saw her, all right. The biggest headache he'd ever encountered had just disembarked. She shook out her incongruously bright yellow skirts and headed directly toward him.

Royal glanced at Graeme. "I presume you do know her."

Still trying to recover from the sensation that an anvil had dropped on top of his skull, Graeme simply nodded.

"Who is she?" Angus asked.

"More trouble than ye can imagine," Graeme growled.

Lady Sabrina Bell marched up to them. "Good afternoon, Mr. Kendrick. Captain St. George informed me that you would be meeting the boat."

She flashed him a smile so joyful and dazzling it almost knocked Graeme off the pier. "It's a pleasure to see you again, sir. And I cannot tell you how *thrilled* I am to be here in Scotland."

Chapter Nine

While not a man easily surprised, by Graeme's horrified expression it was clear Sabrina had accomplished just that. One could hardly blame him for his shock at her sudden appearance, especially after that mortifying series of events at the Pan Theater. Graeme had likely assumed, considering her father's excruciatingly rude behavior, that he'd never see her again. Sabrina had been hoping he'd been as disappointed by that prospect as she'd been.

She just wished Graeme would say something, since the silence between them was now growing rather fraught.

His companions also seemed perplexed by the situation. They exchanged meaningful glances before the younger man pointedly cleared his throat. "Graeme, are you going to introduce us to the young lady?"

"If I do, then I'll have to acknowledge that this is actually happening," Graeme replied.

Drat. This was going to be harder than she thought—and she'd already had to work *quite* hard to get this far.

To cover up her embarrassment, Sabrina began to rummage in her reticule. "Mr. Kendrick, I have a—"

"What the hell are you doing here?" he interrupted, scowling.

The older man, dressed in a kilt and an old tam crammed

onto a generous quantity of frizzy white hair, clucked with disapproval. "Lad, that's nae way to speak to such a bonny lady."

"That's because you don't know her."

The other man elbowed Graeme in the ribs. "Mind your manners, lad." Then he bowed to Sabrina. "Ma'am, I'm Royal Kendrick. I'm this sorry specimen's brother."

The sorry specimen huffed out a derisive snort.

"And this is our grandfather, Mr. Angus MacDonald," Graeme's brother added.

Sabrina dipped a shallow curtsy. "It's a pleasure to meet you, gentlemen. I'm Lady—"

"Lady Sabrina Bell, daughter of Lord Musgrave," Graeme said. "A lady who should be in London, not standing on a dock in Leith with chickens and crates and trunks, some of which are obviously hers. That would explain why there's so much baggage."

"Good God," Royal muttered.

Sabrina refused to rise to Graeme's bait. Irritating him more than she already had was not part of the plan.

Not that she truly knew what her plan was when it came to Graeme Kendrick. She only knew she'd wanted to see him again, and with a determination that had surprised her.

"Most of the baggage belongs to His Majesty," she explained. "At the king's recommendation, I traveled with his household entourage to help organize the domestic details of his visit."

Graeme took his hat off and rubbed his head. The breeze gusting off the loch blew his hair straight up, and a sudden ray of sunlight caught the red, making his tumbled curls glow like flame. It was appropriate, since he appeared ready to spontaneously combust with frustration.

"Sabrina, what *are* you really doing here?" he demanded.

She should have been outraged at the informal use of her name, but instead it sent a glow to lodge right behind her breastbone. While supremely annoyed with her, at least he wasn't indifferent.

"As I explained, I'm part of the king's retinue. His Majesty wished for my father to attend him, but Father's indifferent health made that impossible."

"So ye came instead? How did ye manage to pull that off? Yer blasted da barely lets ye out of his sight."

Graeme was getting upset again. Still, it was best not to give an inch or he'd take a country mile.

"His Majesty was delighted when I volunteered to come instead. Father was, naturally, happy to please the king."

Actually, Father had descended into rather impressive hysterics. Sabrina, however, had managed to calm him down and then convince her royal godfather that she was *dying* to visit Scotland and would do her best to be of assistance to him.

She'd found unexpected allies in Vivien and Aden St. George. Vivien, in particular, had thought it a good idea for her to leave town, given the lingering gossip about Sabrina and Lord Cringlewood. A respite from the *ton* would allow that ugly chatter to die down.

"That reminds me." She dove back into her reticule. "I have a note for you from St. George."

Graeme frowned. "Why wouldn't he just send an express if he wanted to write me?"

"St. George always has his reasons," Royal said in a dry tone.

"That's what I'm afraid of," Graeme muttered as he broke the note's seal.

Sabrina waited patiently while he scanned the missive. His grandfather stood on his toes to read over his grandson's broad shoulder.

"Give over, Grandda," Graeme said, exasperated.

"What does it say?" Mr. MacDonald asked. "More spy business, I reckon?"

Clearly, Graeme wasn't the only blunt member of the family.

"No, and I'll thank you to keep your voice down," he growled.

"Nae one can hear us over all this commotion, laddie. If it's not spy business, then what is it?"

As Graeme muttered a few choice words, Royal covered his mouth, clearly trying not to laugh.

When Graeme finished reading, he slipped the note into his pocket. "Aden wants to remove Lady Sabrina from the king's entourage, and in with us at Heriot Row."

Sabrina almost dropped her reticule. "That cannot be correct. I'm to stay with the king, at Dalkeith Palace."

Rather than staying at Holyrood, the king would take up residence with the Duke of Buccleuch, in his palace just outside the city. Sabrina knew some had been disappointed in that decision, but the king's personal comfort trumped other considerations.

"Aden is clear that you're to stay at Heriot Row for the duration of His Majesty's stay," Graeme said.

"But—"

"Lass, the king won't even be arriving for another three days," Graeme said more gently. "It wouldn't be proper for you to stay at Dalkeith with only the staff."

It was the *lass* that did it. Sabrina found herself quite unable to resist him when he called her that.

"Well, if you think—"

"I do think. Aden also made it clear that I'm to keep an eye on you. To keep you out of trouble."

Her warm feelings abated a jot. "I do not need a baby-sitter."

"Oh, really?"

This was *not* going as she had envisioned. "Regardless of St. George's instructions, which of course I am not obliged to follow, I will be staying with the king."

He scowled. "The king is hardly a proper chaperone, and you clearly need one."

"Now you're being ridiculous. I'm his goddaughter, as you well know. And you needn't make me sound like a . . . a loose fish."

She could practically hear him grinding his teeth. "No, but you have a knack for stumbling into villains and ending up at gunpoint."

Mr. MacDonald perked up. "Gunpoint, eh? What happened?"

"Nothing, really," Sabrina said. "I simply waited for Mr. Kendrick to rescue me."

"Ye didna faint, or screech like a barn owl?"

Sabrina frowned. "What would be the point of that?"

The old fellow gave her an approving nod. "Sounds like ye'll fit right in with the rest of us."

"This is a deranged conversation." Graeme turned to inspect the massive pile of baggage on the docks. "We need to sort out her ladyship's trunks and have them transferred to Heriot Row."

Sabrina tried one more time. "I still think—"

"No."

There was obviously no point in fighting the pigheaded man. Besides, it might be rather fun to stay with the Kendricks. Evidence suggested they were the opposite of boring.

Sabrina was so tired of boring.

And you'll be closer to Graeme.

She ignored that prompt from the little devil sitting on her shoulder. "Very well, but you needn't worry about my baggage. Hannah will take care of it."

Graeme spun back on his heel, looking aghast. "You brought Hannah with you?"

"Of course. I couldn't travel without another female in attendance."

"I thought we agreed you needed a more capable maid."

"She's perfectly capable. Ah, there she is." Sabrina waved a hand.

"What's wrong with the maid?" Royal asked.

"You'll see," his brother grimly replied.

Carrying a large bandbox, Hannah tottered up to them. "My lady, please don't ever make me get on a boat again. That was the worst—"

Hannah broke off with a shriek and dropped the bandbox. "Not him!"

Graeme let out an audible sigh as he picked up the box.

"Hannah, there is no need for dramatics," Sabrina said. "Please recall that Mr. Kendrick did not push me into the river but rather pulled me out."

Royal threw his brother a startled glance. "Someone pushed her ladyship into the water?"

Their grandfather frowned at Graeme. "Och, lad. Upsettin' for both of ye, I ken."

"It was fine," Graeme tersely said. "She wasn't injured."

"That water was quite shallow," Sabrina added.

"But don't forget you was robbed, miss," Hannah unhelpfully said.

"I need to have a quick chat with the steward overseeing the king's baggage," Graeme hastily interjected. "And someone needs to sort out her ladyship's things and assist her maid. Angus?"

"I'm sure ye can take care of all that," the old man said with an airy wave. "I'll stay and keep her ladyship company."

Graeme's gaze went flinty. "Listen, Grandda—"

"Nae, lad. Off with ye, now." Mr. MacDonald made a shooing motion.

"Hannah, please go with Mr. Kendrick," Sabrina said, hoping to forestall an argument.

"Oh, my lady, are you sure you can't go with me?" Hannah plaintively asked as she gingerly accepted the bandbox from Graeme.

"I can help your maid," Royal said. "That way Graeme can finish his business, and then escort you and Angus back to Heriot Row."

Graeme looked visibly relieved, as did Hannah. In fact, she was now staring at Royal Kendrick with a dazzled expression. While he was very appealing in a dark and dramatic fashion, Sabrina preferred Graeme's rugged good looks.

"Thanks, old man," Graeme said.

Royal took the bandbox from Hannah with a wry smile.

As they walked away, with the maid enthusiastically chattering to her escort, Sabrina regretfully crinkled her nose. "I do apologize. Hannah's a good girl, if a bit flighty."

"Och, that's nothing new for our Royal," Mr. MacDonald said. "A charmer, he is. Unlike someone else, ye ken."

That someone's expression was positively thunderous, so another intervention was in order. "I do hope I won't be an inconvenience to your family. Are you sure you have room for me?"

Mr. MacDonald smiled. "Not to worry, lass. We'll squeeze ye in."

"We can give her your room," Graeme said in a blighting tone, "and you can sleep in the mews. Now, make yourself useful and take Lady Sabrina to the carriage. Both of you need to sit quietly and wait for me. And stay out of trouble."

Well, that was a bit much.

"I'm perfectly capable of taking care of myself," she said firmly.

"That remains to be seen." Graeme stalked off.

"Huh." Mr. MacDonald shook his head. "The laddie seems a mite fashed with ye."

She sighed. "I do seem to have that effect on him."

He gave a low chuckle. "Ye can tell me all aboot it as we wait."

Mr. MacDonald escorted her toward a town coach that sported a coat of arms. It was spacious and well appointed, with luxurious red leather fittings and polished brass lamps.

They climbed in, and he settled opposite her. "So, yer the king's goddaughter."

"I am, sir."

"And Lord Musgrave's yer da." Mr. MacDonald stroked his chin. "And would that be the same Musgrave with yon estate in the borderlands?"

"Indeed. Our family seat is in Northumberland."

"Yer da married a Scottish lass. Of the Chattan Clan, if I'm recallin' correctly."

"That is correct."

From everything Sabrina knew about Scots, they were rather obsessive about their history and clan lineage, so she supposed it made sense that he'd know about her mother. And why he'd be so curious.

"And ye have no brothers and sisters, I'm thinkin'," he probed.

"I'm an only child, Mr. MacDonald."

He beamed at her. "Call me Angus, lass. Everyone does."

"Oh, that's kind, but—"

"How did ye meet my grandson?" he interrupted. "Surely not in that river."

"Well . . . yes, that was when I met him. It's more of a pond, though."

She looked away, having no interest in reliving that humiliating experience.

"Och, there's nae need to be embarrassed. When it comes to Graeme, there's always a bit of a story. I ken that he pulled ye out, but how did ye end up in the drink in the first place?"

Clearly, the old Scot was impervious to hints.

But thankfully, Graeme appeared just then, the carriage rocking as he bounded onto the step and climbed in. The roomy interior seemed suddenly crowded as he slid past Sabrina and sat next to his grandfather. Graeme's long, booted legs took up every available inch of space between the seats.

"She was pushed into the Serpentine by a cutpurse," Graeme said as the carriage began to move.

Angus looked perturbed. "I canna be surprised at such doin's in the *Sassenach* fleshpots, but that's a bit of bad luck."

"You have no idea," Graeme said.

"It wasn't my fault, as you know," Sabrina retorted.

"If you hadn't been hanging about the park, waiting for—" He bit off the words, as if they were sour.

"Must we talk about this now?" Royal and Ainsley naturally deserved an explanation regarding her actions, but why did his grandfather or the other members of the Kendrick family need to know?

"I think we have to," Graeme reluctantly said.

"What in blazes are ye talkin' about?" Angus demanded.

"Lady Sabrina was waiting to meet a man when the cutpurse attacked her."

"Obviously not waiting for ye."

"Obviously."

The old fellow clucked his tongue. "Lass, ye shouldna be meetin' up with strange men in parks."

"Unless it was your grandson?" Sabrina countered. When Angus narrowed his gaze, she mentally checked off a point in her favor. "In any case, my maid was with me."

"If ye mean that Hannah, I'd nae think she'd be much of a chaperone."

"Exactly," Graeme said. "As I informed Lady Sabrina at the time."

"Good lad." Angus waggled a grandfatherly finger at Sabrina. "It's a good thing Graeme came along, ye ken."

Sadly, she couldn't deny that fact. "Yes, I do ken."

"Unfortunately, there was more to it than Lady Sabrina's getting pushed into the pond," Graeme said.

His grandfather twisted sideways to look at him. His gaze grew sharp. "What aren't ye telling me, son?"

"First, you need to promise not to get upset, Grandda. Because I'm handling it."

Sabrina held up a hand. "Actually, I already handled it."

Graeme had the nerve to look slightly amused. "Is that what you call it?"

She lifted her chin in silent defiance.

Angus chopped down an impatient hand. "Cut line, the both of ye. What's so bloody mysterious about this fallin'-in-the-pond nonsense?"

"It's about who Lady Sabrina was waiting for before she fell into the pond," Graeme said.

"Well?"

"Again, you need to promise you won't go off."

"I promise I'll throttle ye if ye don't stop skatin' about like a ninny."

Graeme seemed to mentally brace himself. "Lady Sabrina was meeting Lord Cringlewood."

For a good thirty seconds, the old man was speechless. When he recovered, Sabrina soon found herself stunned by the inventiveness of Scottish profanity.

"Ainsley, I'm so sorry," Sabrina said. "I wish I could have spared you this."

Seated opposite her in the family drawing room, Ainsley waved a hand. "Please, none of this is your fault. I'm only grieved that you had to put up with that loathsome creature's appalling behavior."

"I still can't believe Cringlewood had the nerve to return to England, much less to London," exclaimed Victoria, who had plumped down next to Sabrina on the sofa.

"He needed to hunt for an heiress," Ainsley replied.

Sabrina winced. "And I fit the bill."

Ainsley's extraordinary violet eyes warmed with sympathy. "Single ladies with large fortunes will always be prey to fortune hunters. It's rather an occupational hazard."

Sabrina had always assumed her father's disapproval of her suitors had stemmed from his reluctance for her to marry. In light of recent events, she now couldn't blame him for his overprotective tendencies. Her most attractive asset had never been her intellect, personality, or looks. She'd been a fool to think it anything but the size of her fortune.

Victoria patted her hand. "I'll be writing to Aden to ask him what's to be done. Cringlewood cannot be allowed to continue to prey on women."

"Your brother is dealing with the matter, although I'm not quite sure what the arrangements are."

"It sounds like you did an excellent job of handling the pig yourself," Ainsley said. "I wish I could have seen you shove him over that balcony."

"I was lucky that Mr. Kendrick warned me about the marquess, although it was awkward for him to have to violate your family's privacy." Sabrina winced. "And I'm placing all of you in another awkward situation, dropped on your doorstep like this, and with disturbing news, no less."

"Nonsense," Ainsley replied. "We're thrilled you're here."

"And Graeme must have been pleased to see you," Victoria added. "It's always lovely to visit with friends."

Sabrina wriggled her fingers. "In truth, he seemed nonplussed by Aden's note."

"Yes, that was a bit odd of my brother," Victoria said. "I'm surprised he didn't send an express to tell us about the incident with Cringlewood and of your impending visit."

"*I* didn't know I was coming to visit you," Sabrina said with a wry smile. "It was rather embarrassing."

Victoria poured her a cup of tea from a Limoges service on the table in front of them. "Graeme was right to insist you come immediately to Heriot Row."

Sabrina tactfully refrained from mentioning that he'd been ordered to do so.

"I'm excited to have the chance to catch up with you," Ainsley said. "After spending the last three years in a backwater, I rather feel like a bumpkin."

"Halifax is hardly a backwater," Victoria protested. "Nor were you living in rustic solitude. Logan's house sounds charming, from what you told me."

Ainsley grinned. "Springhill Manor is both charming and enormous. It's even larger than the governor's house, by at least two rooms."

"Not that you were counting," Victoria drolly replied.

"I always count. Plus, we were the first residence in Halifax to have built-in water closets."

Sabrina couldn't help laughing—mostly from relief. The discussion about Cringlewood had been distressing for Ainsley, who'd gone white and pinched looking. But after ascertaining that Cringlewood was no immediate threat to her family, Ainsley had been primarily concerned for Sabrina's well-being. Her friend had then launched into a blunt and rather entertaining commentary about what she would do to the marquess if she ever saw him again, and Victoria had chimed in with ideas of her own.

Sabrina fully agreed with their sentiments.

She couldn't help but marvel at Ainsley's resilience and strength, and it made her realize how lucky she was to have led such a sheltered, privileged life. While Father was a dreadful and sometimes selfish fusspot, he'd always protected her with every ounce of his being. Because of that,

Sabrina had the confidence to step out and lead her own life, making the decisions that were best for her.

Decisions, she hoped, that now would include Graeme Kendrick.

A quiet knock sounded on the door.

"Enter," Victoria called out.

Graeme stuck his head in. "Is it safe to come in? Royal is having hysterics out here in the hall."

His brother shoved him aside. "Idiot. I simply want to check on my wife."

Ainsley rose with a reassuring smile as Royal strode to her. For the first time, Sabrina noticed he had a hitch to his step. He gathered his wife into his arms, and they hugged for a long moment. Then he ducked down to look into her eyes.

"Are you all right, sweet lass?"

Ainsley cupped his cheek. "I'm perfectly fine. You, however, are limping, which doesn't please me."

"Och, it's nothing to fuss about."

Ainsley beetled her brows at Graeme, who'd propped a shoulder against the doorframe. "You should not have kept Royal on the docks in this blustery weather. You know it's not good for his leg."

"It was his idea," Graeme replied. "He said it was the only way to get out of that stupid regalia ceremony."

"Regardless, you should have made sure he came promptly home. I am *quite* annoyed with you, Graeme."

He gave her a mocking bow. "Naturally, I am stunned by that assessment."

"I will knock your block off, laddie boy. Don't think I won't."

Victoria winked at Sabrina. "Just an average day in Clan Kendrick, as you'll soon find."

Goodness. They were certainly a forthright and highly informal family.

Royal drew his wife back to the sofa. "You're scandalizing our guest, love. I'm fine, and I don't think we need to air all our dirty laundry at once."

"You couldn't. There's far too much of it," Graeme said, strolling over to fetch a glass of whisky from the mahogany sideboard.

Sabrina rose to join him.

"Would you like something to drink, my lady?" he politely asked her.

"A glass of sherry, if I may."

A slow smile lurked at the corners of his mouth. It was quite a firm mouth, but very attractive.

"Not something stronger? You might need it to survive my family."

She smiled. "Actually, I find them refreshing."

The hint of amusement turned into a grin. "Yes, Ainsley is exceedingly refreshing."

"Especially with you."

"Oh, she specializes in that."

He handed Sabrina a diamond-faceted wineglass containing a generous pour of sherry. As it was barely midday, this was another indication that Kendricks did everything on a large scale.

"Thank you," she said.

"You're welcome." His gaze warmed with a look that pleasantly muddled her insides. "But if you're staying any length of time in Scotland, you'll need to start drinking whisky, like a proper Scottish lass."

"I suppose you're right. If I wish to do things properly, that is."

The emerald glitter of his mesmerizing gaze positively

dazzled her for a moment. Then he blinked and seemed to withdraw, as if mentally closing the shutters.

"And yet I expect that you won't be staying long," he said. "Going back with the king, no doubt."

"Oh, yes. I suppose so."

They stood awkwardly until Graeme made a vague gesture toward the others. "Would you like to sit? A full tea tray is on its way up. I'm sure you must be famished."

And they say women are changeable.

One moment, Graeme had smiled at her with the warmth of a summer sunrise. The next, he'd grown coolly formal. And he was *not* a formal man.

Well, she refused to be daunted by his erratic behavior.

"First, I want to ask you about your grandfather," she said. "I feel terrible that I upset him."

"I'm just sorry you were on the receiving end of an Angus eruption. Those are not pleasant."

She couldn't help but chuckle. "Eruption, is that what you call it? It was certainly colorful."

"It was one of his better ones."

So colorful, in fact, that Graeme had been forced to intervene, although initially without success. Only his threat to toss Mr. MacDonald out of the carriage had finally taken some of the wind out of the old fellow's sails.

When Sabrina had tried to apologize for bearing such bad news, the old man had tersely informed her that it was "nae her fault" and then had fallen into a brooding silence. Graeme had tried to alleviate the tension by pointing out various sights on the way to Heriot Row.

"I do wish I could make it up to him somehow," she said.

"I sent him up to spend time with the bairns. That always calms him down."

"Oh, yes, the children. I hope I get a chance to spend time with them."

Sabrina loved children, but rarely got a chance to interact

with them. Growing up an only child, she'd missed having a sibling or two.

"You'll not have much choice. They rule the Kendrick household."

"That sounds like an immense amount of fun."

"Like the little ones, do you?" he asked.

"I do." She wrinkled her nose. "My father, however, does not. He says they're too messy, too noisy, and they get sick."

Graeme laughed. "He's not wrong, although our bairns are a robust lot. But you'll get the noise and the mess."

"I'll look forward to it."

Warmth once more sparked in his gaze. "Then you'll fit right in, lass."

I hope so.

"Graeme, don't keep Sabrina standing about like a footman," Ainsley called from the sofa. "And you come join the rest of us like a proper human being."

"Yes, Mother," he sarcastically replied as he took Sabrina's elbow to usher her back to the others.

"Oh, Lord, I can't imagine being your mother," Ainsley said in a humorous tone. "She must have been a living saint."

When Graeme's grip briefly tightened on Sabrina's elbow, she glanced up at him.

His expression was bland. "She was all that, and more."

Royal threw him an odd look before smiling at his wife. "Our mother had to be a saint to put up with the lot of us."

Graeme handed Sabrina to one of the sofas, then moved off to the side. "Especially me," he said. "I was a terror."

Ainsley pressed a hand to her chest with mock surprise. "I'm shocked to hear that, although I'm sure Grant wasn't far behind when it came to terrorizing the locals. And I suspect Logan was an absolute fright."

"They couldn't hold a candle to me," Graeme quietly replied. "No one could."

"Our mother loved all of us, lad," Royal said gently. "And you made her laugh the most. She always said you were the most lovable scamp in all of Scotland."

"Did she? I don't remember that."

"I wonder where that husband of mine has got off to?" Victoria said after a moment's odd silence.

Graeme settled into a leather club chair by the fireplace. He seemed to be deliberately sitting away from the rest of them. "Nick came in a little while ago. He was going to change and then come down."

"Oh, dear," Ainsley said. "We'll have to tell poor Nick about Cringlewood. As if he doesn't have enough on his mind with the king's visit."

Royal tucked his wife close. "Graeme and I talked to him about that when he came in. Stop worrying, love."

"You're not to worry about anything, Ainsley," Graeme said. "Aden is handling matters. The marquess has already departed for the Continent, I believe."

"Where it's to be hoped he will meet with an unfortunate accident," Royal grimly commented.

Graeme frowned thoughtfully at his glass. "Travel abroad can be risky. Bandits are especially bad in France, I hear. They have rather spectacular ways of making people disappear, such as shoving them off a cliff."

Ainsley perked up. "Goodness, how dreadful. I imagine such sad events might be rather gruesome."

Graeme gave an insouciant shrug. "Hard to say what might happen to him over there."

Royal's gaze narrowed on his brother. "No suspicion can come back on my wife or the family."

Ainsley patted his arm. "Don't be silly, darling. Aden excels at this sort of business."

"Yes, he's exceptionally talented in that respect," Victoria ruefully said.

Sabrina mentally blinked at the extraordinary and rather bloodthirsty conversation. *Forthright* didn't even begin to describe the Kendrick family.

Royal's gaze, as sharp as broken glass, stayed on his brother. "I mean it. No repercussions for Ainsley."

Graeme's equally sharp gaze didn't waver. "Obviously, although I have no idea what you're talking about. In fact, this conversation never happened at all."

When he cast Sabrina a challenging look, she returned a bland smile. "Did you say something, sir? You do tend to rattle on, so I regret to say that my mind was wandering."

While the others chuckled, Graeme shook his head. "I've noticed how rarely you listen to me."

"But in this case, I actually *am* listening to you."

"Don't make it a habit, or I won't know how to manage you," he replied with a slight smile.

Sabrina felt her cheeks heat up. "As I believe I've mentioned, I do not require managing."

"That's the spirit, Sabrina," Ainsley said. "Kendrick men can be so bossy and interfering."

"We're only that way because we want to protect our lassies." Royal winked at Graeme. "Right, lad?"

"I never boss anyone," Graeme replied. "I'm completely easygoing."

Sabrina choked on her sherry.

"Go down the wrong way?" he politely asked.

"Something like that," she hoarsely replied.

Victoria hauled herself up. "Now that we've got the most pressing issues sorted, and determined that Graeme is *not* bossy, I'd best see what's become of our tea."

"The tea tray will be arriving shortly," said a distinguished-looking man as he entered the room. "There was a minor fracas in the kitchen, thanks to one of the dogs, but Henderson has restored order."

The new arrival had to be Lord Arnprior himself—a handsome man with startlingly blue eyes and jet-black hair.

Victoria heaved a sigh. "Angus promised he would keep those silly dogs under control if they came with us. I suppose I should go speak with him. Again."

Her husband bent to kiss her on the nose. "No, you will sit down and rest."

Her smile was wry. "Nicholas, I do nothing but rest."

Lord Arnprior steered his wife back to the sofa. "And you will continue to rest, my love."

Once his wife was seated, he smiled at Sabrina. "We have a visitor, I see."

"Allow me to introduce Lady Sabrina Bell," Victoria said. "Lady Sabrina, this is my husband, Lord Arnprior."

Sabrina rose and curtsied. "It's a pleasure to meet you, sir. Please forgive the unexpected intrusion."

He bowed. "You're most welcome, although I regret that my scapegrace brother failed to inform us of your impending visit. Had I known, I would have returned home earlier."

"Unfortunately, your scapegrace brother didn't know about her ladyship's visit until she stepped off the bloody boat," Graeme sardonically replied.

Arnprior's eyebrows ticked up a notch, although whether it was in response to his brother's tone or that tidbit of information, Sabrina didn't know.

Fortunately, the butler and the tea trolley arrived, and the next few minutes were taken up with the dispensing of pastries and small sandwiches. When Graeme handed her a full plate, Sabrina didn't even pretend to object. She was famished, and he knew it.

He seemed to know all sorts of things about her, and had since the moment they met. It was both annoying and flattering.

"How was the Regalia Ceremony, dear?" Victoria asked.

"Poor Sir Walter seemed quite anxious about it when we spoke last week."

"It was an immensely ridiculous spectacle," Arnprior replied. "I've never seen so many oddly dressed Highlanders in my life."

"That's because many of them weren't really Highlanders," Graeme said.

"It sounds quite jolly, if you ask me," Ainsley said.

Arnprior grimaced. "Sadly, there was a mishap. In the crush, one of the viewing stands collapsed. There were some injuries."

"How dreadful!" Victoria exclaimed.

"And that, my love, is exactly why you're not to attend any of these events during the king's visit," he said. "I'll not have you putting yourself at risk."

"I can't avoid everything," Victoria protested. "The king won't like it."

"I don't give a tinker's damn about the king," replied her protective husband. "He can get crushed by the mob, but my wife will not."

"His Majesty specifically told me he was looking forward to seeing her ladyship at the reception at Holyrood and at the two balls to be held at the Assembly Rooms." Sabrina smiled at Arnprior. "The guest lists for those events are tightly controlled. No mobs allowed."

"Victoria will be well guarded, Nick," Graeme said. "My word on it."

The brothers exchanged what Sabrina could only describe as a meaningful look before Arnprior gave a nod and went to fetch a whisky.

"Bossy man," Victoria muttered.

"Was Grant with you?" Royal asked Arnprior. "I thought he'd be back by now."

"He was near the collapsed stand, and he helped to pull

out the victims. He arrived home a few minutes ago, and went directly up to change."

Graeme instantly rose. "I'd best check on him."

He was halfway across the room when a man who was quite obviously Grant Kendrick came through the door. The brothers exchanged a brief hug, although Graeme kept a protective hand on the back of his twin's neck.

"All right, lad?" Graeme asked.

Grant mustered a smile. "I'll survive."

Graeme's sharp gaze flickered over him. "No damage done?"

"Not to me. Others weren't so fortunate."

"We'll talk later. For now, come and have a drink and meet our guest."

Sabrina rose to her feet.

"Lady Sabrina Bell," Graeme said, "allow me to introduce my brother, Grant."

Grant bowed over her hand with a polite smile. "It's a pleasure, my lady."

She smiled back. "Likewise, sir."

Although the twins shared an incredibly strong resemblance, Sabrina could easily tell the difference between them. There was a brash, restless energy to Graeme, while his twin seemed quiet—almost solemn.

Until a few short months ago, Sabrina would have laid odds in a betting book that she'd have preferred quiet and solemn to brash and restless. The times had certainly changed.

Once Grant had settled in with a generous whisky and some sandwiches, the conversation again turned to the king's visit. Lord Arnprior asked Sabrina a few gently pointed questions about His Majesty's plans, which she found slightly puzzling. When she flashed Graeme a quizzical look, he simply returned a bland smile.

"I'm quite looking forward to seeing the king," Ainsley said.

"You and half of Scotland," Arnprior commented. "The city is bursting with visitors."

"Let's hope the other half are also looking forward to it," Royal said. "And pray they don't do something stupid."

Sabrina frowned. "Are you expecting trouble? Everything seems quite well planned, from what the king told me."

A sudden silence followed her remark. The various Kendricks exchanged more veiled glances.

"I'm sure everything will be perfectly fine," Arnprior said.

"More tea, anyone?" Victoria brightly interjected.

That fact that Graeme was avoiding Sabrina's eye confirmed for her that there was a problem involving the king's visit. It was a very good thing then, that she loved solving problems.

Chapter Ten

With Nick at the port of Leith taking part in the arrival ceremony, it fell on Graeme and Royal to transport the family to Union Street for the king's official entrance into the city. Given the massive crowds, getting there in time would be a challenge.

"Where is everyone?" Royal asked as he joined Graeme in the front hall. "If we're late, Nick will kill us."

"There was a bit of a brangle over Grandda's choice of attire."

"That sounds alarming."

"I'm sure we're in for a grand surprise. You, though, are entirely on point."

Royal eyed the cockaded hat he loosely twirled on his hand. "Victoria has been nose-deep in that blasted pamphlet. She'd have my hide if I didn't comply with her orders."

Leaving nothing to chance, Sir Walter Scott had issued a pamphlet detailing the appropriate attire and conduct during the king's visit. For the opening processional, "gentlemen of the city" had been instructed to wear blue coats, white waistcoats, and white cotton trousers. The finishing touch was to be a dark hat decorated with a patriotic cockade. Actual participants in the formal procession were dressed in more Highland traditional garb, as befitting the king's Scottish escorts.

Royal eyed Graeme. "You, however, are not on point, and Victoria will not approve."

Graeme had chosen plain attire to help him blend into the crowds of ordinary people. "Fortunately, I convinced her that it was my job to protect the king, not lark about in funny outfits."

"One can hardly walk two feet without tripping over a soldier or a constable. It'll be fine."

Though it was a slight exaggeration, trouble did seem unlikely. Graeme had spent the last three days and a good part of each night roaming the more unsavory parts of town, his ear close to the ground. So far, he'd neither heard nor seen anything of real concern. Even Nick had suggested he was being over-cautious.

No point in taking risks, though. Besides, his work had the benefit of keeping him away from Sabrina, who was proving to be a challenge to his peace of mind.

"I'm sure you're right," he told Royal. "The biggest danger should come from getting squished by a gaggle of idiots or expiring of boredom waiting for the *Sassenach* king."

"There is nothing boring about the king's visit," Vicky said as she marched out from the back hall. "And I will have no more disrespectful chatter, Graeme Kendrick."

He bit back a smile. "Yes, my lady."

Vicky was as nervous as a cat in a thunderstorm. She would be meeting her father for the first time, a man who just happened to be the monarch.

His sister-in-law frowned. "Where are the others? I *will* leave without them, if necessary."

Ainsley appeared at the top of the staircase. "I'm here. And Sabrina—"

"Right behind you," said the lady in question, pulling on her gloves as she joined her friend.

Garbed in a primrose dress with a formfitting blue spencer, Sabrina floated down the stairs in Ainsley's wake. She looked like a bloody angel. For most of his adult life, Graeme had lived surrounded by beautiful women, his sisters-in-law. In his wilder days, he'd been lucky enough to sample the feminine delights of more than one willing, winsome lass or buxom widow.

But those days were long gone. Mostly because of Nick's stern tutelage on the subject, Graeme had thankfully never hurt a woman or taken advantage of one who wasn't eager to take advantage back. Still, he'd yet to meet a woman who truly claimed his heart. And he'd been making damn sure to keep it that way—both for him and for any lassie that crossed his path.

And then he met Lady Sabrina Bell.

It didn't make any sense, given the sort of man he was. But there was something so . . . so shiny and sweet about Sabrina. She reminded him of daffodils dancing in the breeze on a sunny spring morning.

He briefly closed his eyes, shutting out her lovely image and cursing the inconvenience of it all. She was mucking with his brain *and* his heart, and he didn't like it one damn bit.

An elbow dug into his side. "What's amiss, lad?" asked Royal, his gaze bright with amusement and understanding.

"Not a damn thing," Graeme growled.

"Graeme, dear, you're looking a bit dyspeptic," Ainsley said.

Sabrina peered at him with concern. "Are you unwell, Mr. Kendrick?"

Victoria glanced up from her pamphlet with alarm. "I do hope Rowena hasn't passed along the case of the grippe she's just getting over. We don't need it going around the entire household."

"I don't think that's what he's got," Royal said with a smirk.

Graeme contemplated tossing his brother out the nearest window. But that would make a hell of a mess, and then Ainsley would probably toss Graeme out, too.

Victoria patted his arm. "Perhaps it's your nerves. It's a very big day for all of us."

"I'm sure everything will be splendid." Sabrina gave him a reassuring smile. "The organizing has been superb, you know. I'm sure there's no need for rattled nerves."

The lass must think him a complete idiot.

"My nerves are fine, as is the rest of me. I'm simply wondering where the bloody hell—"

"A-*hem*," Vicky interjected.

"—everyone is." Graeme finished. "We're late."

"I'm here," Grant said.

His twin stalked down the staircase, looking massively aggrieved. Graeme couldn't blame him.

"Oh, dear," said Ainsley, trying not to laugh.

"Good Lord, why are you dressed like that?" Royal asked.

"Vicky," Grant tersely replied.

Kitted out in Kendrick plaid with a dress kilt and black coat, Grant also wore a plaid tam more befitting a ride on the moors, and was laden with weaponry, including steel-wrought pistols and a dirk.

Vicky circled him, consulting her pamphlet. "According to Sir Walter, this is the appropriate garb for family members marching with the Celtic Society. But, Grant, where is your broadsword?"

"I am *not* wearing a blasted broadsword," he said with a glower. "I look like a complete moron as it is."

"Only half a moron, dear," Ainsley assured him.

Grant snorted. "Thank you for that show of support."

Vicky flapped the pamphlet. "It says right here that you should be wearing a—"

"I'm sure Grant's outfit is fine," Graeme hastily said. He clapped his brother on the shoulder. "Best get a move on, or you'll miss the procession."

His twin flashed him a grateful smile. "See you later."

"Keep your eyes and ears open," Graeme murmured.

"Aye, that."

"The carriages are ready, madam," Henderson said, approaching from the back hall.

"And now where in Hades's name is Angus?" Graeme said.

"Right here," said his grandfather as he clattered down the stairs.

For a moment, they were all struck dumb at the sight of him.

"Och, that's not good," Royal finally murmured.

Vicky jabbed the pamphlet at him. "Angus, you're supposed to be dressed like Royal, not like a deranged Highlander."

Deranged Highlander was an apt description. Grandda wore the old-fashioned belted plaid, although God only knew where he'd dug it up. Because it was too big, he'd wrapped it twice around his waist, cinching the extra material with a belt. The end still sagged like a bedraggled train and would collect dust as effectively as a mop. He'd finished the bizarre look with a white linen shirt topped with his old leather vest, an ancient pair of boots, and an equally ancient bonnet sporting moth-eaten feathers.

"I'm wearin' the belted plaid, the true outfit of a Highlander," he huffed.

"It's certainly colorful," Sabrina faintly managed.

Ainsley was choking on laughter. "Insanely colorful."

Angus waggled a finger. "I'll have nae sauce, Miss *Sassenach*."

"Mrs. *Sassenach*, if you please. And you're going to give Vicky a fit, which is hardly helpful in her condition."

"Och, she'll nae be faintin' over seein' a proper Highlander."

"You do not look proper. You look . . ." Vicky trailed off, as if words failed her.

"Deranged," Graeme dryly finished.

"I'll nae be wearin' those shabby philibegs that yon Grant is flashing aboot in," Angus retorted.

"You wear a philibeg all the time," Graeme said. "We *all* do. And your ridiculous outfit doesn't even fit."

"Now, see here, yer not too big for me to—"

"What's a philibeg?" Sabrina asked, cutting off the impending Angus eruption.

"It's the short kilt," Graeme answered, scowling at his grandfather. "You know, the one we *all* wear *all* the time."

"Just aboot the house, ye ken."

Ainsley shook her head. "I do believe that may be the biggest whopper you've ever told."

The old fellow scoffed. "Nae, I always tell the truth."

Graeme impatiently checked his pocket watch. "We don't have time for him to change. We're miles late as it is."

And he needed to be out in the crowds, doing his bloody job.

Ainsley patted Vicky's shoulder. "Since Angus will be inside the barouche, no one will be able to tell if it's a belted plaid or a phili-whatever."

"And I'll nae be changin' just to please King Fathead," Angus added.

Vicky capitulated. "Very well, but please stay inside the carriage. I will not have you embarrassing Nicholas or your grandsons."

"I'll be the only proper-dressed Highlander in the entire city, ye ken."

"We *need* to go," Graeme reiterated.

Sabrina glanced at him before taking his grandfather's arm. "I think you look extremely dashing, Mr. MacDonald. Shall we sit together?"

Angus beamed his approval. "Call me Angus, lass. Or Grandda. We consider ye part of the family." He winked at Graeme as he escorted Sabrina to the door.

Ainsley snickered and took Vicky's arm to follow them out.

"And do we consider Lady Sabrina part of the family?" Royal asked Graeme in an innocent tone.

"Oh, shut it," Graeme snapped as he propelled his brother down toward the waiting carriages.

Poor Graeme had been radiating frustration since they departed Heriot Row, no doubt because of Angus. Sabrina, however, liked the old fellow. He'd paid her a great deal of attention, taking her for walks in the parks and filling her with information about Graeme. She enjoyed those chats, although the subject under discussion would be dismayed to hear some of the amusing stories his grandfather had told her.

Angus was clearly matchmaking, as were several other Kendricks. The fact that they were rather obvious was alarming her already skittish prey.

Sabrina swallowed a chuckle at the notion of Graeme as helpless prey. She'd never met a more formidable or competent man, and every moment in his company placed her heart in more danger. She'd avoided such danger in the past, but now it lured her with a siren's call.

She hoped Graeme heard that call, too.

He lifted an eyebrow. "Something amusing, my lady?"

She mentally blinked. "I'm simply enjoying the sights. It's quite the extravagant display."

As the carriage rolled under a festooned lamppost, Graeme swatted aside a fluttering banner that would have taken off his hat. It seemed that every square inch of pillar, post, or brickwork had been decorated with streamers, banners, and placards of welcome. One could barely see the buildings for all the embellishments. It was a festive sight, and the locals were clearly in a corresponding mood as the cheerful din from the crowds illustrated.

"Extravagant understates the case," he replied with a reluctant smile as they passed a young man waving a star-shaped board that read: *You Are Welcome, King!*

Angus stood up and leaned halfway out of the barouche. "Ye ought to be ashamed of yerself," he yelled at the startled fellow. "Dinna be callin' yerself a Scotsman."

Graeme pulled his grandfather back. "Stop embarrassing poor Vicky."

Victoria rolled her eyes. "I'm beyond embarrassment, and I do find myself agreeing with Angus somewhat. It's all a bit much. I only hope we can get through the crowds in time to reach our spot at Picardy Place, near the arch."

The triumphal arch erected at Union Street marked the official entrance into Edinburgh. Sabrina hadn't seen so large a crowd since the king's coronation, and she too hoped they wouldn't miss the royal procession to Holyrood Palace.

Victoria craned up to peer over the back of the carriage. "We seem to have lost Royal and Ainsley."

The couple was traveling separately in Royal's curricle, attended by a groom. Ainsley would join Sabrina and Victoria to watch the parade.

"Royal will look for the footmen I sent ahead to Picardy Place," Graeme said. "If the poor lads haven't been crushed to death, that is."

"I told them to bring cudgels to beat back the crowds," Angus said. "Just in case things got mucky."

Victoria looked appropriately appalled. "You didn't!"

When Angus winked at Sabrina, the countess scowled. "You're ridiculous," she said to her grandfather-in-law.

The old man looked entirely unrepentant.

"I thought we would be driving directly to Union Street," Sabrina said to Graeme.

"Too crowded and too many dignitaries. We'd never get the carriage in."

"Oh, that's disappointing. Will we still be able to see everything?"

"Dinna fash yerself, lassie," he said with a teasing smile. "We'll not have our *Sassenach* ladies missing a moment of the festivities, ye ken."

She blushed like a foolish schoolgirl. Good heavens, she loved his brogue. And when Angus gave her another wink, like a co-conspirator in romance, a warm, happy glow suffused her.

The truth was, she was tumbling quite hard for Graeme Kendrick. She adored it when he smiled at her, especially since he was so sparing in handing smiles out.

"Nicholas put his foot down about being too close to the arch," Victoria added. "He thundered at me for even considering the notion. I told him in no uncertain terms that the king was my father, and that I would sit wherever I liked. Sadly, he was unmoved by my argument."

"Nick has the right of it," Graeme replied. "The crowds will be too thick. You could get stuck in there, especially if something were to—"

He cut himself off, and the three Kendricks exchanged a quick glance. There'd been several of those looks over the last few days, along with abrupt changes of conversation when Sabrina walked into a room.

"Are you expecting trouble?" she asked Graeme.

He adopted a bland smile. It was *quite* annoying how he could so easily mask what he was thinking.

"Not unless you count getting whacked in the head by an errant banner as trouble."

Victoria also smiled at Sabrina. "My husband is overprotective because of my condition. Nicholas is a bit of a worrier, in case you haven't noticed."

"I have, but—"

"And yon pregnant lassie *does* need to use the necessary more than usual," Angus interjected. "We canna be too far from a water closet or—"

"Grandda," Victoria interrupted in a longsuffering tone, "what will Lady Sabrina think of us?"

"That we're untutored Highlanders," said Graeme, flashing Sabrina a charming grin.

"Och, she knows that already," Angus scoffed.

Just as she knew they were deflecting her question. However, since they'd reached Picardy Place and the coachman was angling the carriage into their reserved spot, she let the matter drop.

Victoria shaded her eyes to peer across the plaza. "This is an excellent spot. I can see the triumphal arch just ahead."

"Ah, there's Royal and Ainsley," Graeme said.

When the couple joined them, he opened the carriage door and stepped out so Ainsley could take his place.

"Good God, what a crowd," said the dark-haired beauty as she gracefully flopped onto the seat. "I had to use my parasol on several impertinent fellows just to get through."

Victoria looked concerned. "Was someone rude to you, dearest?"

Royal, an arm propped on the carriage door, flashed a grin. "No, the poor men simply didn't get out of the way fast enough."

"I did say excuse me first," Ainsley said.

"Yes, but it's a bit hard to hear over the crowd, love."

When she gave an insouciant shrug, Royal laughed. "All right, Graeme and I are going to see if we can get closer to the triumphal gate."

"Enjoy yourselves," his wife replied. "But have a care for your leg."

Royal had been injured in the war some years back. According to Victoria, he was now strong and fit, but Ainsley still fussed over him.

Royal leaned in to kiss his wife, lingering more than was strictly proper. When he finally pulled away, Ainsley whispered something that made him chuckle and kiss the tip of her nose.

Sabrina couldn't help sighing. To be so in love . . .

She looked at Graeme, startled to catch him staring intently at her. When his smoldering gaze dipped to her lips, she could almost feel the press of his firm mouth to hers. It made her go weak in the knees—and other places. Sabrina had to resist the urge to shift on the plush velvet seat.

Angus jabbed his grandson. "Would ye like me to step out of the carriage so ye can make a proper good-bye to her ladyship?"

Graeme shot him an annoyed look. "I'm perfectly capable of saying good-bye from here."

"But—"

"Grandda, you need to stay in the carriage and keep an eye on the women. The footmen will also remain, but you're responsible, understand?"

Grandfather and grandson exchanged a look that seemed to transmit an entire conversation.

"Aye, lad," Angus said. "I'll keep a good eye on things."

Victoria smiled at Graeme. "We'll be fine, dear."

"And we'll be too busy watching the parade to think of leaving the barouche," Sabrina assured him.

"Excellent," Graeme said. "We'll come to fetch you once the king passes by. Stay out of trouble, all right?"

Ainsley snapped off a mock salute. "Aye, aye, sir."

Graeme and his brother held a low-voiced conversation before Royal slipped through the crowds, away from Union Street. Graeme went the other way, steadily forging toward the triumphal arch. His imposing height made it easy to follow his progress until he disappeared behind a stand packed with dignitaries.

"That's odd," Sabrina murmured.

"What's odd, dear?" Victoria asked.

"I thought the men were going together, but they headed off in different directions."

"Oh, I believe Royal is fetching us ices," Ainsley said. "It's beastly hot, don't you think?"

It wasn't the slightest bit hot.

"And I suspect that Graeme wanted to check on Grant," Vicky added.

"Aye, to twit him about his missing broadsword," Angus said in a droll tone.

Clearly, the entire Kendrick family was in league with Graeme regarding his mysterious activities, trying to hide whatever it was from Sabrina.

It was silly, really. Sabrina knew better than most what had to be done to safeguard the king. But Graeme's behavior suggested something else. He was deeply worried about something, and was right in the middle of it, obviously.

She leaned across to speak quietly to Victoria. "Is there some sort of specific threat to the king that you're all worried about?"

The countess appeared startled before quickly pressing Sabrina's hand. "There's actually nothing to worry about, my dear. Look around at the security. One can barely move without tripping over a soldier or a city constable."

That much was true. Still . . .

"I'm not entirely sure what Graeme's—I mean, Mr. Kendrick's—role is in any of this. Could *he* be in any danger?"

Victoria's sky-blue gaze warmed with sympathy. "Graeme has gotten himself into a fair amount of trouble over the years and has always managed to get himself out. He'll be fine, I'm sure."

Not a terribly reassuring answer.

Ainsley stood, peering over the growing commotion in the street. "I can see the procession approaching the arch."

A growing din rolled up the street and echoed against the rise of Calton Hill, its looming slopes covered with a multitude of cheering Scots. It was an amazing sight, as if half the country had turned out to give the king a boisterous welcome. Unexpectedly, Sabrina's throat went tight. In this moment, in this explosion of jubilation, she realized she'd never been happier. Scotland, which had been forbidden to her by her father's fretful bigotries, now seemed exactly where she wanted to be. It was a splendid and almost perfect moment.

It needed only one thing—or man—to make it *entirely* perfect. While that would require a bit more work, she'd never been afraid of a challenge.

They all stood now, cheering with the crowds as the Royal Company of Archers marched beneath the triumphal arch.

Well, everyone but Angus cheered. He was glaring at a group of men hoisting a gigantic banner next to the arch. It read: *The Descendent of the Immortal Bruce.*

Angus jabbed a finger at the offending banner. "I might soon be losin' my lunch, ye ken."

"Is that a reference to Robert the Bruce?" Ainsley asked.

"Aye, and if King Fathead is his true descendent, then I'm queen of the faeries."

"I'm sorry, Grandda," Victoria said, "but King George *is*

indeed descended from the Bruce through the Stuart line. Although many generations removed, naturally," she hastily added when the old man began to bluster.

"Still, full marks to His Majesty for trying to correct the mistakes of the past," Sabrina said with a placating smile. "He's very enthusiastic about Scotland and wants his trip to be a splendid success for everyone."

Ainsley patted her shoulder. "That's the spirit, pet."

"Fah," Angus said.

"Look, there he is," exclaimed Victoria.

The king appeared under the arch, traveling in an open carriage. He was hard to miss, the old dear. For one, his portly, imposing figure was garbed in the uniform of a full admiral, and he waved an enormous white handkerchief. Even from a distance, Sabrina could tell he was tremendously pleased. As his carriage came closer, he enthusiastically dispensed smiles and waves to the crowd.

The huzzahs and cries of *you are welcome, King*, swelled in volume as he rolled by. As luck would have it, he glanced over at the Kendrick carriage. Recognizing Sabrina, he gave a cheerful wave, then looked directly at Victoria and lifted his hat in tribute.

The countess had a hand pressed to the swell of her stomach, smiling through her tears at her father.

Ainsley took Victoria's hand. "Steady on, old girl."

"I cannot believe I finally saw him," she choked out.

"And he saw you," Sabrina said. "He's going to be so happy when he properly meets you."

Even Angus seemed touched. "It's a grand thing to see your da, I'll give ye that."

Victoria smiled mistily at him. "Thank you, Grandda."

"You'd best sit down," Ainsley said. "Nick will take a fit if he sees you teetering on your feet."

A few minutes later, the Celtic Society marched by, fol-lowed by the Scottish lords. Grant gave them an enthusiastic wave, and Lord Arnprior doffed his hat to the ladies. All in all, it was a ridiculous, extravagant, and wonderful display. Sabrina wouldn't have missed it for the world.

She only hoped Graeme was safely out of harm's way—if there was any harm to be had—and that he would rejoin them soon.

Royal strode up to the carriage. "What an insane crush. Did you ladies enjoy the show?"

His wife flashed him a sardonic smile. "What? No ices?"

He frowned. "What's that supposed to mean?"

"You were supposed to fetch us ices. Because of the heat," Sabrina couldn't help saying.

"Oh, uh, I seem to have forgotten."

"Obviously," Ainsley replied with amusement.

Victoria shifted uncomfortably on her seat. "It's not an ice I'm longing for at the moment."

"Och, ye need to use the necessary, I'll wager," Angus said.

"Unfortunately, yes," Victoria said. "But we're not supposed to wander off."

Royal waggled a hand. "It'll take some time to get home through this crowd. Sorry, lass."

When the countess grimaced, Ainsley stood and opened the door of the barouche. "Not to worry. There's a lovely teashop just off Union Street, only a block from here. Royal and our footmen can forge a path through the crowd."

"Then I suggest we hurry," Victoria said.

Royal handed her down, and then did the same for his wife.

"You'll stay with Lady Sabrina?" he asked Angus. "Graeme should be back shortly."

The old fellow's smile turned sly. "Aye. The lassie and I have plenty to talk about."

"I'm sure," Royal dryly replied. "But stay in the carriage."

Angus waved him off.

With the two brawny footmen leading the way, Royal escorted the ladies through the crowd and soon disappeared.

"I'd quite like to stretch my legs, too," Sabrina said. "Do you think I might step out? I'll stand right by the coach."

Angus rubbed his hands. "Ye and me both, lass. Why don't we stroll up the block while we're waitin'."

"But Mr. Kendrick—"

"Lass, let's not be forgettin' I raised that lad from the day he was a wee, mewling babe." He grinned at her. "And I'll be happy to tell ye a few more stories about his misspent youth, if ye like."

Sabrina laughed. "Very well, then. We'll stroll, if only for a few minutes."

"It'll be our secret," Angus said with a wink.

Since the procession had passed, the crowds were beginning to thin, allowing them to walk at a slow but steady pace along the row of charming shops. Sabrina had yet to find herself bored in Edinburgh, enjoying the intimacy of the smaller city and the friendliness of the residents.

Angus was relating a shocking but entertaining tale about Graeme and Grant breaking into the poor box of the local kirk when they noticed a commotion ahead of them. A man emerged from one of the stores, shouting. Then a few ladies began shrieking as two little boys—street urchins—forced their way through a knot of pedestrians and dashed into the street, deftly weaving between horses and carriages.

"Constable," someone yelled.

"Och, trouble," Angus said.

Sabrina was so busy craning up, trying to see, that she almost missed the tug on her reticule. Whipping around, she grabbed a bony wrist and found herself staring down into a child's face.

Chapter Eleven

Graeme had spent the last hour roaming the boisterous crowd and had found no cause for alarm. City residents and visitors alike seemed genuinely excited to see the king. A few discontented but mild mutterings had been directed toward the Scottish lords and the policy of the ongoing Clearances, and he'd heard some trenchant, sarcastic comments but nothing more. It seemed he could finally relax. Perhaps he could spend an hour catching up with his twin over a pint of heavy wet.

He'd hardly seen Grant these last two years and missed him, almost as if he were missing a piece of himself. His twin was doing splendidly, and for that Graeme was thankful. By working at Kendrick Shipping and Trade, Grant had discovered an aptitude for organization and business. He'd only needed to get out on his own, away from Graeme and their endless misadventures, to discover his talents.

Just like Graeme had discovered *his* talents. By society's standards, they were not nearly as respectable as Grant's, and that was probably why they suited him so well.

Graeme elbowed his way past two drunken idiots toasting a portrait of the king. In the company of the "gentlemen of the city," Nick had passed by some time ago, which meant the festivities in this part of town had concluded. The king was safely at Holyrood by now, surrounded by his loyal regiments. If all the events associated with the royal visit proceeded as smoothly as today's procession, then the greatest danger might come from hapless spectators toppling off the rocky promontory of Calton Hill.

No point in taking chances, though. He'd venture out after dark to roam the streets and taverns of Old Town, picking up gossip and taking the pulse of the city.

One day down. Nine left to go.

When he reached Picardy Place a few minutes later, the crowds had thinned. He'd gather up his little chicks and see them safely home, as he'd promised Nick. And before Graeme met up with Grant, there might even be time to stroll with Sabrina. She'd yet to see—

He clamped down on his wayward thoughts. Going for a stroll with the lass, as if he were a normal man? Ridiculous. In less than two weeks, she would be sailing back home. There was no point in spending time with her and dreaming foolish dreams of what might have been. Not with the life he led. Not with a woman like her.

His brain properly sorted, Graeme strode toward the barouche that was parked at the other end of the street.

The *empty* barouche, he was sorry to see. The coachman and one groom were there, but no other family member was in sight.

When he spotted Sabrina and Angus a moment later, he exhaled a sigh of relief. They seemed to be having a grand time, chatting like the best of friends. Sabrina obviously didn't give a damn that his grandfather looked like an escapee from a Highland version of Bedlam. Graeme loved the lass even more for her kind, accepting nature.

Not that he *loved* her, though. Not like that. What a stupid thought.

He'd almost reached them when he spotted a commotion farther up the pavement, as if several strollers had been jostled and pushed into one another. A man yelled, and some ladies screamed. A moment later, two urchins burst through the crowd and dashed into the street.

Rum divers, obviously, taking advantage of prime circumstances to pick pockets.

Another boy, dressed in an oversized coat and a woolen cap pulled low, popped out of the crowd a few feet from Sabrina. Graeme broke into a jog as he saw the rascal sidle up behind her. When the boy reached for her reticule, Graeme shoved through a group of university students and ran. He was about to shout out a warning when Sabrina spun around and grabbed the urchin by the wrist, holding fast.

His heart lurched up into his throat. If the boy had a knife . . .

Angus turned and clamped a hand on the urchin's shoulder. "Hold fast now, laddie boy. None of that nonsense."

"Let me go," yelped the struggling boy. "I weren't doin' a damn thing."

The boy kicked out, and Angus staggered. The boy was able to yank free, almost pulling Sabrina off her feet. The urchin turned and promptly slammed into Graeme, who lifted the boy straight off his feet.

"Give it up, lad. You're not going anywhere," he said.

"Let me go, ye bastard!"

The lad wriggled like a worm on a hook. Disturbingly, he barely weighed anything. Underneath the flapping, ragtag coat, he was bony and frail, like a small child.

A string of very adult oaths, however, streamed out of him in a thin, high-pitched voice. Graeme gave him a warning shake to get his attention.

"Don't hurt him," Sabrina exclaimed.

Graeme rolled his eyes.

"If ye put him down, mayhap he'll stop floppin' like a fish," Angus suggested.

Graeme glanced down to encounter a furious and absolutely extraordinary gaze. A blue so light as to be almost silver, the boy's eyes were set in a sharp, thin face the color of bronze.

That silver stare glittered with defiance and something close to panic.

"I won't hurt you," Graeme said. "But you have to stop struggling."

"Shall I call the constable?" asked a clerk who'd emerged from a nearby shop. Various bystanders voiced their approval for such action.

"No," Sabrina firmly said. "He bumped into me. It was an accident."

"Now, lassie," Angus started, "ye ken—"

Sabrina elbowed him into silence.

"We should call the constable," declaimed a thin gentleman, whose tall hat and black garb made Graeme think of a crow. "He's one of those ruffian pickpockets."

Sabrina's intent gaze silently begged Graeme to protect the child.

The boy had stopped struggling, and fear now mingled with resignation in his gaze. Graeme knew terrible things happened to a small, delicate child like him, whether on the streets or in a jail or poorhouse.

"Did this boy pick your pocket?" Graeme asked the crow-like gentleman.

"Well, no, but that's hardly the—"

He turned to the shopkeeper. "And did he rob you?"

"Nae, but—"

Graeme narrowed his gaze on the group of busybodies that had gathered to watch the scene. "Then bugger off before I call the constable on the lot of *you* for causing a disturbance on the king's day."

The clerk turned pale and retreated into his shop, while the crow fellow and his companions huffed off with rapidity.

"That was quite . . . effective," Sabrina commented with a ghost of a laugh.

"Scarin' people off?" Angus said. "A Kendrick specialty."

"Mister, are ye gonna keep me hangin' all day?" asked the boy in a surly voice.

Graeme lowered him, keeping a hand on his shoulder. "Don't even try to run."

"Bleedin' giant," the lad muttered.

Sabrina leaned down, going eye to eye with the child. "No one will hurt you, but I'd like to talk to you for a few minutes, if that's all right."

His mouth twitched. "Do ye *promise* to let me go, then?"

Sabrina held out a hand. "Shall we shake on it?"

The boy stared at her dainty, pale yellow glove. Then his grubby fingers slowly emerged from his sleeve to exchange a handshake. Dirt smeared onto the pristine fabric, but Sabrina seemed not to notice.

"So, we're havin' a chat on the street, are we?" asked Angus.

"No, I thought we would sit in the carriage," Sabrina replied.

Graeme frowned. "Sabrina, if the lad—"

"I have my reasons," she quietly said.

He sighed and gently propelled the lad toward the carriage.

"You don't 'ave to push, guv. I gave my word I wouldn't run."

"I hardly think your word is reliable."

Sabrina reached out a hand to the boy. "Why don't I escort you?"

Graeme mentally rolled his eyes. No self-respecting boy—much less a rum picker—would be caught dead holding a lady's hand in public.

The child hesitated before slipping his little mitt into Sabrina's hand.

"Huh," muttered Angus.

"You may let go now, Mr. Kendrick," Sabrina said.

He shot her a sardonic glance but complied.

The lad didn't try to escape, although he continued to eye Sabrina with wonderment. Graeme couldn't blame the nipper. It wasn't every day a little pickpocket was escorted along a genteel city street by a beautiful young lady.

At the barouche, Graeme waved the astonished groom back to his perch and opened the carriage door. He handed Sabrina in, then, taking no chances, lifted the boy up and plopped him on the opposite seat.

"Ho, mister," he protested. "I ain't no sack a potatoes."

"No, you're lighter than a sack of potatoes." Graeme's heart ached to feel how thin the boy was within the voluminous coat.

Graeme waved Angus in then shut the door, leaning against it from the outside. The boy eyed him with distaste, clearly resenting Graeme's effort to prevent any attempts at escape. Graeme would certainly let him go, but not until Sabrina deemed it appropriate.

She gave the boy an encouraging smile. "What's your name?"

The icy-blue gaze narrowed. "None of yer soddin' business."

Graeme lightly cuffed him on the shoulder—very lightly. "Keep a civil tongue, lad. And refer to her as *my lady*."

She flashed Graeme a warning look. "You can call me Sabrina. And I simply wish to know what to call you. I have no nefarious designs, I assure you."

The boy scrunched up his face. "Come again?"

"We won't turn ye over to the law," Angus said. "Yer safe."

The boy eyed Graeme. "What about the big bloke?"

"The big bloke won't be hurtin' ye either, word of a Highlander."

The boy scowled. "I ain't never been to no Highlands, so that means nothin' to me."

Angus tapped the side of his nose. "It's grand to be a Highlander, laddie. And we're famous for keepin' our word."

For a moment, the lad looked wistful. "I ain't been nowhere but right here."

"Old Town?" Graeme asked.

The older sections of the city were medieval rabbit warrens, as bad as any stew in London.

"Aye. Me and my—" He broke off.

"Your what?" Sabrina gently prodded.

"Nothin'."

"Where are your parents?" she asked.

He shrugged. "Never knew my da. My ma said he were a sailor, from the Indies."

That accounted for the boy's unusual appearance—unusual at least for Edinburgh. London was a hodgepodge of peoples from all over the world. Mayfair and Kensington were ridiculously rarified, but greater London held a vibrant mix of races that jostled along fairly well, depending on the part of town. A couple originally from Jamaica owned Graeme's favorite pub. He counted Mr. and Mrs. Samuels amongst his few real friends in London, always ready to serve up a good pot of stew and a sympathetic ear.

In the world Graeme moved in, people rarely thought twice about such friendships, but in Edinburgh or Glasgow? His own nephew was of mixed heritage, and he'd seen first-hand the bigotry the wee lad had experienced, even with the protection of a family like the Kendricks.

For this child, the challenges of survival would be enormous.

"What about your mother?" Sabrina gently asked.

"She died when my bro . . . when I was little."

Sabrina took his hand. "My mother died when I was just a baby."

The boy tilted his head. His knit cap slipped sideways, revealing thick, dark-copper locks, twisted into a knot at the base of his neck. "What about your da?"

Sabrina smiled. "My father is still alive."

"That's . . . that's nice."

"Yes, it is." She gave his hand a couple of gentle pats. "Now, won't you please tell me your name?"

"Ballantine," he finally said.

"And a fine Scottish name that is," Angus said.

"What's your given name?" Sabrina coaxed.

The lad pressed his lips closed.

"Son, if you're not going to answer the lady's questions, maybe I should haul you off to the clink after all," Graeme said, annoyed.

The boy snorted, obviously feeling confident enough to see it as the empty threat it was.

"No, you won't," Sabrina said.

Graeme rolled his eyes. "Lass, of course I'm not—"

"We can't just let him go without our help. It's much too dangerous."

Of course it was dangerous. Life on the street always was, but she clearly meant something else. "Sabrina, what exactly are you worried about?"

"I'd say it's because yon lad isn't a lad," Angus dryly said.

The boy froze, like a rabbit spotting a fox.

Sabrina nodded. "*He* is a *she*, and I will not allow a little girl to run about the stews of Edinburgh unprotected."

The child bristled. "I ain't little, and I ain't unprotected. I'm head boy, lady. One day, I'm gonna have a gang of my own."

After Graeme picked his jaw off the ground, he took a closer look and wanted to smack himself. Those delicate features were not just the result of youth and frailty.

Angus snorted. "And ye call yerself a spy."

The girl perked up. "Yer a spy? Coo!"

Graeme frowned. "I'm not a spy. And why are you running about, pretending to be a boy?"

She gave a remarkably insouciant shrug. "It's safer, and the lads listen better if'n I acts like them."

"That's awful," Sabrina said, looking rather pale.

The girl bristled. "Lady, I runs the gang and keeps 'em all in order. I'm in charge."

"But—"

Graeme cut in. "What's your name, lass?"

"Tilly," she reluctantly said.

"Mine's Graeme. Graeme Kendrick."

Her eyes widened. "Ye mean like the Laird of Arnprior Kendrick?"

"Yes."

"Coo," she breathed, much impressed.

"Tilly, do you really have to, um, run a gang?" Sabrina asked. "Surely there's something else you'd like to do with your life."

Tilly snorted. "Be a whore like me mam?"

Sabrina flinched, while Angus let out a weary sigh.

Graeme had to help the lass. The case that had almost gotten him killed had involved a girl in danger, and he'd made an epic hash of it. This time, he'd get it right.

"Tilly, do you work from a flash house?" he asked.

She nodded.

"With a fence or a gang leader?"

"Arch rogue," she tersely replied.

Gang leader, then. Children from the stews often fell into the clutches of petty criminals, who lured them in with promises of protection and then exploited them without mercy. It made Graeme want to kill the bastard controlling Tilly.

"For how long?"

"Since me mam died. She worked for him, too."

"You don't have to keep working for him," Sabrina earnestly said. "We can help you do something else."

"Can't."

"Why not?" Graeme asked.

Tilly's expressive face mirrored an inner struggle.

"'Cause I'm tryin' to get me little brother out of the orphanage," she finally blurted out. "Ol' Bill said he'd get Charlie out once I pays off our debts to him. When me mam died, she owed Bill money. Then he took on the raisin' of us, so I owes him, too. But then Bill said Charlie was too little to earn his keep, so he says let the parish take care of him. He's the one who stuck Charlie in the orphanage in the first place."

Sabrina, who'd been looking appalled, rallied. "My dear girl, I can give you whatever money you need."

For a moment, hope flared like a torch in Tilly's gaze. But just as quickly, the light snuffed out. "Can't."

Sabrina frowned. "Why not?"

"'Cause I promised Bill I'd work for him as long as he said," Tilly said. "Bill said he'd tell me when the debt's paid. So it ain't up to me. He said he's been loyal to me, so I gots to be loyal to him."

"But you're a child," Sabrina replied. "Adults shouldn't let children make promises like that."

Tilly scowled. "I ain't no silly bantling, and I don't welch."

Sabrina looked perplexed, but Graeme understood both Tilly's cant and her dilemma.

"The gangs have their own code of conduct," he explained. "If you violate that code . . ."

When Tilly drew a finger across her throat, Sabrina looked ready to bolt up her crumpets.

Graeme quickly pressed Sabrina's hand. "We'll get it sorted, lass. I promise."

"Nothin' to sort," Tilly said. "I run the gang till Ol' Bill says I don't. Once he says I've paid off our debts, I'll run my own rig. Or maybe leave town," she wistfully added. "Start someplace new with Charlie."

Sabrina pressed a hand to her lips before replying. "No child should have to live like that."

"I do all right. And once I gets Charlie out, I'll have enough to take care of him, too."

"But—"

Graeme gave Sabrina a warning shake of the head. She breathed out a frustrated huff but desisted.

Tilly flashed a sharp look at Graeme. "Mister, can I go? Someone'll come lookin' soon enough, and Ol' Bill won't like me jabberin' with ye."

Graeme understood. If someone from the gang saw the child talking to them . . .

Sabrina's frustration finally broke free. "We simply *cannot* let her return to the dreadful situation. We have to help her."

"Do you want me to talk to Old Bill?" Graeme asked Tilly. "I'm sure I could square things away. Convince him to let you go."

Panic flashed across her features. Her gaze darted about, as if she were seeking an avenue of escape.

Graeme held up a quick hand. "It's all right. I won't do anything that would get you in trouble."

"He'd kill me if I let ye even come near him. 'Sides, I'm his best boy. He won't let me go till he's ready." She blew out a disgusted breath. "And I can't get Charlie out on my own. Ol' Bill put him in, and Matron says I'm too young to take him out."

Graeme extracted his billfold. "Let's try this. Forget Bill and what you owe him. Pay the matron your brother's fees, and tell her that the Kendrick family will vouch for the both of you. If you need me to go to the orphanage, I will do that, too."

Tilly jerked a bit. Then she frowned thoughtfully down at her lap, clearly thinking through all the possibilities.

"That might work," she finally said. Her sharp gaze

fastened on Graeme. "And ye'll not be askin' me to pay ye back?"

"Consider it a charitable donation to the orphanage from the Kendrick family."

In a twinkling, the pound notes disappeared up Tilly's sleeve.

"Do you have a bolt hole?" Graeme asked.

When the girl clammed up again, he smiled at her. "I don't need to know where it is. Just that you have someplace safe to stay."

Safe was a relative term in Tilly's world. Children like her usually had secret hiding places, sometimes little more than a corner in an old cellar. Somewhere the adults couldn't reach them.

Tilly scoffed. "Course I have a bolt hole."

"All right." Graeme opened the door of the carriage. "You can go."

Sabrina grabbed Tilly's sleeve. "That's it?" she said to Graeme. "We're just going to let her go?"

Tilly glared at her. "Ye promised."

Sabrina's sweet countenance pulled tight with dismay. "I promised to help you, Tilly. Letting you go back to that horrible man is not helping you."

The girl darted another panicked look around the street. "I gots to, miss, or Ol' Bill will make me pay."

Graeme gently pulled Sabrina's hand from Tilly's sleeve. "It's the best thing for her at the moment. And we can't hold her against her wishes."

"Damn right," Tilly said.

"Och, lassie. Not in front of a lady," Angus said.

Sabrina flapped a hand. "I don't care about her language. I care about her safety."

"I can takes care of myself, never you fear, miss."

"Dammit to hell," Sabrina muttered.

Despite the fraught situation, Graeme had to choke back a laugh.

"Tilly, do you know how to write?" Sabrina asked.

"Course I do. I ain't no dummy."

"I assume you know where the Kendricks live, on Heriot Row? I'm staying there for a little while. If you need help, send me a message. I mean it, Tilly."

"Sabrina," Graeme started to warn.

"Or send a message to Mr. Kendrick or Mr. MacDonald," she hastily added.

Angus waggled a finger. "That's me."

"If I'm not there, one of them will help you."

She stared at Tilly for a moment longer before pulling her into a hug. The little girl froze for a few moments before a thin hand snuck out of her ragged sleeve to rest on Sabrina's back.

When Sabrina finally let go, Tilly gave her a shy grin. "Yer nice, miss. Prolly the nicest lady I ever met."

Graeme heartily agreed with that assessment. Sabrina was so bloody nice it made his heart ache from the loss of something he knew he could never have.

"Away with you, now," he gruffly said, helping Tilly down.

Sabrina leaned over the edge of the carriage. "Remember, come to Heriot Row if you need help."

Tilly favored them with a dazzling smile. The lass would grow up to be a beauty some day if, God and the Kendricks willing, she could escape the same fate as her mother. He'd talk to Nick first, but Graeme had every intention of getting the young lass and her brother safely stowed.

"I won't forget," Tilly said. "God bless ye, miss."

Then she darted away, disappearing in the crowd.

Sabrina slumped in her seat and pressed a hand to her eyes. "God, that was horrible."

. Angus patted her knee. "Och, yer not to worry. We'll sort things out for the lass and her brother."

Sabrina lowered her hands. "But how will you even find her?"

"Yer forgettin' yon laddie's a spy. He'll find the bairn."

"Good Lord," Graeme muttered.

Sabrina huffed out a watery laugh as she fished inside the pocket of her walking gown. "I'm not usually such a watering pot. It's just that her situation was so—" She broke off.

"Something wrong?" Graeme asked.

"My new handkerchief is missing." Her smile was rueful. "I do believe Miss Ballantine picked my pocket while hugging me."

Chapter Twelve

"Are you sure this be the right place, my lady?" Hannah asked, still inside the hackney. "It smells something awful."

After shaking the dirt of the rundown coach from her skirts, Sabrina glanced back at her maid. "We're near the cattle market. Since you're from the country, you should be used to that smell."

"I hate cows," the maid glumly replied.

Sabrina ignored her as she gazed at the sign above the door of a three-story building—one that had seen better days, approximately two hundred years ago.

The oldest part of Edinburgh meandered in a downward, antique sprawl from the castle on its high promontory. The buildings were crowded together and unusually tall, looming over the alleyways and narrow streets that made up Old Town. They cast gloomy shadows even on a bright summer morn.

Historic, yes, but Old Town offered endless opportunities for people to stumble into trouble. Poverty and desperation lurked in the warren of alleys, and so did crime.

You should have told Graeme about this.

She kicked that unwelcome thought to the back of her mind. Tilly's note had been quite clear: come alone, and quickly. Yesterday, the girl had refused any help. Something had obviously changed quite drastically overnight.

"The sign is very faded," Sabrina said. "But I think I can see *Wee* and probably *Dog*, so this must be it."

Tilly had asked to meet at a coffeehouse named the Wee Black Dog. Unless there was a Wee White or a Wee Yellow Dog, this was the spot.

"But, my lady—"

"I cannot go in there by myself." Tilly had said to come alone, but wandering about Edinburgh without even her maid would be truly foolhardy. "Please get out of the coach."

Sabrina sounded a bit testy, but the morning had been a challenge. First, she and Hannah had had to sneak out of the house, and then they'd been forced to walk several blocks before finding a hackney stand.

"Lady, are ye goin' to pay me," the driver asked, "or do I have to call me a constable?"

Mustering an apologetic smile, Sabrina dug into her reticule.

The disreputable-looking fellow suspiciously counted the coins she'd handed him. "Yer not exactly spilling it out, are ye? Jest like a nob. Tight in the fist."

She struggled to keep hold of her patience. "I am paying you exactly what we agreed upon, sir. Besides, your carriage *is* rather shabby. If you thought a bit more about the comfort of your passengers, you might find your business improved."

When the driver made a growling comment about what she should do with her suggestion, Hannah let out a faint shriek and clambered out.

Sabrina refused to be cowed by vulgarity. "Might I also point out that addressing a customer in such crude terms will hardly encourage future business."

The driver gave her a hard look. "Yer daft, lady," he finally said. He snapped his reins, and the coach lumbered off.

At the moment, Sabrina could not disagree with his assessment.

Hannah stared glumly after the hackney. "We should've brought one of them strapping footmen for protection. That Davey is awfully nice."

Sabrina had also been second-guessing herself from the moment they'd left Heriot Row. Hearing from Tilly had been a surprise, and she'd not been prepared with any sort of plan.

Just after dawn, a grubby boy had appeared at the kitchen entrance with a note for Sabrina. The boy had probably been Tilly, which begged the question as to why she hadn't simply asked to speak with Sabrina. Instead, she'd handed over the note to the scullery maid, who'd passed it to the kitchen maid, who'd then handed it off to Hannah.

"We're here now," said Sabrina, "so we just have to make the best of it."

Two laborers brushed by them and went into the coffee-house. The men cast them curious glances as they passed, but looked perfectly respectable in their smocks and breeches—ordinary workers looking for breakfast on a quiet street before starting their day.

"But we're smack in the middle of a slum, my lady," Hannah protested. "As like we'll end up dead, or worse."

Sabrina steered her toward the door. "Hannah, do not address me as *my lady* when we get inside. In fact, don't say anything. Just look like the stout-hearted Englishwoman I know you to be."

"If you say so, Lady Sabrina."

"Don't call me that, either."

"Yes, my lady."

Hopeless.

Several steps led down from the street into a dim, low-ceilinged room. The vision that greeted Sabrina, while certainly uninspiring, was neither threatening nor particularly grim. The Wee Black Dog seemed exactly what Tilly had said in her note—a decent coffeehouse near Edinburgh's cattle markets. Under the enticing scent of coffee lurked the same faint smell of manure that permeated the entire neighborhood. The tables and benches were rough-hewn but clean, and the floor neatly swept. There were small windows set high in the outside wall, but most of the light came from spirit lamps and two large branches of candles on a service counter.

Ignoring curious glances from patrons, Sabrina made her way to the counter, where a young woman with a kind face and a wealth of red hair under a mobcap was stacking oatcakes onto a platter. Hannah, breathing out an aggrieved sigh, trudged along in Sabrina's wake.

The woman looked up with a sharp, assessing glance before reaching under the counter for two coffee mugs.

"Good morning," Sabrina said. "I'm looking for—"

"She's in the back corner. Just let me get ye and yer girl some breakfast, and ye can join her."

"Oh, thank you. But that won't—"

"Ye'll not stand out so much if ye have a cup and somethin' to eat." Her gaze flickered over Sabrina's dress. "Right now, ye stick out like sore thumbs."

Oh, dear. She'd worn her plainest walking dress and a simple straw bonnet in the hope she wouldn't stand out.

"Yer quality, miss, and *Sassenach* to boot. No hidin' that, no matter what ye wear."

"My apologies. I don't wish to cause trouble."

"Och, dinna fash yerself." The woman filled two cups with coffee and added thick splashes of cream, then she began stacking oatcakes and little pots of butter and jam on a battered wooden platter.

"Just coffee will be fine," said Sabrina.

"The vittles are for Tilly, luv. She's too proud to take charity, so ye'll be payin' for it."

"You take care of Tilly?" Sabrina asked as she dug in her reticule.

"I tries to. My name's Emmy, by the by."

Sabrina slid a half crown across the counter. "It's a pleasure to meet you. My name is Sabrina, and this is Hannah."

Emmy blinked in surprise at the coin. Then she nodded her thanks and swiftly pocketed the money before picking up the platter. "The bairn needs help, ye ken. She's in trouble."

"I'm here to make sure she gets help."

"She and her puir little brother." Emmy's friendly gaze turned grim. "The way that bas—" Then she shook her head. "Come along now."

They followed her to a shadowed corner near the fireplace, more a cubbyhole in the wall. A table and two benches were tucked into the cramped space. Tilly occupied the bench against the wall, her cap pulled low over her eyes and her hands wrapped around an empty mug.

Emmy set down the platter. "Yer friends are havin' a bite to eat, and there's plenty for all of ye, darlin'."

Tilly seemed to retreat even further into her oversized coat. "Thank ye."

The woman nodded and returned to her work.

For several long seconds, the girl neither moved nor acknowledged them.

"May we sit down, dear?" Sabrina finally asked.

"I told ye to come alone," Tilly replied in a tight little voice.

"This is Hannah, my maid. She can be trusted."

Those words were met with a fraught silence. Sabrina looked at Hannah, who rolled her eyes.

"I'll takes my coffee and go have a bit of a chat with that Emmy," the maid said. "She seems like a proper sort."

Sabrina gave her a grateful smile and slid onto the bench opposite Tilly.

"Goodness, this looks quite scrumptious," she said, picking up an oatcake. "But I don't think I can eat it all myself, Tilly."

"I am a bit hungry," the child said gruffly. "No time to eat this mornin'."

Sabrina pushed the platter closer to her. "Then you'd best have some."

When Tilly pushed her cap up and reached for an oatcake, Sabrina choked back a gasp. The girl's right eye was puffy and ringed with a smudgy black bruise. Her cheek sported a nasty cut, barely starting to scab over.

"Don't make a fuss, miss," she said in a sharp tone. "It ain't nothin'."

"But you're hurt."

Tilly snorted before shoving one of the oatcakes into her mouth. "Nae. I've had worse than this."

It took Sabrina several seconds to master an upwelling of rage and sorrow. "Did Old Bill do that?"

"Who else?"

Her cynical nonchalance broke Sabrina's heart. "Because you talked to us yesterday?"

"Aye. One of the other kids saw and grassed me out. Ol' Bill said he needed to make an example of me."

Sabrina gripped her mug. "But why?"

Tilly's pale blue eyes glittered with hatred. "I'm supposed to give everythin' to him, but I kept the money yer bloke gave me." The anger in her gaze suddenly turned into a shimmer of tears. "Now I can't get Charlie out."

"He's holding your brother over your head."

"I'm his best earner, miss. He don't want me leavin' him."

Sabrina stared at Tilly's pinched, bruised face. These last few months were teaching Sabrina a hard lesson. For too long, she'd lived in a charming but utterly useless world. Now she intended to change that.

"We'll finish our breakfast, and then we're going to the

Courts to speak with a constable or a magistrate. Then we're—"

Tilly's hand shot out and grabbed her wrist. "No! I ain't no snitch."

Sabrina covered the girl's hand. "I understand you're afraid, but you cannot let that horrible man continue to abuse you. He's a criminal, Tilly. He belongs in jail."

"I'm bent too, miss. They'll put *me* in jail, or the work-house." She grimaced. "And how long do ye think I'll last once it gets out that I snitched on Bill?"

Sabrina fought down a rising sense of frustration. She was in completely over her head. If only Graeme were—

No. She would take care of this. She would make a difference in this child's life.

"Tilly, what exactly do you want from me?"

The girl didn't hesitate. "I need ye to help me spring Charlie from the orphanage. We need to do it this mornin', afore Bill gets wind of it.

"He'll take my brother, if we're not quick about it," the girl added. Her thin fingers tightened around Sabrina's wrist. "I'll pay ye back, miss, I promise. And . . . and I'll pay for that hanky I stole, too."

"Tilly, I don't care about the money or the kerchief. But will they give Charlie to you? You're just a child."

"That's why I need ye to come with me. They'll spring him if yer with me."

Sabrina doubted the process would be that simple. Nothing about this so far had been simple. Still, she had to try.

"Very well, although I'm not quite sure how to go about such things."

And what would happen to the children afterward. She'd like to take them back to Heriot Row, but doubted Tilly would agree.

The girl smiled, then winced a bit and touched her cheek. "Never fear, miss. I has a plan."

"Which is?"

"I'm takin' Charlie to London. We'll lay low for a day or two, then head south."

Sabrina could feel her eyes bugging from her sockets. "Absolutely not."

"Keep yer voice down," Tilly hissed.

Sabrina leaned across the table. "I am not tossing you from the frying pan into the fire. We'll get Charlie out of that orphanage, and then we'll go back to Heriot Row. Mr. Kendrick will know what to do."

Tilly shook her head. "Nah, I gots my own plan. Don't need any nobs."

Sabrina tapped her chest. "Apparently you need this nob."

The girl winced.

"Why were you so insistent in your note that I not tell Mr. Kendrick about our meeting?" Sabrina asked.

Tilly's silver gaze flickered away for a moment. "Don't know him."

"Well, you don't know me, either."

"You ain't a bloke, miss."

Sabrina had to repress the urge to put her head into her hands and start sobbing. That, however, would do nothing to solve their current dilemma.

She dredged up a smile. "Then I suppose we'd best be on our way. Poor Charlie has been in that orphanage long enough, don't you think?"

Tilly's smile blazed to life as she jumped to her feet. "That's grand. It's just off—"

The words died on her lips as she stared toward the front of the room.

Sabrina turned to see a familiar figure looming in the

doorway. And she could feel his masculine ire radiating across the room.

"Drat," she muttered.

Hannah scurried over to join them. "Oh, my lady, it's Mr. Kendrick, and he looks right stormy-like."

The heavy weather was coming straight for them.

Chapter Thirteen

Graeme stalked down the steps, glaring at the woman whose sole purpose apparently was to drive him into jabbering idiocy. And damned if she didn't look annoyed at his appearance, as if *he* were the one engaged in a harebrained rescue mission.

A young woman came out from behind the counter and quickly stepped in front of him. She held up a large wooden tray like a shield. "Ye'd best think twice before chargin' in here like a bully-boy, mister."

Some of the customers rose from their tables. "Ye'll nae be causin' a ruckus with Emmy, ye ken," one particularly burly fellow threatened.

"It's all right, Emmy," Sabrina piped up from the corner. "He won't hurt anyone."

The sturdy young woman eyed Graeme with no less disapproval. "He looks a right ugly customer to me."

He could hardly quarrel with her assessment, since he'd been forced to roll out of bed and pull on whatever clothes came to hand. He gave the lass a placating smile, hoping to look as harmless as possible.

A derisive snort was her response.

"I promise it's fine," Sabrina said. "He's with me."

Emmy reluctantly lowered her tray, still scowling. "Verra

well, but dinna try any funny business with miss, or ye'll find yerself with a bloody great headache."

"I already have a bloody great headache, thanks to *miss*," Graeme replied. "But I'm a Kendrick, if that makes any difference. The lady is staying with my family and is under our protection."

Understanding dawned on Emmy's face. "Och, yer one of them Kendrick twins, ain't ye?"

Apparently, his old reputation was still intact. "Guilty as charged."

The woman snorted. "I'll bring ye a cup of coffee."

"Thank you."

"But no bustin' up my furniture," she added.

The denizens of Old Town obviously had long memories, not that he blamed her for the dig. He and Grant had brawled in more than a few pubs back in their Edinburgh university days.

"What was that about?" Sabrina asked.

"You don't want to know."

She gave him a remarkably cheeky smile. "Actually, I do."

He stared at her in disbelief. "That's what you want to talk about, not this mad scheme? If anyone gets wind of this little escapade, your reputation will be thoroughly shot."

"I did bring Hannah with me," she replied with a hint of apology.

Her maid was currently working hard at trying to fade into the wall.

"Sabrina, this is a very dodgy part of town," he said, getting exasperated. "No respectable lady would come here with only a maid as escort."

She looked down her elegant little nose at Graeme. Since he was looming over her, he found it a neat trick.

"This establishment is perfectly respectable. Besides I'm on an errand of mercy." Her glare was defiant. "I cannot refuse to help this poor child."

Said child had pulled her cap down as soon as she'd spotted him, and had yet to say a word. Embarrassed, probably, and trying to figure out the best way to bolt. Graeme hoped like hell that Tilly wasn't trying to pull a con, taking advantage of Sabrina's kind heart.

"It's all right, miss," the girl said in a muffled voice. "I'll go."

"Stay right there, Tilly," Sabrina replied.

"No, miss. I gots to go now afore it's too late." She started to slide out from behind the table.

Graeme pointed a finger. "Stay."

When the girl froze like a startled fawn, Sabrina scowled at him. At the same time, Emmy thumped a coffee mug down on the table, also giving him the evil eye.

You're making a hash of things, laddie boy.

Summoning his patience, he swung a leg over the bench and sat next to Sabrina. "It's all right, Tilly. Whatever it is, we'll get it sorted."

The child finally lifted her head. Graeme's heart slammed into his ribs when he saw her bruised face, and he had to struggle to control an upwelling of fury. For a moment, he wanted to break not just every piece of furniture in the place, but in the entire damn city of Edinburgh.

"Mr. Graeme is a Kendrick, dear," Sabrina quietly said. "They always keep their word."

Emmy nodded. "Lord Arnprior and his kin are honest and true, even the wild ones like this bloke. Ye can trust Clan Kendrick."

Graeme threw her a sardonic glance. "Thank you."

The woman shrugged and returned to her work.

"I will help you, sweetheart," he said to Tilly. "My word on it."

The girl blushed, embarrassed by his term of endearment, but he also caught her shy smile.

Sabrina patted Tilly's hand. "I told you." She glanced at

him. "By the way, how did you find us? We were quite careful not to be seen."

"Ainsley was up with the baby. She caught a glimpse of you and Hannah scampering down the street."

Sabrina frowned. "But how did you find us here, specifically? We had quite a good start on you, even with the warning."

With his coat flapping, he had been stuffing his shirt into his breeches as he'd bolted out of the house. Luckily, he'd come upon a chimney sweep who'd seen the women heading to the closest hackney stand. The driver remaining there had overheard Sabrina's directions to the driver she'd hired. Graeme had eyed the fellow's broken-down hackney and equally unfortunate nag and had made the decision to run back to the house to fetch Royal's curricle and a groom. He'd wasted a few minutes finding the right coffeehouse, but notwithstanding that inconvenience, finding Sabrina had been as easy as falling off a log.

"It's what I do, lass."

"Your talents are quite remarkable. And annoying," she added with a mutter.

"You cannot imagine how annoyed I'll be if you try anything this hen-witted again."

She'd started to bristle when Tilly came to her defense. "Here now, miss was just tryin' to help me."

"I know, but I worry about her, Tilly. Miss has a knack for finding trouble."

Sabrina shot him an obscure, sideways glance. "Only lately."

He had to repress a smile. "Can we now come to the point of all this drama? I'm assuming Tilly had a run-in with Old Bill."

"Run-in with the ol' bastard's fist," Tilly said.

Old Bill would pay for that, too, Graeme silently vowed. "I wish the both of you had thought to ask me for help."

"This weren't my idea, I can tell you," Hannah finally piped up.

"I never would have guessed," Graeme dryly replied.

Sabrina touched his hand. "I wanted to ask for your help, truly."

"Why didn't you?"

She threw a brief glance at Tilly, who ducked her head again.

Ah. Tilly had forbidden it. Still not a good excuse, but he understood. Sabrina had promised the girl she'd help, and Sabrina was a woman who kept her word, even if it meant marching headfirst into danger.

Graeme gently cupped Tilly's pointy little chin, lifting her face so he could get a better look. "I reckon he took your money, along with giving you that shiner."

"Ol' Bill is quick with his fists, but I don't care about that." Her face suddenly contorted with anguish. "I can't get Charlie out of that bloody orphanage. Bill will get him, and we'll be stuck forever."

"No, we'll fix it," Graeme said.

"I'm sorry I lost your money," Tilly said in a small voice.

He wanted to tell her that the money didn't matter. But to a child like Tilly, money mattered.

"So, what's the plan?" he asked.

The girl perked up. "Yer not mad that I lost yer money?"

"It was stolen from you, lass. And I promise I'll deal with Old Bill at the appropriate time. For now, we have to spring Charlie from the orphanage, I'm guessing."

"Aye, afore Bill gets to him."

"All right. Tilly, you and I will fetch Charlie."

"What about me?" Sabrina asked.

Graeme stood. "I've a curricle and groom waiting outside. You and Hannah go back with him."

Sabrina shook her head. "I'm going with you and Tilly. I promised her I would."

"It's no proper place for a lady," he said. "I'll not have it."

"But miss has to pay what's still owing," Tilly objected.

Graeme reached for his billfold, but let out an exasperated sigh.

"You forgot to bring money, didn't you?" Sabrina said.

"I was in rather a hurry," he sarcastically replied. "You can give me the money, and I'll take Tilly."

Sabrina rose, keeping a firm hold on her reticule. "Hannah, you go home in the curricle with the groom. I'm going with Mr. Kendrick and Tilly."

"Are you sure, my lady?"

"Quite sure."

Hannah bolted for the door.

"Sabrina—" Graeme started.

She laid a hand on his arm. "I need to do this, sir. I *need* to help."

It was foolish beyond belief to let her come, but Graeme had a terrible sense that he would crush something inside her if he said no. He knew what that was like, and how damaging it could be.

Tilly gave an urgent tug on his sleeve. "Mister, please."

"The both of you will do *exactly* as I say, is that clear?" he said.

They returned identical nods.

While Tilly headed for the door, Graeme took Sabrina's arm. "You will do *everything* I say, lass, or I will put you over my knee for a good paddling."

"M . . . Mr. Kendrick," she spluttered. "Really!"

He was biting back a grin when the door flew open and a squat, toad-like man stepped into the room. Dressed in a bottle-green tailcoat, bright pink vest, and tall beaver hat, the fellow looked ridiculous.

Tilly, however, let out a yelp and skidded to a halt right in front of him.

Instantly, the man lashed out and cuffed the girl, knocking her into the lap of a startled customer who managed to keep her from hitting the floor.

"Ye little bitch," the toad growled. "I warned ye not to run."

It took but a moment for Graeme to find himself with a hand wrapped around the man's neck, pinning him to the doorframe with the other hand.

"Old Bill, I presume," he snarled.

Bill gurgled as he desperately scrabbled and thrashed, managing to land a weak kick on Graeme's shin.

Graeme slammed him hard into the door. "Stop struggling, ye bastard."

Sabrina suddenly was at his side. "Mr. Kendrick, you'll choke him to death."

"All right by me," Tilly said as she wiped her bloody nose with her coat sleeve.

Graeme tightened his fingers around Bill's throat, and the man's face turned purple.

A small fist punched him in the shoulder. "Graeme, please stop it. *Now.*"

Her use of his name cut through the killing rage clouding his brain.

She punched him again. "You simply *cannot* kill a man in the middle of a coffee shop."

He glanced down into her pale but determined features. "Are you sure?"

"Quite sure."

She was right, of course. It would be massively inconvenient, involving constables, magistrates, and piles of paperwork. With the king still in Edinburgh, Graeme didn't have time for such nonsense.

He pulled Bill away from the doorframe. "I'll deal with

you later." Then he drilled the toad in his jaw, dropping him to the floor in a graceless heap.

Sabrina blinked. "Goodness. That was effective."

"Should keep him down for a while." He glanced at Emmy. "Sorry about the mess, lass."

Emmy shrugged. "I'll have a couple of the lads dump 'im out back in the alley, then I'll close up. That should give ye a head start."

"I'm obliged."

Tilly joined them and gave Bill's leg a kick. "Still say ye shoulda killed him."

Sabrina extracted a plain linen handkerchief from her reticule and handed it to the girl. "That would have been inappropriate, dear, and most unhelpful."

"You're taking all this mayhem rather well," Graeme said.

Sabrina shot him a wry look. "I seem to be growing immune to mayhem. My poor father would be horrified."

"Och, lass, he'd just blame it on me." Graeme ushered her and Tilly up the stairs to the street.

In the end, it had been almost ridiculously easy.

After a ten-minute walk, they'd reached the Orphan Home for Friendless Boys, a tall, soot-stained building with a forbidding atmosphere. Graeme had asked Sabrina—instructed her, more accurately—to let him do the talking. For once, she'd been happy to do so.

A porter had ushered them into a small parlor to wait for the matron and the superintendent. Although covered in ghastly brown wallpaper that amplified the grim atmosphere, the room was tidy and respectably furnished.

As Tilly had warned them on the walk over, the superintendent had proven to be the problem. Supercilious and suspicious, he'd initially resisted their attempts to have Charlie released into their care. The matron, a kind and rather motherly sort, had advocated for the boy's release, but was ordered to keep silent by her superior.

Graeme had been deferential up until that point, as deferential as a Kendrick apparently could be. But then he'd undergone a startling transformation. Sabrina had always seen him as a man more comfortable in the shadows than in the ballrooms of Mayfair. Not rough, but no typical gentleman, either. Much of the time, one would never have guessed him a son of one of the noblest houses in Scotland.

And yet that is precisely what he became at the orphanage. He assumed an air of authority as impressive as his height, informing the superintendent that he would be consulting with his brother, Lord Arnprior, as to certain irregularities he suspected in the home's management. Graeme had then thrown out thinly veiled references to Lady Arnprior's close relationship with the king. The combination had the superintendent's resistance crumpling like a used serviette. Sabrina had then handed over a few banknotes, and the deed was done.

When she'd stood to join the others in fetching Charlie from the orphanage's workroom, Graeme had narrowed his aristocratic gaze on her and suggested she remain in the parlor. Much to her surprise, Sabrina had found herself dropping right back into her chair.

Graeme Kendrick could be impressively masterful and dominating, and it was *quite* annoying that she found such behavior so attractive.

Fifteen minutes later, they were back on the street. Charlie, a darling, red-haired boy with his sister's eyes, clung to Tilly.

"I knew ye'd spring me, Tilly-willy," he said in a tearful voice. "But I was afraid I'd die afore ye got me out o' there."

"Nae, love," Tilly gruffly replied as she hugged him. "I'd never let anything happen to ye."

Graeme crouched down in front of the boy. "Did someone in the orphanage hurt you, Charlie? The superintendent?"

The child rubbed his eyes with his nubby, oversized sleeve. Sabrina made a mental note to provide both children with new clothing.

"Not him, though he's a scaly one. Some of the bigger boys used to give me a drubbin' 'cause I'd stick up for—" He grimaced and swallowed any further remark.

"Stick up for me," Tilly finished. "'Cause of what I look like."

Sabrina felt her stomach tighten with anger, but Graeme simply ruffled the boy's hair.

"You're a brave lad, Charlie," he said. "Good for you."

Sabrina couldn't help bristling. "Sir, that hardly seems the appropriate—"

"So, what's the plan?" Graeme interrupted, giving her a warning glance as he rose to his feet.

She bit back a tart observation and took a moment to collect herself. "Perhaps Tilly and Charlie might return to Heriot Row with us? Then we could have something to eat and a chat about . . ."

She trailed off as identical expressions of disbelief registered on the children's faces.

"Actually, I was asking Tilly what her plans were," Graeme said.

Sabrina went hot with embarrassment, but forced herself to ignore it. "They're children, Mr. Kendrick. They need adults to help them formulate a proper plan."

"The adults haven't been doing such a good job of it, so far."

"Aye, that," Tilly agreed. "And I got a plan, miss, remember? Me and Charlie are goin' to London."

Sabrina couldn't help planting her hands on her hips. "And I told *you* that London was much too dangerous for children on their own. Especially children without any means of support."

"You could give us more blunt, miss," Charlie suggested. "Tilly says you have lots."

"I do, but—"

"We wouldn't need much," Tilly wheedled. "Just enough for the stage and to get us set up in London."

"And just how do you intend to support yourself?" Sabrina asked.

When brother and sister exchanged a furtive look, she shook her head. "Absolutely not. I am *not* providing the means for you to fall back into your criminal ways."

"But it's what I'm good at." Tilly gave a fatalistic shrug. "I don't know how to do anythin' else."

"An' I'm practicin' real hard how to be a rum diver," Charlie proudly added.

Sabrina threw Graeme a confused glance.

"Pickpocket," he replied.

When Sabrina glared at him, she got the distinct impression he was trying not to laugh.

"Do you think you might try making a useful suggestion?" she snapped.

"I'm waiting for yours."

"Very well. The children should go to school and be trained in respectable professions."

"As what?" Tilly pointed a finger at her face. "I ain't exactly respectable lookin', 'specially in a place like this."

She meant Edinburgh, or anywhere in Scotland, for that matter, where her mixed-race parentage counted against her. That was utterly heartbreaking, and Sabrina wished she could take in the children herself. Her father, however, would pitch an apoplectic fit.

"I ain't gonna lose Charlie again, if someone tries to say he ain't my brother," Tilly defiantly added.

"London is a splendid idea," Graeme said.

Sabrina gaped at him. "Are you mad? A pair of friendless children there? They'd be eaten alive."

"They're not friendless because they have us. And I can send them to Aden. He's dealt with children in these circumstances before. Remember Tommy?"

"Of course. He was the boy with you that morning in the park."

"He also came from a"—Graeme slanted a glance at Tilly—"difficult background. Aden and Vivien are very good at helping such children."

"Who's this Aden bloke?" Tilly asked, suspicious.

Graeme gave her a reassuring smile. "A good friend and a good man. He and his wife can give you shelter and help you get set up."

"Respectably," Sabrina firmly said.

"Of course." Graeme leaned over, so he and Tilly were on eye level. "You have more options than you think, lass. You and Charlie can have a good and proper life together. Aden and Vivien can help you figure out what that might look like and keep you safe, too."

Tilly scrunched her mouth sideways for a few moments before glancing down the lane. "All right, but we can't stand around here jawin' about it. No tellin' when Bill gets back on our trail."

Graeme straightened. "Splendid. We'll figure out the arrangements later. Meanwhile, do you have someplace to hole up?"

"We can stay with Emmy. We'll be safe there, for now."

"Be off with you then. I'll come to the Wee Black Dog in a few days and hammer out the details."

Leave them unprotected until then? "I cannot feel comfortable with them staying there, Mr. Kendrick. The children would be safer with us."

When Graeme shook his head, Sabrina wanted to whack him with her reticule.

Tilly also shook her head. "Nae, miss. We'll be better with Emmy. She'll see to us."

"But—"

"They'll need some money," Graeme said, cutting Sabrina off.

The children looked at her with wide, expectant eyes. Silently fuming, Sabrina extracted a few guineas from her change purse.

"Coo," said Charlie in a reverent voice.

"Have Emmy buy you some new clothing. You'll need it for London." Sabrina shot Graeme a scowl. "Of course, I could have—"

The coins disappeared inside Tilly's coat. "Thanks, miss, for everything."

She threw her arms around Sabrina's waist and gave her a brief, fierce hug before taking her brother's hand. They ran down the lane into a narrow close, disappearing from sight.

Sabrina rounded on Graeme. "That was decidedly unhelpful of you."

"Which part? When I saved you from Bill? Or when I got Charlie out of that bloody orphanage? Or when I'll be making arrangements for them to go to Aden and Vivien?"

Well, that was annoying. True, but annoying.

"And I did not appreciate your order to remain in the parlor," she said, switching tack. "I am not a child, Mr. Kendrick. I do not wish to be bossed like one."

He began leading her toward the main thoroughfare. "I was trying to protect you. That damned place was not something any gently bred young lady needed to see."

"I appreciate the sentiment. But I decide what I need to see, not you."

"Sabrina—"

She pulled her arm from his loose grasp. "My entire existence has been sheltered and comfortable, while children like Tilly and Charlie . . ." Her throat went tight.

Graeme took her hand and gently tucked it into the crook of his elbow. "I understand, lass. You feel helpless."

"Incredibly helpless," she said with a little growl.

"As do I, at times. But there is much you can do to help." He glanced down at her with a lopsided smile. "You've got quite a pile of blunt at your disposal. Use that to make a difference."

"And I will, starting with *that* dreadful place. The superintendent is clearly not a good man."

"Och, I'll be talking to Nick about the orphanage. He'll see to it."

"And Old Bill? Will you take care of that?"

"Old Bill's criminal reign will soon be coming to an end."

"Painfully, one hopes."

He laughed. "As painful as I can make it."

"Splendid."

"For a sheltered miss from Mayfair, you're rather bloodthirsty. It's quite thrilling," he teased.

"While I am naturally delighted that you find me so entertaining, don't think you can divert me, sir. We should not have let the children out of our sight. Until Old Bill *is* dealt with, they're in danger, even with Emmy."

"Tilly's as smart as they come. She wouldn't go to Emmy if she didn't feel secure there."

They stepped out into Cowgate, a wide street running through Old Town. Carriages and carts rumbled by in a continuous stream, while merchants, shoppers, and day laborers hurried about their business.

Graeme stuck up an arm to flag down an approaching hackney.

"But—" She had to bite back her question when the carriage pulled over.

"Heriot Row," Graeme said to the coachman.

When Sabrina started to climb into the hackney, her foot slipped. Glancing down at her half boots, she sighed. They were smeared with a gruesome-looking muck. "Oh, blast. These are brand new."

"Let that be a lesson to you. No more sneaking off to Old Town."

"And, as I said—" She gasped when Graeme wrapped his hands around her waist and lifted her straight up into the hackney and onto the seat.

"That was hardly necessary," she snapped when he climbed in beside her.

"Apparently it was. Anyway, I'll buy you a pair of new boots."

"I do *not* need you to buy me boots."

Graeme bent forward to inspect his own footwear. "Actually, I think you should buy *me* new boots. What in God's name was in that alley? It's disgusting."

"Stop trying to change the topic."

He had the nerve to give her an exceedingly warm smile that threatened to knock every sensible thought from her brain. "I thought we were finished with that topic, except for the part where you keep haring off on these deranged missions."

"There was nothing deranged about it. And the children should have returned to Heriot Row with us. Instead, *you* sent them haring off without any protection whatsoever."

"Lass, it's only for a few days. Besides, Tilly is better at surviving in the stews than you could ever imagine."

"I don't want to imagine it. And while Tilly may be very resourceful, Charlie is only a little boy."

Graeme began to look a wee bit irritated. "I truly don't mean to insult you, Sabrina, but you're like a little lamb wandering off into the woods compared to Tilly *or* Charlie. That boy survived an orphanage, remember."

She gave him the haughtiest look she could summon. "That comparison is exceedingly insulting. I am a grown woman, and I have proven more than once that I am quite resourceful in a pinch."

Graeme's demeanor transformed to decisively annoyed. "Some of that resourcefulness stems from the fact that you're rich, Sabrina. And that's grand, as far as it goes. But you can't just pay people to do what you want or manage them into compliance. Frankly, it's arrogant to think that you can. Tilly knows her own mind, and she knows what she wants. If she'd wanted to come to Heriot Row, I would have made that happen. But she didn't. I respect that decision, as should you."

For a generally taciturn man, he could certainly deliver an effective lecture. If Sabrina were a better person, she would admit that he'd landed more than a few home points.

Apparently, though, she was *not* a better person, at least when it came to Graeme Kendrick.

"You think I'm arrogant? Well, that's rich, coming from you. You're the most arrogant, interfering man I've ever met."

He twisted sideways, looming over her. Green thunderbolts all but shot from his gaze. Truly, his eyes were the most extraordinary she'd ever seen. They held a startling emerald clarity that yet hinted at untold, turbulent depths. For an alarming moment, she fought the temptation to yank his head down and kiss him to see if he tasted of those same turbulent but dangerously enticing depths.

"It's a damn good thing I'm interfering," he growled, "since you have a talent for getting yourself into insanely tight spots."

Like this one. They were wedged together on the seat, and it was impossible not to feel the length of his muscled thigh pressed up against her. The fact that Sabrina had no desire to escape this particular tight spot was a shocking but not unexpected revelation.

"May I remind you that I was also respecting Tilly's wishes? She made a point of asking me to come alone."

"And wasn't that a good decision?" he sarcastically replied.

She pointed a gloved finger at his nose. It was a very nice nose, long and aquiline and as arrogant as the rest of him. She was tempted to kiss it, too.

Idiot.

"I was in complete control of the situation this morning."

"And would you have been in control when Old Bill stormed in?"

"Of course not," she replied, trying to be fair. "But we would have been gone by then. Your arrival was the cause of our delay."

His retort was delayed by a sharp turn that threw her halfway across his lap. When Graeme muttered a curse, she felt her cheeks flame with heat—and not from his salty oath. No, it was the state of his lap that startled her. What she felt there was shockingly prominent. It seemed a bizarre reaction to an argument, although Sabrina had to confess to ignorance in such matters.

Letting out an aggrieved sigh, he set her away from him. In the confines of the carriage, it was barely an inch between them.

"Sorry," he said.

She thought it best to misunderstand him. "Apology accepted. As I said, without your interruption, Tilly and I would have been gone before Bill arrived."

"Did it never occur to you that Old Bill might have followed you? He'd have surely guessed Tilly's intentions. Then what?"

Sabrina opened her mouth to reply but realized that he was correct—again.

"I do wish we knew his last name," she said. "It's ridiculous to keep referring to the man as Old Bill."

"Lass, can you *never* ask for help?" Graeme said, exasperated.

She hesitated. "Not very easily, I admit. I've been running my father's household since I was fifteen. I'm used to making decisions on my own."

"You might try it now and again. Just for the novelty, if nothing else."

So much for her olive branch. "Really, Mr. Kendrick. I find you quite rude."

"And ye'll find somethin' else if ye keep tryin' my patience."

"What, pray tell, is that?" she snapped back.

He clamped one hand on the back of her neck and the other on her shoulder and pulled her in. They were so close that her eyes crossed as she tried to focus on his irate but excessively handsome features.

"This," he growled.

His mouth took her with a gentle ferocity that soon stunned her into limpid compliance. It was a sensual plundering, and one she had no desire to resist. His lips moved with searing demand, taking exactly what he wanted—which was exactly what she wanted to give. Sabrina melted into his embrace, opening to his kiss with an eagerness that was quite shocking on her part.

She'd been kissed a few times, stolen pecks behind a potted plant or after a waltz, from suitors more nervous than she. But those experiences barely registered, not when compared to the sensual storm that was Graeme Kendrick.

With a happy sigh, Sabrina snuggled against his brawny chest, letting the storm wash over her. His kisses were hungry, ravishing yet tender, so tender she felt a momentary prickle of tears. But then he deepened the kiss, sucking on her lower lip before giving it a nip that sent a shiver coursing through her body.

Hesitantly, Sabrina moved her lips over his, tasting him back. She was inexperienced, but he was wicked temptation itself, thrilling her to the marrow of her bones. Graeme was turning her life upside down, obliterating her comfortable, safe existence.

Thank God.

They were like chalk and cheese in so many ways, and yet somehow they seemed right.

Growing bold, she teased him with the tip of her tongue. He groaned, the sound a low rumble as he pulled her halfway onto his lap. She dug her fingers into his neckcloth, eagerly opening to his exploration, oblivious to everything but the feel of his mouth and the brawny body wrapped around hers.

He murmured his approval, the sound vibrating through her like a bass note of pleasure. Suddenly, his mouth gentled, and the kiss grew even more sensual—slow, wet, and luscious, a promise of things to come. One kiss flowed into another, a stream of caresses that clouded her mind and turned every muscle and nerve languid with desire.

When Graeme sucked her tongue into his mouth, Sabrina found herself clinging to him like a bird clings to a branch in a winter gale. But she wanted more, much more. Moving her hands to the back of his neck, she slid her fingers through his silky, soft locks—the only soft part on that massively hard body. When she snuggled closer, he groaned into her mouth. It was a delicious sound, one that made her squirm with a need to plaster her entire body to his.

Throwing caution to the proverbial winds, she wrapped her arms around his neck and pressed tight, chest-to-chest. Graeme suddenly froze, as if an arctic wind had swept through his veins and turned him to a block of ice. Every part of him went stone-still.

Then he unlocked their lips and slowly retreated, or at

least tried to. After all, she was attached to him like a limpet. He reached up and unhooked her arms and pulled them away. Without a word, he carefully placed her hands back on her lap. Then he turned forward, putting as much distance between them as he could. In such tight quarters, that meant they were still thigh-to-thigh, and she could feel the tension gripping his muscles.

Mystified, Sabrina stared at his grim profile. His jawline was taut as piano wire, and his high cheekbones were glazed the color of brick. He also seemed to be trying to catch his breath.

She understood, because she felt like he'd sucked all the air out of her lungs. Like her, he seemed stunned, but not in a good way.

Drat. Men were so dreadfully complicated.

"Goodness, that was rather surprising," she said, trying to rally.

Sabrina winced at her dementedly bright tone. But she couldn't get a read on the blasted man. Was he angry with her? True, they'd been arguing just before he had kissed her. But he *had* kissed her.

"Not that surprising, but certainly inappropriate," he gritted out, refusing to look at her. "My apologies."

Had he truly not noticed how eagerly she'd responded to him? "Thank you, but no apology is necessary."

When he shot her a startled look, Sabrina gave him a tentative smile. "I didn't mind."

"You should mind. I took advantage of you."

"I don't believe you did, in fact."

He muttered under his breath as he opened the door of the hackney.

"What are you doing?" she asked.

"We've arrived at Heriot Row, in case you failed to notice."

She had failed to notice because he'd been kissing her

with what she'd assumed was unbridled enthusiasm. His current behavior, however, showed no such enthusiasm.

"Mr. Kendrick, you're much too—"

He all but catapulted down to the pavement.

"Blast," she muttered.

Graeme helped her down. That's when she noticed his neckcloth had fallen victim to *her* enthusiasm. His shirt had been pulled rather askew, as well.

"Oh, dear," she weakly said.

He glanced down at her. "What's wrong? Besides the obvious," he added.

Rather unnecessarily, she thought.

She waved a vague finger at his chest. "You look rather, um . . ."

He glanced down and let out a sigh, then made an unsuccessful attempt at rearranging his clothing. Sabrina crinkled her nose, then paid off the coachman while Graeme silently fumed.

"Come along, you," he said as he hustled her up the steps to the house.

"Your manner is rather disobliging, sir. I did nothing wrong."

"I'm aware of that, my lady. The fault for this unfortunate incident is entirely mine."

She gave him an encouraging smile. "I wouldn't go that far."

Graeme extracted a key from an inside pocket. "I would."

Sabrina didn't bother to hold back an aggrieved sigh. Really, men could be *such* blockheads.

When he opened the door, he breathed out another curse.

"Now what's wrong?" she asked.

"Guess."

She didn't need to guess, because both Ainsley and

Angus were standing in the entrance hall, clearly waiting for them. And wasn't that just jolly splendid?

Ainsley rushed over to greet them. "Finally! We were expecting you ages ago. I was afraid something had happened."

Angus inspected his grandson's rather disheveled state. "Looks like something did happen," he dryly commented.

Sabrina forced a smile. "It's been *quite* the lively morning. Mr. Kendrick had to deal with some very bad characters."

"Who apparently didn't like his neckcloth," Ainsley said. "Or your hat, dearest."

When Sabrina reached up, she found her straw hat tipped halfway off her head. "How did that happen?" She hastily straightened it.

"I can hazard a guess," Angus said.

"Just don't, Grandda," Graeme snapped. "I'm going upstairs to change and try to forget this morning ever happened."

"We did save two children, you know," Sabrina called after him as he stalked off. "That's worth remembering."

She'd found their kiss memorable, too. Sadly, he did not seem to agree.

Graeme cast her an irate glance over his shoulder, then bounded up the stairs and disappeared.

"I'd best go see why the lad is so fashed," Angus said.

Ainsley threw a meaningful glance in Sabrina's direction. "As if we don't already know."

"Aye, but Kendrick men, ye ken. They canna get it right the first time."

Sabrina frowned. "Get what right the first time?"

The old fellow chuckled. "Ye'll find out soon enough, lass." Then he clattered up the stairs after his grandson.

Ainsley turned to her. "Now you can tell me exactly what pitched Graeme into such a lather."

Sabrina held up her hands. "I'm not really sure. One minute we were arguing, and the next minute we were . . ."

"Kissing?"

"It didn't last very long," she said in a rueful tone.

Ainsley scoffed. "Angus is right. Kendrick men are so thickheaded that it's a miracle they manage to get married, much less reproduce."

"You and Royal managed it."

"My husband is the only man in this family with any brains. After all, he fell in love with me, didn't he?"

"I do not believe that Graeme is in any danger of falling in love with me, however."

Ainsley took Sabrina's arm and steered her toward the stairs. "Come along, dearest. It's time you got your first lesson in how to manage a Kendrick male."

Chapter Fourteen

Ainsley gracefully dropped into a chair and began stripping off her gloves. "Gracious, but it's hot in here. I thought I was going to keel over while talking to the king."

Graeme gingerly settled into the spindly chair on the other side of the supper table. He'd spent the last hour prowling every inch of the Assembly Rooms. Since he'd found no trouble, he decided he'd earned some time with his family. The Kendricks had staked a claim to a large table at the edge of the ballroom and settled in for the evening.

He moved aside a vase stuffed with heather and greenery meant to evoke the Highlands and winked at Ainsley. "You and Georgie looked quite cozy. The old boy was flirting with you, obviously."

Royal glowered at him. "My wife doesn't get cozy with any man but me, and that includes the king."

"Sadly, I must admit that Graeme is correct," Ainsley said. "The king is a terrible flirt, even at his age. He simply can't help himself."

"Any man—even one so decrepit as our esteemed monarch—is inclined to flirt with you, sweetheart," Royal gallantly said. "I only hope you didn't flirt back."

"I am a loyal subject of the Crown," Ainsley responded. "I must do my duty, as should we all."

"I'm not bloody flirting with him," Royal said. "I almost lost a leg at Waterloo. I've done my bit."

"This is a ridiculous conversation," Nick said. "And please do not tell me the king was engaged in flirtations while Victoria was sitting right next to him."

Ainsley laughed. "I'm teasing. George has been on his best behavior."

"Instead of acting like a *Sassenach* twiddlepoop, as Angus would say," Graeme said. "Speaking of which, where is the old boy? We need to keep an eye on him, so he doesn't do anything especially stupid."

"Like challenge the king to a duel to redress our defeat at Culloden?" Royal wryly asked.

Graeme snorted. "I just don't want Angus embarrassing Vicky."

"Angus went with Grant for some fresh air," Nick said. "Can't say that I blame him, given the heat and the crowds."

Ainsley flapped her fan so vigorously that her dainty curls blew straight back off her forehead. "I wish they'd waited for me."

"Do you want to leave?" Royal asked with concern. "We can try to find a hackney."

"Good luck," Graeme said. "It's a mob scene out there. Half of Edinburgh is milling about on the street, waiting to see the king."

"And it's not good form to leave before His Majesty, don't forget," Nick added.

Graeme would be happy to insult old Georgie, if it meant he could go home and get much needed sleep. This assignment was turning out to be worse than his last one, since he'd yet to get his hands on even one piece of decent information regarding potential plots. Even worse, Sir Walter Scott and the king's advisors were determined that George spend as much time as possible out in public. Every time he stepped foot outside, the king was at risk. But from whom or what, Graeme hadn't a clue.

It was as frustrating as hell.

"Honestly, I can't wait for it all to be over," Ainsley said. "Friday was the absolute worst."

In addition to the other events, there'd been a massive military review at Portobello Sands. The locals had poured in from miles around, with crowds estimated at thirty thousand. The king had arrived by carriage, but had then mounted a gray charger and ridden slowly down the regimental line, creating an excellent target for a potential assassin.

Graeme had shadowed the king as best he could. Grant and Royal had also patrolled the crowd, alert for trouble. Under the circumstances, protecting the monarch was an all but impossible job. If someone had wanted to kill George he'd have had a cracking good chance to do so.

Fortunately, the review had gone splendidly, and the crowds had been delighted. Later that evening, the Peers' Ball had taken place at the Assembly Rooms. The crowds had turned out for that event, too, with thousands blocking the streets to watch carriages disgorging ladies in their finest gowns, and men dressed in tartans, bonnets, and shields, and all sorts of Highland nonsense meant to honor the king.

Despite the sheer pandemonium, that event had been wildly successful as well.

Aye, Graeme had been run off his feet, but at least he'd had a solid excuse to avoid Sabrina. After that disastrous episode in the carriage—and the most enchanting kiss of his life—he'd stayed far away from her. Tonight had proven trickier, since the Caledonian Hunt Ball was a long-standing family tradition. Nick had ordered Graeme to attend, and as a family member, not as a bloody spy lurking behind potted plants, as his brother had trenchantly put it.

Fortunately, Sabrina had been much engaged by the royal

entourage. She'd spent most of the evening in George's company, as had Vicky.

"Mob scene or not, if my wife wishes to leave, we're going," Royal said to Nick. "And old Georgie can bloody well go shoot himself if he doesn't like it."

Graeme flashed the startled guard behind their table a placating smile before turning back to his family. "Can the members of this blasted family go one day without making seditious remarks? It'll be a miracle if we don't end up in prison."

"Angus will take the fall for us," Royal said. "You know he loves to play the martyr."

Ainsley waved down a passing waiter and ordered a tray of champagne. "Sadly, we're stuck for the duration. His Majesty wishes to speak with me again before he leaves."

"Oh, splendid," Royal said. "More flirting with my wife."

Nick gave Ainsley a stern look. "No flirting in front of Victoria. She's in a delicate state."

"Maybe Sabrina could flirt with him for a while," Royal commented. "Give my poor wife a break."

Graeme scowled. "Don't be disgusting. She's his god-daughter."

Royal smirked. "And is that the only reason it bothers you, laddie?"

"Oh, sod off."

Nick jabbed him in the shoulder. "Watch your language. I'm sure Lady Sabrina has no desire to flirt with the king, regardless."

Ainsley put a finger to her chin. "I do believe she wishes to flirt with someone, though. I'm not sure who."

Graeme repressed the impulse to tear his hair out.

Fortunately, the waiter arrived with their drinks, diverting the inane discussion.

"Vicky seems to be having a grand time with her father," Royal said to Nick.

Both Vicky and Sabrina were seated with the king across the room, watching the dancers. Sabrina was chatting away with her usual, cheerful enthusiasm, while Vicky and the king seemed to be mostly listening and laughing. The lass seemed to have that effect on most people. She made them . . . happy.

"The king's been very attentive to Victoria," Nick replied. "Neither of us expected the invitation to have the ladies for a private tea at the palace."

"That invitation almost gave Vicky a nervous fit," Ainsley said. "Fortunately, Sabrina managed the whole episode remarkably well. She got Vicky and the king talking about life at Castle Kinglas, and things went swimmingly from there."

"Lady Sabrina manages everything well," Nick said. "She'll make a splendid wife for a very lucky man."

Ainsley winked at Graeme. "If that man would actually put in an appearance now and again."

"*That* man has been run off his feet keeping Vicky's father safe, in case you failed to notice," Graeme tartly replied.

"Poor Sabrina," Ainsley said with a dramatic sigh. "She's barely seen you since that *very* interesting carriage ride the other morning."

Nick perked up. "What carriage ride?"

Graeme scowled at Royal. "Can't you keep your wife under control? She's being immensely irritating."

"I won't even try." Still, Royal took pity on him by switching topics. "I'm glad for Vicky's sake that the king's visit is going well. But I'll also be glad when this madness concludes. I feel like we're trapped in an unending Highland pageant."

"And the bloody music," Graeme said. "If I have to listen to one more reel I'm going to shoot myself."

Ainsley laughed. "You do all look splendid tonight,

though. Except for Angus. Vicky and I did our best with him, but to no avail."

Nick and Royal were wearing the dress kit of the Black Watch, their former regiment, and Graeme and Grant had donned Kendrick plaid. Their grandfather, unfortunately, had again chosen to wear the traditional belted plaid, and he'd also dug up a moth-eaten matching bonnet not seen in decades. Since almost every other man at the ball had on the short kilt, along with appropriate evening kit, the old fellow stood out like a bull at a garden party.

"At least he's not lugging around the ceremonial broadsword," Royal said. "He might have used it on some poor soul who offended him."

"Like the king?" Ainsley said with a grin.

"God, don't even joke about it," Graeme absently replied.

He'd just caught sight of his twin at the bottom of the room, making his way toward their table. Alarmingly, Grant was alone.

"Where's Grandda?" Graeme asked when his brother arrived. "I thought he was with you."

Grant took the empty seat next to him. "Well . . . he rather got away from me."

Nick frowned. "What does that mean?"

Grant jerked his head toward the opposite side of the ballroom, where King George was sitting. Vicky and Sabrina were still with him, as was . . .

Angus.

The old fellow was planted directly in front of the king, talking a mile a minute and waving his arms. As one, the family members stared at the scene of impending mayhem, bereft of speech.

Ainsley recovered first. "I feel a swoon coming on for the first time in my life." Clapping her fan shut, she leaned over and jabbed Grant's hand. "How could you let this happen, you nincompoop?"

"That actually hurt." Grant rubbed his hand. "Look, have you ever tried controlling my grandfather? He was right behind me, but when I turned around the slippery old codger was gone."

"Are we absolutely sure he's not got a ceremonial dirk or knife?" Royal asked.

"Darling, this is no jesting matter," Ainsley said.

"Who said it was a jest?"

Sighing, Nick rose. "I'd best go see if I can smooth over whatever madness he's no doubt spouting at the king."

Graeme stood, too. "I'll go with you. If nothing else, I can bodily cart him off."

He was only half joking. Thanks to Angus, the family could be facing social annihilation.

Ainsley scowled up at Graeme. "This is all your fault. You should have known Angus would do something like this."

"We can apportion blame later," Nick said. "For now—"

Graeme peered across the room. "Hang on. I'm not sure there's actually a problem. In fact, they just seem to be chatting. Quite amicably, it appears."

Royal also stood and stared across the room. "Good God, you may be right."

As they watched, dumbfounded, the king roared with laughter and clapped Angus on the arm. Their grandfather chuckled and then pointed at the dancers twirling before them. He seemed to be explaining something while George attentively listened.

"This cannot be right," Nick said.

"I still think we need to go over there. Just in case it goes sideways," Graeme said.

"We'll stay here and hold down the fort," Grant said.

"And hide under the table if Angus erupts," Ainsley added.

Graeme and Nick were barely halfway across the room

when Sabrina rose from her seat next to the king and offered it to Angus. The old fellow immediately accepted and recommenced a lively conversation with George.

Sabrina exchanged a few words with Vicky, who was looking utterly bemused, then glanced up and met Graeme's eye. Flashing a wry smile, she held up a finger, clearly telling them to wait.

It took but a few moments for her to slip through the crowds to join them at the edge of the dance floor.

"Not to worry," Sabrina said with an impish smile. "No Angus eruptions on the horizon."

For a moment, Graeme gave in to the selfish impulse to drink her in. She reminded him of sunshine in her cream-colored, spangled gown, with her guinea-gold hair tumbling gracefully down her neck. He had to resist the urge to tug on one of her glimmering curls. In fact, he wanted to tug her into a dark corner, where he could explore every inch of her sweet body.

Aye, she'd bewitched him, all right. Graeme could only be grateful there were no dark corners nearby, and that his big brother was there to play chaperone.

Nick eyed the tableau on the other side of the room. "Angus must be in his cups. It's the only explanation."

"And not a very reassuring one," Graeme said.

"He seemed quite sober to me," Sabrina replied. "He and His Majesty are simply having a nice chat."

"What could they possibly chat about that didn't involve Angus's going off about some old Highland grievance?" Graeme asked.

"Right now, they're talking about the dancers. Your grandfather is explaining the steps and the meanings behind the older dances."

Nick grimaced. "Och, that's no good."

Graeme knew what he meant. Some of the old songs

contained elements of protest against English oppression of the Highlands.

"I'd best get over there," Nick said.

"There truly is no need to worry, sir," Sabrina replied. "They're getting along like blazes."

"As in this room could be burning down at any moment," Graeme sardonically replied.

She huffed out a chuckle. "Indeed, no. But Victoria does wish for you to join her, Lord Arnprior, though I assured her everything would be fine. His Majesty has taken quite the shine to your grandfather."

The two old fellows now had their heads together, as if exchanging confidences. Vicky had a hand clapped over her mouth, trying not to laugh.

"That is the most stunning thing I've ever seen," Graeme said.

"I might never recover from the shock," Nick added before he went to join his wife.

Leaving Graeme alone with Sabrina was awkward, considering what had happened the last time they'd spoken.

Or kissed, more accurately.

"Ah, would you like to join the others at the table?" Graeme asked.

"There's no one at your table," she gently pointed out.

Damn. He spotted Grant at the refreshments table, but Ainsley and Royal had disappeared. They had probably taken the opportunity to sneak out to avoid potential mayhem.

Graeme eyed the petite beauty standing patiently before him. It would be impolite, not to mention scandalous, to abandon her on the edge of the dance floor. Nor did he wish to settle in for an intimate chat at their empty table.

She raised a golden eyebrow. "Would you care to dance, sir?"

Surprised, he frowned. "Do you actually know any Scottish reels?"

That was all the blasted orchestra was playing tonight, along with other traditional Scottish tunes. It felt like a damn gathering of the clans.

"Well, no," Sabrina replied.

Graeme had to grin. "Then why did you ask me to dance, you daft lass?"

"Because you seem rather at a loss as to what to do."

That was certainly true. "Actually, I should be getting back to . . ."

"To what? Lurking about, doing your mysterious spy work?"

"I haven't a clue what you're talking about."

Her smile was adorably smug. "Since you are currently free, perhaps you could take me for a stroll in the hall. I could use a breath of fresh air."

He glanced around the spacious room, assessing the situation. The king was under ample protection, as safe here as when he was locked away in his bedroom, guards stationed every ten feet. The Assembly Rooms were secure.

"I'll tell you what the king said to your grandfather," Sabrina added in a coaxing voice.

She was temptation incarnate. Graeme told himself it *would* be good to know what Angus was up to, just in case.

"It would be wise to know, I suppose."

Her smile curled into a full-on grin. Aye, she was a bright, sunny day, a dram of fine whisky, and a lingering kiss all rolled into a delicious package that was well nigh impossible to resist.

She tucked a hand in his arm as they headed to the main corridor. "There are some window alcoves. Perhaps we could open one of the windows and get a breeze."

The alcoves were at the mostly deserted end of the hall and

lit only by the occasional wall sconce or branch of candles.
Curiously, Graeme found himself raising no objections.

Idiot.

He allowed her to lead him to the last window. Sabrina was
a masterful little thing, which he found quite stimulating. His
cock was also finding the situation quite stimulating, which
was a trifle embarrassing, especially while wearing a kilt.

"It's blessedly quiet here," she said. "All that piping does
get a bit much."

"Spoken like a true *Sassenach*."

She chuckled as she fumbled with the window latch.

"Allow me," he said.

Instead of backing out of the way, Sabrina settled onto
the window seat, primly folding her hands as he stretched
beside her to grasp the latch. The lass certainly didn't mind
being close to him. Of course, he'd reached that conclusion the other day, when she'd so enthusiastically returned
his kiss.

He swung the window open. When a cool breeze fluttered in, Sabrina closed her eyes and lifted her face, letting
the air wash over her.

"That's better," she murmured.

It was indeed better, since it would take but a heartbeat
to lean down and capture her pretty mouth in a ravishing
kiss. It was madness to be this close, breathing in the delicate scent that drifted up from her smooth, pearly skin. He
wanted to press his lips to the base of her throat and nibble
his way along her bare shoulder to the poof of her little
sleeve. Then he would push down that silly poof, and . . .

When her eyes opened, Graeme jerked back, banging his
shoulder against the window frame.

"Goodness, Mr. Kendrick. Don't hurt yourself."

He mentally sighed. The lass was melting his brain and
turning him into a clumsy oaf.

"I'm fine. Perhaps we'd best stroll toward the ballroom. It's a wee bit secluded down here."

"Nonsense. Another couple just walked by us a few moments ago."

He leaned out to look. Sure enough, a man and a woman had just strolled past on their way back to the ballroom.

"And you call yourself a spy," she teased.

"Apparently a bad one." He propped his shoulder against the window frame. "All right, so tell me what George and my grandfather were talking about. Angus is not a fan of *Sassenachs* in general and royal ones in particular. Especially not that royal one."

"I've been working on your grandfather. I told him how excited the king was to be here, and how much he wished to make up for the mistakes of the past."

Graeme raised his eyebrows. "And Angus bought that?"

"It *is* true that the king is very enthusiastic about Scotland. I may have exaggerated a bit on the other point."

He laughed.

"I also told him how much His Majesty has been looking forward to meeting Victoria." Sabrina wrinkled her nose. "Angus was blustery about that at first, since the king has ignored her all these years. Fortunately, that is no longer the case."

"Thanks to you, from what I hear."

"I simply smoothed the way. The king and Victoria did the rest."

"You did more than that, lass. You not only helped bring Vicky and her father together, you apparently managed to convince Angus that old George isn't his mortal enemy. That elevates you to sainthood in our family."

"I do have a talent for managing fussy old men," she said with another adorably smug smile.

Graeme was truly beginning to love that smile.

"You have a talent for managing more than just old men." He deliberately let his voice go deep and rough.

She blushed, and he had to resist the impulse to trace the path of her rising color with his fingertip.

"Do . . . do you want to know what else your grandfather and the king talked about?"

He blinked when he realized he'd started to lean over, as if to kiss her. "Oh, ah, absolutely."

Sabrina carefully patted her curls, obviously composing herself. "It was a bit awkward when Angus first appeared, since he was looking grumpy. But Victoria immediately introduced him and informed the king that Angus knew more about Highland traditions and culture than anyone she'd ever met."

"Smart lass. That's my grandfather's weak spot."

"He seemed a bit flummoxed, to tell you the truth."

"Probably because he wanted to pick an argument with Old Georgie. But Vicky spiked his guns."

"If so, it worked."

Graeme shook his head. "But I can't see Grandda giving over that easily. It's still a bit of a mystery."

"I believe the real breakthrough occurred when the king informed Angus that he was the first real Highlander he'd met since coming to Scotland. In fact, according to His Majesty, your grandfather is the very definition of a true Highland warrior."

Graeme practically choked. "In that deranged outfit? He looks completely mad."

"Not according to the king. He said that your grandfather's belted plaid was heroic in the extreme. He only regretted that Angus was unable to complete the outfit with a dirk and a broadsword."

"Och, he did not say that."

"He did, indeed. In fact, I would now say that your grandfather is the king's new favorite."

Graeme stared at her as his brain tried to process the absurdity of that sentence.

A moment later, he burst into laughter, grabbing on to the window frame to keep from doubling over. Her assertion was the most hilarious thing he'd ever heard in his life.

"Mr. Kendrick," Sabrina said, "perhaps you shouldn't laugh *quite* so loudly. We don't want to attract undue attention."

"Of . . . of course," he choked out, trying to get himself under control. But he couldn't seem to manage it. Every time he thought of Angus larking about with the king . . .

Sabrina frowned. "Mr. Kendrick, really. You must contain yourself."

He found her stern look hilarious, too.

"You started it with this ridiculous story," he gasped.

She rose to her feet, alarmed. "Mr. Kendrick. You need to stop laughing, or you will force me to take action." For good measure, she wagged an admonishing finger at him.

"Do your best," he choked out as he tried to get himself under control.

"Very well, you leave me no choice."

She clamped her hands around his head, yanked him down, and planted her lips to his. Graeme sucked in a breath, both in laughter and surprise, and the kiss turned inadvertently and immediately intimate.

And hot, so hot it practically knocked him off his feet, taking her with him. To keep from falling out the window, he pulled her tightly against his chest. Her hands slid to his neck as she stretched up to deepen the kiss.

Aye, and what a kiss it was. Sabrina had learned a thing or three about kissing during that illicit interlude in the hackney. Innocent yet bold, she explored his mouth, sending a bolt of pure lust straight to his groin.

Unable to resist, Graeme planted a hand on the base of her spine, bringing her lovely curves to his lower body. He nudged against her, his erection pressing into the slight, soft round of her belly. She trembled, gasping against his lips, momentarily freezing in his embrace.

Ye randy bastard, let her go.

Reluctantly, he was about to do so when her gasp turned into a luscious whimper. Sabrina nestled even closer as she nuzzled his mouth with sweetly sensual kisses. What little brain remained in his head proceeded straight south, focusing on the one thing that mattered—him inside Sabrina, with her body wrapped around his.

Skin to skin, and as soon as possible.

It was madness, and he knew it. He didn't give a damn. The only thing in the world was Sabrina, kissing him with a joyous abandon that was all her, setting him on fire. If there'd been a curtain hanging in the bloody alcove he'd have pulled it shut, stripped her naked, and spread her wide, burying his face between her silky thighs.

That lascivious image dragged a groan from deep in his chest. He pulled Sabrina higher and gently rubbed against her, his cock pressing into her sweet, intimate notch. At the same time, he surged into her mouth. She trembled and dug a hand into his collar, eagerly tasting him back. Graeme ravished her mouth with hot, deep glides of his tongue. She took every bit of him, and gave it back in good measure.

And still it wasn't enough.

Instinctively, his hand slid to her luscious backside, his fingers curling into the fabric of her dress. The material was a whisper of silk, and hardly any barrier at all to the feel of her supple body. He craved more. He craved every damn inch of her, tonight, tomorrow, and for as long as he could bloody well keep her.

He deepened their kiss. Sabrina all but climbed up his torso, clinging to him until there wasn't a spot of daylight between them. He reveled in the swell of her breasts and the feel of her soft, delicious curves. Graeme cupped her, nudging a thigh between—

An eruption of giggles from the corridor locked them into a frozen embrace, mouth to mouth. Sabrina's eyes popped wide with alarm.

"Hell's bells," complained a masculine voice. "I don't know where you lost your confounded bracelet, Eugenia. We've been all over the rooms. I suppose we should check these blasted window alcoves, too."

Sabrina squeaked into Graeme's mouth and started to pull away.

"Hush, love," Graeme murmured, his lips brushing her cheek. "Don't move."

She shivered, as if suddenly cold, but stayed where she was, securely held in his embrace.

Where she belonged.

He ignored that wild thought to focus on the couple now less than ten feet away. As usual, he and Sabrina were skirting on the brink of disaster.

"You silly man, I haven't lost my bracelet," a young woman chortled. "I simply wanted to get you off on my own. Perhaps we can take a little stroll about the corridor?"

The man brayed with laughter. "I say, that's crafty of you. But the king's about to leave, and we don't want to miss that."

Sabrina's mouth puckered into a grimace.

"Drat," said the young woman. "We can't possibly miss that. My mother would be dreadfully annoyed."

"Lord, I don't need that. Bit of a dragon, your dear mamma."

The woman laughed, her reply muffled as she and her escort retreated.

With a sigh, Sabrina disengaged from Graeme's embrace. Regretfully, he let her go.

"We should go back, too," she said. "His Majesty will be wondering where I am."

Now that her lush mouth was no longer fused to his, Graeme's brain was beginning to function again. "I suspect he won't be the only one, unfortunately."

Sabrina deftly rearranged the ribbon under her bodice—which, naturally, brought his gaze down to her breasts. Then she shook out her skirts.

"Nonsense," she said. "We've only been gone a few minutes. No one noticed, I'm sure."

She'd just kissed him until his eyeballs practically rolled back into his head. With the exception of her pink cheeks, however, she seemed remarkably unaffected.

"I certainly noticed," he acidly replied.

She shot him a sharp glance and then went back to checking her skirts. "Oh, bother. This fabric wrinkles at the slightest touch. I do hope no one notices."

"Is that all you're going to say?" Graeme demanded.

She tilted her head. "What do you want me to say?"

"Lass, we were just kissing like maniacs in a secluded alcove. A very secluded alcove."

Her smooth brow crinkled. "Do you want me to apologize?"

"No," he growled.

"Do *you* want to apologize?"

"I should, except you were the one who kissed me first."

"I certainly didn't notice you objecting."

"Uh . . . did you want me to?" he asked.

She ignored his response. He didn't blame her, since he sounded like a moron.

Carefully, Sabrina patted her shiny curls. "How does my hair look?"

Graeme had the sense he was staring at her like a dumb ox. She truly didn't seem the least bit disconcerted by their passionate kiss.

"Er, fine?"

She rolled her eyes. "You're hopeless, Graeme Kendrick."

"You wouldn't be the first *Sassenach* to make that observation."

"I am shocked to hear that."

With a sigh, he took her hand and led her back to the ballroom.

Chapter Fifteen

The dratted man was avoiding her again.

Sabrina had thought they'd made excellent progress at the Caledonian Hunt Ball, when Graeme had literally swept her off her feet into the most thrilling moment of her life. His passionate kiss in that secluded alcove had muddled her insides and resolved all doubts.

She was in love and wanted to spend the rest of her life with Graeme Kendrick.

At the time, she'd thought it best to make light of that kiss instead of overwhelming him with an impetuous declaration of her feelings. Nor had she wished to raise a fuss about improper behavior—hers, for the most part. For a man who engaged in so reckless a profession as spying, Graeme had turned out to be a high stickler about kisses and such.

In retrospect, she'd underplayed her hand. That he'd turned skittish again was now frustratingly clear. For the last few days, Graeme had managed to be where she was not, with annoying consistency.

"Are you not enjoying the play, Lady Sabrina?" murmured Grant Kendrick.

She'd been so lost in thought about the man who was driving her demented that she'd forgotten about the one sitting next to her in the Theatre Royal box. Ainsley and Royal were seated in front of them, watching the performance, while Angus was . . . Well, she didn't know where the old fellow had gone off. Sabrina was so distracted by her mental meanderings that she'd not seen him leave.

She dredged up a smile for Grant, who was so like his twin and yet not. "It's an outstanding performance. Sir Walter has outdone himself."

The command performance of *Rob Roy* was one of the final engagements of the king's visit. His Majesty was seated in the royal box with members of his entourage, including Lord and Lady Arnprior. Graeme was somewhere in the theater, too. Sabrina had caught a glimpse of him coming in, but he'd yet to join the rest of the Kendrick family in their box.

That was discouraging, since the clock was ticking down. Soon, she would be leaving Edinburgh with the king.

"I particularly liked that last scene," Grant added. "What did you think of it?"

Sabrina realized she couldn't remember a single thing about any scene in the blasted play. "I'm forced to admit I haven't been paying attention. How dreadful of me."

Grant's smile was wry but kind. Physically, he and his brother were all but mirror images, and there was obviously a profound connection between them. They seemed to need no words to understand each other, sometimes exchanging looks that obviously contained entire conversations.

But there were great differences, too. Grant was a gentle giant, quiet and kind. A peaceful sort of person, he seemed most content in the company of his family. Graeme, in contrast, had a restless energy often barely contained. Underneath that gentleman's exterior lurked a Highlander warrior, fierce and dominating and even a wee bit uncivilized.

If Sabrina had a brain in her head, she'd prefer the peaceful gentleman to the hard-bitten warrior. Sadly, it would appear she did not have much of a brain when it came to Graeme Kendrick.

"You are the opposite of dreadful," Grant replied. "It's my stupid brother who's dreadful for neglecting you."

"There's absolutely no reason for Mr. Ken . . ." She trailed off when Grant raised a sardonic eyebrow.

How mortifying. She'd done a splendid job of hiding her feelings from Graeme, but not from the rest of his family.

"I'm his twin," Grant explained. "I practically live in his head."

"That must be interesting."

He grinned. "It can be rather confusing at times. But I know exactly where he wishes to be at this very moment. And it's where he *should* be, if he weren't so pigheaded."

"No, it's me," Sabrina said with a sigh. "I annoy him."

Graeme seemed to bring out the worst in her—or the best. Honestly, she couldn't decide which.

"You do annoy him, but not for the reasons you think."

She gave Grant a quizzical smile.

"He's afraid of you," Grant explained.

Sabrina choked on a startled laugh. "That cannot be. I'm neither intimidating nor very special."

"You are very special, indeed, Lady Sabrina, and Graeme is painfully aware of that fact."

She tried to ignore the pleased fluttering behind her breastbone, as well as the conviction that this was a highly inappropriate conversation. Grant was Graeme's brother— his twin, which made it even worse.

Yet that also meant talking to Grant was the closest thing to talking to his brother. And since Graeme wouldn't talk to her . . .

"Mr. Kendrick's actions don't seem to reflect such an opinion," she cautiously replied.

"He doesn't think he deserves you."

She blinked. "What an odd notion for him to take up. His brother is an earl, and the Kendricks are a distinguished family."

Grant raised an eyebrow. "Is it odd?"

Sabrina couldn't help scowling. "Your brother is a brave, kind, and incredibly decent man. Any woman with a grain of sense should realize that."

He nodded. "While I happen to think my brother deserves the world, he doesn't see it that way."

"Why not?"

"It has much to do with our family's past." Grant frowned. "And more recent events, I suspect, although I'm not entirely sure."

"I suppose you couldn't give me a hint?"

"It's Graeme's story to tell, I'm afraid." Grant flashed her a wry grin. "I think with a wee bit of effort, you might be able to winkle it out of him."

"If only he would stay in one place so I could try," she joked.

"Och, he's a hardhead, but don't give up. Graeme may think he wants you to run up the flag and surrender, but he actually doesn't."

"That's a bit confusing."

"Welcome to life in Clan Kendrick." Grant's green gaze turned serious. "I think you're the best thing that's ever happened to Graeme, my lady. It won't take much for him to realize that. He just needs a little push."

"A very large shove, rather," she said with a sigh. "At least one can't accuse him of fortune hunting."

"No, Graeme doesn't care about money."

"Unfortunately. Otherwise perhaps I could bribe him into marrying me."

When she clapped a hand over her mouth, appalled by her tactless remark, Grant laughed.

Ainsley twisted around to smile at her brother-in-law. "Well, have you convinced her yet?"

Grant waggled a hand.

Sabrina grimaced. "Goodness, this is embarrassing."

"Embarrassing people is a Kendrick specialty," Ainsley said.

"So I have noticed."

"And I've noticed how difficult it is to watch this bloody play with you lot chattering like magpies," Royal said.

"This play is entirely silly," Ainsley replied. "Besides, you've been eavesdropping, too."

"I leave that particular activity to you, my love."

"Only because you know I'll share everything with you later." Ainsley winked at Sabrina. "No secrets in this family, as you'll soon find out."

Sabrina shrugged. "I don't suppose I'll have a chance to find out, since I'll be returning to London with the king."

"Vicky and I both feel you should remain with us for the summer. That will give us plenty of time to mount a campaign. Graeme won't stand a chance against our combined forces."

Did Sabrina say embarrassing? Utterly mortifying, more like it.

She mustered the remaining shreds of her dignity. "You're all so kind, but I cannot throw myself at a man who is not interested in me."

"Disinterest is not the issue," Ainsley said. "I can assure you of that."

Assurances or not, Sabrina had her pride, and she refused to chase after a man who couldn't make up his mind about her. "It doesn't—"

She broke off when Angus slipped in through the door. "We've got trouble," he said.

Royal leaned forward, peering in the direction of the royal box. "Is it the king?"

"Is Vicky all right?" Ainsley asked quickly.

"They're all fine," Angus said. "It's Graeme."

Grant jumped up. "What's wrong?"

Angus handed Sabrina a note. "This came for the lass."

The messy blob of sealing wax on the back of the crinkled parchment was already broken.

She flashed Angus an exasperated glance. "You read it?"

He shrugged, clearly unrepentant.

Irritation was replaced by horror as she scanned the cramped handwriting.

"Aye, the lad's been kidnapped," said Angus.

"My God," Ainsley gasped.

"By Old Bill." Sabrina's heart was racing so quickly it was hard to talk. "And he's demanding a ransom." She handed the note to Royal.

"How did you get this?" Royal asked Angus.

"I'd lost sight of Graeme. I was worried, so I went outside to the carriages to look for him. That's when this scaly fella showed up. Said not to make a fuss or Graeme would get plumped. Said to bring the note to the lass."

Sabrina tried to think past the cold terror that had settled in her brain. She didn't need to understand much cant to know what *plump* meant. If she didn't pay the ransom, Graeme would be murdered.

"I'm going to get Nick," Royal said. "Then we'll—"

"No," Sabrina snapped. "It clearly states that *I'm* to bring the money to the Wee Black Dog, and I'm to come alone. I'm to do so within the next hour, or the consequences will be . . ." Her throat closed.

Ainsley rested a hand on her shoulder. "Kendricks are exceedingly hard to kill, pet. We'll figure it out."

"The Wee Black Dog's not far from here," Grant said in a low voice. Fortunately, the noise from the stage was loud enough to cover their fraught conversation. "If we get Nick, and the footmen from the carriage—"

Sabrina chopped down a hand to stop him. "The note is *very* clear. No raising the alarm. I will *not* endanger your brother's life."

Grant shoved a frustrated hand through his hair, making it stand straight up. He looked so much like his twin that Sabrina wanted to burst into tears. This was her fault. Graeme had been right about Old Bill all—

You can blame yourself later.

"You all need to trust me," she firmly said.

"We do," Ainsley said. "But Graeme will kill us if we just let you waltz into danger."

"The decision isn't up to him."

Royal let out a low curse. "If you want to pay the ransom, let me go instead."

"Dinna think that'll work," Angus said. "Old Bill's fashed that Sabrina took away his best rum diver, so he wants to lord it over the lassie for getting a jump on him. No tellin' what he'll do to Graeme if we don't do as the bastard says."

"Splendid," growled Royal. "Nothing like a spot of revenge to keep everything orderly."

At least Tilly and Charlie were safely out of Bill's reach. They had departed for London yesterday. But if anything happened to Graeme, Sabrina would absolutely die.

She stood and began to gather her things. "We need to leave immediately."

"Hang on," Grant said. "We need a plan."

"Not to mention fifty pounds," Royal said. "I doubt any of us are carrying such a sum on our persons."

"I am," replied Sabrina. "I have it in my reticule."

Ainsley blinked. "You do?"

"It's rather a habit of mine."

Sabrina always carried quite large sums of money, even though some might deem it foolhardy. It gave her a sense of security, and of freedom. Because she was not at home, and with life in Edinburgh a wee bit strange, she'd taken to carrying extra, just in case.

Thank God.

"Good for ye, lass," Angus said. "Like a true Scotswoman, always prepared."

"Then shall we go?" she prompted.

"We still don't have a plan," Grant protested. "We have no idea who this Bill idiot has with him, and don't know the layout of the place."

"I was there last week, so I can provide the necessary information," Sabrina impatiently said. "Now, can we *please* be on our way before your brother is murdered? That is not what I had in mind for him."

"All right, we'll come up with something on the way." Royal glanced at his wife. "You'll hold down the fort and explain things to Nick at the interval?"

Ainsley gave a nod. "Sabrina, give me your jewelry. There's no need to offer additional temptations."

Sabrina unpinned her ruby brooch and stripped off her bracelets. She kept her garnet earbobs on. They weren't terribly expensive, and might come in handy if further negotiations were necessary.

"Royal Kendrick, you be careful," Ainsley said, pulling him down for a swift kiss.

"Always."

"And keep Sabrina safe, or I'll murder the lot of you," she added.

Angus opened the door. "Come along, lass. We'll follow yer lead."

Sabrina threw her opera cloak around her shoulders. "Leading is what I do best."

In the almost thirty minutes it had taken to secure the Kendrick town coach and then make their way to the coffeehouse,

Sabrina had been dying inside. At least the extra time had given her a chance to fully explain the situation and the layout of the Wee Black Dog, and had allowed them to come up with a plan.

Angus, naturally, had wanted to charge in, pistols blazing, which had almost given Grant a fit. Royal, on the other hand, was cool-headed and decisive and had quickly devised a strategy. She saw much of Graeme reflected in the Kendrick family—he'd inherited the courageous but reckless tendencies of his grandfather, along with the strength and intelligence of his brothers. As a group, the Kendricks seemed well nigh unstoppable.

The men had made it clear that they were exceedingly unhappy with her participation in their hastily contrived scheme. Sabrina, however, refused to budge. Old Bill held her responsible for Tilly's departure and was seeking to humiliate her. If an embarrassing and even risky scene could save Graeme's life, she would happily suffer it.

Sabrina would suffer far more than that for Graeme Kendrick.

When the carriage pulled up, Royal glanced out the window. "Grant and I will make our way around to the back of the building and hope we find another way in."

Sabrina grimaced. "I'm sorry. I wish I'd been more observant in that respect."

Angus patted her knee. "The lads will find a way in."

Grant handed her down from the carriage. Even in daylight, this particular laneway had been dark and uninviting. Now the gloom was positively Stygian, with only fitful candlelight flickering in the occasional tenement window. Past the light thrown by the carriage lamps, the night was inky-black.

The groom came around and handed Royal a pistol.

"Sorry, sir," he said. "I've only got the one extra."

"It'll have to do." Royal checked the weapon. "You need

your weapon, since I want you to stay with the coach and keep an eye on the alley."

"Aye, Mr. Royal."

"I've got a knife," Grant said, extracting a wicked-looking blade from an inside pocket of his greatcoat.

"And I've got a little popper," said Angus, pulling out a small pistol.

Sabrina thought back to her first meeting with Graeme. "You certainly are a well-armed family."

"Ye can never be too prepared," Angus replied, winking at her.

"Grandda, best put that away," Royal said. "We don't want to spook anyone before we get the lay of the land."

"I'm nae booby. Not my first rescue, as ye well ken."

"I ken," Royal dryly replied.

Clearly, the Kendricks had an interesting history. It occurred to Sabrina that falling in love with one of them might be a risky proposition in more ways than one.

Too late now.

"Lady Sabrina, are you truly ready for this?" Grant asked.

"I am," she firmly said.

"You're a brave, fine lass," he said with a wry smile. "My brother probably doesn't deserve you, after all."

"Och, Graeme is the best of ye," Angus snorted. "Now be off, while yon lassie and I do our part."

Royal tapped his grandfather's arm. "Take care of her. Just keep everyone talking until we find our way in."

"Aye, that."

When Royal and Grant disappeared into the shadows, Angus took Sabrina's arm and led her into the alley.

She did her best to steady her suddenly erratic heartbeat. Despite her bravado, she felt monstrously out of her depth. True, she'd faced down Cringlewood and also helped rescue Tilly and Charlie. But this was different. Now she was walking straight into the jaws of a dangerous trap, one where a life was at stake.

Graeme could already be—

"Dinna think aboot it," Angus said, cutting into her panicky thoughts. "It's always the worst before the fight. That's when the nerves jangle ye."

"I'm hoping we avoid the fighting bit."

"Aye, bribery is good, trickery better. But if the fightin' starts, just do as Royal said."

"Hide under a table?" She wrinkled her nose. "That seems rather cowardly."

"Yer a brave lass, especially for a *Sassenach*, but yer nae used to fightin'."

"Don't forget that I pushed Lord Cringlewood over that balcony."

He chuckled. "That ye did. But I'm thinkin' ye'll manage to talk us out of this wee spot of trouble. Royal and Grant are just for backup."

That seemed wildly optimistic. But since she and Angus were now standing in front of the Wee Black Dog, there was no more room for doubt. They'd run out of time, and she could only pray that Graeme hadn't.

There was just enough light from the windows of the coffeehouse to illuminate her companion's calm features. Angus gave her a measuring look and lifted a bushy white eyebrow.

Sabrina pushed open the door and stepped down the stairs, stopping on the last one. When she cast a swift glance around, her heart sank.

Emmy stood behind the counter, grim-faced, while a bulky man with unruly whiskers kept her under guard. Old Bill sat at a table in the center of the room, flanked by two young men—very young, hardly more than sixteen. Their hard, thin features and the clubs they held in their hands more than made up for their appearance of youth.

Even worse, Sabrina didn't see Graeme.

Angus nudged her off the bottom step and into the room.

Old Bill scowled at her from his seat. "I told ye to come alone, ye barmy chit. Who's this old goat?"

Angus bristled but remained silent.

"Unfortunately, sir, I could not make my way to this part of town without assistance. As I'm sure you can see, my elderly companion is hardly a threat," Sabrina answered.

"I couldna let the puir lass come by herself," Angus dolefully said. "I'm just a harmless old grandda, ye ken."

When Sabrina caught a quiet snort from the dark cubbyhole at the back of the room, relief almost took her out at the knees. She would recognize that snort anywhere. After all, she'd heard it directed her way often enough.

"Where's the Kendrick lad?" Angus asked.

"Back here. Tied up like a Christmas turkey," Graeme replied.

Sabrina took a quick step forward. "Mr. Kendrick, are you—"

Angus pulled her back to murmur in her ear. "He's tellin' us his situation. That he canna help."

Bill twisted around to glare at the nook. "Shut yer gob, or I'll clobber ye."

"I believe you already have," Graeme replied in a hard voice.

One of the boys waved his club. "Want me to cosh him again, guv?"

"If you dare to hit Mr. Kendrick, I will not give you a single shilling," Sabrina snapped. "And then I'll take that blasted club and cosh *you* over the head."

Bill loudly guffawed. "I said barmy? Complete loony, more like."

"Easy lass," Angus whispered. "Stick to the plan."

Sabrina drew in a breath to steady her nerves and her

fury. "All right . . ." She frowned. "I cannot keep calling you Old Bill."

"I dinna care what ye call me. After tonight, ye'll nae be seein' me again." He flashed a smile, one that sported a number of missing teeth. "And if ye ever do, ye'll be wishin' the good Lord ye hadn't."

"The only business you have with the good Lord is to ask His forgiveness for your truly wretched behavior," she replied. "Before I give you the money, I will also have your word that you will abandon your criminal enterprise and cease using children for your nefarious activities."

"Good God," Graeme muttered.

Sabrina couldn't blame him, since she had sounded rather demented. But she was simply following the plan. To keep Bill talking and distracted until the others found their way in.

Fortunately, Bill rose to the bait. "Ye can sod off, lady. The only thing yer getting from me—if ye pays up—is the big Kendrick oaf." He glared in the direction of the cubbyhole. "And yer welcome to him. The bastard broke one of my bowman's arms."

Sabrina seized the opportunity to prolong the discussion. "Why in heaven's name would a pickpocketing gang need a bowman? That sounds entirely deranged."

Angus smothered a chuckle. "Bowman is cant for thief."

"Aye, and a nasty break it was, too," Bill snarled. "I'll be havin' to pay an old sawbones to fix it."

"That is most unfortunate," Sabrina said. "But as long as Mr. Kendrick didn't break a child's arm—"

"Of course I didn't break a child's arm," came the irritated interruption from the back.

"Then I'm sure the bowman deserved it," Sabrina finished. "Kidnapping Mr. Kendrick was thoroughly illegal Mr., er, Bill."

"Everythin' I do is illegal," the gang leader replied,

shooting her a disbelieving glare. "And now I'm down another man, on top of ye stealin' away my best earner. Ye owe me, girl, and ye'll pay up or yer gent here will get the worst of it."

As if for emphasis, one of his young guards waved his club.

Sabrina pointed a finger at the lad. "You should be ashamed of yourself, young man. Going around hitting people, when you should be in school or learning a trade."

The lad sneered. "I gots a trade, lady. I'm a thief."

"Thieving is not a profession with a future, I assure you. In fact, you will likely be transported before you're much older. Or worse, I'm sorry to say."

When the young man took a menacing step forward, Angus whipped out his gun and leveled it.

"Stay put, laddie," he calmly said.

"Want me to shoot 'im, Bill?" asked the bewhiskered guard, who had also pulled out a pistol.

"Not unless ye wants to be stuck like a pig," Emmy said with grim satisfaction.

Apparently, while Whiskers had been retrieving his weapon, Emmy had unearthed a knife and was now pressing it under her former guard's ribs.

The big fellow threw her a startled glance. "Come on, Em. No threats now, ye ken. We're friends, ain't we?"

"No," the girl snapped.

"Could we please refrain from murdering one another?" Graeme barked. "You all need to put down your blasted weapons."

"Glad someone is talkin' sense." Bill actually sounded almost amused.

Sabrina felt ready to jump out of her skin. Nor could she draw out this absurd conversation much longer. If Royal and Grant didn't soon appear, it was likely someone would be shot or knifed—accidentally, most likely, given the way the evening was going.

"Girl, did ye bring the money or not?" Bill demanded.

"Best hand it over," Angus advised in a low voice. "Looks like the plan went sideways."

She sighed and opened her reticule, extracting the thick bundle of pound notes.

"Blimey," exclaimed one of the lads.

Even Bill looked impressed. "Bring it 'ere."

She shook her head. "First let Mr. Kendrick go."

"Not until we're paid and on our way."

"It's fine, Sabrina," said Graeme. "Angus, take the money and give it to Bill."

"Nae," the gang leader snapped. "*She* gives it to me or the deal's off."

After a fraught silence, a quiet snarl emerged from the cubbyhole. "If ye touch a hair on her head, I'll throttle ye. Then I'll rip out yer guts and set them on fire."

Bill went a bit pale, which was understandable. Graeme's low, lethal tone was terrifying.

Perversely, it made Sabrina quite lighthearted.

"Not to worry, Mr. Kendrick," she said. "Old Bill doesn't frighten me in the least."

She marched up to the table and held up the wad of notes. But when he grabbed for it, she pulled it out of his reach.

"First, I'll have your word that you will leave Tilly and her brother alone," she said.

He gave her a sour look. "Aye, ye have it. She was gettin' to be more trouble than she was worth. Too cheeky by half."

"Yes, abusing children tends to make them cheeky," she replied in a withering tone. "Which is why I will also have your word that you will cease recruiting children."

"Oh, aye, and just how am I supposed to support myself?"

"I am about to hand over fifty pounds—that's more than enough to help you get started in a respectable business."

He snorted with disgust.

"And the Kendricks will know if you employ children again. They *will* put a stop to it."

"Oh, lass, I'll be puttin' a stop to Old Bill, regardless," drawled Graeme. "Count on it."

Annoyed by his unhelpful interruption, she glanced at the cubbyhole and got a terrific shock. From her new angle, she could now see Graeme. With his face cut and bruised, he looked like he'd been dragged backwards through a thorny bush. He also looked mad as hornets and ready to throttle everyone in the room, including her.

It took her a moment to recover. "Please, sir. Let me handle this."

After a tense couple of seconds, Graeme nodded.

She turned back to Bill, who was regarding her with no small measure of surprise. Sabrina didn't blame him. In no scenario could she have ever envisioned negotiating with a crime lord, even a minor one. But since meeting Graeme Kendrick, life had consisted of one surprise after another.

"Do we have a deal?" she asked. "No more recruiting children?"

Bill seemed to ponder that for a few moments. "I'll be losin' a powerful lot of blunt without the kiddies. And I've gots to pay for a sawbones, ye ken. For my bowman."

Breathing out an exasperated sigh, Sabrina unhooked the garnet bobs from her ears and threw them onto the scarred tabletop. "These should fill the gap."

Bill swiped them up with a grin. "Hand over the money, and we've gots a deal."

"I'll have your word as a . . ." She couldn't bring herself to call him a gentleman.

Bill spit on his hand and extended it. "On my honor as a thief."

Regretting the loss of her best pair of gloves, Sabrina shook his hand. Then she placed the money on the table.

He picked up the notes and stood. "And I hope never to see ye again."

"One can certainly hope," she tartly replied.

Bill strolled to the door, followed by his young guards. They gave Angus—still holding his pistol—a wide berth. Whiskers came around the counter to join his leader.

Sighing with relief, Sabrina turned toward Graeme. He'd managed to climb to his feet, despite being wrapped by a great deal of rope.

"You will, however, be seeing me again, Bill," Graeme said. His eyes were glittering emerald shards. "And there will be a reckoning."

Bill paused by the door. "I'm thinkin' not."

Sabrina went to work on the big knot binding Graeme's wrists behind his back. "He's leaving. Don't start trouble," she hissed.

Graeme kept his focus on the gang leader. "And why should I not hunt you down and kill you?"

She struggled with the insanely complicated knot. "Because it would be illegal?"

Graeme cast her a brief, incredulous look.

"And because I'm gonna do you a favor," Bill said. "More rightly, I'll be doin' yer lady a favor."

Sabrina blinked and straightened up. "What do you mean?"

"I like a lass with spirit, and ye got plenty. Although yer costin' me plenty, too," he added with a chuckle.

Angus impatiently waved his pistol. "Get on with it, man."

"Grandda, put that bloody gun away before you shoot someone," Graeme snapped.

"Amateurs, the lot of ye," Bill sneered. "And ye, mister, thinkin' yer so clever, askin' yer sneaky questions all about the town."

Sabrina took one look at Graeme's furious expression and hastily intervened. "What is it you wanted to tell me?"

"Them rumors about plots and such—they ain't about George," Bill said. "No one cares about them old grievances against the *Sassenachs* anymore. Leastways not enough to kill a tubby old king."

"Then who and *what* are the rumors about?" Graeme asked.

"It's about the Clearances," Bill said. "It's about them Scottish lords and ladies and who they're kickin' off their lands." Then he pointed at Sabrina. "It's about her. She's the one I reckon's got the target on her back, not the king."

Chapter Sixteen

"Almost got it," Grant muttered as he cut through the ropes around Graeme's wrists.

Graeme could hardly feel his hands anymore. His legs had also been tightly lashed, and he hoped he didn't topple over once he was free.

"I'm sorry, lad," Royal said. "I'm ashamed we so thoroughly let you down."

"Not your fault, brother. Besides, her ladyship was more than up to the task."

Sabrina, who hovered right behind Royal, didn't seem to notice Graeme's sarcastic tone. "Are you sure you're all right? That looks like a terribly nasty blow to the head."

"My head is thankfully very hard."

"Hardest head in the family," Royal said.

Graeme ignored him to scowl at Sabrina. "You had no business putting yourself in danger. Have you no brains, woman? You could have been killed."

When he thought of what could have happened, Graeme was torn between shaking Sabrina until her molars rattled and pulling her into his arms for the rest of eternity.

"I had everything perfectly under control," she replied. "There is no need to starch up, sir."

"Starch up? See here, you daft—"

"Got it," Grant exclaimed, cutting through the last of the hemp.

Though Graeme had tried with everything he had, there had been no way he could free himself. And they'd bound him so tightly he'd had no chance of reaching any of his knives.

What a thoroughly embarrassing disaster.

"Thanks, lad," he said to his twin. The blood rushed back into his hands, making them tingle and burn. He shook them out.

"You can't really blame Lady Sabrina, old fellow," Grant said. "She was simply following instructions."

"Instructions that could have gotten her killed."

"Instructions that, if not followed, could have gotten *you* killed," she pointed out. "And *you* might try being a wee bit grateful. I am down a considerable sum of money *and* my garnet earbobs, you know."

Graeme definitely wanted to shake her, but had the feeling he'd fall down in a heap if he tried. "I will pay you back the money," he said as Grant steadied him. "But may I point out that toting a small fortune in your reticule is an open invitation to robbery."

"Which I believe just happened, thanks to you," she said in a snippy tone.

Emmy thrust a cloudy glass into his hand. "Drink this. It might help."

Graeme managed to dredge up a smile. By all rights, the young woman should be clobbering him over the head for putting her at risk, not giving him a dram.

"Thank you." He shot the whisky down.

It was a rough brew, but quickly sent heat to his limbs and helped dull the ache from his throbbing head.

"In all fairness to Sabrina," Royal said, "we did construct a workable plan. But one can hardly fight one's way through a gang of children."

"Especially children with pistols," Grant added in a gloomy tone.

Royal and Grant had burst in immediately after the departure of Bill and his henchmen. Although they'd found the back door easily enough, they'd encountered an unexpected obstacle—street urchins, armed to teeth. Graeme's brothers had tried to wheedle, argue, and bribe their way into the coffeehouse, but the children had refused to budge. They'd faded away only when a whistle from the street, signaling Bill's departure, had called them off.

By that point, there'd been nothing to do but cut Graeme free.

Graeme sighed. "Och, I didn't exactly cover myself in glory. The clever brats fooled me, too."

One, a girl of about eight, had lured him out of the theater lobby with a tale about some of the children needing his help to escape Bill's clutches. When Graeme had taken the chance of slipping out to the side alley to talk to the child, he'd been promptly coshed from behind and shoved into a waiting hackney. By the time he'd come out of his daze, he'd been securely bound and under guard.

He shook his head in self-disgust, wincing when pain throbbed behind his temples. Emmy thrust another fortifying glass into his hand.

"I swear," he muttered, "children are better at lying than spies are."

Angus snorted. "Laddie, have ye talked to yer nieces and nephews lately? No one tells whoppers better than the little ones."

"Except for you, Grandda," Grant said.

"Aye, it's a talent."

Sabrina was once more studying Graeme with a worried frown. "Mr. Kendrick, do you think you can walk now? You must return to Heriot Row and call for the surgeon."

Graeme touched his head. The bleeding had stopped. "I'm fine."

"But you obviously took a terrible blow," she said, tightly clutching her reticule.

Graeme couldn't help but give her a reassuring smile. "There's no need to worry, lass. They stunned me, but I never lost consciousness."

Royal stepped closer to inspect Graeme's cut and look at his eyes. "No dizziness or blurred vision? No nausea?"

"None."

His brother nodded. "You'll do, but we should get home before anything else can go wrong."

Oh, things had gone wrong, all right, if what Old Bill had told them was remotely true. And Graeme's instincts told him that Bill's information was more right than wrong.

If so, Sabrina was in danger, and it meant that Graeme had to get her out of Scotland—for his sake, as well as hers. The very notion of anything happening to her all but incapacitated him.

Not a particularly effective condition for protecting anyone.

As if hearing his thoughts, Sabrina narrowed her gaze on him. It was amazing how well those innocent, peacock-blue eyes could read him.

"And we *are* going to have a full discussion of Old Bill's warning," she said. "I didn't understand much other than the part in which I'm the likely target of a plot, not the king."

Royal threw Graeme a startled glance. "What? Why?"

"Because of the Clearances, apparently," Sabrina said before Graeme could answer. "And something murky about smuggling."

Grant sighed. "Of course it was murky. Murky is all we do."

"Let's just get safely away, shall we?" Graeme said.

"Grant, can you escort Emmy home and compensate her for any damages?"

The young woman waved a hand. "Och, ye've done enough by helping Tilly and Charlie."

"I'll see you home, just to be sure," Grant said.

"And we'll also make sure Bill doesn't bother you again," Graeme added.

"I reckon the old bastard will be clearin' town. He'll be wantin' to avoid more trouble with the Kendricks," Emmy said.

Grant flashed Graeme a quick smile. "I'll take care of it. Just get yourself home in one piece, all right?"

Graeme nodded and reached for Sabrina. Instead, she took his arm and began steering him across the room.

He sighed. "Lass, just once do you think you could let me manage the rescuing?"

"Naturally, I would be happy to, if given the chance."

"Happens she's right," Angus said as he followed them to the door. "Not much rescuin' on yer end."

"That is not the point, Grandda," Graeme groused.

"I am sorry to disoblige you, sir," Sabrina said as he extracted his arm from her surprisingly firm grip and nudged her up the stairs to the street. "But I'm not sure what else I could have done to avoid the situation, other than let you get murdered."

They stepped out onto the dark street. Graeme held her back for a moment, casting a swift glance in both directions. The north end of the alley, leading further into the tight warren of tenements and closes, was deserted. At the other end waited the Kendrick carriage, with their coachman and groom patiently standing guard.

Nonetheless, Graeme curled a protective arm around Sabrina's shoulders and pulled her against his side. He would take no chances with her, not until she was safely out of harm's way.

Which also meant safely out of his life.

And that was for the best. The sweet, wonderful girl was much too good for the likes of him.

She startled a bit before settling under his arm. Oddly enough, and despite the lingering danger, Graeme felt his tense body also begin to settle. It felt right, having her in his arms. The part of him that had always been restless suggested it had found what it needed to be at peace.

Sentimental twaddle.

He picked up the conversation in a quiet voice. "Sabrina, what you did was kind and brave, but also foolhardy. You should have stayed in your box at the theater, and let my brothers manage things."

"If you ask me," she said, "the lesson from this evening's adventures is to stay away from theatrical productions. I swear I am never going to the theater again."

He gave her an incredulous look. "That's your lesson from this debacle?"

"I was not the one who was tricked by a small child and kidnapped, after all."

"Aye, our Graeme was not at his best this evening," Angus said from behind them.

"Again, not the point, Grandda."

"Then what is, sir?" Sabrina asked.

He'd rather lost the point, so he simply shut up and marched her to the carriage. Though young Bobby's eyes went wide when he saw Graeme, the groom quickly let down the steps and opened the door.

"No trouble at this end?" Royal asked, joining them.

"Nae, Mr. Royal," said Bobby. "Saw a bit of a scurry at the other end of the alley but thought it best to stay here, like ye said."

"Good man."

Angus clambered in, then reached down a hand to Sabrina.

Royal followed them inside. Graeme again gave a quick but thorough perusal of the surrounding area, but all was quiet.

"All right, let's be off," he said, climbing in.

He took the seat next to Royal, across from Sabrina. She was still looking miffed. Well, hurt, actually. He could read her, too, and he saw the hurt in her blue gaze. She'd risked her life for him. However foolish, her actions had been courageous and selfless.

"Sabrina, it practically kills me that you put yourself in harm's way for me," he bluntly said.

She blinked. "Was that an apology for biting my head off?"

Graeme sighed. "Probably."

"And likely the best you'll get from him, I'm afraid," Royal said, amused.

"He's embarrassed, ye ken." Angus reached over and patted his knee. "Ye've been under a strain, lately, what with the plotting and such. It's nae wonder yer a mite off yer game."

"I am not off my game," Graeme growled.

"That bump on your forehead states otherwise," Royal said.

"As for you," Graeme said, rounding on his brother, "did you and Grant lose your bloody minds? How in God's name could you allow Sabrina to walk into that rolling disaster? What if something had happened? The king would have seen us all hang, as would her father."

Royal held up his hands. "Grant and I tried to talk her out of it."

"Happens the lass didna give us much of a choice," Angus added. "Plus, she was the one with the blunt, laddie."

"The lass is well able to speak for herself," Sabrina said. "And it's true that I did not give them a choice. It was clear from Old Bill's note. . . . And really, I am so tired of calling him Old Bill—"

"Since you're never going to see him again, it doesn't matter what you call the bastard," Graeme interrupted.

"Now, children," Royal said. "No fighting in the carriage."

"Oh, sod off," Graeme snapped.

Sabrina bristled like a hedgehog, which he found rather adorable.

"Everyone was doing their best under trying circumstances," she said in a frosty tone. "Bill had threatened to *kill* you, and I was the only one with enough money on hand to provide a ransom."

"Och, he wasn't going to kill me."

She lifted a challenging eyebrow. "Do you wish we'd taken that chance?"

"When it comes to you, yes," Graeme snapped. "My brothers and my grandfather know how to take care of themselves. You, however, have no experience in dealing with the criminal underworld, despite your demented insistence otherwise. You have put yourself in danger, time and again. It's got to stop, Sabrina, before things truly go wrong."

Rather than accepting his entirely justified reprimand, Sabrina leaned across the gap, her eyes glittering with blue fire. She wagged a finger at him, mere inches from his nose.

"You are not my father, sir, so you may keep your lectures to yourself. In fact, I suggest you keep your interfering opinions to yourself from now on. Furthermore—"

Graeme clamped his hands around her slender shoulders and dragged her closer, until they were all but nose to nose. "Do you not understand, you daft lass? You could have been killed. Killed. Can you even begin to comprehend what that would mean to me? To *anyone* who loves you?"

Her mouth dropped open, and her eyes actually crossed as she tried to focus on him. For a long moment, they stared at each other, both panting as if they'd raced up the hill to Heriot Row on foot.

Royal broke the charged silence. "There's no need to roar, Graeme. You all but blew the ribbons out of the poor girl's hair."

"And ye'd best put her back down on the seat," Angus said. "Unless ye'll be puttin' her on yer lap, instead."

Graeme blinked, and Sabrina flushed a fiery red that was visible even in the dim light of the carriage lamps. Since he *had* practically yanked her onto his lap, he carefully eased her back onto the opposite bench, smoothing the folds of her opera cloak down over her arms.

"Sorry," he muttered, feeling like ten times a moron.

"It's fine," she replied in a breathless tone. "It's been an upsetting evening for all of us. You're a little . . ."

"Fashed?" Royal dryly finished.

Graeme cut him another dirty look but refrained from rising to the bait.

"It was distressing for all of us, ye ken. But ye have to admit her ladyship did well." Angus beamed at Sabrina. "Yer a born negotiator, lassie. Ye had Old Bill on the ropes, ye did."

Graeme made a concerted effort to remain calm—not easy, since his family was driving him crazy. "Yes, but you also lost a considerable sum of money and your earrings. I'm truly sorry for that."

Although obviously still rattled, Sabrina gave him a shy little smile. It made him long to pull her onto his lap and kiss her into melting submission. Thank God he wasn't alone with her, because he probably wouldn't have been able to resist the temptation.

"The money is nothing," she said, "and the earrings were not particularly special. Certainly not compared to securing your safety."

"Still, I'll pay you back."

"It's not necessary—"

"A Kendrick always pays his debts," Angus interrupted. "It's part of the code."

She frowned. "What code?"

Graeme rolled his eyes. "I haven't a clue."

"Ainsley will see to replacing your earbobs," Royal added. "And we won't take no for an answer. As annoying as my little brother is, my family would have been quite distraught if he had been injured. We owe you an enormous debt of gratitude."

Her smile turned wry. "When you put it like that, I cannot refuse, can I?"

"You cannot," said Graeme, "so don't even try."

"Grand," said Angus. "So, just like Robbie Burns said, *all's well that ends well.*"

Sabrina pressed a hand to her lips.

"That wasn't Robbie Burns, Grandda," Royal said.

"Aye, it was. In fact—"

"It doesn't matter who said it," Graeme interrupted, "because it's not ended yet. There's still the issue of Sabrina's safety."

Royal sighed. "I'd forgotten about that."

"I certainly haven't." Keeping Sabrina safe was all Graeme could think about.

Angus patted his knee again. "Laddie, ye've got to relax and let us help ye, or yer poor head will explode from the strain."

Fortunately, before the contents of Graeme's brain could splatter all over the inside of the family town coach, they pulled up in front of Heriot Row. The groom opened the door, and Angus clambered out, followed by Royal.

"After you, my lady," Graeme said.

Sabrina hesitated and then touched his hand. "All jesting aside, we need to discuss what Bill told us."

"I'm aware," he grimly said. "And what he said was no jest, I'm sorry to say."

She sighed. "How annoying. Well, I suppose we'll just have to deal with it."

"*We* are not dealing—"

Royal stuck his head in. "Are you two coming?"

Graeme followed Sabrina out, trying to ignore the throbbing behind his temples. The lass would surely be the death of him. For such a sunny, sweet-tempered woman, she could be insanely stubborn. And much too fearless. Over the years, he'd learned that a wee dose of fear was just the ticket for staying alive.

Lady Sabrina Bell? She didn't know the meaning of the word.

The door to the house flew open. Nick loomed in the doorway, fists propped on his hips. He scowled over the heads of everyone, directing his ire right at Graeme.

"You'd best have a good explanation, laddie boy," Nick barked. "Victoria and I had the devil of a time trying to explain to the king why you'd all disappeared. Especially Lady Sabrina."

Ainsley appeared a moment later and shoved him aside. "Move, Nicholas." She took Sabrina's hand and drew her into the hall. "Are you all right, dearest?"

"I'm fine," she said, giving Ainsley a hug. "Poor Graeme, however, is not."

"Let me look at that cut." Nick took Graeme by the chin, frowning with concern.

Graeme suffered the embarrassing inspection, since it would have turned into an argument if he had refused. It was all rather ridiculous, given that he topped his big brother by a few inches and outweighed him, too. The Laird of Arnprior could be a fussy old hen when it came to his siblings.

In many ways, Nick had been more father than brother to all of them, especially the younger ones. And he'd been a better parent than the old earl, for damn sure. Their father had been a stern-tempered man, sometimes even a harsh one. A few times, Graeme had been on the receiving end of the old earl's hand, one that could strike a punishing blow.

Nick, though? He would always be there for Graeme and all his brothers, no matter the trouble or pain.

"Should we send for a physician?" Sabrina asked in a worried voice. "He took an awful blow to the head."

"Did you lose consciousness?" Nick asked. "Or feel nauseated?"

Graeme pushed away his brother's hand. "Hell and damnation, it's just a bump. I'm perfectly fine."

"I don't think there's any lasting damage," Royal said. "Except to his manners."

"That's a hopeless cause," Ainsley said with a twinkle. "But the poor man could probably use a sit and a wee dram, I imagine."

"That's the first sensible suggestion I've heard all night," Graeme replied.

"That's because I'm smarter than all you Kendricks." Ainsley glanced at Sabrina. "Pet, as much as I'd love to hear about your misadventures, perhaps you'd best take yourself off to bed."

Sabrina shook her head. "I'm not the least bit tired. Besides, we need to have a discussion with Lord Arnprior."

Nick, who was still trying to look at Graeme's head, glanced over at Sabrina. "I'm happy to discuss anything with you, but I'm sure it can wait till morning. You must be exhausted."

Sabrina gave a stubborn shake of the head. "No, it cannot wait."

Nick arched an eyebrow at Graeme.

"'Fraid not, old man," Graeme said. "We've got a situation on our hands."

His big brother sighed. "Of course we have."

"Graeme Kendrick! What have you done to yourself?"

Garbed in a gigantic wrapper that did nothing to conceal

her pregnant state, Vicky descended the stairs like a stately schooner coming into port.

"Victoria, you're supposed to be in bed," Nick said in an exasperated tone.

Ignoring her husband, she waddled up to Graeme. "You look terrible. We need to send for a doctor."

"We've already ascertained that Graeme has an exceedingly hard head and has suffered no lasting injury," Ainsley said.

Graeme dropped a quick kiss on the top of Vicky's frilly nightcap. "I'm fine, Mother. I promise."

"You are a dreadful boy," she said with a reluctant smile. "You're sure?"

"I'll be even more sure when I finally get that drink everyone's been promising me."

He took Sabrina's elbow and nudged her toward the stairs. "Up with you, lass. The sooner we talk this out, the sooner you can get in—"

He had a sudden and extremely tantalizing vision of Sabrina in bed. With him. *Under* him, more precisely.

She shot him a questioning frown.

"The sooner you can plan your departure," he finished.

Sabrina pulled her arm away. "I'm not going anywhere until someone explains why I'm in danger."

"What's this?" Nick said. "Lady Sabrina is in danger?"

"Not out here," Graeme said. "Up to the drawing room, everyone."

Henderson, as usual, had anticipated all needs and was waiting up there, drinks organized.

"I've ordered the tea tray, my lady," the butler said to Vicky as he handed Graeme a hefty glass of Scotland's finest. "I'll bring up a basin of hot water and some cloths. Mr. Graeme's wound needs to be cleaned."

Graeme shook his head. "No need. It can—"

Henderson, naturally, was already halfway out the door.

"Bunch of old biddies," Graeme muttered.

"It's because they love you," Sabrina said in a quiet voice. "And they worry about you."

He glanced down at her, surprised by the comment. "They worry too much."

She tilted her head. "Someone has to, since you clearly don't worry about yourself."

That cut a little too close to the bone. "Worry is a waste of time."

She frowned. "That's a silly—"

"Let's get started, shall we?" he interrupted.

Her delicate jaw clenched, she allowed him to steer her to the sofa where Vicky was already ensconced.

Nick stood in front of the fireplace, arms crossed over his chest in his best laird-of-the-manor stance. "All right. Exactly what happened tonight?"

Graeme settled into an armchair, weariness dragging at his bones. God, he was tired of this. He was tired of everything.

"Do you want me to explain?" Sabrina softly asked him.

You're not tired of her.

He smiled at her. "No, I'll do it."

He swiftly explained the evening's events, with Sabrina and Royal filling in the holes. Shortly after Graeme started, Henderson came in with a basin and a few cloths. Ainsley rose to take them.

"Don't mind me," she said as she wet a cloth and gently wiped Graeme's face.

Graeme paused, startled at the amount of blood on the white towel.

"Aye, ye got a right, proper knock," Angus said.

Graeme couldn't help but grimace. His poor family. He caused them no end of trouble and worry.

"Sorry," he said to Nick.

His brother's smile was wry and understanding. "It's all right, my boy. We'll get through it together."

While Ainsley cleaned him up, Graeme finished relating events. His family listened with few interruptions.

"That is quite something," Ainsley finally said. "And huzzah for you, Sabrina. You are the true heroine of the tale."

"Don't encourage her," Graeme said. "The lass could have gotten herself killed."

"Och, yer just jealous she got to do all the rescuin'," Angus teased.

"Lady Sabrina's bravery is commendable," Nick said. "And we must be thankful that this unfortunate situation gave us a measure of warning."

Sabrina clasped her hands together, clearly frustrated. "But a warning of what? The Clearances? I confess I'm not as informed as I should be on that issue."

"A number of landowners have been seeking to increase the profits from their land," Nick explained. "They do so by evicting longstanding tenants and crofters, turning the land over to sheep or cattle farming."

She frowned. "Are the tenants compensated?"

"Generally not."

"Then what happens to them?"

Nick hesitated.

"They're tossed from their homes, left to fend for themselves," Ainsley said grimly.

Royal sighed. "Blunt as always, my love."

"I fail to see the point in sugarcoating it. It's a horrendous, shameful situation."

Sabrina sucked in a quavering breath. "Is my father engaging in those sorts of practices?"

Graeme flashed his brother a warning look.

"I'm not familiar with every situation where Clearances are occurring," Nick gently replied. "But I've heard some talk of such regarding your father's estates."

His brother knew *exactly* where things stood with Musgrave's estates. Nick always knew these sorts of things. He was trying to soften the blow for the poor girl.

Sabrina looked ill. "I . . . I don't know what to say."

"It's not your fault, lass," Graeme said gruffly. "Your da certainly isn't the only one doing it."

"But your family isn't. Not the Kendricks."

"No."

For a few seconds, she appeared shattered. Then she unclasped her hands, smoothed down her skirts, and straightened her spine. "While I'm not trying to minimize the situation, I suspect my father is unaware of how things stand. He has very little to do with Lochnagar Manor, which has been the case for years. It's always been overseen by his business manager in Edinburgh, and by an estate steward."

"Not an uncommon situation with absentee landlords," Nick agreed.

If Musgrave didn't know his own business, it only confirmed what a nodnock he was, as far as Graeme was concerned.

"What does this have to do with Sabrina?" Vicky asked. "And smugglers? I don't really understand that bit."

"That's what probably made her the target," Graeme said. "Old Bill was annoyingly vague, but I suspect one of Musgrave's tenant families has been running a smuggling rig. Apparently, they were evicted along with the rest of the crofters. That, obviously, did not sit well with the smugglers. But I'll need to look into it more to get a true sense of it."

Royal shook his head. "It must have been a hell of a rig, if they're bent on murder."

"Mayhap it's not murder," Angus said. "Mayhap it's ransom they're after. Kidnappin', not killin'."

Graeme thought about it. "That makes sense, Grandda.

More than this ridiculous assassination plot I've been chasing like a dog after its tail."

"Assassination?" Sabrina asked in a faint voice.

"We thought the king might be under threat," Graeme explained. "That's why I came north in the first place."

After processing that bit of information, she shook her head. "That still doesn't explain why . . . Oh, I see. My father was supposed to come north with the king, not me."

"Aye, and when you showed up instead, you became the target."

"But how would a bunch of silly old smugglers even know Lord Musgrave was supposed to come north?" Ainsley asked, waving her arms.

"That's an excellent question," Graeme said. "It's quite possible this could be a crime of opportunity. Many Scottish lords—or ladies—would make an inviting target for both revenge and ransom. And many of them are in Edinburgh right now, all here for George's visit."

"So, Sabrina might not be the target," Vicky said, looking hopeful.

Graeme wasn't prepared to go that far. In fact, his instincts were telling him that Old Bill had the right of it. But how could he prove it?

"Possibly," he reluctantly said.

"Probably, I hope," Sabrina replied. "Regardless, I am deeply disturbed to hear there may be Clearances on my father's estate. I intend to investigate that situation."

"How? You're going home in a few days," Graeme said.

Her dainty chin took on a defiant tilt. "I will not be returning home until the situation is resolved to my satisfaction. His Majesty will have to do without me on the trip."

Oh, and wasn't *that* all Graeme needed? Sabrina putting herself right into the thick of things, where she would be most vulnerable.

He carefully put down his glass and stood. He crossed his arms over his chest and scowled down at Sabrina.

And noticed how remarkably unimpressed she looked.

"This is not up for debate, Sabrina," he said. "You *will* be returning to London."

She stood and crossed her arms, mirroring his pose. "Your opinion notwithstanding, sir, that will not be happening. I'm remaining in Edinburgh."

"The hell you will," he growled. "If I have to drag your pretty arse onto that blasted boat myself, that's exactly what I'll do."

Ignoring her outraged gasp and the resigned sighs of his relatives, Graeme stalked from the room.

Chapter Seventeen

Sabrina morosely eyed the trunks lined against the wall of her bedroom. In two days, she would depart with the king. Her life in London—her privileged and utterly boring life—beckoned once more.

Sadly, Graeme seemed especially eager for her departure, and the reasons didn't truly matter. If he had feelings for her, he wasn't prepared to act on them. Sabrina wasn't prepared to chase after him like a silly miss entirely lacking in dignity.

She picked up the crystal glass she'd snuck up from the drawing room and took a cautious sip, wincing at the bracing heat of the whisky. Tonight's disturbing events, ending with that embarrassing scene with Graeme in front of his family, continued to pluck at her nerves like a deranged harpist. The whisky, she hoped, would be medicinal and calm her down. So far it had failed to do the trick, but she was willing to soldier on to the bottom of the glass.

Graeme's parting and highly insulting shot had certainly thrown the cat amongst the pigeons. After a stunned pause, everyone in the room had started talking, all of them offering highly opinionated observations. A lively argument had ensued, giving Sabrina her chance to slip from the room. That she'd done so undetected only confirmed how upset the family was by Graeme's behavior.

If she had a brain in her head, she would happily depart and leave the poor Kendrick family in peace.

But the situation at Lochnagar Manor demanded some kind of action from her. A clear injustice was taking place on her father's estate, one she could not ignore. If Graeme truly cared for her—and she'd thought he did—he would see how much it meant to her to correct that appalling situation, and he'd offer to help. The more she thought about it, the more it seemed that Graeme Kendrick didn't think much of her at all, and that was an awful notion to contemplate.

Sabrina forced another mouthful down, wondering how Scots could refer to whisky as smooth. When she stood up from her dressing table, she wobbled.

The medicine, it would appear, was working.

She tipped her head back and swallowed the rest, struggling not to cough. All good medicines were the same, nasty but effective. She hoped this one would be effective in helping her to forget blasted Graeme Kendrick.

When a quiet tap sounded on the door, she peered at the clock on the mantel. Who would be knocking at this late hour?

Certainly not blasted Graeme Kendrick.

"You're an idiot," she muttered as she headed for the door.

For some reason, it seemed farther away than it appeared.

When she opened it, she blinked at Ainsley, dressed in a frilly wrapper and matching nightcap. Her friend glanced down at the glass in Sabrina's hand.

"It's entirely medicinal." Sabrina was quite proud that she barely slurred her words.

"It would appear you've had a good helping of the medicine."

"I think I deserve it after that dreadful scene," Sabrina responded in a dignified tone.

She then turned and tripped over the hem of her dressing gown, flailing to regain her balance.

Ainsley steered her toward one of the floral armchairs by the fireplace. "Sit, pet, before you fall down."

"Nonsense. I never do silly things like that. I'm an absolute paragon of control, and I never put a foot wrong. *Everyone* says so."

"Then you met Graeme, and it's impossible to maintain one's dignity around a Kendrick."

Sabrina gratefully sank into the chair. "You seem to manage it."

Ainsley, taking the chair opposite, raised a sardonic brow.

"All right," Sabrina admitted. "You're as bad as the rest of them."

"It's why I'm so perfect for this family. As are you, I might add."

"Unfortunately, the only one whose opinion matters in that regard doesn't agree."

"Kendrick men are insanely stubborn. The term 'jingle-brains' was invented specifically for them."

Despite her gloomy mood, Sabrina giggled. Obviously, she was tipsy enough to find their conversation more than slightly absurd.

Ainsley smiled. "That's my girl. I was worried when you snuck out of the drawing room. Not Sabrina-like at all."

"It seemed the smart thing to do at the time."

"Graeme's ridiculous tantrum was very upsetting for you. I was tempted to give him a good slap. Unfortunately, he managed too quick an exit."

Sabrina wrinkled her nose. "Wise of him, given the subsequent discussion."

"Indeed. It's never a pretty sight when Angus and Nick go at it. But then Vicky started yelling, which is fairly rare. That sent Nick into a lather, so he ordered the rest of us upstairs to our rooms."

"Oh, dear. Is Victoria all right? I hate the notion of upsetting her."

"Vicky is fine. She was still ringing a peal over Nick's head as he carted her upstairs."

"Lord Arnprior must rue the day I showed up on his doorstep. I've been a great deal of trouble."

"Darling, you're an absolute angel compared to the rest of us. And Nick is simply overprotective. As is Graeme, I might add."

Sabrina blew out an exasperated sigh. "I rather think he's trying to rid himself of a bothersome female who has made his life a trial. I suppose I cannot blame him."

Ainsley leaned forward. "Sabrina, he's trying to get rid of you because he's protecting you. Your little adventure tonight put a proper scare into him. Graeme is terrified you might be harmed."

"Because the king would have a fit, as would my father," Sabrina morosely replied. "Yes, he made that clear."

Ainsley jabbed Sabrina's knee. "No, silly. The poor man is besotted with you. All he can think about is getting you out of harm's way. And in his current frazzled state, that means getting you right out of Scotland."

That sounded cautiously hopeful. "Besotted, really? He's certainly not acting like it."

"Kendrick men lose their minds when they fall in love, which results in very erratic behavior." Ainsley snorted. "And they say women are emotional. What nonsense. Men turn into wrecks when they fall in love, at least our men do."

"That sounds quite lovely, but there's only one problem."

Ainsley cocked an eyebrow. "That Graeme isn't your man? Oh, he most certainly is. Royal says he's never seen the poor lad so rattled, and Graeme is not the sort to get rattled. In fact, he's turned much too silent and grim since he took up this spy nonsense."

"He does strike me as a serious, disciplined man," Sabrina replied.

"Graeme was always a good-natured hellion, but he's

become much too serious these last few years. Fortunately, that's beginning to change, because of you."

Sabrina gave Ainsley a tentative smile. "And that's a good thing?"

"A very good thing." Ainsley cast a pointed look at the trunks. "Which is precisely why you cannot run away."

"But if Graeme doesn't wish to . . ."

"Oh, he wishes to. Trust me, he wishes *very* much." Ainsley waggled her eyebrows.

Sabrina could feel herself blush. This was a rather improper and embarrassing conversation.

"Then what's holding him back? It's one thing to keep me from harm. It's quite another to push me out of his life, which he has done repeatedly."

"Because he's a moron?"

"Then perhaps it's best I'm leaving. One doesn't wish to marry a moron. One might end up with frightfully stupid children as a result."

Her lame attempt at a joke had the opposite effect, since the idea of children with Graeme brought a sudden sting of tears to her eyes. Sabrina had never been in love, nor had she ever thought seriously about having a family of her own. Now she *was* in love, and she wanted a houseful of rambunctious little sons and red-haired little girls—with Graeme.

Ainsley studied her with a warmly compassionate gaze.

When a few tears slipped free, Sabrina extracted a handkerchief from the pocket of her wrapper. "I am never drinking whisky again." She wiped her nose. "It's turned *me* into a moron."

"Sabrina, Graeme loves you, but he's frightened of hurting you—and of getting hurt in return."

"He should know by now how I feel about him. I've made it embarrassingly clear."

"Graeme is worried he won't be able to protect you."

Ainsley pointed a finger. "Not an unreasonable concern, under the circumstances."

"Then he should help me face the threat and solve the problem," Sabrina groused. "Not send me away."

"Agreed. But there's another issue, one which is more pressing, I believe."

"His life as a spy?"

"Actually, I think he'd happily give up that life for you, except . . ."

"Yes?"

"Graeme doesn't think he deserves you. He feels unworthy of your love."

Sabrina remembered what his brother had said. "Grant suggested something similar the other night."

"He's a smart one, our Grant. Graeme is afraid you'll reject him, once you really know who he is."

"I do know him. He's a kind, brave, and thoroughly worthy man."

"He doesn't feel that way. Graeme has spent years trying to make up for what he considers to be . . ." Ainsley frowned for a moment. "His failings, for lack of a better term."

"I don't understand."

"I suppose Grant didn't tell you why Graeme doesn't think he's good enough for you?"

"No. He said it wasn't his story to tell."

Ainsley rolled her eyes. "Typical. Kendrick men are also ridiculously secretive. Graeme certainly won't tell because he's worried you'll think poorly of him. But I do think you need to know why he thinks that way, regardless."

"All right, but I could never think poorly of him," Sabrina replied.

"Good for you. But hold on, because it's going to get a bit rough for a few minutes."

Sabrina drew in a deep breath to calm her suddenly shaky nerves. "I'm ready."

Ainsley nodded. "Angus has told you bits and pieces, but he's mostly been talking around the edges. You're aware, of course, that Nick and Logan are the offspring of the old earl and his first wife."

"Yes. Angus told me that his daughter was the old earl's second wife."

"Correct. The second Lady Arnprior was devoted to her husband and her new family. From what Royal tells me, she was truly a saintly woman. Life at Kinglas, for the most part, was happy."

Sabrina ticked up an eyebrow. "For the most part?"

"The old earl was quite old-fashioned and expected much from his sons. He could be rather hard on them." Ainsley let out a sigh. "Especially Graeme."

"How . . . how hard?"

"Hard enough to leave a mark, now and again."

Sabrina mentally cringed. While he'd no doubt been a handful, she could easily imagine Graeme as an adorable, fiery-haired imp. The notion of raising one's hand to a child broke her heart.

"Poor little boy," she softly said.

"Unfortunately, it's sometimes the way of things between fathers and sons. But you mustn't think it was truly bad. Lady Arnprior was a splendid mother, and the family thrived." Ainsley hesitated. "Until they didn't."

"What happened?"

"Lady Arnprior died giving birth to Kade, the youngest boy, and the effect on the family was profound."

Sabrina had few memories of her own mother—flashes of golden hair, softly scented kisses, and glimmers of barely remembered smiles. Mamma's passing had echoed down through the years, taking a toll on her father, and through him to her.

"Yes, I can imagine."

"Lord Arnprior never recovered. He died two years later, after a fall from his horse. Nick became laird and clan chief, although he'd effectively been running things since his step-mother's death."

"I cannot imagine the pressure on the poor man."

"It gets worse, I'm sorry to say. Not long after his father's death, Nick married his childhood sweetheart."

Sabrina blinked. "I didn't realize he'd been previously married."

"It was a sad situation. Nick's first wife was not in good health and died young. They had a lovely little boy, though. Nick was devoted to wee Cameron, as were his uncles. The lad was their shining light through very dark times."

Sabrina's stomach turned hollow as a bell. Lord Arnprior now had only one child, Rowena. "What happened?"

"Cameron died in a drowning accident at Castle Kinglas. Nick wasn't there, but the brothers were. They tried to save little Cam, but Logan, Royal, the twins . . . Well, there was nothing to be done. That final tragedy essentially destroyed Nick and the family."

It took Sabrina a few moments to choke back tears. "I'm so, so sorry. Poor Lord Arnprior."

Ainsley let out a weary sigh. "Indeed. Nick felt unable to remain at Kinglas after the tragedy, so he joined one of the Highland regiments and went off to war. Royal joined the same regiment to keep an eye on his big brother. Nick thank-fully emerged from that carnage without a scratch, but my poor husband barely survived."

Sabrina winced. "I knew he was injured, but I had no idea how badly."

"Royal hates being the object of anyone's pity."

"I can understand that. But where does Graeme fit into this? Did the twins fight in the war, too?"

"The younger lads remained at Kinglas, with Angus in

charge. In hindsight, it was not the wisest of decisions, especially when it came to the twins. Angus could never bring himself to discipline the lads. Not after all they'd been through."

"I cannot blame him," Sabrina quietly said.

"Everyone else did, unfortunately. The twins left a trail of mayhem, from Kinglas to Glasgow to Edinburgh. God only knows what would have happened to the family if Vicky hadn't appeared on the scene." Ainsley flashed a brief smile. "She always says the twins were her biggest pedagogical challenge. Eventually, she prevailed and transformed those Highland hellions into gentlemen. For the most part, anyway."

"Thank goodness for Victoria. The Kendricks now seem happy and at peace. You're certainly all very comfortable with one another."

Ainsley actually laughed—a relief, after such a sorrowful tale. "By that you mean we're a pack of interfering busybodies."

"Dearest, I would never be so rude."

"You should, because it's true. But not everyone is happy. For some Kendricks, the wounds of the past have yet to fully heal."

"Graeme," Sabrina said. "I can understand how the effect of such losses would linger. But he was caught in a terrible maelstrom of events, none of his making, so why does he feel so responsible?"

"He believes his reckless, rakehell behavior made things worse for the family." Ainsley snorted. "He's not wrong about that. But he was young and desperately unhappy, and that is a bad combination."

Ah. Now it all made perfect sense. "Graeme feels he must atone for past sins."

Ainsley tapped the side of her nose. "On the mark. He

doesn't feel worthy of you and is therefore determined to cut off *his* nose to spite his face."

Sabrina waved her arm, almost knocking over her glass. "It's so ridiculous. I'm nothing special."

"Pet, you are very special, and Graeme knows it. We all know it, which is why we want him to marry you."

"But if he ships me off to England, I'll never see him again." Sabrina scowled. "He'll make sure of it."

"If there's one thing I've learned about Kendrick men, it's that one cannot let them gain the upper hand. You have to control the situation, Sabrina. Show Graeme who's in charge."

"Which means . . . not going back to England?"

Ainsley tilted her head. "Do you wish to go back?"

Sabrina pretended to think about that. "I don't believe so. In fact, I'm quite certain I wish to spend the rest of the summer in Scotland."

"Splendid response."

"There's just one problem. What guarantee do we have that Graeme will remain in Scotland? He could simply pull up stakes and return to London, leaving me here to mope like a silly old thing."

Ainsley's grin was the definition of sly. "One thing Graeme won't do is leave you unprotected. So we'll have to put the dear boy in a position where he'll be forced to protect you—up close, and in a very personal manner."

That sounded rather undignified. Then again, when it came to Graeme Kendrick, Sabrina had misplaced her dignity some time ago.

"How do you suggest we accomplish that?"

"We're going on a trip, Sabrina. You, me, Royal . . . and Graeme."

Chapter Eighteen

The king was on board his yacht and on his way back to London. More important, at least from Graeme's point of view, Sabrina was safely away as well. Not that he'd seen her today or had the opportunity to make a formal good-bye. Apparently, she'd already boarded the boat well before Graeme had arrived at the docks.

He couldn't help scowling as he stalked through the fashionable streets of New Town. For once, Sabrina had avoided him, instead of the other way around, and had done so very effectively these last few days. He'd only caught a glimpse of her at the service of thanksgiving prior to the king's departure, the last official event of the royal visit. Now, she was gone without a word or even a look of farewell.

Not that he blamed her after that ridiculous scene in the drawing room the other night. He'd been a complete ass, and she'd deserved an apology. Still, her departure was for the best. Graeme had no room in his life for such a bonny, sweet lass. And sooner rather than later, she would have concluded he wasn't fit to carry the train of her gown, much less marry her. That realization would have been painful and humiliating for both of them. So, now he'd do his best to forget her and those incredible, passionate kisses that had knocked him off his pins, and get on with his life and the job.

He'd get over her, just like he always got over everything that disturbed the chosen course of his life.

Liar.

He sighed, slowing to a halt as he reached the Kendrick mansion. While it was true that Sabrina had upended his life, he had to admit it had been ripe for disruption. These last few years, his work had filled up all the empty hours and spaces of his life, giving him everything he thought he'd needed. Sabrina had changed that by knocking him off his axis. But in an odd way, she'd also knocked him back on.

Now she was gone, and that was the way it needed to be. *Pull yourself together and get on with it.* He needed a good, dangerous mission to keep his mind from the lass.

As he started up the steps, the door opened, and Grant appeared. "All right, laddie? You're looking a bit fashed."

"Just thinking."

His twin lounged on the doorstep, a sly grin shaping his mouth. "Thinking of anyone in particular? A lady, perhaps?"

Graeme stopped one step below him. "No, and you can sod off with the rest of them if you even mention her name."

For two days, his family had relentlessly pestered him about Sabrina. Nick and Angus had been the worst. His grandfather had sighed gustily, lamenting Sabrina's impending departure and making annoying comments about *missed opportunities* and *love's labour's lost*, whatever the hell that meant. Nick had simply lectured, insisting that Graeme apologize for his rude behavior. Graeme had finally pointed out that Sabrina was avoiding him, so his family could just bugger off and leave him alone.

After that, everyone had.

"All right, then I won't," Grant replied. "Where's Nick?

I thought you went to the docks with him to see the great and glorious departure of our great and glorious king."

"He stopped to see his banker on the way home. I decided to walk and have a think about the next steps on this blasted case. Just because the king is gone, it doesn't mean it's solved."

Actually, Graeme had been in such a foul mood after discovering he wouldn't have a chance to say good-bye to Sabrina that Nick had thrown him out of the carriage. Big brother had suggested that a long walk up the hill might encourage Graeme to cease acting like an addlepated chucklehead.

"Anything useful come to mind?" Grant asked.

"Not really. It's not as if I have anything solid to go on."

"Perhaps you might write to Lady Sabrina's father. His lordship could give some guidance."

"Not a chance. That man can't stand me."

"Then have Aden speak with him."

Graeme snorted. "Lord Musgrave, did you know someone is trying to murder you, or possibly your daughter? Oh, and you might have smugglers on your lands, not to mention you're a wee bastard for evicting your tenants."

"I'm sure Aden can phrase it more elegantly."

"Doesn't matter if he serves it up on a gold platter. Besides, I doubt the old fellow even knows what's going on up at Lochnagar. Man's a complete ninny."

Grant flashed a grin. "That's no way to talk about your future father-in-law."

"I'll toss you down these blasted steps, laddie boy. I'm stronger than you are, don't forget."

His twin relented with a laugh. "Sorry. I shouldn't be ribbing you."

"Especially since yon *Sassenach* has set sail, ye ken," Graeme dryly replied.

"We'll see," Grant cryptically replied.

Graeme frowned. "See what?"

"Never mind. If neither Musgrave nor Aden can help, there's got to be something that will resolve this blasted nonsense."

His twin was holding something back, and that was annoying. They had never held anything back from each other, though that had changed over the last few years.

Graeme had been the one holding back, and from all his family, not just Grant. It felt odd and wrong.

"I'm not sure what to do next," he finally said. "Not something I enjoy admitting."

"Aye, you never like to admit you might be wrong."

"Because I'm never wrong."

Grant rolled his eyes.

"This is different, though," Graeme added. "I swear I can see the answer at the edge of my vision, but when I turn, it's not there."

"Maybe it's not at the edge. Maybe it's right in front of you. And it's not *it*. It's *her*."

"Och, it's bad enough to have both Angus and Nick riding me. I don't need you piling on as well." When his twin raised an incredulous eyebrow, Graeme sighed. "Sorry."

"I always stand with you, no matter what the rest say," Grant said, very seriously.

"I know. Even when I don't deserve it."

"And you don't deserve Lady Sabrina? She clearly has feelings for you. And you just as clearly have feelings for her. That is splendid, if you ask me. Not something to be avoided."

"You know why it won't work," Graeme tersely replied.

Grant blew out an exasperated sigh. "And you know how I feel about this issue. But clearly I have failed to convince you. Which is insulting, since I'm your twin."

"It's not that, ye ken," Graeme gruffly replied. "Your opinion matters the most."

While it was true that Grant knew him better than anyone, it was also true that Grant refused to find any fault in Graeme. Because his brother's love and loyalty was boundless, it made him a bad judge of character when it came to his twin.

"You need to stop punishing yourself for these stupid imaginary crimes," Grant insisted.

"They're not imaginary."

His brother actually began to look annoyed, which took some doing. "If you'd simply talk to Nick or Royal—"

"God, no. They don't need me mewling like a gouty old bachelor."

When a thumping sound came from inside the hall, Grant quickly straightened up. "Royal understands our family better than anyone. And he saw everything, too. I can think of no one better to explain exactly why you deserve to be happy, like the rest of us."

Graeme eyed his twin. "And are you happy?"

"I'm not unhappy, which means I'm in better shape than you."

When another thump sounded from inside, Graeme frowned. "What the hell is going on in there?"

When he started to brush past, Grant held up a hand. "Promise to speak with Royal, will you, laddie?"

Graeme shrugged. "I promise, not that it matters. With any luck, I'll never see Sabrina again."

"Bad luck then, I'm afraid."

"What are—" The words froze on his tongue as a familiar feminine voice, giving orders, of course, floated out to them.

Graeme pushed his smirking twin aside and stalked into the hall, where he encountered an enormous pile of luggage and Lady Sabrina Bell. She was directing two footmen in the proper disposal of trunks and bandboxes.

"What the hell are you still doing here?" he barked.

Sabrina turned to him with a blindingly cheerful smile. "Ah, Mr. Kendrick. Did everything go well at the docks? No problems, I hope?"

"The only problem is that you're not on the bloody yacht with the bloody king."

"Graeme, do stop yelling," Ainsley said as she joined Sabrina.

Both ladies wore carriage dresses, half boots, and plain bonnets, as if garbed for travel. Of course, the mountain of luggage suggested travel was imminent. Just not to England, apparently.

"Why isn't she on the boat?" he asked his sister-in-law.

"Because I am not returning to England," responded the lady herself.

For the first time in his life, Graeme understood the phrase *gnashing one's teeth.* "We talked about this. You cannot be here."

"No, you talked about it. We, in fact, never had that chance."

"Because you've been avoiding me."

Royal appeared from the back hall, also garbed for travel. "What's all the yelling about?"

"It's just Graeme, dear," Ainsley replied. "The usual."

"Of course I'm yelling. And if someone doesn't tell me—"

"You'll what?" Ainsley interrupted. "Storm off in a huff? Then you'll never find out what the plan is."

Graeme shook his head. "You really are a pain in the arse, you know."

She smiled. "It's rather my mission in life when it comes to you, dear boy."

Ignoring her response, Graeme turned back to Sabrina, who studied him with a polite regard. That, naturally, spiked his temper again. Unfortunately, the *Sassenach* was impervious to bluster, yelling, and attempts to intimidate.

He forced himself to mirror her calm attitude. "If it please your ladyship, would you care to tell me why you've remained behind?"

She rewarded him with her sweetest smile. "A civil conversation, then. Finally."

"Not for long, if I don't get some answers."

"We're going on a trip," she said.

"I can see that. Where?"

"To Lochnagar Manor."

Graeme stared at her. "What in the—"

"The carriage is here, Lady Ainsley," said one of the footmen. "Should we start loading up?"

"Yes, please."

Graeme held up both hands. "Nobody is doing anything until I get some answers."

Ainsley waved the footmen over to the pile of luggage. Not surprisingly, the lads jumped. Everyone *always* jumped when it came to Ainsley.

Graeme narrowed his eyes on Sabrina. "Lass?"

"As I said, we're going to Lochnagar Manor. My family's ancestral holdings."

She said it slowly and distinctly, as if he were dim-witted. And at the moment, he felt rather dim-witted. "And why would you be doing something so foolish?"

"There is trouble on my father's estates, and his tenants have suffered as a result. I need to correct that."

Graeme leaned in until he and Sabrina were almost nose to nose. "And have you forgotten the bit about smugglers and someone trying to kill you?"

She responded with a disdainful sniff. "I cannot be swayed by the vague ramblings of Old Bill. It's likely all stuff and nonsense, anyway."

"Well, I can be swayed. And if you had a particle of sense in that pretty head of yours, you would be, too."

Sabrina scowled up at him. "Now, see here—"

Ainsley patted her arm. "Don't even try, pet. When our lad gets into a snit, it's hopeless to try to reason with him. Besides," she said to Graeme, "that's why you're coming with us. You're going to protect Sabrina."

"And I'm going to protect Ainsley," Royal said, comically waggling his eyebrows.

"Finally, big brother weighs in," Graeme said with heavy sarcasm. "Why the bloody hell would you agree to so deranged a plan?"

Royal clapped him on the shoulder. "There's nothing deranged about it. Lady Sabrina wants to visit the ancestral pile, which is completely understandable since she's already here in Scotland. And Ainsley and I thought a nice holiday would be just the ticket."

Graeme could feel his eyeballs practically falling from his skull. "Have you completely lost your wits? And what about your children? Surely you're not suggesting we drag them"—he stepped aside to avoid a footman carrying a teetering pile of bandboxes—"along with us."

"Don't be daft," Angus said as he bustled into the hall. "I'll be stayin' here to look after the wee ones."

Graeme glowered at him. "So you're in on this, too, are you?"

His grandfather scoffed. "Yer seein' plots everywhere. It's simply a wee holiday."

"You're insane," Graeme said before turning back to Royal. "Do you really expect me to believe this nonsense? For one thing, you never leave your children."

His brother looked annoyed. "You know how much we love our children, but it's been years since Ainsley and I have been alone together. I'd say we've earned a bit of a romantic interlude."

His wife dramatically batted her eyelashes. "Very romantic, I'm hoping."

"Count on it, lassie," Royal said with a comic leer.

"Please, you're making me ill," said Graeme.

Angus elbowed him in the ribs. "Ye could take a few lessons in wooin' from yer brother, ye ken."

"Grandda, if you don't shut up, I will toss you out the closest window."

"Fah," Angus replied, curling a lip at him.

Graeme scrubbed his forehead. "Where's Victoria? Surely she and Nick did not agree to this mad plan."

Grant snapped his fingers. "Right, Victoria is having a nap. She said to tell you good-bye and not to worry about anything. And to have fun."

"Are you telling me Nick was in on this?" Graeme exclaimed. "I spent the entire damn morning with him, and he never said a blasted word."

Grant frowned. "Yes, that is rather odd. I wonder why?"

Graeme flashed him a sour look. "Don't even try."

"You could use a little holiday, old boy," Grant quietly said. "You've been working awfully hard these last several months."

"Aye," said Angus. "Yer tetchy. Like a fractious old biddy, ye ken."

Graeme glared at Sabrina. "If you think—"

"Ah, Henderson, there you are," Ainsley interrupted as the butler came down the stairs with a large carpetbag.

"Is that mine?" Graeme demanded.

"I had Henderson pack your things." Ainsley checked her pocket watch. "Now, we really do need to be on our way."

"I do *not* need you making decisions for me, Ainsley."

"Stop blustering, Graeme, or I will box your ears."

"You know she will," Royal said.

Graeme closed his eyes, struggling with his temper. When he opened them, he met Sabrina's gaze.

She was looking a bit crestfallen. Even sad and quite lost, truth to tell. And that made Graeme feel . . . awful.

"It's all right, Mr. Kendrick," she said quietly. "You don't have to come. I'm sure we can manage things on our own."

Graeme whipped off his hat, resisting the temptation to hurl it at the nearest vase. Instead, he scrubbed a hand over his head before turning to address the butler.

"All right, Henderson, you can load up my bag with the rest of the luggage."

"Very good, sir."

"And *you* will do absolutely everything I tell you to do," Graeme sternly said to Sabrina. "Is that clear?"

She nodded. "Yes, Mr. Kendrick."

"Which includes not haring off alone on any mad schemes."

"No mad schemes." Sabrina gave him a tentative smile. "I do think it will be fun. I've always wanted to see the Highlands."

Graeme couldn't even think how to respond. They were riding into God knows what, with no plan and no help. It was the definition of insanity.

Ainsley took Sabrina's arm. "Come along, pet. Our carriage awaits."

As the ladies swept out the door, Royal nudged Graeme. "It will be fun, you know, especially in the company of such lovely ladies."

"It will be the opposite of fun, and you know it."

Angus heaved a dramatic sigh. "Fun is what ye make of it, lad. So start makin' it."

Graeme turned on his heel and stalked out the door.

Chapter Nineteen

The small coaching inn had fallen quiet for the night. With Ainsley and Royal safely ensconced in their room, that meant Sabrina could finally have a frank and private talk with Graeme. It was long overdue, and she wouldn't sleep a wink until she cleared the air between them.

Since their group's departure yesterday, Royal and Ainsley had done their best to maintain sensible and lighthearted conversations. Ainsley had related hilarious stories about the Kendrick family, including escapades by the twins while visiting Canada. It was good-natured and harmless and Graeme hadn't seemed to mind. But he steadfastly refused any attempt to include him. With every mile north, he'd grown increasingly grim and silent.

Still, as Ainsley had predicted, their diabolical plan had worked. Once Graeme had realized that Sabrina was going to Lochnagar, he obviously felt he had no choice but to go with her. He would never leave her unprotected. Sabrina knew that for certain.

Her plan had thus far been a success, but at what cost? Even with her sitting two feet from Graeme in the confines of their traveling coach, he'd felt miles away. Sabrina was beginning to worry that she'd won the battle but lost the war.

In fact, she was beginning to doubt this whole venture—and herself. And doubting herself was a rare and unwelcome feeling.

She tiptoed down the hall to Graeme's door, halting in front of it. She strained to hear any sound at all through the oak panels.

Nothing.

Perhaps she'd waited too long and the dratted man was asleep, worn out from his efforts to avoid her. He'd refused to eat with them, insisting that the ladies and Royal sup upstairs in a private parlor while he remained on guard in the taproom. Sabrina had thought it a ridiculous precaution. No one could have any idea they were on the road. But Graeme had been maddeningly insistent.

After supper, he'd practically barked at her to retire to her bedroom and lock her door. But since it was a lovely evening, she'd instead suggested they take a quiet stroll down one of the nearby country lanes, just to stretch their legs. When he'd reacted with an annoying degree of incredulity, Sabrina had protested that it was much too early for bed.

"Then read a book," Graeme had tersely replied before stalking off to check the locks on the ground floor windows, much to the bemusement of the poor innkeeper and his good wife.

That had been *quite* enough. Sabrina was going north, and if the great spy continued to be such a grump, he could take himself back to Edinburgh forthwith.

She raised a hand to knock when the door suddenly opened. Startled, she jerked back, almost losing her balance. Graeme snaked out a hand to steady her.

"Careful, lass, or you'll fall on your arse."

Sabrina composed herself. "I would never be so clumsy as to fall on my, er . . . as to fall down in so undignified a manner."

He raised a sardonic eyebrow. Really, he had a talent for making her feel like a twit.

He also had a talent for looking splendid, even in his current state of dishevelment. While still dressed in breeches and boots, Graeme had discarded his topcoat and unbuttoned his vest. His shirt was partially open, exposing his throat and a portion of muscled chest. When he propped a forearm on the doorframe and stared down at her, Sabrina's mouth went as dry as a day-old muffin, and her knees as wobbly as blancmange.

Apparently, the sight of such masculine pulchritude disordered her brain, because all she could do was stare like a besotted ninny. How she'd fallen in love with this Highland hellion in so short a time still astonished her.

Of course, why wouldn't a woman fall in love with a hellion who was brave and smart, kind to women and children, and was also *quite* excellent with babies? Sabrina again had a sudden desire to have babies with Graeme—several, if she were lucky.

Amusement sparked in the back of his emerald gaze. Sabrina would have found that annoying but for the delicious smile that curled up the corners of his mouth.

"Is there something I can help you with, my lady?"

She blurted out her first thought. "How did you know I was standing out here? I was very quiet."

"Never mind that. Why the devil are you even up? You should have been asleep ages ago."

"Mr. Kendrick, it is not yet eleven o'clock," she tartly replied. "Hardly the middle of the night."

"We'll be up at the crack of dawn and back on this blasted journey. That is why you need to get your sleep instead of creeping about like a footpad."

"I did not creep. I walked like a perfectly normal person."

"Sabrina, there is nothing remotely normal about you."

She jabbed a finger in the direction of his formidable chest. "Now, see here, sir—"

"No, you see here. You shouldn't be wandering around the halls at night. It's not safe."

"If it's so unsafe, perhaps you'd best let me come in."

All humor gone, his eyes narrowed to slits. "Bad idea."

Sabrina lifted her chin, and they engaged in a staring contest. But after several seconds, it began to feel absurd.

Fortunately, before she felt too ridiculous, floorboards creaked at the end of the hall. Muttering an oath, Graeme pulled her inside and closed the door.

"This is entirely daft," he said. "Not to mention foolhardy and massively inappropriate."

Sabrina folded her hands at her waist, trying to look dignified. "I need to talk to you."

"We can talk in the morning."

"Would you be more disposed to speak with me in the morning? I think not."

"I'm less disposed to speak with you now."

Sabrina put up her hand. "Let me guess. You need to do one more patrol, just to be sure that nonexistent villains are not lurking in the shadows. By the way, even if said villains do exist, they would have no idea we're staying at this particular inn."

"First, they likely do exist. Second, it wasn't my idea to go belting off to the Highlands. That, lass, is on you." He strode past her to the fireplace, grabbed the poker, and began jabbing at the smoldering fire.

Sabrina mentally girded her loins. "Mr. Kendrick, you must desist from such ill-tempered behavior. I find you to be quite the grump, and it's quite annoying."

He straightened up and stared at her in disbelief. "You're annoyed? I'm trying to safeguard you from impending doom, and *you're* annoyed. How the hell do you think I feel?"

She crinkled her nose. "Annoyed?"

He snorted and shook his head, rather like a bull getting ready to charge. And what he would likely do was charge her right out of his room.

She mustered a placating smile. "I admit we were rather assertive in our efforts to persuade you—"

"I believe *dragooned* would be a better term."

"No one dragoons you anywhere, sir. You're the most—" She was about to say pigheaded, but that would likely result in her immediate ejection from his room.

"You were saying, Lady Sabrina?" he asked with sarcastic politeness.

"I was going to say that you are the most strong-willed person I've ever met. I doubt anyone could force you to do anything."

"Except for you, apparently."

He took her arm and steered her to the leather club chair in front of the now cheerily burning fire. He'd obviously stoked it for her comfort.

"All right, lass. Sit yourself down and say your piece."

He retreated a few steps to lean against the fireplace mantel. Still he loomed over her, his broad shoulders, brawny frame, and long legs backlit by the flickering from the grate.

Really, the man was ridiculously impressive. Overpowering, really. And they were alone, in his bedroom. They'd been alone before, but never under such intimate circumstances.

"Well?" he prompted. "What's with the skulking about and the inappropriate nighttime visits?"

Sabrina decided it was a waste of time to be shy with Graeme Kendrick. "I never skulk. As for inappropriate, desperate times call for desperate measures."

He frowned. "What does that mean?"

"We will be arriving at my father's estate tomorrow. I wish to know how you plan to proceed."

His frown deepened into one of puzzlement.

She twirled a hand. "With your investigation, I mean."

"Well," he said, drawing out the word into a long, sardonic syllable, "I rather thought I'd wait until someone tried to kidnap you and then arrest them."

"Can you actually arrest people?" she doubtfully asked.

Graeme rubbed an exasperated hand over his face. "I was joking, Sabrina."

"I knew that."

"You bloody well did not. And I'm hoping we can avoid the kidnapping part—or worse—which is why I objected to this mad venture. It's making me insane to see you keep putting yourself in danger."

Instead of offending her, his words made her flush with pleasure. "I have every confidence we will avoid such calamities."

"I wish I shared your confidence. But we're going in blind. We have no idea of the troubles that could await us."

She also suspected they were walking into a mess, but one that had more to do with her father's neglect than with any real threat to her.

"I know, but I think you worry too much."

"And you don't worry enough."

"I find that it generally does no good. It only makes one grumpy," she pointedly added.

"Sabrina—"

"I have to do this, sir. With or without you."

He tilted his head. "Why?"

"You know why."

They're gazes locked and held with an intensity Sabrina felt in every part of her body. It seemed as if Graeme were trying to read both her mind and her heart. It was disconcerting, and . . . wonderful.

Wonderful because he truly cared about what she thought.

"It's because you're a kind, good lass," he finally said.

"Because you want to make things right. But sometimes you can't make them right, Sabrina, no matter how hard you try."

She suspected that last bit was more about him than her.

"It's still important to try, though," she said. "And besides, I don't think this is one of those times. If there has been mismanagement at Lochnagar, I can fix it. What else am I to do with all this money I have? Father and I are disgustingly rich, you know."

"I do know," he dryly replied.

And it clearly bothered him.

"Then you also know my family is responsible for the people who depend on us for their very well-being. And if my father is not capable of carrying out that responsibility, it falls on me to do it."

"I don't think that's necessarily—"

"Are you suggesting I'm incapable because I'm a woman?"

He scoffed. "You're a force of nature, Sabrina. I pity the man who stands in your way."

"Then don't stand in my way."

"I'm not."

"Yes, you are."

"You are absolutely impossible to argue with." He glowered down at her.

"I'll take that as a compliment."

"Lass—"

"Would Lord Arnprior allow a similar situation on his estate?"

Graeme blew out a frustrated breath. "Of course not. But Nick can take care of himself."

She flashed her most winning smile. "And I have you to take care of me, do I not?"

While he studied her with a narrowed gaze, her heart thumped. Then he finally gave a nod—rather reluctantly, but a nod for all that. It made her shaky with relief.

"Thank you, sir. I am deeply grateful."

He gave her a flourishing bow. "I live to serve, my dear lady."

I hope so.

What she really hoped for was a good-night kiss. How to prompt such a display, however, eluded her.

Graeme started for the door. "It is now officially late, so I'll escort you to your room."

She jumped to her feet. "Wait. There's . . . there's something else we need to discuss."

His sigh was resigned. "Which is?"

Could she really do this?

"Sabrina," he started in a long-suffering voice, breaking the silence.

"I have feelings for you, Graeme."

He froze. For a few seconds, the candles seemed to flicker and grow dim. Sabrina had to resist the urge to squeeze her eyes shut.

"Feelings?" he asked. "As in . . ."

Drat. Why did he have to make *everything* so difficult?

"Yes, feelings, as in emotions. As in the kind men and women have for each other when they . . . like each other. Quite a lot," she defiantly added.

He looked more puzzled than anything else. "I see. And just how do you expect me to respond to that?"

The lass had all but dropped an anvil on his head. Her words certainly had that effect, knocking every sensible thought from his brain.

It was the fault of those blasted feelings she kept talking about. Feelings like the ones that urged him to sweep her up, carry her to the damn bed—which was *right there*—and make love to her. For their entire deranged conversation, he'd been forced to exert every ounce of willpower to keep his hands to himself.

And now, alone in the shadowed intimacy of his bedroom, was she offering herself to him?

He might as well shoot himself and be done with it.

Sabrina blinked, obviously startled by his tepid response—one that had taken every ounce of what little restraint he had left. Then her fine, golden eyebrows snapped together in an imperious scowl. She smartly covered the short distance between them and then jabbed a finger to his chest.

"For one, I would expect you to respond with a degree of courtesy befitting a gentleman."

"Lass, you just propositioned me. I'm rather at a loss."

Her cheeks burned with a bright heat. "I did no such thing. I told you how I feel, and I would expect you to do the same. After all, you have been rather free with your kisses on more than one occasion. Were you, in fact, simply dallying with me?" She sniffed. "That is hardly the behavior of a gentleman."

Now *that* was annoying.

"Let me point out that on at least one of those occasions, *you* kissed me."

"Very well, but you didn't exactly fight me off. You responded with a great deal of enthusiasm, if memory serves."

"Because I am clearly a moron who forgot he was a gentleman. And let that be a lesson to you, I might add."

She blinked again and took a step back. Sabrina no longer looked angry or even imperious. She looked . . . wounded.

And that made Graeme feel like a total blighter. "I'm sorry. That didn't come out right. In case you've failed to notice, I'm not the most eloquent of men."

"Oh, I noticed. And I will add that it's not exactly the

done thing for a woman to profess her feelings. It was horribly difficult. And embarrassing," she added under her breath.

"Och, not for a brave lass like ye," he said, trying to lighten her mood.

Her lips went flat with disapproval.

"Sabrina, what exactly do you want from me?" he asked, feeling at sea.

After staring at the floor for a few moments, she lifted her gaze. It shimmered with a mix of emotions that scared the hell out of him.

"I want to know how you feel about me," she whispered.

He knew he should hustle her right to the door and out of the room. But with the hurt in her eyes and the wee softness in her voice, he couldn't reject her. At least not without explaining why.

"Sit ye down," he said, gently steering her back to the chair.

She grumbled a bit but complied, perching on the edge of the seat as she smoothed her pretty blue skirts over her knees. Her hands trembled, just a bit.

Graeme felt ready to jump out of his skin. His stupid brain—along with his cock—was urging him to take her immediately to bed. That would settle both their nerves in no time.

Instead of giving in to his reckless need for her, he moved back to the fireplace and propped a shoulder against the mantel.

"I wish you wouldn't do that," Sabrina groused.

"Do what?"

She waved a vague finger. "Stand there, looking so . . . so manly. It's distracting."

Graeme bit back a smile. That was the bossy little lass he'd come to love.

His brain tripped.

Love.

Yes, he loved Sabrina, and wasn't *that* a bloody awful turn of events? He'd known it for days, of course, while doing his best to shove the truth into a deep, dark hole. Now her brave declaration had brought the overwhelming feelings right to the surface.

Feelings. The one thing guaranteed to blow up in his face.

"Well?" she asked. "Are you going to just stand there like a sphinx? I am not leaving this room until I get an answer."

"Standing here like a sphinx would be my preferred option. But since you insist, I will admit that of course I have feelings for you, goose. I should think I've already made it obvious enough."

Her mouth twisted sideways a bit. "Well, you haven't. With the exception of those, um, interludes, you've been a complete grump. Does that not suggest the opposite of feelings, at least good ones?"

He leaned forward and braced his hands on his knees, so he and Sabrina were only a few inches apart. "I've got feelings, lass. And they're bloody strong. If you had any idea just how strong, you'd turn tail and run."

Sabrina's lovely blue eyes popped wide, but then she mustered a pert response. "I'd bet you a bob I wouldn't."

He tapped her nose before straightening up. "And I'd lose that bet, God help me."

When a cheeky little smile curled up her mouth, the band of steel around his chest gave way. Sabrina was sunshine itself, joyful and confident by nature. Graeme hated that he made her doubt herself. But she *should* turn tail and run, because he was no damn good for her. And was it even love she felt for him? In her mind, he probably represented some sort of romantic hero, not the deeply flawed man that he really was.

"Well, then," she said, "why have you been so . . ."

"Grumpy?"

She nodded.

"Let me ask you a question first. How do you really know you have deep feelings for me?"

She scrunched up her face. "What sort of ridiculous question is that?"

"There's nothing ridiculous about it. You've been a very sheltered young woman."

"Nonsense. I've been running all my father's households for years. I am no green girl, sir."

"Managing your dear old da does not mean you know what it's like to be in love."

"And you do?"

"Uh . . ." She'd marched him neatly into that corner.

"So, there," she said, rather unnecessarily, he thought.

"Sabrina—"

"Graeme, I know how I feel because I *feel* it."

He frowned. "Feel what?"

"My emotions, you booby. In fact, I'm sure of those feelings because they fail to dissipate even when I'm vastly annoyed with you. Like now."

"You do rather look like you might bash me over the head with the poker."

"It's precisely because I *do* love you that I want to knock some sense into you. If I didn't care so much, it wouldn't matter."

"That doesn't make . . ." He scratched his chin. Actually, it made perfect sense. Graeme frequently wanted to bash his older brothers or toss them out the window, especially when they acted like interfering old biddies. But that didn't mean he loved them any less.

"Graeme, I am not some silly miss just out of the schoolroom. Nor am I drifting about in some romantic Highland dream. Our experiences together have been dreadfully uncomfortable and sometimes quite frightening." Sabrina blew out a frustrated breath. "In fact, there has been a distinct lack of romance."

"Hang on," he couldn't help saying. "That ride in the hackney was romantic."

"You yelled at me. Besides, that hackney smelled like a goat pen."

"But you were fairly enthusiastic about that kiss."

She hesitated before giving him an uncharacteristically shy smile that wrapped silken tendrils around his heart. "It *was* a very nice kiss. Almost as nice as the one at the Caledonian Hunt Ball."

He sighed. "Oh, hell, you're right. We do have feelings for each other."

"And is that such a dreadful thing?"

"It is for me."

Sabrina looked blank for a moment before practically exploding out of her seat. "What a dreadful thing to say, Graeme Kendrick. Take it back!"

"You're not getting my meaning, lass," he protested.

"Then try explaining it to me."

Since she looked ready to grab the poker, Graeme captured her hands. He sucked in a calming breath, trying to find the right words but finding himself distracted by her delicious scent. She reminded him of wildflowers and honey, and a summer day in the Highlands. Everything about her muddled his brain.

"Sabrina, it doesn't matter how I feel, because what I feel isn't . . . isn't right. You are the sweetest, prettiest, nicest girl in England, and I would give you the world if I could."

"I already have quite enough of the world," she responded in a surly tone. "What I need is you."

"But that's the problem. I'm not good enough for you." He tried to muster a wry smile. "These days, I'm barely good enough for anything, much less such a bonny lass."

She went from surly to soft in an instant. "Graeme Kendrick, you are a perfectly wonderful man. Why would you say such a thing?"

"I'm afraid you don't know enough about me."

"I know that you're kind, brave, and intelligent. You care about the innocent and the helpless, and you will do anything to protect them, even risking your own life."

Such extravagant praise made him uncomfortable. "Och, ye'll nae be turning me into a hero."

"But you—"

"It's my job, Sabrina. Which brings me to another point. My work is dangerous, and I refuse to put you in harm's way."

"In this case, I believe I'm the one putting you in danger."

When he opened his mouth to refute her statement, she lifted a sardonic brow.

"You are incredibly annoying," he said, gently pressing her back into her seat. Much easier to think when he wasn't touching her.

"Ha, so I'm right," she replied.

"Only in this case. The type of work I do—"

She twirled a hand. "Yes, it can be dangerous, but Aden and Vivien manage it. Surely there are other spies who get married."

"I'm not a spy," he automatically said.

"Then there's not a problem, is there?" she sweetly replied.

She was running rings around him. She was right that there were any number of agents who had families. Most of them had retired, however, or gone into other work. But he knew he was good at what he did—better than good—and he couldn't think of a damn thing he could do with his life except . . .

Marry Sabrina.

"Your da is one," he said. "He hates me. I'm Scottish *and* a younger son. With not a shilling to my name, in fact."

"You have a perfectly respectable competence, care of your two older brothers. Not to mention the income from your work."

"Who the hell told you that?"

"Ainsley, of course."

He was truly going to have to murder his sister-in-law.

"It's hardly a fortune. Not up to your father's standards by a long shot."

"It's not up to my father. And I have money enough for the both of us."

"Sabrina—"

She pulled a face. "Why did I have to fall in love with the one man who isn't a fortune hunter—in fact, who holds my fortune against me?"

"I don't hold your fortune against you."

"You do. It makes you feel unequal, or not as good in some stupid way."

It did, but he could get over it because she was worth it. What he couldn't get over . . .

"Sweetheart, I'm not worthy of you. There are things I've done, things that can never be undone."

She shook her head. "I don't understand."

"I have blood on my hands. Blood that can never be washed off."

"You mean you've killed people."

He nodded, hating to even say it.

"Bad people?"

He snorted. "I generally make it a point not to kill good people."

"Then what is the problem?"

The problem was one he couldn't put into words, especially not to her.

After several seconds of fraught silence, Sabrina came to her feet. Damned if she wasn't studying him like a specimen under glass.

"So, the answer must be that you are a coward, afraid of a wee *Sassenach*. Even worse, afraid of her father, an elderly hypochondriac." She sighed. "I must admit to feeling disappointed, after all the buildup. Highlanders are apparently all flash and no bang, rather like a squib gone awry."

He narrowed his gaze. "So, it's ferocious you want, is it?"

She curled her lip in a delicate little sneer. Even though Graeme knew she was baiting him, it worked. That blasted *Sassenach* sneer worked.

"Aye, then ye'll have it."

She squeaked when he yanked her against his chest. But when he tipped up her chin and took her mouth in a decidedly ferocious kiss, Sabrina enthusiastically threw herself into the spirit of things. So enthusiastically that when she flung her arms around his neck, Graeme stumbled back into the mantel.

"Oh, oh, sorry," she gasped. "Are you all right?"

"Stop talking."

He held her jaw while he devoured the most luscious set of lips this side of Hadrian's Wall. After a few moments, he was convinced they were the most luscious lips south of the wall, too. She lured him in with a siren's call he could no longer resist.

Graeme had been resisting her for weeks. Now she was finally in his arms, kissing him like mad, ravishing him with a sweet, sensual urgency. Aye, she was a treasure, one he longed to claim.

So, claim her.

He let a hand drift down to her arse, gently squeezing her. Those curves were so delicious that he cupped her with both hands, kneading her pretty bottom as he nudged her with his rapidly burgeoning cock.

Sabrina swayed, as if unsteady on her feet.

Too much, you idiot.

Mentally sighing, he forced himself to ease off. Sabrina

sank back on her heels, resting her head on his chest as she sucked in a shaky breath.

"All right, love?" he murmured as he cuddled her.

She looked up, a wavering smile parting her kiss-swollen lips. He'd been a wee bit *too* ferocious, it seemed. But Sabrina was temptation beyond all earthly reason.

"Just a little wobbly in the knees." She curled her hands into his shirt. "I hope you don't mind if I hold on to you. It's all a bit . . . overwhelming."

It killed him to say it, but he did. "Lass, should I stop?"

"Graeme Kendrick, I practically had to hold a dirk to your throat to get you to kiss me. Why would I want you to stop?"

He raised his eyebrows.

"We're simply kissing," she said with an exasperated sigh. "There's no need to be squeamish because I got wobbly."

"I beg your pardon, my lady."

He cast a quick glance over his shoulder at the bed.

Bad idea.

However . . . "I think I have a solution for your wobblies."

She perked up. "Yes?"

Letting her go, he strolled to the club chair and settled into it, shifting to accommodate the now-massive erection straining against the fall of his breeches.

Sabrina stalked over, looking adorably stern. "And what am I supposed to do, pray tell?"

"This."

He wrapped his hands around her waist, picked her straight up, and plopped her onto his lap. She squawked, landing in a bit of a sprawl. Graeme carefully positioned her to straddle his thighs, which hiked up her gown and brought her pretty breasts to his eye level.

Even more delightfully, her round backside was now snug against his erection, with nothing between them but the fall of his breeches and her thin gown. The temptation to slip a hand under that gown and play with her dainty feminine flesh was, again, almost irresistible.

He would resist that, at least for now. But the thought of her tight channel clenched around him was so enticing that he flexed his hips, nudging against her once more. He couldn't hold back a groan as her bottom pressed onto his cock.

Sabrina's eyes popped wide. "My . . . my goodness."

Graeme trailed a hand down to her thigh to play with the top of her garter. "Does this position take care of your wobbly knees?"

Her laugh was shaky. "Not really, but at least I won't collapse onto the floor."

"I'm hoping you're going to collapse on me."

He gently cupped her chin and brought her down for a kiss. With a happy sigh, Sabrina draped her arms around his shoulders and nestled close. Her mouth was honey and heat, and Graeme knew he could spend hours just kissing her.

But right now he had other plans, ones that included her breasts. To his way of thinking, it was long past time he got a good look at them.

When he gently bit her lower lip, she wriggled her delicious bottom, which did tremendous things for his erection. Leaving her mouth, he nibbled his way along her delicate jawline, gently nudging up her chin as he moved down her throat.

He paused to kiss and lick the tender hollow where her pulse fluttered. When she swayed, he slipped an arm behind her back to hold her steady. With his other hand, he gently tugged on her bodice. The tops of her breasts plumped up over the lace trim, delicious treats ripe for his mouth.

And just below that trim were her nipples. Already stiff, they pertly thrust against the fabric of her stays.

"Och, lass," he murmured. "That's the prettiest sight a man could ever see."

When he curled a hand around her breast, Sabrina let out a sweet whimper that turned into a moan when he tweaked her nipple through the layers of clothing. God, she was responsive. He couldn't wait to get her naked and underneath him.

She dug her nails into his shoulder. "Oh, Graeme!"

He rubbed his palm back and forth across the tight point. "Does that feel good, my darling girl?"

When she gave a frantic little nod and again wriggled her bottom, Graeme felt a lascivious grin curl up his lips. He tilted her back over his arm. Her breasts popped out even more, both nipples almost fully in view.

Bending over her, Graeme dragged his mouth over her plump curves. He dipped his tongue beneath the trim of her bodice to lick the taut point of one of her nipples.

Sabrina trembled in his arms. "Oh, oh," she gasped.

She clamped a hand to the back of his head, keeping his face nestled against the swell of her breasts. Graeme could hardly breathe, but it was a sacrifice he was more than willing to make.

He'd hooked his fingers into the top of her bodice, about to tug it fully down, when a knock sounded on the door.

"Laddie, are you awake?"

Sabrina jerked in shock, toppling sideways. Graeme caught her as she instinctively flung out an arm, hitting the small table next to the chair. It crashed to the floor, along with the branch of candles and a half glass of whisky.

Royal banged again. "Graeme!"

"Oh, God," Sabrina gasped. "Don't let him come in."

"Royal, stay—"

His brother barged into the room.

"What the—" Royal stopped dead. "Oh, hell."

Graeme kept a firm hold on Sabrina as she started to scramble off his lap.

She swatted at him. "Let go."

"You'll fall on your arse if I do."

"I will do no such thing," she huffed.

After Graeme set Sabrina on her feet, she turned and glared at Royal. "And you, sir, should not barge into rooms without permission."

"My apologies, Lady Sabrina," he dryly responded. "All that crashing about gave me the wrong impression. I feared someone was attacking my brother."

"Someone was attacking your brother," Graeme said as he stood. "Quite nicely, I might add."

"Honestly," Sabrina huffed.

"Sweetheart, you might want to . . ." Graeme pointed at her disheveled bodice.

She glanced down at herself and let out a horrified squawk. Turning her back, she went about setting herself to rights.

"What are you doing here, anyway?" Graeme asked his brother.

"I was just checking on you." Royal narrowed his gaze. "And not a moment too soon, apparently."

"Mr. Kendrick and I were simply discussing the arrangements for our arrival at Lochnagar Manor," Sabrina tossed over her shoulder.

"And you both had to sit in the same chair to do so?" Royal asked.

"That was an accident," Sabrina said.

Graeme pressed a hand to his mouth, trying to stifle a chuckle.

"Don't you dare laugh," she threatened, turning around to glare at him.

"Indeed, my lady," said Royal. "This is hardly a laughing matter."

"Well, maybe just a little bit," Graeme said.

For a moment, he thought Sabrina would belt him, but she stalked right past him.

"Good night, Mr. Kendrick," she snapped at Royal. "In the future, I suggest that you wait to be invited into a room."

She stormed out.

"She has a point," Graeme said. "You do have an unnerving tendency to barge in at the most inconvenient times."

His brother righted the table. "You must be thinking of Angus. Besides, it would appear my timing was excellent. Not that I blame you, but that was not the way to go about it, lad."

Graeme closed the door. Now that Sabrina was gone, he felt deflated—in more ways than one.

Even worse, he was ashamed to have embarrassed the sweet girl and put her in such a dodgy position. "Royal, what are you doing here? It's almost midnight."

"Ainsley was worried about you."

Graeme retrieved the candlestick and picked up the glass, which had managed not to break. Sad waste of whisky, though. He could use a dram.

Or ten.

"Worried she's not driving me completely insane?"

Royal sat on the padded bench on the other side of the fireplace and absently rubbed his thigh.

"Ainsley loves you and worries about you, Graeme. We all do."

That made his heart pinch, so he decided to ignore it. "Is your leg all right? I knew this trip would be too much for you."

"My leg is fine, and stop trying to change the subject."

"I don't even know what the subject is, so how can I change it?"

His brother rolled his eyes. "Idiot."

"That does seem to be the general opinion around here."

"You do realize you're going to have to marry the lass now."

Graeme scowled. "But nothing happened."

Royal ticked up an eyebrow.

"Well, nothing much."

"Nothing much is more than enough."

"Not if you keep your blasted mouth shut. You can be sure I won't be blabbing about it, and neither will Sabrina."

"Sure about that, are you?"

Graeme frowned. "Why would she say anything?"

"Because you love each other?"

Graeme shook his head. "In this case, it's not a good enough reason."

"You mean that *you're* not good enough," Royal gently corrected. "Or so you think."

Those words clawed at his guts. Graeme sank into the club chair, struggling to manage his emotions. It was hellishly hard, because a hint of wildflowers and passion still lingered around him.

"I know I'm not," he tersely replied.

"You don't know a bloody thing. Of course you're good enough for Sabrina. Why you fail to see that is beyond me. Whatever minor sins you've committed are long in the past."

"Not according to—" Graeme bit off the words.

"According to our father?" Royal quietly finished.

"They weren't minor sins, either, as our esteemed parent made clear."

Royal frowned. "What are you talking about?"

"About Mother. It was partly because of me that she . . ." Again, he couldn't say the words.

"What?"

"That she died."

Graeme winced at the stunned expression on his brother's face, then looked away. But at least the secret was finally out. He'd promised Grant that he would speak with Royal and tell him the truth. He'd kept to his promise, and the deed was done.

All that now remained was for the final blow to fall.

"Graeme, look at me," Royal said.

When he reluctantly met his brother's gaze, he saw only compassion and affection.

"That's errant nonsense, laddie," Royal said. "Please explain to me how a little child was responsible for Mamma's death."

"I was a hellion. Even as a lad, I caused trouble."

"We all did."

"Not like me."

Royal scoffed. "Have you met our brother, Logan?"

"You know I was the worst." Now that he'd pulled down the dam, it all wanted to come out, like an ugly, raging torrent. "Mamma was delicate. She needed peace and quiet. She didn't need a little bastard cutting up the peace and causing trouble. And that's exactly what I did. It was a strain on her nerves and on her health."

"Father actually told you that?"

Graeme thought back to that horrific night. He had been seven, and it had been a few weeks after Mamma's death. He'd cried himself to sleep, then awakened from a nightmare. He'd turned to Grant, seeking comfort. But his twin, who'd barely been able to sleep for days, ill with grief, was finally slumbering. Graeme had found his little robe and had gone to look for his grandfather. But Angus wasn't in his room, so Graeme had wandered about until finding himself in the library.

Where his father sat, disheveled and bleary-eyed, behind his desk.

Father had always been a tower of strength, a laird and clan chief who never wavered from duty. But on this night, he'd seemed just a weary old man, riven with sorrow. Graeme had wanted to comfort his da and receive comfort in return.

Instead, the earl had unleashed a verbal hammering so ugly it had nailed Graeme to the floor. It only ended when Angus rushed into the room. After exchanging a few sharp words with Father, Angus had swept Graeme into his arms and taken him up to bed. He'd tucked him in and stayed by his side, holding his hand until he fell asleep.

From then on Angus had appointed himself Graeme's special protector, never again mentioning what had happened that awful night.

"Laddie?" Royal's gentle prompt brought Graeme back to the present.

"Father told me exactly that." He tried to sound like he didn't care.

Royal leaned forward, his gaze intent. "Listen to me, Graeme. Our father was a stern man, but a good one. But after our mother died, he became as angry and bitter as arsenic. He fell into a whisky bottle and never climbed out. And his anger poisoned *everyone*."

"Not Nick."

"Even him. That's why Nick wanted Angus at Kinglas. We needed someone to love us, and that was Grandda."

"But I was—"

"Did you know Father also blamed Kade for Mamma's death?"

That was another punch to the gut. Poor, wee Kade had barely survived the birthing and had then been robbed of his mother.

"That's insane," Graeme said.

"As insane as blaming a little boy like you for her death."

Graeme frowned into the peat fire. His brother patiently waited him out.

"But before that," Graeme finally said, "Father claimed I drove Mamma crazy with my antics. Said I was too much for her."

Royal snorted. "We all got that lecture, especially poor Logan. Father tore a strip off him on a regular basis."

"I . . . I don't remember that."

"You were very young. And I think you've forgotten the way things were before our mother died."

"Like what?" Graeme cautiously asked.

"Like who taught you to ride?"

His father.

"And how to fish."

"Father," he slowly said.

"And how were those times? Did he act like you were a burden then?"

Graeme reached through the haze of time and sorrow to recover those moments. He remembered the praise from his father when he tied his first lure and caught his first pike. He remembered the rides on his little pony, Father patiently teaching him how to properly jump a fence. Memories lurked in that haze. Dim, but there.

"No, they were . . . nice times."

"Father wanted us to be good men, good Highlanders. You were a bit of a challenge, so he was harder on you, although not as hard as he was on Logan. But Father loved us, laddie, in his own way. He truly did."

"I guess I'd forgotten that."

"There have been many rough years since, Graeme. It's a wonder we can remember any good times."

Graeme gazed at his brother, the kindest man he'd ever known. Royal had given up so much for his family. "*You* remember."

"I'm too stubborn to forget. And what I also haven't forgotten is how much Mamma loved you." Royal stood and pressed a hand to Graeme's shoulder. "You were never a burden to her, my boy. Our mother loved us with all her heart and soul. That was her gift to the family. Do not dishonor her memory by thinking otherwise."

He winced. "That's what I've been doing, is it?"

"Aye, and running away from the rest of us." Royal snorted. "All this spy business, lad. Time to give it up, ye ken."

Graeme scowled, grateful for the chance to shove down the emotions that were choking him. He felt like he'd been drowning in bloody feelings since Sabrina had bulled her way into his room.

"It's what I'm good at, ye ken," he sarcastically replied. "What else can I do?"

"Sabrina might have a suggestion or two."

"Oh, sod off."

Royal laughed and headed for the door. "Actually, I'm off to bed. Dawn will come early, followed by another spectacular day on these deplorable Highland roads."

"This mad scheme wasn't my idea, remember?"

His brother paused, a hand on the doorknob. "One more thing."

Graeme rolled his eyes. "Yes?"

"You're good enough for anyone, including Lady Sabrina."

Chapter Twenty

Sabrina winced as they rattled through another patch of dreadful road on the approach to Lochnagar Manor. Even their well-sprung carriage couldn't smooth out the ride on lanes more suited to donkey carts.

Graeme peered out the window into the darkening gloom. "I see a stone gate up ahead. Looks like the entrance to a courtyard."

Ainsley, leaning against her husband's shoulder, sat up with a grimace. "Thank God. My backside has been screaming at me for hours."

"You'll feel better after a nice bath," Royal said. "Then I'll give you a soothing massage, if such treatment is necessary."

"Darling, your massages tend to be rather more stimulating than soothing," Ainsley flirtatiously replied.

Royal winked at her. "Exactly."

"You two are revolting," Graeme said.

"Ridiculous. We're simply an old married couple," Ainsley said. "Not even remotely revolting."

Graeme cast Sabrina a sideways glance. "Her ladyship might think otherwise."

"Oh, I've been too busy reading my book to notice anything out of the ordinary," Sabrina replied in a bright voice.

She had no intention of appearing a buttoned-up prude, especially not in front of Graeme.

"You might try to spare my blushes," Graeme complained to his brother. "You know how shy I am about this sort of thing. A veritable babe in the woods."

Sabrina started to laugh but bit her tongue when the carriage hit another enormous hole. She almost slid off the seat.

Graeme latched on to her. "Hang on, lass. Don't want ye hurtin' yerself."

"Thank you," she breathlessly said, righting herself.

He let her go as the coachman slowed down after the horrific bump.

"Best keep hold of her, Graeme dear," Ainsley said with a twinkle. "These roads are dreadful."

"I should be happy to hold on to her as long as required," Graeme said, "but I believe we're at the gates of Lochnagar Manor."

"You're no fun," Ainsley said.

Graeme snorted. "I am devastated to hear that."

Ainsley rolled her eyes. "We're on holiday. Remember?"

"Is that what we're calling it?"

Sabrina mentally sighed. Graeme's mood had considerably improved since that exciting interlude in his bedroom, but he'd still not mentioned a word about it. Although, when she'd come down for breakfast, he'd pulled out her chair and given her a wink before fetching her tea and scones. It was a remarkable change from his previous attitude.

The carriage passed under a high stone arch into a spacious courtyard. When they came to a halt, Sabrina tried to get a look at the manor house through the gathering dusk.

Graeme's smile was encouraging. "Ready to survey your domain, my lady?"

"As ready as I'll ever be."

"I'm ready to sleep in a hut," Ainsley said, "if it means getting out of this blasted carriage."

"You in a hut. I'd love to see that," Graeme said.

When Ainsley stuck her tongue out, Sabrina laughed. And suddenly she was incredibly grateful that Ainsley, Royal, and Graeme had come with her on this mad journey.

"I know this is a dodgy situation," Sabrina impulsively said, "but I'm so happy you're all here. Thank you."

Ainsley patted her knee. "Wouldn't miss it for the world, pet."

Graeme winked at her. "We'll get it sorted, lass. Dinna fash yerself."

She smiled at his teasing, then glanced out the window. "What's taking so long?"

Royal started to open the door of the carriage. "I don't— ah, Bobby, there you are," he said to the groom. "What's amiss?"

"There's nary a light on in the place, Mr. Royal. Looks right deserted."

"That can't be right," Sabrina said. "Our Edinburgh business agent sent an express to the housekeeper. They should be expecting us."

"We'll check it out," Graeme said. "You ladies stay here."

"I refuse to stay in this coach a second longer." Ainsley squeezed past her husband to take Bobby's hand and hop down.

Rolling his eyes, Royal followed his wife out of the carriage.

Graeme eyed Sabrina.

She sighed. "If you want me to wait in here, I will."

After all, she had promised to follow his orders.

"Och, with Ainsley stomping about, you might as well get out. If there are any lurking villains, hopefully they'll shoot her first."

"I heard that," Ainsley called. "You beast."

Sabrina smothered a chuckle as Graeme helped her down to the uneven stones of a central courtyard.

"Careful, lass," he said, keeping a hand under her elbow.

When she smiled up at him, his gaze had turned smoky with heat. Sabrina's breath caught in her lungs.

He bent his head close. "I've been thinkin' about last night too, ye ken."

Goodness. Perhaps there was hope for them yet.

"Graeme, stop mooning at Sabrina and go knock on the door," Ainsley ordered.

"I thought we wanted them to moon at each other," Royal said.

Sabrina couldn't help wincing. As matchmakers, Royal and Ainsley were as subtle as fireworks on the king's birthday.

Graeme scowled at his brother. "You go knock on the door. I'm going to scout around the back of this bloody building and see if there's any sign of a working stable. If not, we'll have to head back to that village."

"If that was a village, I'm the Queen of Sweden," Ainsley commented.

"I wish you were in Sweden," Graeme retorted as he headed toward the corner of the manor house.

"Ha, ha. Very amusing," Ainsley called after him.

"It won't be very amusing to go back to that village," Royal said as he started across the courtyard.

"It seemed almost as deserted as this place," Ainsley remarked.

"Dunlaggan isn't really a village, from what I understand," Sabrina said. "More of a hamlet."

Only a few miles from Lochnagar Manor, Dunlaggan was just a small collection of cottages and shops along one main street, with a small town square and a church with a vicarage. It had taken but a few minutes to travel through it, and they'd barely seen anyone. A few curtains had twitched in windows, and she'd seen one elderly gentleman hobbling along with his dog. He'd cast a suspicious glance at the carriage, then accelerated with surprising speed to disappear into the lone pub.

"I must say that your manor house is quite splendid," Ainsley said. "A bit rundown but still impressive."

Sabrina drew in a calming breath, gazing over the vista north of the house. This was her mother's childhood home, where Mamma had roamed the gardens and glens and lived in sight of the craggy, dramatic Highlands. Something quietly sorrowful stirred just behind Sabrina's breastbone. If Mamma had lived, Sabrina's life would have been so different.

She turned to see Royal mounting the imposing stone staircase that led up to the massive front door, set between matching turrets. Lochnagar Manor was a classic tower house, built with sturdy blocks of multicolored stone. Though the building was simple and almost stark, the stone and architecture blended in a pleasing symmetry in keeping with the windswept landscape.

Unfortunately, it also looked deserted. Its unlit windows showed no signs of life inside. Sabrina's heart sank. Had she made a dreadful mistake after all?

Ainsley pressed her shoulder. "Hang on, old girl. The lads will sort it out."

As Royal banged on the door, the other coach carrying Hannah, one of the Kendrick footmen, and the baggage, rumbled into the courtyard.

"We'd best not unload anything," Sabrina said, "until we're certain someone is actually here to let us in."

"Royal and Graeme will get in, and we can always chop up the furniture and use it for fuel and huddle in front of the fireplace. Won't that be romantic?"

"Very romantic. Especially when we have nothing to eat or drink."

Her friend crinkled her nose.

Royal glanced over his shoulder. "Sorry, ladies. There doesn't seem to be—"

A creaking of hinges cut him off, and the massive oak door swung open. An elderly woman stood in the doorway, neatly dressed in a gray gown with a tartan shawl draped over her shoulders and tucked into a belt, from which hung a large set of keys.

"Apologies, sir. I was in the back of the house." She looked past him, and her eyes widened. "Are ye my Lady Sabrina's party?"

"Unless you were expecting another group of interlopers to descend upon you," Royal wryly said.

When the poor woman eyed him with alarm, Sabrina hurried to the bottom of the steps. "Are you the housekeeper? I am Lady Sabrina."

The woman gave a stiff curtsy before coming down the steps to greet her. "Aye, my lady. I'm Mrs. Wilson. I'm that sorry, but ye caught us at sixes and sevens."

"But my father's business manager sent an express post, informing you of our arrival. I do hope there's no problem."

"I only got the missive yesterday, my lady. And we've nae had visitors in ever so long, so we're shorthanded." She grimaced. "We're always shorthanded, sad to say. We'll do our best, but the house is a wee bit rough at the moment."

"As long as there's a hot bath and plenty of whisky, I'll be fine," Ainsley cheerfully interjected.

Mrs. Wilson's thin features wrinkled up like a spider's web. "Ah . . ."

Ainsley sighed. "Please tell us that you at least have the whisky."

"That we have, and plenty of it," Mrs. Wilson replied in an oddly morose tone.

"Never mind the baths for now," Sabrina said. "I presume you have enough rooms to accommodate us."

"Aye, but they're not ready, my lady. Many of the rooms

have been closed up since the death of yer grandparents. We've not had visitors since then."

Sabrina blinked. That had been over fifteen years ago. No wonder the poor woman was so unprepared.

"We'll adapt," she said. "Our servants can help, and Mrs. Kendrick and I will assist you in getting organized and preparing the rooms."

"Oh, huzzah," Ainsley sardonically remarked.

Hannah, who'd climbed out of the second coach and was standing next to Ainsley, heaved a dramatic sigh.

"We'll talk later about how many servants are required," she said to the housekeeper. "I'm sure we could hire some from Dunlaggan?"

Mrs. Wilson looked cryptic. "Maybe."

While Sabrina had not expected trumpets and banners, this reception seemed downright bizarre. Something was wrong, and she intended to find out exactly what that something was.

But first they needed to unload and settle in as best they could before dark fell completely.

"Mrs. Wilson, are the stables able to accommodate—"

"I've got it sorted," said Graeme as he strode back into the courtyard.

Scurrying behind him was an eager lad of about twelve, dressed in baggy breeches and a smock. Shuffling in their wake was an elderly fellow in a leather jerkin and boots, calmly puffing a battered clay pipe.

"Mr. Wilson, there ye be," the housekeeper said with relief. "Her ladyship has arrived."

"I've got eyes to see, wife. Not to mention yon fella there." He jabbed his pipe in Graeme's direction. "He's been barkin' orders since he showed up."

"They only received our express yesterday," Sabrina said to Graeme. "It's not their fault."

"Believe me, those stables won't be ready for days," he

replied in a grim tone. He looked to Bobby. "Can you help Mr. Wilson and . . ."

"Brian, sir," the young lad chirped up.

Graeme nodded. "Bobby, after we've unloaded, please help the lad and Mr. Wilson get the horses settled for the night."

"Aye, Mr. Kendrick."

Graeme glanced at Mrs. Wilson. "Do you have any footmen?"

"Nae, sir."

Sabrina blinked. "Not even one?"

"Any maids? Cooking staff?" Graeme tersely said. "Any staff at all?"

Mrs. Wilson's mouth puckered up, as if the question posed a problem without an answer. "It's nae easy to hire servants in these parts. I do most of the cookin', and we have a scullery maid. And a Dunlaggan girl helps when needed. She's comin' tomorrow to tidy the bedrooms and wait on the ladies."

"We're going to need more help than that," Ainsley said, casting a glance at the growing pile of luggage Bobby and the footman were unloading.

Sabrina felt rather overwhelmed, and she *never* felt that way. There might not be family in residence, but there was still a manor house and grounds to be maintained. According to their business manager, the estate was still turning a profit, so there should have been more than enough resources for general upkeep. Unfortunately, Father's former business manager had retired only two months ago at the venerable age of eighty-five, leaving an unorganized mess in his wake for the new manager to sort out.

Graeme muttered a curse. "All right, we'll help our men unload the carriages. Hannah can help Mrs. Wilson get our rooms ready, while Lady Sabrina and Ainsley start assessing what we'll need to survive in this benighted place."

Ainsley let out a ladylike snort. "Well, aren't you the bossy one?"

That simply deepened his scowl.

Oh, dear. Grumpy Graeme had reappeared. And he *was* being rather bossy. Then again, he was a man who was good at giving orders, especially in difficult situations. Sabrina could sympathize, because she liked to give orders, too.

"Let's hope it's not benighted," she said. "In fact, it looks like a splendid old place. I can't wait to see the rest of it."

"I've seen the necessaries and the rooms at the back of the house," Graeme tartly replied. "And there is nothing splendid about them."

Mrs. Wilson brightened. "The ladies will nae be havin' to be usin' the necessaries. We have indoor water closets, put in just before my lady's grandfather passed. Although they've nae been cleaned in several a year," she added.

Hannah let out a quiet moan, and even Ainsley looked a bit daunted.

"We'll worry about that later," Sabrina said. "It's getting quite dark, and I don't want anyone tripping while unloading the carriages."

"If it's dark, at least no one can shoot at us," Ainsley joked.

Mrs. Wilson, who seemed to have a penchant for alarm, looked exceedingly rattled. "That is nae laughin' matter, ma'am. There be bad folk in these parts."

"And you and I are going to talk about that, Mrs. Wilson," Graeme said, "as soon as we get everyone inside and settled."

Sabrina decided it was time to reassert control. "Mr. Kendrick, I am the owner of Lochnagar Manor, and I will—"

"Bully for ye, lass. Now, get yerself inside before I dump ye over my shoulder and carry ye in."

She bristled. "*Mr.* Kendrick—"

He pointed a finger toward the door. "Now."

"You too, Ainsley," Royal ordered.

"Men," his wife replied in a disgusted voice before following the housekeeper up the stairs.

Sabrina glowered at Graeme, who was decidedly unimpressed by her show of defiance. Then she headed up the stairs and through the front door, Hannah trailing morosely in her wake.

They found themselves in a massive, circular hall lit by one branch of candles. It looked positively haunted in the dim light. Sabrina swore she could hear the leathery rustle of batwings up in the eaves.

Ainsley propped her hands on her hips and eyed the cold, uninviting space. "Well, this is quite . . . something."

"That's one way to describe it," Sabrina replied.

Hannah crowded close, as if expecting howling ghosts to jump out of the shadows.

"I hate Scotland, my lady," she moaned. "It's something awful."

At the moment, Sabrina could not bring herself to disagree.

Chapter Twenty-One

Sabrina looked up from her lists, as she basked in the sunlight streaming through the east-facing windows of the family dining room. It was the first truly bright day since their arrival.

And the first moment she didn't feel run off her feet.

Although truly a splendid house, Lochnagar had been woefully neglected. For three days, they'd all been working almost without pause to make the manor habitable. Sabrina had the distinct impression Mrs. Wilson was still surprised that they'd decided to remain. The woman obviously had great affection for Lochnagar and had done her best for the old place, but it was clear she had yet to trust Sabrina. As Lord Musgrave's daughter, Sabrina was the source of many of the estate's problems from the housekeeper's point of view.

Father likely had no idea how bad the circumstances were, since he'd relied so heavily on his former business manager and various estate stewards to handle the work. Those gentlemen had much to answer for, including years of willful mismanagement.

Much to Sabrina's extreme surprise, Lochnagar no longer even had an estate steward. According to Mrs. Wilson, the latest one had lasted for less than a year and had decamped six weeks ago, without explanation. There were mysterious circumstances that the rest of the staff refused to discuss.

It was much the same with the servants hired from the hamlet, a remarkably stubborn and reticent group of Scots. That they didn't trust Sabrina wasn't surprising, but they'd been equally close-mouthed when Graeme and Royal had tried to elicit information.

The answers to the problems of Lochnagar remained frustratingly elusive.

Graeme and Royal had been riding the estate and speaking with tenants, both to ascertain the damage done to the land and to sniff out potential nefarious deeds. So far, they'd come up empty when it came to such deeds.

Sabrina went to the mahogany sideboard and poured a cup of tea from the French silver tea service. The sideboard, a handsome piece of furniture from the Queen Anne period, had seen better days. The tea service, however, had been jealously guarded by Mrs. Wilson and was in good condition.

The small dining parlor was one of the nicest rooms in the house with an old-fashioned beauty enhanced by carved oak paneling. The woodwork throughout the manor was in generally excellent condition, as were the timbered ceilings and much of the plasterwork. The views were magnificent too, especially on the east side. Sabrina could gaze out over the glens to a small loch glittering in the distance.

The formal dining room, by contrast, was cavernous and grim, with its old-fashioned furniture and faded portraits of gloomy ancestors. The exception was a portrait of her mother, a sweet painting of a golden-haired, laughing girl in a riding habit. Sabrina had been forced to blink back tears when she first spotted it.

Graeme, who'd accompanied her on that first tour of the house, had handed her a handkerchief. "Silly to have such a bonny lass stuck in with these gloomy guts," he'd said.

He'd then plucked the painting from the wall and carried

it to Sabrina's bedroom, hanging it over the small fireplace. His thoughtfulness had made her cry a bit, too, although she'd had the sense to do that after he'd left the room.

Returning to her seat, Sabrina once more tackled her seemingly endless lists of linens, and inventories of plate, crystal, and silver. It would take her weeks to sort it all out. But those lists were a small part of the myriad of problems confronting her—including what would happen with Graeme. He'd taken to avoiding her again, which was more than a little vexing.

When the door opened and Ainsley walked in, Sabrina smiled, grateful for the respite from her work.

"I suppose it's too much to ask for coffee," Ainsley said, going to the sideboard. "I would kill for a strong cup of coffee."

"I put in a large order of supplies, but they have yet to arrive."

Ainsley joined Sabrina at the table. "I thought Halifax was the back end of the world. It would seem I was wrong."

Sabrina winced. "I'm sorry, dearest."

"Nonsense, it's been a grand adventure. Besides, all these early nights are giving me quite a bit of quality time with my husband. He certainly knows how to put it to good use."

"Lucky you," Sabrina muttered.

Ainsley patted her hand. "Don't despair, pet. Graeme will come around. It must be hard to concentrate on romance when one is worried that the object of one's affection might be the target of a plot."

"That is a depressingly sensible viewpoint. Unfortunately, we seem no closer to solving the mystery than when we got here."

"And that means Graeme is still too fashed for romance."

"He's too fashed to even let me step out of the blasted house. I suggested we go for a ride yesterday, and he all but bit off my head."

"He can be an idiot, our Graeme."

Sabrina mustered a smile. "I shouldn't be ungrateful. He's doing his best to protect me."

"Then do something *inside* the house."

"Such as?"

"Sneak into his bedroom and force him to be romantic."

Sabrina couldn't help laughing. "I think I'd best stick to my lists. How goes the battle with the water closets? You are an absolute angel for taking on that job."

"Aren't I, though? But I'm just supervising. Patty has been doing most of the work. That girl is both sturdy and good-tempered, which are excellent qualities when dealing with plumbing."

"Still, I cannot thank you enough. It's a rather grue-some job."

"Sabrina, I lived in Canada. I had moose camped out in my garden. This is nothing."

"Moose? That sounds alarming."

"You have no idea. By the way, unlike everyone else at Lochnagar, Patty is quite talkative. I've gleaned quite a few interesting tidbits from her."

Sabrina perked up. "Such as?"

"Why don't we wait for the men to join us? They came in a few minutes ago, and Mrs. Wilson said she would pro-vide a cold collation as soon as they washed up."

Sabrina glanced at the clock, startled to see it was well past noon. "Goodness, I'd completely forgotten about food."

"Understandable. You've been preoccupied with bringing this blasted house back from ruin. But you're not to overdo it, my dear." Ainsley waggled her brows. "Graeme won't like that."

"He's barely been around to notice what I'm doing, the dratted man."

"How annoying." Ainsley reached for a cheddar and chive scone left over from breakfast. "I'll say one thing for Mrs. Wilson. She's an excellent baker."

"Actually, Hannah made those. She's been very eager to help in the kitchen."

"No doubt because she wanted to avoid water closet duty."

"We all wanted to avoid that. Fortunately, Hannah and Mrs. Wilson get along surprisingly well."

"Because they both have gloomy temperaments, dragging doom around behind them like dirty dusters."

"They're not the only ones."

"You're referring to Graeme. In his case, the word is grumpy."

"Or grouchy."

Ainsley laughed. "Grouchy Graeme. That's the perfect nickname. I can't wait to start using it."

Sabrina put up a hand. "Please do not. He'll never talk to me again."

"Who will never talk to you again?" Graeme asked.

She carefully put down her cup before turning to see him coming through the doorway, Royal right behind him.

Ainsley scrunched her nose. "Kendricks are always flitting about like ghosts instead of properly stomping in like the giants they are."

Graeme went to fetch a cup of tea, while Royal dropped a kiss on his wife's head before sitting down.

"If I were a ghost," Royal said, "I'd be sure to moan and wail in a dramatic fashion, clanging my bloody broadsword against the stone walls of the manor."

"That is disgusting," Ainsley said. "I forbid you to engage in such behavior, even when you're dead."

Sabrina smiled. "Lochnagar could use a good ghost."

"You'll be sure to lose Hannah if one pops up," Ainsley replied.

Graeme took a seat. "A distinct advantage. And I repeat, who will never talk to you again, Sabrina? Is there a problem with one of the servants?"

The man was truly a dog with a bone.

"It's nothing," she said.

He narrowed his gaze. "Lass—"

"My dear, hardly anyone in this blasted house will talk to any of us," Ainsley smoothly interrupted. "It's quite frustrating, as I'm sure you know."

Royal grimaced. "We do. We've spent the last three days trying to pry information out of the tenants and villagers. Tight-lipped as oysters."

"One would think the remaining tenants would be eager to talk about the problems on the estate," Sabrina said. "We've made it clear we want to help."

"They've heard that before, from your former estate manager, for one. After he then handed out a number of eviction notices, one can say that trust in outsiders became nonexistent."

"But you're Highlanders," she protested. "Surely they should be willing to speak with you."

"Highlanders or not, we're still outsiders," Graeme replied.

"Did you try the brogue?" Ainsley asked. "That usually does it."

Royal snorted. "Graeme put on a brogue so heavy even I could barely understand him."

"One of the crofters laughed at me," Graeme dryly said. "I am truly losing my touch."

Ainsley patted his arm. "Never mind, dear. It's time to give up all this spy business. All this skulking about can't be good for your health."

"My health is just fine, thank you." He looked at Sabrina. "The real problem is that they know Royal and I aren't the ones in charge."

"That would be my father."

"Yes, and no one trusts an absentee landlord, a *Sassenach*, no less."

Sabrina put down her teacup with a sigh. "It all sounds rather hopeless, doesn't it?"

Graeme waggled a hand. "Not quite. We finally had a bit of success with one of the oldest crofters, Stan MacTavish. He manages a large herd of coos."

"What are coos?" Ainsley asked.

"A species of Highland cattle," Sabrina replied. "Hardy, and an excellent source of income."

Graeme flashed her a smile. "Correct. You should be able to have a nice chat with Mr. MacTavish about it. He was willing to speak to us because he's crusty enough not to give a damn what anyone thinks of him. He also feels safe from eviction, since your father apparently wishes to expand his cattle holdings."

"And what did Mr. MacTavish have to say?" Sabrina asked.

"First, let me tell you what's been nagging at me," Graeme said. "Why did your father replace the previous estate steward in the first place? Mr. Hugo had served as steward here for years."

"I assumed it was because he wouldn't follow orders to enact the Clearances," Sabrina replied.

"According to MacTavish, such was not the case. Hugo cleared tenants, but seemed to do so in a very selective manner."

Ainsley snapped her fingers. "Maybe some of the crofters were bribing him."

"Possibly," Graeme said. "While MacTavish was forthcoming about his dislike for Hugo, he was vague on details regarding the man's sudden departure from Lord Musgrave's employ."

He fell silent, frowning thoughtfully into his teacup.

"He's not the only one who's rather vague," Sabrina prompted.

"Let's just say he hinted at illegal operations on the estate," Graeme said. "Ones that Hugo was involved in."

"What sort of illegal operations?"

"Brewing whisky."

Ainsley rested her chin in her palm. "Oh, like you and Grant once did?"

Graeme rolled his eyes. "That was just a hobby. This is something else entirely."

"Something that possibly involved smuggling," Royal added. "But MacTavish wouldn't go any further than that."

Sabrina let out a sigh. "Oh, splendid. Is this still going on, do you think?"

Graeme shook his head. "We've been all over the estate, and I've seen no evidence of it. Stills are difficult to hide."

"Agreed," said Royal. "So, your father's now-retired business manager finally gave Hugo the boot. The new estate steward began to more vigorously enforce evictions, which presumably included the smugglers."

"Which would make them quite angry," Sabrina said.

Ainsley cocked an eyebrow. "Angry enough to exact vengeance on Musgrave?"

"It's all speculation at this point," Graeme said.

"Do we even know the names of the people involved in this activity?" Sabrina asked.

"MacTavish claimed some confusion on that point," Graeme dryly replied.

Sabrina tapped her fingers on her teacup. "We have no proof at all of smuggling, then."

"I'm positive there was an illegal operation and that Hugo was involved," Graeme said. "The problem is that locals are more likely than not to protect smugglers, since they hate the taxes on the legal brews and anything that smacks of *Sassenach* law. It makes it difficult to investigate."

"Although MacTavish suggested both Hugo and the mysterious smugglers were not popular with the locals," Royal added. "That's fairly unusual."

"Still," Sabrina said, "that sounds mostly like hearsay, and certainly no proof of a plot to kill me."

"Sabrina," Graeme said. "You must—"

She held up a hand. "I'm truly not trying to be difficult. But Lochnagar needs us, Graeme. I cannot pull up stakes and abandon these poor people without solid evidence that I'm in danger."

"It's to your credit that you want to help, but your father—"

"My father is the cause of this state of affairs. That being the case, I mean to stay here and set Lochnagar back on a path of good management."

"I can possibly shed some light," Ainsley said. "Patty was quite gabby this morning about nefarious activities at Lochnagar."

Graeme sighed. "And when did you plan on sharing this?"

"When you stopped talking. Which took quite a long time, as usual."

"Then perhaps you can enlighten us now, love," Royal said, forestalling his brother's scowling retort.

"Patty's father, as you know, owns the pub in Dunlaggan, which is a locus of gossip. Fortunately, Patty likes to spread that gossip. I was quizzing her about Mr. Hugo's replacement, a certain Mr. Francis. Our Patty developed tender feelings for Mr. Francis, and was quite desolate when he bolted from Lochnagar."

"Did she say why he left?"

"He was afraid, apparently. Patty believes there was skullduggery afoot, and that Mr. Francis was determined to curtail it through evictions. In doing so, she thinks he brought someone's wrath down on his head, enough to necessitate a quick exit."

"Did she mention the names of the, er, skullduggers?" Graeme asked.

"She suffered a convenient memory lapse at that point."

"Does Patty know where Mr. Francis currently resides?"

"Alas, he did not return her feelings, so he did not impart that information."

"Apparently, he did not impart that information to anyone," Sabrina said, troubled by Ainsley's information. "How inconvenient."

"I'll run him to ground," Graeme said. "In the meantime, Royal will be taking you and Ainsley back to Edinburgh. You'll leave tomorrow."

Royal lifted an eyebrow. "We will?"

"Yes."

"No," Sabrina said.

Graeme directed her a stern look. "Did you not hear what Ainsley just said? Francis was obviously run off under threat. Lochnagar isn't safe for you."

"Mr. Francis left almost two months ago. And you just noted, you've found no actual evidence of an illegal distillery or a smuggling operation, merely hints by MacTavish. Right now, all seems quiet, which suggests the smugglers are long gone." Sabrina shrugged. "And as nice as Patty is, one can hardly call her a reliable witness."

Royal nodded. "All good points. Doesn't really sound like there's much cause for immediate panic."

"Oh, that's a helpful assessment," Graeme sarcastically replied. "Since when did you turn into an inquiry agent?"

Ainsley whacked Graeme on the shoulder. "Don't be disrespectful to your big brother."

"I'll tell him whatever he needs to be told. And you ladies will do exactly as I say."

Well, that was a bit much. "I appreciate your concern and care, sir," Sabrina said, "but without more specific information and a credible threat—"

"Credible threat," Graeme interrupted. "What would you find credible, Sabrina, a pistol held to your back? Again?"

"Without a credible threat," she firmly went on, "I refuse

to turn tail. The people of Lochnagar—my people—have been abandoned too many times. I will not repeat that pattern."

"Well said," Ainsley piped in. "Graeme, you and Royal will simply have to do your job and protect us."

Before Graeme could explode, the door opened, and Mrs. Wilson entered. Hannah followed, trundling a wheeled cart with their luncheon.

"Oh, excellent," Ainsley said. "I'm famished."

When Graeme shot his brother an incredulous look, Royal gave a shrug. "Might as well give it up, old boy. The ladies have made their decision."

"The hell they have," Graeme said, jumping to his feet.

Mrs. Wilson eyed Sabrina with alarm. "My lady, do ye want us to come back?"

"It's fine, Mrs. Wilson," Sabrina said. "Please serve luncheon."

Graeme fixed Sabrina with an irritated glower. "Insane, the whole lot of ye," he said before stalking out of the room.

"But you've not had any lunch," Sabrina called after him.

"That's all right," Ainsley said, reaching for a dish. "More for us."

Chapter Twenty-Two

Sabrina had been forced to sneak out of her own house, thanks to Graeme. Sensible precautions were one thing, but he'd fully departed the realm of sensible some time ago. Yet again he'd ordered her not to step foot outside.

After the gentlemen had left on another search of manor lands, Sabrina had gone to the stables and saddled up a mare. Unfortunately, bringing a groom along was not an option, since Bobby had also ridden out with Graeme and Royal.

She made a mental note to hire another groom as soon as possible.

Slowing the mare to a walk, Sabrina passed through the gates and turned onto the main road to the hamlet. From this vantage point, she had a splendid view of the dramatic landscape of rolling glen, with glimmers of a loch in the distance and craggy peaks beyond them. Less than a mile away was Dunlaggan, the picturesque hamlet so closely tied to the estate.

As she gazed out over the beautiful vista, her throat went unexpectedly tight. Sabrina had always taken a great deal of satisfaction in running her father's households, but this was something entirely different. She felt a newfound sense of pride in Lochnagar, her mother's birthplace and the ancestral home of her clan. Deep in her bones, there was a sense of belonging she'd never before experienced.

Lochnagar had fallen asleep these many years, like a princess in a fairy tale. But now, the lovely old girl was awakening from her slumber. And Sabrina couldn't walk away, no matter the trouble or potential for danger.

She urged the placid mare into a canter and soon reached the outskirts of the hamlet. There, she encountered only a lad with an adorably gap-toothed grin leading a cow to a paddock.

Dunlaggan's simple stone cottages were neatly maintained, with scrubbed stoops, painted shutters, flower-filled window boxes, and even the occasional door sporting a bright blue or red. For all the troubles plaguing the estate, the hamlet's residents clearly had a great deal of pride.

But the local folk seemed exceedingly wary. As she passed, matrons scurried inside before she could say hello, and two elderly gentlemen on a bench in front of the pub subjected her to a narrow inspection. They barely bobbed their heads when she smiled and gave them a cheery wave.

Sabrina could only hope her potential source of information proved to be friendlier.

She halted in front of a gray-stone manse, the largest house in the hamlet. It was tucked in a pretty pocket garden beside the village kirk. Casting a quick glance around to ensure her privacy, she gathered up her skirts and swung off in an awkward dismount. The mare snorted and eyed her with a degree of disdain but didn't balk.

"You're an old dear with excellent manners." She rubbed the horse's ear before looping the reins around a convenient hitching post.

Pushing through the knee-high gate, she walked to the front door and rapped the knocker. When there was no answer, she rapped again. Again, there was silence, but for the buzzing of bees and the rustle of leaves in the gentle afternoon breeze. Two mullioned windows opened out over the garden, so she hoped someone was home.

She was about to rap a third time when a quick footstep sounded from inside. The door swung open to reveal a young man in shirtsleeves and a neat leather vest, with sleeve protectors tied around his forearms. He held a pen and rather owlishly blinked at her, as if his thoughts were far away and she was something of a surprise.

Then his expression cleared, and he flashed a charming smile. "My dear ma'am, please forgive me. My housekeeper has stepped out for a moment. Have you been waiting long?"

His gaze was so warm and his expression so friendly that Sabrina couldn't help but smile back. "Just a moment or two. I'm sorry to disturb you."

He opened the door wide. "No, indeed, Lady Sabrina." He flashed a grin. "We have very few visitors to Dunlaggan, and certainly none that look like you."

When he then flushed, his smile turning into an expression of comic dismay, she chuckled as she stepped inside.

"And I take it you are Reverend Brown."

"I am, my lady. Please forgive my impertinence. My housekeeper, Mrs. Adair, has described you in detail, as have some of the villagers." His smile returned. "I only returned to Dunlaggan yesterday, and I've heard talk of nothing else. Everyone is quite excited."

She paused in the low-ceilinged hall as he shut the door. "I'm not quite sure *excited* describes my reception."

He cast her a quick glance before gesturing down the hall. "Won't you join me in the back parlor? It's quite the nicest room in the house and not nearly as cluttered as my study. Mrs. Adair would have a fit if I allowed a visitor into my study in its current state."

"We certainly cannot upset Mrs. Adair."

He again flashed his very attractive smile. "A good housekeeper is a treasure, as I'm sure you know."

They entered a neatly furnished room with a comfortable mix of floral fabric wing chairs, round tables holding books and vases of mums, and a faded settee in red velvet. Sabrina perched on the settee while Mr. Brown took one of the wing chairs.

The vicar was a tall man with an athletic frame. With his strong features, friendly smile, and glossy dark hair, he was attractive, though not as brawny and handsome as Graeme, of course. Few men were. Still, Mr. Brown had an engaging smile and an open countenance that immediately put her at ease.

"Can I offer you something to drink?" he asked. "You've caught me a bit off guard, but I'm sure I could rustle something up."

"No need, sir. I had luncheon just before I came."

His gaze twinkled with humor. "Thank goodness. If you must know, I'm hopeless in the kitchen. Mrs. Adair barely lets me step foot in the room. She says I'm a menace to the domestic arts."

Sabrina laughed. It felt good to laugh and enjoy a pleasant conversation with a man who wasn't barking at her. "Then we must be thankful I've already eaten."

"And please forgive my appearance, my lady. I was working on my Sunday sermon."

"I should have sent a note down first, but I needed to speak to you with some degree of . . ." Sabrina hesitated. "Urgency."

He turned serious. "Actually, I intended to call on you later today. I've been in Kinloch Laggan for the last few weeks, at my other parish. Kinloch is my primary living and keeps me busy. Not that Dunlaggan doesn't have its challenges," he dryly added.

"Have you been vicar in Dunlaggan for some time?"

"About two years. The Kinloch parish is within the purview of the head of the Chattan clan. When he appointed me to that parish, he asked that I be assigned to this living as well. Your father had no objection."

"So you were here when Mr. Hugo was still the estate steward."

"Yes," he tersely replied.

"Do you mind if I ask your opinion of him?"

"The man was a complete scoundrel. We generally avoided each other."

Drat. Would this be another dead end?

Mr. Brown grimaced. "I don't mean to sound rude, my lady. I truly believe, though, that Mr. Hugo cared little for Lochnagar and its tenants. However, he did seem to have the trust of your father's business manager in Edinburgh."

Sabrina clenched her gloved hands in her lap. "I apologize. My father's health has been uncertain, and he turned his Scottish concerns over to his manager. With unhappy results, I'm afraid."

"No apology is necessary. There are a fair number of absentee landowners in the Highlands, and some are better than others. Now, there is little doubt that change is coming to this part of Scotland, Lochnagar included."

"And I intend to reverse the changes that have hurt the tenants and the locals, as best I can."

He gave her a relieved smile. "That is splendid news, indeed."

"But as you say, there are challenges. The villagers and even the manor staff are quite wary. We know something criminal took place under Mr. Hugo's supervision. We've also deduced that the new estate manager, Mr. Francis, was apparently frightened off."

"That was my impression, as well."

Sabrina clapped her hands in frustration. "But no one will talk to me about it."

Mr. Brown sighed. "The people of Dunlaggan can be remarkably reticent. And it would be worse for you, the daughter of an absentee landlord, and a *Sassenach*, no less. I'm afraid I must counsel patience."

"It's hard to be patient when there's skullduggery afoot on your own lands. And aside from Mr. Hugo, I don't even know the names of those involved."

"I know who they are and what they've been doing," the vicar calmly said. "It's not exactly a secret."

It took a few moments for Sabrina to muster her wits. "You know about the smuggling, then?"

"Everyone knows about it, my lady."

"Yet I obviously know very little," she tartly replied.

He winced. "Forgive me. I'd assumed that Mrs. Wilson would have informed you of some of the details."

"Not a word. One of the older crofters did tell us that someone was brewing whisky and likely running a smuggling ring."

"A very successful smuggling ring, one that was primarily to the benefit of Mr. Hugo and the Barr family, one of your former tenants."

Sabrina frowned. "I saw the Barr name in the estate records. They had been tenants for at least two centuries."

"Yes, and exceedingly respectable farmers in the older generations. That apparently changed when your grandfather died. With Hugo's assistance, the younger Barrs formed an illegal partnership that ran successfully for several years."

"And no one tried to stop it?"

He shrugged. "As long as the rents were coming in and the estate was producing revenue, I suppose no one cared."

"What about the authorities?"

"Illegal distilleries in the Highlands are hardly uncommon, I'm sorry to say."

She thought of Graeme and his brother. "So I have come to understand."

"Circumstances only changed when Mr. Francis was brought in to step up the Clearances. The Barrs were one of the first families to be evicted." The vicar grimaced. "To say they were unhappy is a vast understatement."

"Does anyone know where the Barrs are now?"

"If some do know, they're not telling me."

She blinked. "They don't trust you?"

"It's not that. Some of the locals are afraid of the Barrs. Afraid of what they're capable of doing if anyone talks. Others simply feel loyal to the old Highland ways. Under the circumstances, it's hard for them to know who to ask for help."

Sabrina stood. "I can help, so perhaps they'll talk to me."

Mr. Brown rose with her. "I hope so. These are difficult times for Dunlaggan and Lochnagar."

"Thank you, sir. You've been incredibly helpful."

The vicar bowed. "Whatever I can do, please do not hesitate to ask."

She tilted her head. "Actually, there is something you can do."

"Name it."

"You can escort me to the pub and introduce me to the locals."

His eyebrows shot up in comical surprise. "Uh, you wish to go to the pub?"

"I certainly do."

No luck at the vicar's house, which was incredibly annoying. The blasted man wasn't home, and the housekeeper hadn't a clue where he was.

Annoyed was understating the case. Graeme was skating on the edge of panic. He couldn't believe Sabrina had disobeyed his instructions and gone out by herself.

He'd given Ainsley an earful about that, but she'd simply yelled right back at him. Fortunately, his sister-in-law had climbed down from her high horse long enough to tell him where Sabrina had gone and why.

Graeme needed to keep better track of the lass, apparently every bloody moment of the day and night.

Night watch would be fun.

He ignored his moronic brain and trotted his horse back through the hamlet, slowing as he approached the Deer and Hound, the only pub in town. He'd stopped in a few times since their arrival and had been met with a wall of silence and suspicion. Today probably wouldn't be any better, but at least someone might have spotted the vicar, with or without Sabrina. Graeme only hoped the two of them weren't wandering about the countryside, looking for clues. Sabrina clearly thought of herself as something of an investigator. While there was no doubt the lass was sharp as a pin, amateurs always caused trouble.

Sabrina had a knack for causing trouble without even trying.

Graeme dismounted in front of the pub. As usual, an ancient lounged out front, smoking a pipe. There were always one or two of the old boys stationed there, keeping an eye on the street. Graeme rather imagined they did it in shifts, because he'd never once passed by without falling under the scrutiny of one of the local Methuselahs. The results of their perusals were invariably disapproval.

"Good afternoon. I'm Graeme Kendrick."

"I ken who ye are."

The old fellow vigorously pulled on his pipe, then blew out an impressive cloud of foul-smelling smoke. Enveloped, Graeme coughed.

"Ye'll be lookin' for the lass," he added.

"Know where she is?" Graeme hoarsely asked.

Methuselah jerked his pipe toward the door. "She and the vicar are havin' a wee chat with Monroe and just about everyone else in the hamlet." He puffed out another cloud. "Gossips, the whole lot of 'em."

Graeme waved a hand through the billowing brimstone. "I suppose you're above that sort of thing."

"I already ken everythin'. Ye might try rememberin' that, laddie. Save yerself some time."

Graeme mentally rolled his eyes. "I will do that, Mister . . ."

"Get ye in before yon lassie causes more trouble."

"Yon lassie is your lady," he replied. "You might consider treating her with the respect she deserves."

A skeptical snort was the only reply.

Hopeless.

The sooner he got Sabrina away from this deranged corner of the Highlands, the better.

Pushing open the door, Graeme blinked and then promptly picked his jaw up off the floor.

Sabrina sat at a table in the center of the rustic, timbered room. With a pint in front of her, she was talking to Monroe, the publican, and three other men. One, a young fellow in a sober black suit, was obviously the vicar. The others were the local butcher and a crofter from Lochnagar. Scattered at the surrounding tables was probably half of Dunlaggan, straining to hear the earnest conversation.

Graeme stalked over to Sabrina.

Startled, she glanced up and then let out a quiet sigh. "Oh. I wasn't expecting to see you."

"I'm quite surprised to see you as well. Without an escort," he pointedly added.

"Ah, but I do have an escort. Mr. Kendrick, may I introduce Mr. Brown. He's the vicar here in Dunlaggan."

The young man stood and executed a polite bow. "It's

a pleasure to meet you, Mr. Kendrick," he said with a warm smile.

Sabrina beamed at the vicar. "Reverend Brown has been ever so kind and helpful."

The vicar pressed a hand to his chest. "It is my honor to help you, my lady."

Graeme shoved his hand into his greatcoat pocket, resisting the impulse to rearrange the man's perfectly straight nose.

"I hate to contradict a lady," Graeme said, "but I don't believe Mr. Brown escorted you from Lochnagar to the village. Unless he made prior arrangements to sneak you out of the house, that is."

The vicar looked wounded, and that actually made Graeme feel guilty.

"Sir, I never sneak, especially with ladies." He resumed his seat with a great deal of dignity.

"Happens that's true," said the butcher. "My Betsy has been tryin' to sneak off with yon vicar for months, but he's as skittish as a virgin on her weddin' night." He good-naturedly elbowed Brown, who was now looking appalled. "Nae luck for my poor Betsy, ye ken."

"Mr. Harrison, I have the utmost respect for your daughter. Indeed, for all the ladies in the village," Brown protested.

"Of course you do, my dear sir," Sabrina said before frowning at Graeme. "Anyone with a brain can see that."

Splendid. Now she thought him brainless.

Graeme made an effort to wrestle his temper under control. "My lady, may I suggest we return to Lochnagar? It's getting late."

She glanced at the old case clock sitting on a shelf behind the bar. "It's barely four o'clock. Besides, we're having a very interesting conversation, which you should be part of."

"You can tell me all about it on the way home."

She crossed her arms and raised an eyebrow.

Mentally cursing, Graeme gave in, hooking an empty chair with his foot and swinging it over to the table.

"Can I be gettin' ye a pint, sir?" Monroe asked.

"Another time, thank you. I really must be getting her ladyship home as soon as possible."

Sabrina cast the barkeep an apologetic smile. "You must excuse Mr. Kendrick, sir. He's rather a worrier, I'm afraid."

Oh, he'd give her something to worry about, once he got her home.

"I'm simply concerned for your well-being, my lady. You shouldn't be riding around an unfamiliar neighborhood without an escort."

"This neighborhood, as you deem it, is my family's ancestral lands. Besides, the hamlet is barely a mile from the gatehouse. I'm sure I was never in any danger."

"I'm actually quite good at measuring distances," Graeme replied. "And a mile is certainly long enough for something to happen to an unescorted young woman."

Sabrina looked ready to argue, but the vicar turned and earnestly pressed her gloved hand. "Mr. Kendrick is correct, my lady. Given the present circumstances, it's best you exercise caution."

Sabrina blew out an exasperated breath. "It seems overly cautious to me. After all, no one seems to know if the Barrs have even remained in the vicinity."

Graeme frowned. "Who are the Barrs?"

"The smugglers," Sabrina explained. "The ones brewing illegal whisky on Lochnagar lands."

Monroe solemnly nodded. "Aye, right bastards they are, too. Beggin' yer ladyship's pardon," he said.

Graeme felt the hairs bristle on the back of his neck. "You were discussing the smugglers? In here?"

She looked puzzled. "Why wouldn't I?"

Hell and damnation.

Because half the bloody village was in the pub, and one or more of the locals might be in cahoots with the damn Barrs, whoever they were. If so, the Barrs would soon know that Sabrina was on to them.

"What else have you been discussing with the villagers?" he asked, trying to keep a level tone.

Several people shifted uncomfortably and exchanged furtive glances.

"How to improve the situation at Lochnagar, for one thing."

Sabrina sounded a trifle mystified. She had no bloody idea how bad this could be.

"Like stoppin' them bloody Clearances," someone called from the back of the room. "Will ye be doin' that, or do ye need your da's permission?"

Sabrina peered around, trying to identify who'd spoken. "It's my intention to stop—"

"And what about them Barrs?" interrupted a middle-aged woman in a mobcap. Graeme recognized her as the daughter of one of the remaining crofters. "They're a bad lot, and who's to say they willna be comin' back?"

Sabrina bristled. "*I* say."

"And how will ye be doin' that, so foine a lady as yerself?" the woman sarcastically replied.

"That's no way to talk to her ladyship," the vicar said in a reproving voice. "She deserves our respect and consideration."

"The way her da has been *considerin'* us all these years?" The woman snorted. "She's just another do-nothing *Sassenach*, if ye ask me."

Monroe stood. "That's enough out of ye, Jennie Robertson. I'll nae have ye insultin' her ladyship in my pub."

Sabrina also stood. "It's fine. I—"

"I'll insult who I please, Dan Monroe," the woman retorted.

Almost instantly, everyone in the pub started talking—yelling, really—either at Monroe, Jennie Robertson, or the vicar. And many were now on their feet, waving their arms and arguing on top of one another. If there was one thing Highlanders were good at, it was arguing.

And fighting.

It was obviously time to go.

Graeme took Sabrina's arm, propelling her to the door. She started to bluster, but he continued, dodging various patrons and getting her outside.

"Was that really necessary?" she snapped.

"Yes."

"Things dinna go as planned, I take it," said Methuselah from his bench.

"That is an understatement, I'm sorry to say," said the vicar, who'd followed them out.

Graeme rounded on him. "What in God's name were you thinking, man? Anyone could have been in that bloody pub, listening in."

"Anyone was," Methuselah cryptically replied.

Sabrina jabbed Graeme in the chest. "You leave poor Mr. Brown alone. He's been nothing but helpful, and I'm grateful to him."

"He's a bloody fool," Graeme said. "Landing you in the middle of that scene."

She jabbed Graeme again. "Everything was fine until you walked in."

"No, Mr. Kendrick is correct, my lady," Brown surprisingly said. "I should have known better, even though you seemed so very determined."

"You were simply trying to help, sir. Unlike some people," she tartly added.

When Brown flashed her a rueful, charming smile—one Sabrina returned—Graeme's faintly stirring instinct to forgive the man went up in the proverbial puff of smoke.

"Well, this *unhelpful* man is going to get you back to the manor house, where you'll be safe." He again took her by the arm. "Where's your horse?"

"Behind the pub," said the old man. "I'll fetch it."

He rose with surprising alacrity and disappeared around the corner of the pub.

"I suppose I should make my good-byes," the vicar morosely said.

"I suppose you should," Graeme responded.

Sabrina's glare all but torched him. "I swear I'm going to murder you," she hissed under her breath.

"I'm sure Mr. Brown will be happy to give you absolution," Graeme replied.

Now looking thoroughly alarmed, Brown gave a hasty tip of his round-brimmed hat. "Good day, Lady Sabrina. I'll be in touch."

He rushed off, all but leaving a dust trail in his wake.

"You are truly an awful man," Sabrina said to Graeme.

For the last few minutes, his instincts had been telling him to get her back to the house as soon as possible. Now, they were all but blowing trumpets in his ear.

"You love me anyway," he replied as he scanned their surroundings.

"Ha. In your dreams," she muttered.

That was exactly his dream, that Sabrina would love him. But he'd have to keep her alive first.

"Mr. Brown is incredibly well-mannered and kind, which is more than I can say for you." Sabrina gave a haughty little sniff. "In fact, I like him very much."

"Oh, do ye, now? And what, exactly, does that involve?

More secret visits to the parsonage? More pints of ale in the local pub?"

"I will visit whomever I please." She jabbed Graeme in the chest again. By now, his cravat was likely demolished. "And you have nothing to say about it."

He leaned in so close that her peacock-blue eyes practically crossed. "Oh, I'll have something to say about it, lass. Count on it."

She blinked, then a slow smile curved up her lush mouth. "Well, I do believe you're jealous, Mr. Kendrick."

He straightened. "Don't be ridiculous. And where is that damned . . . ah, finally."

"Here be yer horse, my lady," Methuselah said as he rounded the corner of the pub.

"Thank you," Sabrina replied.

She still wore that smug little smile. Cheeky lass. The hell of it was he loved that about her.

The old man held the mare while Graeme boosted Sabrina into the saddle.

She settled her skirts. "Thank you, Mr. Chattan."

Graeme cocked an eyebrow at the old man. "You're a Chattan? You're a member of Lady Sabrina's clan, then."

"Aye, and ye'd best be gettin' the lady home. My nose is twitchin', ye ken."

"Mine, too," Graeme dryly replied.

Despite his annoyingly cryptic comments, Chattan seemed to know quite a lot. Graeme would have to further their acquaintance.

He untied his horse and vaulted into the saddle. "Let's go lass. No dawdling."

"You are so annoying." She took off at a trot down the street.

"Ye have yer hands full with that one," Chattan commented.

"Aye, that."

Graeme cantered after her, coming abreast as they left the hamlet. She made a point of ignoring him.

"So," he finally said, "are you going to tell me, or do I have to pay my own secret visit to Reverend Brown?"

"You'd probably give him a conniption, you're so rude."

He bit back a smile.

"Very well," she said with a dramatic sigh. "You'll just pester me until I tell you."

"Me, pester? Never."

His amusement faded as she related what she'd discovered. And while it was the first true break they'd had, it also confirmed his fears. If the Barr family was still in the vicinity, they were a danger to Sabrina and anyone else who might cross them.

Still, he needed more information. As soon as he got her safely home, he would ride back to Dunlaggan and try for a frank talk with Mr. Chattan.

"Unfortunately," Sabrina added, "no one seems to know where the Barrs are. But it's clear some of the villagers are still afraid they might return. They are apparently *not* nice people."

"Oh, you think?"

"There is no need for sarcasm, Mr. Kendrick."

She looked so very proper and pretty, with her stylish riding habit and jaunty plumed hat. If the situation hadn't been so dire, Graeme would have found a nice cozy meadow and proceeded to engage in some very improper behavior that would involve removing both habit and hat.

"There's every reason for sarcasm, since I just pulled your pretty arse out of a near riot."

"It was not a near riot, and you simply *must* cease referring to my posterior in that way."

"And you must cease taking risks with your life."

She shot him a veiled look. "The way you do with your life?"

He snorted. "That's different, and you know it."

"That last time I looked, you were made of flesh and bone, just as I am."

"I'm trained to do this, lass. You are not."

They turned from the main road into the drive that led past the gatehouse and up to the manor.

"I assure you," she said as they passed between the imposing stone gateposts, "I have no desire to take unnecessary—"

Chips of stone exploded from the post closest to Sabrina as the sound of a shot echoed. Her horse shied, but she brought the mare quickly under control.

Graeme wheeled his horse around, blocking her as best he could. "Sabrina, get down and behind that post."

"Where is it coming—"

Suddenly, more chips exploded from the gatepost as another shot slammed into it. Graeme threw himself from his horse and dragged Sabrina from her saddle. He forced her into a crouch and pushed her behind the post and out of range—he hoped—of the shooter.

He ran a quick hand over her dark green riding habit, checking for blood. The shots had hit the post, but stone chips had exploded everywhere.

"There's no need to grope me," she breathlessly said. "I'm uninjured."

"Are you sure? I took you down fairly hard off your horse."

She nodded, her golden hair coming loose from its pins. "Other than losing my hat, everything seems to be fine. And that was someone shooting at us." She grimaced.

"Yes."

"Drat. How would anyone even know where to find us?"

Graeme snuck a quick look around the pillar. He saw

nothing and thankfully heard no shots. "Lass, the entire village knew where we were going."

"Yes, but I didn't see anyone leave the pub, did you?"

"I just wanted to get you out of there." And he should have been more careful.

She sighed. "Well, this is most inconvenient. Both our horses have bolted. I'm assuming you're armed, however."

He extracted his pistol from the special leather sleeve strapped to the back of his waist.

Sabrina rummaged in a pocket and pulled out a small lady's pistol.

Graeme blinked. "When did you get that?"

"After you were kidnapped. It seemed a sensible precaution."

"Do you know how to use it?"

She rolled her eyes.

He snorted. "I'm hoping it won't come to that. There've been no more shots, so perhaps our attacker has taken himself off."

Thankfully, the shooter had not been much of a marksman either.

"He might be moving into a different position," she warned.

Graeme hadn't wanted to frighten her by mentioning that, but his lass was both smart and courageous. And while she was looking a bit pale, Sabrina was not the sort to succumb to hysterics.

"I don't think we should stay here to find out," she added.

"Agreed. We'll try for the ditch by the—"

He broke off when he heard the sound of galloping horses.

Dammit. Was it to be a kidnapping then?

"Stay behind me," he said as he checked his pistol and cocked the hammer.

"Graeme," called a familiar voice. "Are you there?"

"Oh, thank God," Sabrina muttered.

Graeme leaned out to look up the drive. "We're here."

Royal cantered up, cutting off the road to join them behind the shelter of the gatepost. He quickly dismounted.

"Did I bloody well hear shots?"

"You did," Graeme replied. "Fortunately, they went wide."

Royal cursed. "Bobby and I were cutting across the east meadow when we heard them. Then we saw your horses pelting up the drive. I told Bobby to round them up and stay clear until I got the lay of the land."

"Mr. Kendrick, you could have been seriously hurt," Sabrina said, perturbed.

Royal shook his head. "I got a good look as I came down the drive, and I saw no one."

Graeme pointed to a stand of trees on the other side of the main road, about a hundred feet away. "I'm betting the shooter was there."

Royal cocked a brow. "Want me to go take a look while you get Sabrina back to the house? You can take my horse."

"I absolutely forbid it," Sabrina said. "Ainsley might kill me if I put you in harm's way."

"She *would* kill me," Graeme said. "Besides, I think he's gone. Your loudly announced heroic Highlander routine probably scared him off."

"You're welcome," Royal sarcastically replied.

"Let's get Sabrina back to the house," Graeme said. "I don't want to take any chances."

She grimaced. "We can't leave Royal out here by himself."

"I'll send you with him and walk back."

She grabbed the lapel of Graeme's greatcoat and shook it. "You are not staying here by yourself. It's too dangerous."

"Och, lass, no need to panic," he gently said, taking her hand. "I'll be fine."

"I'm not panicking, but I'm not letting you risk your life."

Sabrina had gone dead white, and her pupils were huge. Not once had she shown signs of being scared for herself. But for his sake? She looked frightened to death.

"Lass, it's my job, remember? I'm supposed to protect you. That was the deal."

"It was a bad deal, and I rescind it."

"Not to worry," Royal said. "Rescue is on its way."

Bobby was trotting down to meet them, leading one of the runaway horses. Wilson was leading the other.

"Mr. Wilson was riding back from the blacksmith and saw the commotion," said the groom. "Is all well now, Mr. Graeme?"

"Well enough to get back to the house." Graeme led Sabrina to her horse. "Royal, you ride on the other side of her. Bobby, you and Wilson take up the rear. And we're going to ride fast, all right?"

Wilson sighed. "Trouble, I ken. Them Barr fellas?"

"You knew about them?" Sabrina asked in a disbelieving voice.

"Everyone knows about them, my lady."

"Then why—"

"Later," Graeme said.

He boosted her into the saddle, then swung up onto his horse. Royal moved into position on the other side of her.

"I don't think my horse is built for speed," Sabrina doubtfully said.

"Old Nellie will ken she's going back to her stall," said Wilson.

Sabrina looked at Graeme, then flicked the reins and

broke into a canter. Quickly, she accelerated to a gallop. He and Royal kept pace on either side of her, with Graeme prepared to take her reins or sweep her out of her saddle at the first sign of trouble.

But she rode fast and had an excellent seat. Within a few minutes, they were sweeping under the stone arch to pull up into the courtyard. Only then did Graeme let out a breath he imagined he'd been holding for ages.

He swung down and went to assist Sabrina with her dismount.

"That was surprisingly easy," she said with a smile.

"There was nothing easy about any of that."

"You know what I mean." She twirled a hand. "It could have been much worse."

Now that she was out of immediate danger, Graeme had the luxury of getting angry again. He'd been angry before they'd been shot at, and now he felt like a volcano about to blow.

He took her by the elbow and marched her to the staircase fronting the house. "It was bloody bad enough, Sabrina. This nonsense has to stop."

"There is no need to manhandle me, sir," she protested.

"Apparently, there is."

The door opened, and Ainsley came out onto the top step. "Graeme, why are you manhandling Sabrina?"

"Because she won't do as she's told."

"Because *she* is not a child," Sabrina snapped. "I know exactly what happened, and why it's a problem."

"That remains to be seen."

"I'll just take the horses around to the stables, shall I?" called Royal.

"Royal Kendrick, get up here this minute," Ainsley shouted. "Your brother is being an idiot, and you need to control him."

Graeme ignored Ainsley as he hustled Sabrina into the hall, right past a startled Mrs. Wilson and into the main drawing room.

When he finally let go, Sabrina made a show of shaking out her skirts. "Really, Mr. Kendrick, your behavior—"

"Seems a wee bit over the top," said Ainsley, joining them. "Graeme, is this really necessary?"

"Well, they *were* being shot at," said Royal as he strolled in. "So I can't blame the lad for being fashed."

Ainsley gasped. "Shot at? Sabrina, are you all right?"

Sabrina gave her a tight smile. "I'm fine. Mr. Kendrick pulled me out of harm's way."

Ainsley shot Graeme a questioning look.

"No one was injured. By the time Royal came along, the shooter had fled the scene."

"Thank goodness." Ainsley scowled at her husband. "I would have been most annoyed if any of you had been shot."

Royal gave her a hug. "Och, no worries. We're indestructible."

She gave him a shove. "You Kendrick men always say that, but it's not true. None of us is."

"Exactly the point I've been trying to make to her blasted ladyship," Graeme said. "This would not have happened if Sabrina hadn't gone gallivanting off to have a cozy chat with that nincompoop of a vicar."

"He's not a nincompoop. He's nice. And handsome," Sabrina added in a snippy tone.

Ainsley grinned. "How handsome?"

"*Very.*"

Graeme was sure that lava would begin flowing from his ears at any moment. "May we please stay on point?"

"Which one?" Royal asked.

"The only one that matters—Sabrina and Ainsley leaving

for Edinburgh in the morning. It's obviously no longer safe for them here."

Sabrina frowned thoughtfully, as if considering his assertion. Then she shook her head. "No."

Graeme waited a few seconds. "That's it? Just, no?"

"No, Mr. Kendrick?"

"Sabrina—"

"Graeme's not wrong, my lady," Royal said, firmly cutting him off. "Getting shot at is no joking matter."

"But the shots went wide." She looked at Graeme. "Noticeably wide."

He'd noticed that, too—not that it mattered. "The next one might not be wide. You'll leave under Royal's escort. I'll stay behind and get to the bottom of this."

Sabrina thrust out a hand. "I will *not* leave you alone. You need people you can trust."

"I can handle it." Graeme glanced at Ainsley. "I suggest you ladies go upstairs and pack. You need to leave at first light."

"May I suggest you cease giving orders in *my* house," Sabrina exclaimed.

Graeme closed the distance between them. "When I agreed to this stupid venture, I distinctly recall you promising to obey my orders."

She tilted up a defiant chin. "Because I expected your orders to make sense."

"Good God, Sabrina. Someone was shooting at you!"

"But how do you know the Barrs are actually trying to"—she whirled a hand—"actually kill me?"

"Because they have no bloody reason to kill me, ye daft girl."

Royal frowned. "Who are the Barrs?"

"The smugglers," Sabrina said. "The tenants evicted by Mr. Francis—the ones who threatened him."

"My point exactly," Graeme said. "They're dangerous."

"And that's exactly why I cannot leave," Sabrina retorted.

"That makes no bloody sense."

Sabrina blew out a breath and glanced up at the ceiling, as if searching for patience. "I think we can agree that the Barrs are still in the vicinity."

"Those bullets whizzing past our heads suggest as much," Graeme grimly replied.

"Yes, but I'm not the only target. They've got most of the residents of Dunlaggan terrorized as well."

"At Lochnagar, too," Ainsley said. "The servants are obviously afraid to say anything."

Royal snorted. "Except for Wilson, quite suddenly."

"Perhaps he's finally had enough," Sabrina said. "Perhaps everyone has finally had enough. My father has neglected these people for too long, with dire results. It's my responsibility to set things right."

"You can do that later," Graeme said.

Sabrina tilted her head. "Would your brother, Lord Arnprior, flee under similar circumstances?"

"Of course not, but he sure as hell wouldn't let Vicky hang about in harm's way."

"Actually, dear," Ainsley said, "I'm quite sure Vicky would insist on staying with Nick, come hell or high water. Nor would I leave Royal to face danger alone, either."

Graeme scowled. "That is an incredibly unhelpful intervention."

"Happens she's right, lad," Royal said. "Let's not forget that Ainsley did save my life."

"I don't care if she's right about other people. Sabrina is not staying."

"I am most certainly staying," Sabrina calmly replied. "If I let the Barrs run me off my own lands, no one in Dunlaggan or Lochnagar will ever trust my family again. This is my responsibility. I am incredibly grateful for your help, but I will not abandon my people."

Ainsley nodded her approval. "Perfectly sound reasoning."

"No, it's not." Graeme looked at Royal for backup.

His brother spread his hands. "If she cuts and runs, it could make things worse."

"If she doesn't run, she'll continue to be a damn target."

"Then we'll simply have to protect her," Royal said. "And get this damn situation sorted as quickly as possible."

Graeme looked at the three of them, all lined up against him. "You're all deranged." He pointed at Sabrina. "Especially you."

Then before his head truly did explode, he turned on his heel and stalked from the room.

Chapter Twenty-Three

Graeme stood in the quiet shadows of the empty corridor. The rest of the house was finally abed, but Sabrina was awake. Light seeped out from under her bedroom door. He suspected she was probably making a list of insults to pile on his head over breakfast.

Every one deserved.

He'd apologized so many times in his life he'd lost count, so it wasn't the apology that worried him. It was the possible aftermath that had him fashed and hesitating out here in the hall. When she knew everything, she could very well reject him, and that scared the hell out of him.

He rapped on the door, more loudly than he'd intended. Graeme had pursued ruthless killers through London's rookeries without batting an eyelash, yet now he was acting like an anxious old bachelor. And when the hell had that happened?

When a pretty English lass turned your life upside down.

The lass who'd made his life worth living again.

The door swung open, and Sabrina scowled up at him. "Are you trying to wake the entire household?"

She was dressed in the daintiest wrapper he'd ever seen, a frippery of cambric, lace, and ribbons that skimmed over her lovely curves. Sabrina wouldn't realize it, of course, but she was backlit by a roaring fire, rendering her robe semi-transparent.

She was truly going to kill him.

"Mr. Kendrick, are you going to stand there like a booby all night or say something?"

"Sorry, lass. Didn't mean to knock so loudly. Maybe my nerves got the best of me."

"You don't have any nerves. You are the most insensitive, ill-tempered man in the world."

Graeme tried to look soulful. "I'm here because I owe you an apology for my insensitive, ill-tempered behavior."

"And did you come to this decision all on your own?"

"I confess that I had a wee bit of help in that direction."

She let out a delicate snort. "Ainsley."

He flashed a smile. "She threatened to shoot me."

"A forced apology is not welcome."

When Sabrina started to shut the door, he stuck a booted foot in the gap. "I didn't need Ainsley to tell me, daft girl. It might surprise you to know I figured out I was a dolt all on my own."

"Yes, it would surprise me."

He wedged his foot in a bit more. "May I come in? So as to facilitate the making of the apology?"

"That would hardly be appropriate, sir."

"That never stopped you before, my lady."

When she rolled her eyes and swung the door wide, he bit back a smile.

"All right but you can't stay. It would be most improper."

He shut the door and leaned against it. "We're not in the habit of being proper, are we?"

Her gaze flickered over him. Graeme wore only boots, breeches, and a shirt unlaced at the throat. She'd seemed to find the combination appealing last time, and he'd decided the situation called for a wee spot of manipulation.

"I like what you're wearing," he said.

Sabrina glanced down at her body, as if she'd forgotten how she was attired. A fiery blush reddened her cheeks.

Graeme waved at her frilly, beribboned nightcap. "Especially that cap. It's like a topper on a wedding cake."

"You're a twit, Graeme Kendrick."

She stomped over to a needlepointed armchair by the fireplace, plopped down, and primly folded her hands in her lap, doing her best to look stern. But her pretty bare feet and the outline of her nipples through the delicate fabric of her nightclothes ruined the effect. Graeme felt a surge of heat in his groin as he settled his shoulder against the solid wood mantel of the fireplace.

"Aren't you cold? No slippers, lass."

She tucked her feet under the lace-trimmed hem of her wrapper. That was unfortunate, since Graeme liked looking at her toes. He rather thought he'd like to nibble them, too.

Well, at least the nipples were still in view, pert and begging for attention. Sabrina would have a heart attack if she knew just how pert they currently were.

"I never get cold," she said. "And it's barely the beginning of September. It's still summer."

"And it's still the Highlands. And that's quite the fire for someone who isn't cold."

The blaze was all but roasting his backside. Then again, the rising heat in his body was just as much the result of the salacious images pouring into his brain.

Her continuing scowl did nothing to dampen that heat. He wanted to use all his skills to replace that grumpy expression with one of sensual ecstasy.

"Are you going to make your apology?" she demanded.

"Absolutely." He was about to launch into his prepared speech when he finally took full notice of the bed on the other side of the long, low-ceilinged room. "Good God."

She glanced over her shoulder to follow his gaze. "It's

ridiculous, isn't it? I practically have to call a hackney to get from one side to the other."

The obviously ancient bed was the sort of thing an entire family could sleep in. Four thick, heavily scrolled posts rose up a good ten feet to support an enormous wooden canopy that curved up into a carving of a crown. The bed would befit a Renaissance prince, one who would lounge in bed while receiving his court.

It was also the perfect bed for entertaining a royal mistress—or a pretty little *Sassenach*. Graeme could easily imagine spending a day or three in that bed with Sabrina.

"Apparently," she added, "it was built for Mary of Guise, who was married to a Scottish king in fifteen-something-or-other. How it ended up at Lochnagar is a bit of a mystery."

"Everything about this place is a mystery. But I have to admit it's growing on me. It's got good bones."

"I think so, too." Then she pulled a face. "I hate that my father has neglected it."

Graeme hunkered down, lacing their fingers together. "That doesn't make you responsible for what happened here. Nor do you need to fix it all at once."

She tried to tug her hands away. "Are you actually going to apologize, or are you about to lecture me again? If it's the latter, you can leave."

He took one of her hands and turned it over, pressing a kiss to the inside of her wrist. Her pulse jumped against his mouth.

"Of course I'm going to apologize." When he licked her delicate skin, she startled a bit.

"Then perhaps you'd best get on with it," she said rather breathlessly.

He let go of her hand and cupped her delicately determined jaw. "Lady Sabrina Bell, I sincerely apologize for saying such idiotic things. I hope you realize that my . . ."

"Bad temper?" she prompted.

"My bad temper stemmed from concern for you. I most sincerely and humbly beg your forgiveness."

The corners of her mouth twitched. "It *was* a rather volatile situation. I was not at my best, either."

"Och, ye were both bonny and brave, like a true Highland lass, ye ken."

She giggled.

"I, on the other hand," he continued, "apparently succumbed to a bout of hysterics, which no doubt accounted for my . . ."

"Raising your voice?"

He nodded.

She scoffed. "You don't have a hysterical bone in your body. As for the yelling, it merely seems to be a Kendrick family trait."

"True enough. You need to get better at yelling."

Her blush deepened. "Does . . . does that mean I might be a member of your family some day?"

He leaned in and feathered a kiss across her lips. "Only if you accept my apology."

She sucked in a wavering breath. "That sounds like blackmail to me."

"I'm very good at underhanded tactics, in case you failed to notice."

"Oh, I've noticed."

She slipped her arms around his neck, pulling his head down. She gave him the sweetest of butterfly kisses before slipping her tongue out to taste him. Graeme murmured his appreciation, gently cupping her cheek as she teased along the seam of his lips.

But when she pressed closer, he sighed and slowly pulled back. Before they went any further, there were things she needed to know.

Her eyelids fluttered open, her peacock-blue eyes soft and hazy with desire.

"Why are we stopping? Is something wrong?" Then her gaze snapped into focus. "Something *is* wrong. What?"

The words still eluded him. With her in his arms, nothing else seemed to matter. But she had the right to know everything, good and bad. And even if the bad had been in service of the good, it had stamped a mark on his soul.

"I have to tell you something, and it's not very pleasant." He huffed out a bitter laugh. "That's an understatement. It's bloody awful."

She stroked his hair, smoothing the locks she'd disheveled only moments ago. "I won't shrink from it."

"You say that now—"

"Just tell me."

Her tart command almost made him smile. "Yes, my lady."

"You don't look very comfortable, though. Do you want to sit in the other chair?"

He settled onto the floor, crossing his legs tailor-style. "I'd rather stay close to you, if you don't mind."

She took one of his hands and plopped it onto her lap. "I won't let go."

He quietly began. "I had a case last winter that was probably the hardest of my career."

"Harder than this one? Because this one seems an absolute mess."

He cracked a brief smile. "This one is only hard because it involves you, sweetheart. It scares the hell out of me that something could happen to you."

She squeezed his hands. "Then we'll simply have to make sure nothing happens to me."

"Aye, that. Anyway, this other case . . . it involved children, little girls. They were . . ."

"Just say it, Graeme," she gently urged.

"They were sold into prostitution, to brothels, mostly. Some of them catered to men with money and connections, including aristocrats."

Sabrina closed her eyes for a few moments. When she opened them again, they glittered with fury. "Sometimes I wish I never had to set foot in London again."

He kissed the back of her hand. "There is evil everywhere, love, but I take your point. London can be rather a sewer."

"Honestly, these stupid Lochnagar smugglers are nothing compared to monsters that harm children," she fiercely said.

"True, enough."

"Was it a case you worked with Aden?"

"Yes, and three other agents. Aden always prioritizes cases in which women or children are subjected to danger or degradation." Graeme flashed a wry smile. "And he doesn't care whose toes he steps on, either."

"Good for him. And good for you, too."

He grimaced. "Eventually, yes. But things went sideways at one point. We were tracking a gang that was preying on children in the stews. On orphans mostly, ones who lived on the streets. But a family named Watson in Bethnal Green also came to my attention. The father occasionally ran errands for one of the madams at the center of the whole thing. Watson did the occasional nasty job for her, but nothing that would necessarily bring him to our notice."

"Then what did?"

"Mrs. Watson. She was the break in the case. They had a girl of ten. She was a beautiful child and caught the attention of the madam, who offered Watson a considerable sum for the girl to work in her brothel."

Sabrina had already gone pale, so he'd spare her the more horrific details. She needn't know that with the father's eager agreement, the madam had arranged the sale of the daughter at auction, the kind that attracted the vilest sorts of men.

"The girl's mother stumbled upon the plan. In a panic, she went to a pub owned by a friend who was a former inquiry agent. The pub is often frequented by Bow Street Runners, which is how the matter came to our ears."

Sabrina dug her nails into his hand. "Please tell me that you got to the child in time."

"We did, but just barely. The poor woman had very little information to go on, other than the night the girl was to be turned over to the madam."

"Why couldn't you just arrest the madam?"

He shook his head. "It's not that easy, I'm afraid." Too many people in high places enjoyed the services of such establishments.

"It should be easy," Sabrina said with a scowl.

He kissed her hand again. "True. As well as trying to rescue this child, we wanted to bring down the ring. That meant we had to both find the child, who had already been taken from her mother, and also catch the gang leaders in the act of procuring the girl."

While Graeme had wanted to go after the girl, Aden and the other agents had thought tracking the madam would be more efficient. In the end, they'd decided to do both.

"What did you do?" she gently prompted.

"I discovered Watson's hiding place. I should have gone for help then, but I was afraid of losing the girl if the bastard got spooked." Graeme sighed. "Watson had told his daughter that she was to be a fancy lady's companion, and that she would finally have nice clothes and lots to eat. The poor thing had no reason to doubt him. After all . . ."

"He was her father." Sabrina's gaze was soft with compassion.

"And children tend to believe their fathers."

"What happened next?"

He'd found father and daughter holed up at a grubby tavern owned by the madam. Graeme had taken down two armed guards before he even got to the father. And Watson himself had been a right nasty piece of work, almost as big and burly as Graeme.

"I had to fight Watson in front of that terrified little girl. She was convinced I was a bad man attacking her father." He snorted. "She whacked me over the head with the chamber pot. Gave me quite a nasty lump."

Sabrina winced. "Oh, dear. But you prevailed."

"It was a near thing. Watson got ahold of one of my knives, but I finally managed to kill him." Graeme let out a weary sigh. "He gave me no choice. The bastard almost took me out."

Sabrina looked stunned. "Thank goodness you were able to wrest the knife from him."

"Only after he used it on me." Graeme hesitated, not wanting to say the words. But he knew he had to tell her everything. "And that's not how I killed him."

"Then how . . ."

"I strangled him to death. With my bare hands, and in front of that poor, screaming child, I murdered her father."

Horror clouded Sabrina's brain. But Graeme looked so heartsick, she forced down her roiling emotions. "I'm so sorry you had to suffer such a terrible thing, Graeme."

"It was the wee lass who suffered. To lose her da like that . . . her screams . . ." He closed his eyes.

The poor man blamed himself. The things he'd seen and done, the weight of it all . . .

Sabrina took his face between her palms. "Look at me, dearest."

When he opened his eyes, the sorrow in his gaze wrenched her heart.

"You did *not* murder that man," she said. "You killed a

monster and saved a child. By any measure, you did the right thing."

"The wee lass didn't think so." He blew out a disgusted breath. "I should have found a way to get her out of there first, or gone for help. To make sure—"

"Stop. You always blame yourself, and I'm not having it anymore. You're the bravest, kindest man I know, even if you are pigheaded and high-handed. So enough of this nonsense."

A tiny smile edged the corners of his mouth. "Pigheaded, am I?"

"And rather thick, if you think this would make me turn away from you. You saved a child from a life of horror and degradation. That is incredible."

"I just hope she understands that, someday."

"Is she safe and with her mother?"

"Yes."

"Then she will, when she's old enough. And even if that child hates you for the rest of her life, it doesn't matter. You *saved* her. That is what matters."

He frowned. "I never quite thought of it that way."

"It's time you did. And I won't hear any more bottleheaded notions about your not being good enough for me. *I'm* not good enough for you."

He scoffed. "Don't be daft."

She went nose to nose with him, as he'd done to her on more than one occasion. "I love you, Mr. Kendrick. I'd given up hope that there were men like you in the world. I'm *so* happy to be proven wrong."

He looked blank for a moment. Then green fire sparked in his gaze. In one graceful movement, he unfolded his legs and stood, pulling her with him. Sabrina found herself swept off her feet and into his arms.

"What are you doing?" she asked.

"I'm taking you to try out that ridiculous bed. I just hope I don't lose sight of you once we get in there."

She huffed out a laugh. The relief she felt that he'd finally shared his deepest secrets—finally trusted her—was overwhelming. As was her love for him. Being able to say it, straight out, was simply wonderful.

"I must warn you that it's not very comfortable," she joked, trying to master her wobbly emotions.

He set her down on the high mattress. "It doesn't look comfortable at all. But I'm hoping we'll find an appropriate strategy."

She circled her arms around his neck as he untied the laces of her cap. "Do you have a specific plan in mind?"

"I'm a spy. I always have a plan."

"Does that plan include a conclusion to your spying career?"

His smile was wry. "Sooner rather than later, I expect. That's if your father doesn't murder me first."

"You leave Father to me. Now, tell me the rest of your plan."

He went to work on the laces of her wrapper. "The first part is to get you out of all these frilly things. The second part is to make love to you for the rest of the night."

Her heart thumped. "All night? Won't you be exhausted in the morning?"

He flashed a wolfish grin as he began to ease the wrapper down her arms. "I'm prepared to make that sacrifice."

Suddenly, she felt out of breath. "That's quite no . . . noble of you."

Graeme's hands froze. "What's wrong?"

"Nothing, really."

Sabrina stood on the edge of a cliff, about to leap into a world that would forever change. It was thrilling but also daunting.

He grimaced. "I didn't even ask you. You should give me a swift kick to the bollocks and shove me out of the room."

She choked on a laugh. "That would hardly be helpful. I've always understood that injuries to certain parts of the male anatomy can be rather discouraging."

"Downright deflating. But I *am* a cad for rushing you, love. I apologize."

"No. I want this more than I've ever wanted anything."

"Yes, but . . ."

Sabrina let out an exasperated sigh. "All right. Let me ease your maidenly qualms."

"It's *your* maidenly qualms I'm worried about."

"Shockingly, I don't seem to have any."

"Well, I do. I'm an exceedingly proper fellow, not to mention rather shy when it comes to this sort of thing."

It was so ridiculous she was hard-pressed not to laugh. But it was also a moment too serious for laughter.

Sabrina took one of his hands between hers. It was big and calloused, the hand of a strong, competent man who would do anything to protect her and the family they would build together.

"Graeme Kendrick, will you marry me?" she asked.

His eyes glittered like polished emeralds. Then he blinked a few times and cleared his throat.

"Sorry, it's rather dusty in here," he gruffly replied.

"You are such a booby," she tenderly said.

"It's not every day a fellow gets proposed to by such a lovely lady. It's . . . it's . . ."

She raised an eyebrow. "Disconcerting?"

"No, it's splendid. But are you sure, my darling girl? Really, truly sure?"

That hint of vulnerability twisted her heart. That she held such power over him was rather terrifying. Of course, he held the same power over her.

"I'm sure. And I do hope you're not going to embarrass me by rejecting my suit. I would never live it down."

Relief and joy flooded his gaze in equal measure. "I'm not that big an idiot." He leaned down and feathered a brief kiss across her lips. "Yes, Lady Sabrina Bell, I will marry ye. With all the love and gratitude in my wretched soul, even though I do not deserve ye."

She sniffed, trying to hold back a few tears. "You more than deserve me, you silly man. And now that we have that settled, can we please get back to your plan?"

"Which part?" he teased.

"This part." She started to yank his shirt out of his breeches.

"You're a bossy little thing, aren't you?"

The shirt snagged on a button. "Get used to it."

He laughed. "Here, let me help you." He pulled his shirt over his head and dropped it on the floor.

Sabrina felt her mouth sag open. "My goodness."

A shirtless Graeme was a sight, quite on par with the Elgin Marbles. His muscled chest was dusted with golden-red hair that narrowed in a silky line to the waist of his breeches. As for what was behind those breeches . . . that was obviously impressive, too.

He tapped her jaw shut. She hadn't even realized she was gaping at him.

"Your turn," he said.

"I'm acting like a ninny, aren't I?"

He kissed her nose. "Not at all, love. And I promise I won't do anything you don't want me to."

For such a rugged, hard-bitten man, Graeme was remarkably tender. He'd always put her needs first, and he'd done that from the moment they met. It was simply who he was.

"Actually, I think I'd like to do everything."

"I am delighted to hear that," he replied as she pulled off her wrapper and handed it to him.

Sabrina now wore only a sleeveless chemise, a whisper of cambric. Graeme's avid gaze curled her toes and made her insides grow muddled.

He reached out to cup one of her breasts. When he rubbed a thumb across one nipple, Sabrina swallowed a gasp. Then he tugged on the rigid tip, and she cried out at the sharp, delicious sensation.

Embarrassed, she clapped a hand over her mouth.

"Sorry," she muttered when he grinned and pulled her hand away.

"Sweetheart, make as much noise as you like."

"But Ainsley and Royal are just down the hall. They might hear us."

"They're probably doing the same thing right now."

She flapped a hand. "Not helping."

"No one can hear, I promise," he said in a soothing tone.

"You must think I'm a booby."

"I think you're utterly adorable."

He leaned down to nuzzle her lips. Sabrina's eyes drifted to half-mast as she rested her hands on his broad shoulders. His skin was hot under her fingers, the muscles as hard as rock.

"And I like it when you make noise," he added, waggling his eyebrows. "Feel free to scream, in fact."

"I am *not* the screaming type, sir."

His emerald gaze glittered. "Oh, I do love a challenge."

Sabrina lifted her chin, trying to look pert. Inside, she was a bundle of nerves and excitement. Because, really, what could be more exciting than Graeme Kendrick making love to you?

"Challenge accepted, Mr. Kendrick."

His sudden grin should have warned her. The next

moment, he had her flat on her back, and was standing between her legs. He swooped down and sucked on her nipple through the fabric of her chemise.

Sabrina gasped at the hot, wet feel of his mouth. Within seconds, she was writhing beneath him. When he gently bit down, she almost *did* scream. It was the most incredible sensation she'd ever felt.

Graeme pulled back, his hands propped on either side of her shoulders. "Just think how that will feel when you're naked."

She sucked in a wavering breath. "I'm still not going to scream."

"Lassie, you're going to be screaming down the rafters before the night is out."

"You are a truly dreadful man."

He grinned and straightened up, her wrapper a crumpled ball in his hand. "Let's get you out of that chemise and prove just how dreadful I am."

She struggled up into a sitting position. "All right, but you're making an absolute mess out of that very expensive robe of mine."

He shook it out before turning to carefully drape it across a nearby chair. When the light from the crackling fire caught his back, gleaming on his bronzed skin, Sabrina let out a gasp—and not one of pleasure.

Graeme quickly turned back. "What's wrong?"

She had to swallow before she could answer. "Your scar."

He grimaced and reached for his shirt. "Sorry. I forget how gruesome it looks."

She scrambled off the bed. "No, let me see."

"Sabrina—"

"Hush."

She gently ran her fingers over the thick scar, where the knife had sliced into his body. Although fully healed, the flesh was still puckered and red, and the scar would never truly fade. It would always be a haunting reminder of that grim day.

As she gently pressed her lips to the mangled skin, tears gathered in the corners of her eyes.

"Please dinna cry," Graeme gruffly said when she straightened up and faced him. "It's just a stupid, big scratch. I'll put my shirt on if it bothers ye."

Sabrina threw her arms around his waist. "I don't care how it looks, you big idiot. I care that I could have lost you before I even found you."

"I survived, sweetheart. I'm just fine."

"You are not to be injured like that again, do you hear? I couldn't bear it if anything happened to you."

He eased her to arm's length, one eyebrow tilted up. "And now you know how I feel when you throw yourself into harm's way."

"Point taken," she grumbled. Then she gave him a little shake. "But promise you'll be more careful from now on."

"I promise I will always come home to you." He kissed the tip of her nose. "Now, may I suggest we get back to the part where I make you scream?"

Her emotions were so tangled she didn't know whether to giggle or burst into tears. She compromised by letting out a little snort. "If you insist."

"Oh, I do insist."

He swept her into his arms and carried her back to the bed. Putting her down, he then pulled her chemise up and over her head. Sabrina blinked at finding herself so quickly naked.

His eyes blazed with green fire as he trailed his calloused fingertips across her shoulders. Sabrina shivered.

"You are the most beautiful thing I've ever seen," he growled.

She resisted the impulse to clap her hands over her

private parts. But this was Graeme, the man she would marry. The man she loved. There was no need to hide.

"Thank you." She mustered a smile.

"You're welcome. Now, up with you, my brave, *Sassenach* angel."

He plopped her on the bed, all in a sprawl. She started to scramble to the head of the bed. Graeme, however, gently pushed her back down, leaving her legs dangling over the edge of the mattress.

She frowned. "Aren't you getting in bed with me?"

"Soon."

Then he curled his big hands around her thighs and pushed them apart, stepping between them. Sabrina's mouth went dry. To be so exposed . . . It was embarrassing and exciting, all at once.

Graeme cupped her feminine parts. "Och, that's lovely," he rumbled.

She felt herself grow soft and damp. When he slipped a finger along the tender seam, rubbing her, she gasped and clutched at the bedclothes.

"That's it, my angel," he crooned as he continued to play with her.

He teased her with slow, delicious strokes, setting her on fire. Instinctively, Sabrina clenched her thighs around his hand as tiny contractions rippled through her core.

She'd never felt anything like it, and they'd barely begun to make love.

When he pulled away, Sabrina couldn't hold back a regretful sigh.

Graeme's chuckle was wicked. "We'll get back to that, my sweet. I have a few other things to attend to first."

She came up on her elbows. "Like what?"

He didn't answer. Instead, he stood between her spread legs, staring at her. Then he cupped his hand around the huge erection pushing against the fall of his breeches, and stroked himself.

Sabrina almost fainted. Because Graeme standing between her legs, half-naked and rubbing himself, was the most stimulating thing she'd ever seen. When he finally did get naked and enter her, she probably *would* faint.

And, suddenly, the idea of touching him seemed very stimulating, too. "Would . . . would you like me to do that?"

"Later," he rasped out.

Then he pushed her legs even wider and came over her, his mouth once more going to her breasts. But this time, she *was* naked, and the sensations defied description. Sabrina fell flat onto the mattress with a loud groan—she didn't care who heard it—as he lavished attention on her body.

Graeme cupped her breasts in both hands, plumping them up. Then he went from one to the other, sucking and tonguing her, teasing her until she *was* ready to scream. Her nipples burned with intense pleasure, so hot and tight she thought she would die.

When he gently bit her, she let out a cry, digging her fingernails into his back.

Graeme lifted his head. His hair tumbled over his brow, and his cheekbones were flushed with color. Like her, he seemed short of breath.

"I do believe that was a scream," he said.

"N . . . no," she managed. "Certainly not a scream."

"Ah, then let's try again."

He pressed a quick, searing kiss to her lips, and then started to make his way downward. He nibbled her neck, making her giggle. Then he gently pinched her nipple, holding it tight while he sucked on it. Sabrina bit down on her lip, refusing to scream.

"Stubborn lass," Graeme murmured.

Then he slipped lower, kissing and licking his way down

her body. His hands continued to play with her breasts, building her arousal.

When he slipped away, she dazedly looked up to see him on his knees on the floor. He glanced up at her, his eyes a fiery glitter, before slowly pushing her legs wide.

"Ready?" he asked in a husky voice.

Whatever it was he had in mind, she was certainly ready for it.

"Yes," she whispered.

When he dragged his tongue over her most intimate parts, she *did* almost faint. Never in her wildest dreams had she ever imagined a man would do such a thing.

And never had she imagined that anything could feel so wonderful.

For long minutes, Graeme lavished attention on her sex, driving her wild. He kept one hand planted on her thigh and the other on her belly, holding her down. His command of her body somehow made the pleasure more intense.

And he teased her, the brute, bringing her several times to the brink before easing back. Sabrina didn't know whether to whack him or clamp her hands on his head and keep him pressed firmly against her aching sex.

But she wasn't in control, Graeme was. And she loved every minute of it—until he pulled back.

"Why . . . why are you stopping?" she all but wailed.

"Because I need to be in you, Sabrina," he rasped out. "And I think you're more than ready to take me."

He helped her to scoot up higher on the bed, onto the pillows. Every muscle in her body trembled, weak with longing for him.

Graeme sat on the edge of the bed to yank off his boots, then he stood and unbuttoned the fall of his breeches, freeing himself.

Sabrina's mouth went dry as dust. "My goodness," she managed.

It seemed to be the only thought her addled brain could muster.

Flashing her an almost sheepish smile, Graeme stripped out of his breeches and dropped them onto the mattress. Then he joined her on the pillows. He gathered her close, his body hard, hot, and enticing. Sabrina felt a jumble of nerves, and yet she'd never felt more cherished.

"Ready, love?" he asked again.

She tilted her face up to kiss him. "I love you, Graeme Kendrick," she whispered, letting that be her answer.

Emotion darkened his gaze, and he blinked a few times. "Aye, that, my darling."

He settled her on her side, facing him, their bodies all but fused together. Then he lifted her leg and placed it on top of his thigh, so she was open to him.

"Hang on to me," he murmured.

He slicked a hand over her, making her tremble. When he notched his erection against her, Sabrina curled her hands over his shoulders. Then he began to push, breaching the tight entrance of her body.

Sabrina didn't scream, but she did almost yelp. Because it hurt, and quite a bit.

"It gets better," he gritted out.

"Soon, I hope," she gasped.

He paused for a moment, then flexed his hips. She felt a sharp sting, and then he was inside. *All* the way inside. Sabrina sucked in a deep breath, forcing herself to relax.

After several long moments, the pain began to ease into an almost-pleasant ache. And something else replaced her discomfort, something . . . extraordinary.

Graeme inside of her, reaching so deep she could almost feel him touching her heart.

He rested his forehead on top of her head, gasping like he'd just run a race. Sabrina curved a hand around his neck, then cautiously lifted her leg and settled it higher on his muscled thigh.

Even better.

"God, Sabrina," he groaned.

She kissed his chin. "This is certainly something, I must say."

"It certainly is," he ground out.

"Are you all right?" she asked after a few moments of fraught silence.

Graeme choked out a laugh, which she felt all the way to her core. "I'm supposed to ask you that."

She took stock of her body. "I'm quite well, actually."

He tipped up her chin to kiss her. "God, lass, I love you."

"How much?"

When he nudged her, she gasped.

"This much," he said.

Then he began to move. He started slowly, giving her time to catch up with him. When he cupped her bottom, tilting her toward him, Sabrina moaned. Because *that* felt wonderful, and somehow was exactly what she needed. Her arousal built, and her entire body began to tremble.

Graeme stroked into her, his breath coming in hard gasps in her ear. She clutched him, digging her nails in as she wavered on the edge. So close . . . so close . . .

Then he gave her a last, hard nudge, and she tumbled. Waves of pleasure swept through her body, her inner contractions clenching around his erection. When she cried out, Graeme gripped her bottom and held himself tightly against her, his breath hissing from between clenched teeth. He poured himself into her. Sabrina buried her face in his neck as the last remnants of pleasure rippled through her body.

And as her love for him rippled through every bit of her heart and spirit. Graeme was inextricably a part of her in a way she'd never dreamed possible.

She lay quietly in his arms, the intensity of the moment easing into a deep, settled peace. Then Graeme rolled onto his back, bringing her to rest in an undignified sprawl on his broad chest. She was sure to be a sweaty, absolute mess, but she didn't care. She was completely and utterly happy.

"All right, love?" he murmured.

Sabrina nestled her cheek against the crisp hair of his chest. "Aye, that."

The rumble of his laugh vibrated through her entire body.

"Are you?" she thought to ask a moment later.

His hand drifted down to her bottom, sending a sensual shiver up her spine.

"Never better, which I suppose was your plan all along. First, you would lure me into your bed and have your way with me. Then, when I could no longer think straight, you'd propose marriage. It's a wicked lass, you are."

Sabrina trailed her fingertips over his flat stomach, making him twitch. "You'll recall that I proposed before I had my way with you, and you responded in the affirmative."

"That's because I was already imagining the wicked ways. It turned my brain to mush."

Sabrina propped her chin on his chest. "I hope you don't mind."

He lifted his head and an incredulous eyebrow. "Do I look like I mind?"

"No, but . . ."

"But?"

"I did plan to propose," she admitted. "Which was rather forward of me."

"Ye are a cheeky, managing type, ye ken."

When she nipped his chest, he twitched again.

"And how long has this plan been in the works?" he asked in a husky murmur.

"Since that night at the theater, in London."

This time, he went up on his elbow, dislodging her a bit. "Really?"

She wrinkled her nose. "I hope you don't mind."

He nudged her. "Do I feel like I mind?"

His erection had started to burgeon again. "You do not."

"I'm surprised because I was a complete prat to you that night," he said.

"Not so much then, although you were indeed a complete prat several times after that. I almost gave up, but I'm too stubborn to admit defeat."

He huffed out a laugh before dropping his head back to the tumbled pillows. "I apologize for being such a thickhead, and for making it so hard on you."

"Ainsley explained that Kendrick men are rather thickheaded when it comes to love, and that one must be persistent."

"She's not wrong. We're not the easiest lot to manage."

"I'm quite good at managing things, as you've learned."

"Yes, and I've noticed you're rather smug about it, too."

She let out a dramatic sigh. "I'll try not to be *too* managing."

"Excellent, though I can think of one way you can manage me, any time."

In an instant, Graeme had her on her back, bracing his arms around her shoulders. Sabrina gasped, her eyes going wide at the feel of his erection against her thigh.

"Already?" she squeaked.

"Well, I still have to get that scream out of you."

He leaned down and nipped the tender skin of her neck. Sabrina moaned as desire ignited like dried kindling to a spark. When Graeme shifted, moving down her body, she arched her back and spread her arms wide, reveling in the luxurious sensations—

A sharp, ominous crack sounded above them. Graeme jerked up to stare at the heavy wooden canopy over their heads.

"What the—"

As another crack rent the air, Graeme wrapped himself around Sabrina and rolled them right off the bed. They crashed to the floor in the span of a breath before the entire canopy detached from the posts and fell with the screech of splintering wood. The bedposts flew outward, landing on the floor with a resounding thud.

Sabrina lay on top of him, stunned but unharmed. When he'd rolled them off, he'd cushioned her fall with his body.

"Are you all right?" Her voice came out in a screech.

He blinked up at her. "I think so."

"Did you hit your head?"

Carefully, he sat up, bringing her with him. "Not really, mostly my elbows and arse. Are you all right?"

"You're a very effective cushion. Let me look at your arms."

She twisted around to get a look at one of his elbows. The skin had split and was bleeding.

"That needs to be cleaned and bandaged," she fretted.

"Lass, it's nothing."

He was staring grimly at the massive canopy, splintered at the edges but mostly still in one heavy piece.

Sabrina closed her eyes and leaned against him, feeling faint. If he'd not had such quick reflexes . . .

He cuddled her. "Are you sure you're all right?"

She opened her eyes and forced a smile. "Just rather stunned, and grateful not to be as flat as a griddlecake."

They heard a rush of footsteps in the hall before someone banged on the door.

"Sabrina, what happened? Are you all right?" called Royal.

"We're fine," barked Graeme. "Just give us a moment."

"Sabrina, I'm coming in," Ainsley said through the door.

"Wait," Sabrina shrieked.

Graeme winced. "Och, lass, my ears."

"Sorry." She patted his cheek before scrambling to her feet. "Wait a moment, Ainsley. I'm coming."

She retrieved her wrapper. Graeme pulled on his shirt before grabbing the blanket they'd kicked to the floor and wrapping it around his waist.

"My breeches are under that bloody canopy," he said with a grimace.

"Will you two open up?" Royal ordered.

Sabrina hurried to the door, opening it enough to look out. Royal had thrown on breeches and a shirt, while Ainsley was dressed in a rather ugly flannel wrapper.

Sabrina blinked at her. "You, in flannel?"

"One always wears flannel in the Highlands, dear."

"Can we postpone the fashion discussion," Royal impatiently said. "What the hell was that noise? And what the hell is Graeme doing in your room?"

Ainsley's gaze flickered over Sabrina. "I think we know the answer to question two."

Before Sabrina could respond, Davey came rushing down the hall. The footman was fully dressed and carried a pistol.

"Everything all right, Mr. Royal? I heard a terrible crash."

Sabrina leaned out a bit, still keeping the door mostly closed. "Everything's fine. Part of my bedframe collapsed."

When Ainsley bit her lip, obviously trying not to laugh, Sabrina scowled at her. "It's not what you think."

"If you say so."

"It's fine, Davey," Royal said. "Go back downstairs."

The footman tactfully nodded and retreated back down the hall.

"Why is Davey running around with a pistol?" Sabrina asked.

"Graeme and I have some of the servants on rotating watch."

"Kendrick men always like to be prepared." Ainsley waggled her eyebrows. "For anything."

Royal ignored his wife. "Are you going to tell us what happened? That sounded like the entire ceiling of your room fell in."

"Let them in, Sabrina," Graeme said from behind her.

She sighed and opened the door.

Royal and Ainsley gaped at the bed.

"Good God," Royal finally said. "That is . . ."

"Insane." Ainsley whacked Graeme in the arm. "You and furniture. What in God's name were you up to in that bed?"

"Nothing," he protested. "The damn thing just up and collapsed."

"He's right," Sabrina said. "We truly weren't doing anything."

The other couple exchanged an incredulous glance.

"Well, almost nothing," Sabrina amended. "Certainly not enough to cause *that*. Graeme saved us, too. If he'd not moved so quickly, we . . ." She had to swallow.

Ainsley winced in sympathy. "How horrific. And not very romantic, I must say."

"Rather the opposite," Sabrina gloomily replied.

Royal glared at his brother. "I'm not best pleased with this situation, laddie, for a number of reasons."

Graeme rolled his eyes. "No need to get fashed, since we're getting married. Sabrina proposed to me. Before the collapse, fortunately."

Ainsley gave Sabrina a hug. "Congratulations, darling. That is splendid news."

"Thank you. It is rather exciting, isn't it?"

"This conversation is entirely beside the point," Graeme impatiently said. "We need to talk about why that blasted canopy collapsed." He pointed a finger at his sister-in-law. "Do *not* say it again."

Ainsley mimicked locking her lips and throwing away the key. Royal moved closer to inspect the collapsed bed.

"It's very old," said Sabrina. "I suppose the joints might simply have worn out."

"I suppose that's possible, given how neglected the whole place has been," Royal said.

"I'm not so sure." Graeme pointed at the canopy. "Have a look."

One corner where the canopy had separated from the bedpost looked clean, almost as if sliced through.

"That break looks very clean." Royal inspected the other corners. "The others are splintered."

"Wood rot?" Sabrina had seen it before in some of the truly antique pieces at their estate in Northumberland. Age, dampness, and poor maintenance all took their toll.

Graeme looked grim. "That seems implausible to me. The difference is quite marked."

The floor seemed to tilt a bit, perhaps a trick of the flickering firelight.

"What are you suggesting?" Sabrina faintly asked.

"Are you saying someone tampered with the joints in that corner?" Ainsley asked in a horrified voice.

Royal, back to inspecting the first corner, stood up with an aggravated sigh. "The wood seems crumbly around the joint, but it's hard to say for certain."

"Tampering seems pretty damn likely to me," Graeme said, "given everything else going on around here."

"Who knows you sleep in this room?" Royal asked Sabrina.

"Everyone. It's where the mistress of the house always slept."

"Oh, Lord," Ainsley sighed.

Sabrina pressed a palm to her forehead, where a headache was beginning to form. The most wonderful night of her life, and it seemed it had almost ended in murder.

Chapter Twenty-Four

Ainsley regarded the enormous breakfast with a jaundiced eye. "I can't believe I'm saying this, but I'm not even hungry."

Sabrina grimaced in sympathy. "Mrs. Wilson and Hannah made an extra effort, too. Hannah seems to believe that rare beefsteak, coddled eggs, and kippers will smooth over my brush with death."

"If you have any affection for me, do not mention kippers. Although I do think I could manage one of those cheddar and chive scones. Oh, and pass the butter, please."

Sabrina passed the requested items. For herself, she was sticking with dry toast and tea.

"I'm sorry if I kept you awake last night," she said. "I hope I didn't snore."

"Ha. You didn't sleep a wink, I swear." Ainsley slathered a generous helping of butter on her scone. "How could one, after all that commotion?"

Graeme had moved Sabrina into Ainsley's room. Naturally, she'd have preferred to share Graeme's room, but the dratted man had insisted and all but dragged her there. The ladies had been ordered to lock themselves in the bedroom, while the brothers patrolled the house for the rest of the night.

Sabrina thought it an overreaction. Even if her bed had

been tampered with—an uncertain conclusion—there was no way to know when it had occurred or who had done the deed. She refused to believe it could have been anyone from the household staff.

Sabrina had returned to her own room shortly after dawn to get dressed and had found Hannah standing by the bed, moaning and wringing her hands. When the girl had spotted Sabrina, she'd shrieked so loudly she'd brought *everyone* running from all corners of the house.

Sabrina's life was turning into a French farce.

"I'm sorry about this morning," said Sabrina. "You'd finally gotten to sleep, and then Hannah had to start screaming."

"That was at least mildly entertaining. Poor Hannah thought you were a ghost."

"Yes, and it was vastly amusing when the servants wrestled the blasted canopy off my bed and discovered Graeme's breeches and my nightgown."

Ainsley snickered into her teacup. "It's certainly been an interesting adventure. Such is frequently the case with Kendricks."

"This one is all me, I'm afraid."

"That's why you're perfect for Graeme. You're clearly as much trouble as the rest of us."

Perhaps too much trouble. What with this mess and the prospect of facing her father's certain resistance to their marriage, Sabrina couldn't really blame Graeme for having second thoughts. He'd not even kissed her good night after hauling her off to Ainsley's room, nor had he showed one iota of affection this morning.

At this point, she found circumstances more depressing than interesting.

A quiet knock sounded on the door of the breakfast parlor.

"Enter," Sabrina called.

Mr. Wilson stepped in. "Ye wanted to see me, my lady?"

"Yes. Did you have a chance to look at my bed yet?"

"Aye, my lady. That canopy made a right mess, but not to worry. My missus will get it sorted nice and tidy. And if ye canna sleep there, she can move ye to one of the other rooms. Why, the blue bedroom is grand, ye ken. Rob Roy himself slept there, and a great honor it was."

"I meant did you actually examine the bed," she patiently replied. "To ascertain why the canopy failed as it did."

Wilson stared at his boots, as if lost in thought.

"Any conclusions?" Ainsley prodded.

"I reckon it could be wood rot. Yon bed is almost as old as the house, ye ken."

"So . . . not tampered with?" Sabrina asked.

He frowned. "Hard to tell."

She resisted the impulse to throw a scone at his head. "But you think it more likely to be rot, than someone weakening or cutting into the joint."

He pondered that for a bit, then finally nodded. "Aye."

"Thank goodness," Ainsley said. "We have enough problems without worrying about some villain trying to murder us in our beds."

The old man waggled his head, looking like a marionette on a broken string. "Mr. Kendrick ain't wrong to be worried for my lady. There's some not fair happy to see the mistress back in the house."

Ainsley snorted. "Yes, the shooting of bullets would suggest as much."

Sabrina pressed a hand to her temple. Why was it so blasted hard to get a straight answer from anyone? "Mr. Wilson, do you have any idea if the Barrs have remained in the area?"

"Well, ye ken I canna be certain," he hedged.

"Anything you could tell us. Even a rumor of such."

"Well, I have my suspicions that yon—"

He broke off at the sound of footsteps in the hall. Graeme stalked into the room.

"Wilson, what are you doing here? Is there a problem?"

"Nae, sir." The old man scuttled backwards out of the room, almost colliding with Royal.

"Where's he rushing off to?" Royal asked.

"What was he doing here in the first place?" Graeme said.

Sabrina closed her eyes, making an effort to wrestle her temper under control.

"Lass, what's afoot?"

She opened her eyes, taking in Graeme's scowl. He resembled an angry bull, ready to start snorting and pawing at the faded roses on the old wool carpet.

"And a good morning to you, dear sir," she replied in a sugary-sweet tone. "How kind of you to join us for breakfast."

A rueful smile etched the corners of his mouth. "Forgive me, sweetheart. I'm a complete brute."

He tipped up her chin and brushed a lingering kiss across her lips.

"That's better," said Ainsley. "I was beginning to worry about Graeme's romantic skills."

"After what we saw last night, I believe there's no need to worry," Royal commented.

"Yes, feel free to put any such worries to bed," Graeme dryly said.

"So to speak," Ainsley said with a wink.

Sabrina winced. "That's a dreadful pun."

While her cheeks had gone hot, she felt an almost staggering degree of relief at Graeme's display of affection.

He fetched a plate of food from the sideboard and came to sit beside Sabrina. She smiled at him, no doubt looking like a besotted schoolgirl. And how could she help it? She was madly in love, and he loved her back. It was simply glorious, even if someone might be trying to murder her.

He smiled and tapped her nose, then reached for the teapot. "So, what was old Wilson doing in here?"

"I had asked him to take a look at the bed. He does most of the carpentry and repair work at Lochnagar, so I thought his opinion would be useful."

Royal looked up from the pile of ham and scones Ainsley had stacked on his plate. "And?"

"He thinks it's more than likely wood rot."

Graeme frowned. "What about tampering?"

"He thinks tampering is improbable. The bed is likely the oldest piece of furniture in the house, so rot makes sense."

"My parents had a positively ancient dining room table, going back to the time of Charles II," Ainsley said. "It collapsed during my oldest brother's engagement party. Wood rot. Made a dreadful mess."

"That must have pleased you," Royal said.

"Since my brother is a thundering ass, I felt a small degree of satisfaction."

"But no one was trying to kill your brother at the time, I imagine," Graeme said.

Ainsley wrinkled her nose.

"It would be quite difficult to sneak into the house and sabotage such a big piece of furniture," Sabrina pointed out. "One would have to saw or drill through part of the joint, or inflict some other sort of damage. That would surely attract attention."

"But the house was practically deserted until our arrival," Graeme pointed out. "It's not entirely unreasonable to assume that someone could have snuck in to do just that."

"But how would anyone even have known I was coming?" Sabrina protested. "Mrs. Wilson only had a day's notice."

"I admit it's a short timeline, but hardly impossible."

"But Mrs. Wilson was here."

"If Mrs. Wilson was in the kitchen, you could set off a cannon upstairs and she wouldn't hear it," Graeme said.

"None of the Lochnagar servants heard the bed collapse last night, did they? And that made a hell of a racket."

Ainsley sighed. "Drat. What do the servants have to say about all these nefarious doings, anyway?"

Royal snorted. "Very little, as usual."

"So where does that leave us?" Sabrina asked.

When Graeme and Royal exchanged a long glance, her heart sank.

"No," she said firmly. "I am not leaving. If Ainsley doesn't feel safe, Royal should certainly take her back to the city. But I'm staying put."

"Nonsense. If you stay, I stay," Ainsley stoutly replied.

"Ainsley," Royal warned.

When his wife put up an imperious hand, he rolled his eyes.

"Are you sure, dearest?" Sabrina asked. "I don't want to put you in danger."

"Just to be clear, pet, I'm not the one in danger. That would be you."

Sabrina grimaced. "Yes, well—"

"Which is why you're returning to Edinburgh," Graeme cut in. "I've spoken to the Kendrick staff, and they can be ready to leave before lunch. I've also instructed Hannah to begin packing your things."

Irritation tightened Sabrina's stomach. "You certainly had no right to do that."

"I have every right. I'm going to be your husband, and it's my job to protect you."

"Thank you, but—"

"It would be my duty to protect you, anyway," he added.

"Your job, you mean," she groused.

"It's more than a job, but yes. Can you imagine what your father would say if he knew there'd been not one, but two attempts on your life?"

"We have no idea if what happened last night was an

attempt. As for the shooting incident, that entire episode still strikes me as very odd."

"Yes, I've always found it odd when people shoot at innocent young women," Graeme said.

"There's no need for sarcasm, sir. Even you must admit the shooter was inept. Those shots went wide by a good ten feet. I know because I measured them."

"And when did you go down and perform these measurements?" Graeme asked in a rather bone-chilling voice.

"Before dinner last night," Sabrina said.

"Don't look at me," Ainsley said when Graeme scowled at her. "I didn't know about it."

"I didn't go alone," Sabrina added. "I brought Mr. Wilson and Brian with me. Wilson helped me perform the measurements, and Brian kept a lookout."

Graeme covered his eyes with a hand. "A stable boy and an old man. That is just splendid."

"Nothing happened. And I wanted a closer look."

"Sabrina, it's no surprise the shots went wide, since there was no close protection where the shooter could hide. He had to take his chances from that stand of trees, a good hundred feet away. He'd have to be a very good shot to hit the mark."

Sabrina could not help feeling irritated by his rather sound logic. "But both shots went almost *identically* wide."

Graeme simply shrugged, obviously unimpressed with *her* logic.

"Maybe they were shooting at you," she couldn't help saying.

"Don't be silly."

Royal sighed. "Let's all admit to being silly this morning, shall we? But truly, Sabrina, it might be best if you and Ainsley returned to the city. Someone is definitely playing ugly bugger."

"Yes, but if someone *is* hell-bent on revenge, what's to

stop them from attacking me on the road? After all, they know I'm here, and why wouldn't they be watching us?"

"That's why Royal is going back with you," Graeme said. "Along with our groom and footman to guard you."

Sabrina stared at him, aghast. "And leave you unprotected? Absolutely not."

"I'll be fine."

"You will be a target, skulking about in unfriendly territory." She shook her head. "I refuse to turn tail and run. If you wish to send for additional men to help guard the estate, please do so. But I am not leaving you here on your own."

Now Graeme looked downright thunderous. "Sabrina—"

"I'm not abandoning my people, and I am certainly not abandoning you."

"Honestly, Graeme," Ainsley said, "I hope you realize how lucky you are to win such a splendid girl."

"I do. Which is why I'm trying to keep her alive, so I can marry the splendid girl instead of burying a bloody corpse."

"That is a revolting image," Sabrina said.

He switched his glower back to her. "It certainly is, which is why you're leaving this damn place today."

"I will do no such thing."

Graeme stood, drawing himself up to his full height, like a Highland warrior about to go on a rampage.

"Sabrina Bell, you are going to be my wife, which means you'd best start obeying me when I decide something is in your best interest."

Outraged, Sabrina jumped up, struggling to find the words to respond to that piece of masculine idiocy.

Royal snorted. "You've stepped into it now, laddie boy."

"With both feet," Ainsley added.

"Graeme Kendrick," Sabrina said, "this is *my* house and *I* am in charge here. Not to mention the fact that I'm rich and can do what I want."

"What the hell does money have to do with it?" Graeme demanded.

Since she had no idea why she'd said such a silly thing, she ignored his question. "The pertinent fact is that I have as much right to order you around as you have to order me."

"It might be helpful if nobody ordered anybody around," Royal put in.

"Darling, stop being so reasonable," Ainsley said.

"This is a ridiculous conversation," Graeme snapped.

"I agree," Sabrina retorted.

He turned on his heel. "I'm going—"

Sabrina shoved past him. "You stay there. This time, I get to storm out of the room."

From his vantage point overlooking the loch, Graeme had been scanning the large shed, the nearby pier, and the surrounding glen for almost an hour.

He'd finally caught a damn break.

The smuggling actually *was* taking place on Lochnagar lands, and most likely from this small loch. It butted up against one tiny corner of the estate, and eventually emptied out into Loch Laggan. From there, casks of illegal whisky could be transported to Inverness, Islay, and even Galway. The surrounding landholdings were too fallow for anything but a few crofters and sheep, so the remote location was perfect.

Just this morning, he'd stumbled across the entire operation, including a distillery setup in a well-hidden cave only a half hour's walk to the loch. That had been the only bit of good arising from his fight at breakfast with Sabrina. Graeme had been so furious he'd stormed out of the house and gone on yet another search of estate lands, to get away from everyone as much as to do more sleuthing.

Once again, he'd been a thundering idiot to his darling

lass and undoubtedly owed her another apology. But since his splendid albeit frustrating fiancée was determined to stay at Lochnagar, it was imperative to make the place safe for her.

The shed appeared well maintained, which suggested the Barrs used it as a hideout. The small fishing boat tied up to the pier was probably used to move supplies in and whisky out.

Graeme straightened up from behind the shelter of the large blackthorn bush. Since there were no signs of life, he would scout the shed and, with any luck, find some clue as to when the Barrs would return. Then he'd set a trap and roll the bastards up once and for all.

After checking that his horse was securely tied to a nearby bush, he headed along a narrow, gorse-filled ravine that ran almost to the shed. Aside from the ravine and the patch of bushes at the top of the hill, there was little cover. So far he'd not seen a soul, but there was no point in taking a chance.

When he reached the end of the ravine, he climbed up and quickly covered the remaining ground to the back of the shed. He tugged on a sash window. It was locked, but certainly big enough for him to climb through. A quick jab of his elbow broke the glass. He unlocked the window and raised the sash, then pushed aside the burlap curtain and hoisted himself through.

With only one other small window by the door, also covered with burlap, little light seeped in. Impatiently, Graeme dragged aside the other curtain. Sunlight streamed in, falling directly onto several dozen small casks neatly piled up to the ceiling. It didn't take a genius to deduce what was in them.

He strode across the shed and rapped on a few of the casks. Full, and the scent told him they contained prime Highland whisky, ready to be smuggled. From the marks on the floor, there'd been more casks stacked out to the middle of the room. Having engaged in a bit of illegal brewing himself, he was reluctantly impressed by the size of the operation.

The Barrs seemed to have established a roaring business in their corner of Lochnagar. No wonder they were so fashed by their eviction. This type of rig took years to build and couldn't be easily moved or replaced.

The shed also served as living quarters, with a bed against one wall and two smaller cots tipped on their ends in a corner. A roughhewn table with benches took up the center of the room, and a small peat stove stood by the door. A set of shelves contained dishes, glassware, and cooking utensils, along with basic foodstuffs like flour, oats, and tea.

The stove, with its neat stacks of peat, was ready to be lit.

Got ye, ye bastards.

Grinning to himself, Graeme continued his search, finding tattered maps of the surrounding lochs and rivers with smuggling routes marked out in pencil. Even more rewarding was a cache of ledgers. He shook his head at all the careful notations of buyers, shipments, and receipts—evidence that the bloody rig had been running for years, carefully recorded for posterity.

He took one of the ledgers and started for the window, but quickly froze, straining to hear.

Hell and damnation.

Oars slapping against water, then the scrape of wood against the pier.

Time to make a run for it.

He all but hurled himself out the window, landing hard on his side. Getting up, he managed only a few steps before someone clamped hands on his back and pulled him down. Graeme and his assailant landed in a sprawl in the dirt.

Rolling over, he lashed out a boot. The man howled and doubled over, clutching a hand to his groin.

Lucky kick.

Graeme started to push up, but another man jumped him from behind. The bastard was bloody heavy, too, all but knocking the breath out of him. Graeme writhed and managed to drive an elbow into the man's gut.

When the attacker grunted and loosened his grip, Graeme heaved and was able to throw him off. Coming up onto his knees, he drove his fist into the man's face. With a scream, the big bloke collapsed to the ground, clutching his bloody nose.

Graeme shot to his feet, reaching for the pistol inside his coat.

"Leave off, ye bastard," snarled another man in a thick Highland brogue, shoving the barrel of a gun to his skull.

Graeme sighed as his own weapon was confiscated.

"And ye two idiots," barked his captor. "Get yerself out of the dirt before I shoot ye, too."

"He broke my nose, Jackie," whined the big fellow.

"And he broke my nuts," moaned the other one.

"I'll break yer heads if ye don't get up. Bloody useless, ye are. Dinna know why I keep ye around."

The one who'd taken a shot to the groin gingerly climbed to his feet, still cupping himself. He was a tall, skinny lad with a bad complexion, and probably not yet twenty.

"That hurt bad, ye ken," he said to Graeme in a wounded tone.

Graeme shrugged. "Sorry."

The heavy-set fellow lumbered unsteadily to his feet. "My mam willna be pleased about my nose, mister. She doesna like me gettin' hurt, ye ken."

Graeme barely repressed a snort. "My sincere apologies to your mother."

"Och, idiots," came a mutter from behind him. The pistol retreated from Graeme's skull. "Put up yer hands and turn around."

Doing as told, he faced a thickset, middle-aged man with brown hair streaked with gray. He had a canny look, sharp features, and a shrewd, hazel gaze.

"Jackie Barr, I assume?" Graeme drawled.

"Aye, and ye be one of them blasted Kendricks." Jackie shook his head in disgust.

Graeme flashed a smile that was all teeth. "That's right. And if anything happens to me, my clan will hunt you all down and kill you all in a most unpleasant way."

"No killin', Jackie," protested the big bloke. "Ye promised my mam."

"I'd like to kill *ye*," Jackie said in a disgusted tone.

"But I'm yer cousin."

"We canna be killin' no one, including a Kendrick," the skinny lad added. "Ye'll bring the law doon on us."

"Who cares?" Jackie retorted. "No reason to stay in this bloody country, anyway. I'll just shoot the bastard and throw him in the loch, and then it's away, I am."

"Since there are Kendricks in Scotland, England, Germany, and North America, you're out of luck, I'm afraid," Graeme said. "My family will hunt you to the end of the earth."

"Och, Jackie, that sounds bad," said the lad.

"Shut yer trap and fetch some rope from the boat," Jackie snapped.

The lad hobbled around the side of the shed.

The big fellow was now holding a grimy kerchief to his nose. "There's nae need to snap at poor Dickie. He's just a lad."

"And what's your name?" Graeme asked.

"Don't tell—" Jackie started.

"Magnus, sir. Magnus Barr."

"Hello, Magnus. I'm Graeme Kendrick."

"I'd say pleased to meet ye, but for my nose."

"Sorry about that. You almost crushed me to death, though."

Jackie made a disgusted noise. "Magnus, why don't ye just tell him where we live?"

Magnus frowned. "Ye want me to?"

Jackie shot Graeme a sour look. "Ye see what I have to work with?"

"How sad for you. Still, it's not exactly a secret that your entire family is involved in this little venture. The villagers certainly know."

"And they'll keep their bloody mouths shut, or else," Jackie growled.

"They've already started talking, I'm afraid."

"Because of that skinny *Sassenach* bitch. She's the cause of all our trouble."

Graeme's mild sense of amusement was instantly snuffed out. "You'll be lucky if I don't kill *you* for taking those shots at her."

Jackie snorted. "Och, we were just tryin' to scare her. I'll nae be goin' to the gallows for bloody Musgrave and his kin."

Magnus heaved a sigh. "But she's nae one for scarin'."

"No, she's very brave," replied Graeme.

Jackie muttered a curse, clearly losing patience with the inane conversation. What he didn't lose, unfortunately, was his focus on keeping his pistol pointed at Graeme.

"Dickie, where the hell are ye?"

The lad scuttled up, carrying a length of rope. "Ye needna yell, Jackie."

"What took ye so long?"

"I can barely walk, ye ken." He glared at Graeme.

"Sorry, lad. It was just a lucky shot," Graeme said.

Dickie blinked, then gave Graeme a tentative smile.

Clearly, not all the Barrs were as bloodthirsty as Jackie. The poor lads actually seemed quite decent—a factor Graeme intended to exploit.

"Magnus, tie Kendrick up, good and tight, then get him into the shed," Jackie ordered.

The big man followed his cousin's instructions, tying the blasted ropes very tight. Graeme had no hope of wriggling free. He'd have to talk his way out of this one.

Fortunately, a plan was already taking shape in his brain.

Magnus steered him around to the front of the shed. Graeme mentally cursed when he saw two other men on the pier loading barrels into a second boat. It was now five against one.

"How'd you know I was here?" Graeme asked Jackie after Magnus led him to a bench inside.

"Saw your horse as we were comin' in to meet the boat. Then the broken window."

"Still running your rig on Lochnagar lands, obviously."

"Nae," Dickie earnestly replied. "We were evicted."

"He knows we were evicted, ye twiddlepoop," Jackie said. "He means now."

Dickie brightened. "Oh. We been stayin' with kin, just on the other side of the loch."

"Aye," said Magnus. "My mam's family be crofters on the next estate."

When Jackie shook his head in disgust, Graeme could almost sympathize.

Almost.

"So you were still able to run the rig by coming across the loch and avoiding most of the estate," Graeme said. "Makes perfect sense."

"Until ye showed up," Jackie said. "We were just up and runnin' again, but ye lot sent it all to hell."

"The eviction must have hurt."

"It was a pain in my arse, but we were managin'." Jackie

pulled a bottle down from the shelf and brought it back to the table. He poured a dram into a cloudy-looking glass and shot it down in one go.

"I could use one of them," Magnus hopefully said.

"Ye'll nae get anything until those casks are loaded," Jackie said. "Get to work. Ye too, Dickie."

The two men exchanged an aggrieved look, then started hauling the casks out the door.

"You've obviously been running this rig for some time," Graeme said. "Since the death of Lady Sabrina's grandfather, I imagine."

Jackie scoffed. "Longer than that. My da was doin' it for years, while old Chattan was alive."

Old Chattan was obviously Sir Robert Chattan, Sabrina's grandfather. "And Chattan didn't mind?"

"My da kept it small. Supplied the estate and the pub. Barely made a penny on it, the barmy old coot. Didna want to offend Chattan or cause any trouble with the law."

"Not you, though."

"Wasna goin' to have Chattan lordin' it over me." He flashed an ugly grin. "Fortunately, the old fool kicked off shortly after my da."

"And then Mr. Hugo showed up. That must have made things easier."

"Aye. Musgrave didn't give a damn about the place. But Hugo." Jackie tapped the side of his nose. "He was a canny one. He knew where the real money was."

"What about the old business manager, the one in Edinburgh? Was he in on it, too?"

Jackie rolled his eyes. "That old loony? As long as Hugo kept the rents comin' in, he didna care."

Sabrina had been right. Musgrave's disregard for Lochnagar, benign or not, had caused a great deal of misery.

"But something changed."

Jackie poured another dram. "That twit of a manager in

Edinburgh finally got suspicious when my family wasna evicted, so he up and fired poor Hugo. He said Hugo wasn't enforcin' the Clearances like Musgrave wanted, and if he found any dirty dealings, he'd bring in the law. Hugo disappeared right quick after that."

"As did Mr. Francis, eventually," Graeme dryly replied.

Jackie laughed. "Och, that dandy prat. Thought to get rid of us, he did."

"Well, you were evicted."

"Poncy fool even threatened us. Francis said he would complain to Musgrave if we tried to use Lochnagar lands. Said Musgrave was an important man." Jackie snorted. "And close to the king, as if we give a shite about that."

"So, you threatened Francis and scared him off."

"Oh, aye," Magnus said, who'd just clomped back in to retrieve another cask. "Told him we'd gut him and throw him into the loch. Silly bugger believed us."

Jackie snorted out another laugh.

"But that wasn't enough. You needed to scare Musgrave off, too. That's why you started those rumors of a plot against him."

"Aye."

Graeme couldn't help a bit of professional curiosity. "How did you get the rumors started?"

"Used our contacts on the smuggling routes. We run our stuff into Argyll, Inverness, even Edinburgh. Easy enough to drop a word here and there, and then it spreads."

"You made it sound like it was about the Clearances, not smuggling."

"Lots of people angry over the Clearances, so it made sense." Jackie shot Graeme a hard look. "Can ye blame them?"

"No. But it was never about that."

Jackie shrugged.

"And what about the threats to the king? Was that another distraction?"

Dickie, who was dragging a cask across the floor, flashed a grin. "Och, we was just larkin' about with that one. Havin' a bit of fun."

Graeme glared at him. "You spread rumors about killing the king, just for fun?"

"Oy, dinna be draggin' that cask," Jackie barked. "Pick it up, ye lazy oaf."

Dickie bristled. "I ain't lazy, Jackie. My arms are gettin' tired."

"I'll make 'em more than tired if ye break a cask."

Graeme sat there, stunned into silence. For a month, he'd been driving himself crazy over an assassination rumor that had turned out to be a damn joke. No wonder it had proved so elusive.

He throttled back the urge to bang his head on the table. "The threat to Musgrave wasn't a lark, though."

Jackie shrugged. "If we scared him good and proper, we figured he'd leave us alone. Especially after Francis skived off."

Graeme narrowed his gaze. "You bloody well *shot* at Lady Sabrina."

"I wasna tryin' to hit her," Magnus earnestly said. "I'd never shoot a woman."

"But the silly bitch must be too stupid to get scared," Jackie said with disgust.

Once he was free, Graeme would take a great deal of satisfaction in pummeling Jackie into the dirt.

"And what about the bed?" he asked. "How'd you pull that off?"

Jackie frowned. "What bed?"

"The bed in Lady Sabrina's room. The wooden canopy collapsed onto it."

Magnus and Dickie exchanged confused looks.

"I dinna ken what ye be talkin' about," Jackie said.

If this situation weren't so horribly deranged, Graeme would have laughed. Sabrina was right. It had been wood rot, after all.

"So, your plan was to scare Musgrave, terrorize the locals into silence, and continue your business on Lochnagar lands."

"Aye, that's about the size of it," Jackie smugly replied.

"Far be it from me to criticize," Graeme said, "but that is a remarkably stupid plan."

Magnus nodded. "My mam didna like the plan one bit, ye ken."

"Shut up about yer mam," Jackie snarled, "or I'll bash yer stupid face."

Graeme leaned across the table, ignoring his throbbing hands. "Look, I've done a bit of illegal distilling myself. But you've been terrorizing innocent people and risking lives. It has to stop."

"Musgrave threw us off our lands and ruined our business," Jackie retorted. "What the hell else were we supposed to do?"

"Go legitimate. The British government is starting to legalize operations as big as yours. In fact, they're encouraging Highlanders to obtain licenses for legal breweries."

Dickie dropped a cask. "What?"

"Dinna be dropping the goods," Jackie roared.

Dickie and Magnus ignored him.

"Ye mean we can do this, legal-like?" Magnus asked in a disbelieving tone.

"Yes."

"Bollocks," Jackie spat out. "Dinna believe him, lads."

"Word of a Highlander and word of a Kendrick," Graeme said. "Parliament is looking to put an end to the smuggling, *and* they know there's a demand for a higher quality brew.

Everyone knows that means Highland whisky, made by Highlanders."

Graeme was all in favor of the government's new direction. The smuggling trade would always find a way around the law. It was much better to bring the illegal distilleries into the fold, an elegant solution for everyone involved.

"Coo," breathed Dickie. "Wouldna that be somethin'?"

"In fact, I suspect Lady Sabrina would be willing to partner with you."

If not, Graeme would. After all, he was already familiar with the business model.

"If ye think I'll be doin' business with some bleedin' *Sassenach*, yer out of yer bleedin' mind," Jackie sneered.

Magnus still looked hopeful. "But my mam—"

Jackie pounded the table, rattling the glassware. "If ye dinna shut up about yer mam, I'll toss her into the bloody loch."

Magnus looked shocked. "Jackie, she's yer auntie!"

"Och, shut yer trap." Jackie glared at Graeme. "I ain't stupid, ye ken. Musgrave willna be workin' with the likes of me. He'll see me hanged first."

Likely true, since Jackie had threatened Sabrina. To Musgrave, that would constitute a hanging offense.

But Magnus and Dickie were clearly harmless and eager for a way out.

Divide and conquer.

Graeme shrugged. "You have a legal and profitable way out of this mess, but if you want to toss that chance aside, it's your choice."

"Yer damn right it is."

Dickie breathed out a sad sigh. Magnus now looked both morose and swollen.

"So, what's the plan?" Graeme asked. "You've got to know you're done here."

"Aye, this is our last run." Jackie looked thoughtful, but then suddenly flashed an evil grin. "But I gots a new plan, thanks to you. And it's a good one."

He shoved to his feet. "Dinna ye worry, lads," he said to his kin. "I'll be gettin' us a good haul, and then we'll be shakin' the dirt of the Highlands from our boots."

Chapter Twenty-Five

Sabrina had been pacing the carpet in the drawing room for the last half hour. By now she knew every faded line and squiggle in the Persian design.

"Come have a dram," Ainsley said from the chaise, where she was working on her needlepoint. "It'll calm your nerves."

"You said that when I had my first dram. It didn't work." Sabrina had no intention of getting tipsy when Graeme might be in trouble and needing her help. "He should have returned at least a half hour ago to change for dinner. But no one has seen him since that stupid fight."

"We're keeping country dinner hours, remember? He likely just lost track of time."

After the horrid scene at breakfast, Sabrina had stormed up to her bedroom and had to storm right out again, since the servants were still cleaning up the mess. By the time she'd retreated to the garden and done a bit more stalking around the overgrown paths, she'd begun to feel entirely foolish about her tantrum.

The fact that Graeme had acted like an idiot didn't excuse the silly things she'd said. This soon-to-be-marriage business was certainly turning out to be complicated.

"He's obviously off looking for various Barrs and other

villainous types," Ainsley said. "Kendricks hate standing still when there's a problem. They'd rather run off half-cocked than sit and have a sensible discussion."

Sabrina sighed and dropped into the closest chair. "I know I'm acting silly."

"You're acting like a woman in love, and Graeme is acting like a man in love. It takes some getting used to."

"But what if he is in trouble?"

"Graeme is the one member of this family who *is* almost indestructible. He has survived more mishaps than you can imagine."

"One's luck does eventually run out."

"He doesn't survive out of luck. Graeme is very capable. And very smart. He's really quite formidable." Ainsley pointed a finger at her. "Do not tell him I said that. He'll get a swelled head."

Despite her anxiety, Sabrina chuckled. "He already has one."

"It's an act. He's really just a very nice boy."

"He is rather nice, isn't he?"

"Yes, and perfectly capable of looking after himself. He'll be fine."

Except he hadn't been fine when Old Bill had gotten his hands on him. Graeme occasionally did reckless things. Sabrina had the feeling this could be one of those occasions.

When Royal came in, she twisted in her chair.

"Anything?" she anxiously asked.

"I'm afraid not. Brian confirmed that he went out riding shortly after breakfast and has not been seen since."

"Drat the man," Ainsley said. "What do you want to do?"

"I told Bobby to saddle up a few horses. We're going to go out and look for him."

Sabrina stood. "I'm going with you."

Royal frowned. "I don't think that's a good idea. Graeme

would kill me if I let you come along, especially if there turns out to be trouble."

"I don't care."

Ainsley put aside her needlepoint. "Dearest, I don't think—"

Mrs. Wilson stuck her head into the room. "My lady, the vicar is here. He's insisting—"

Mr. Brown slid by the housekeeper. "I'm sorry to be impolite, Lady Sabrina, but we have a problem."

"Is it Graeme?" she asked.

The vicar solemnly nodded. "Unfortunately, it would appear that Mr. Kendrick has been kidnapped by the Barr family."

Sabrina pressed a hand to her suddenly roiling stomach. Royal muttered a curse.

"Do we know if he's unharmed?" Ainsley quickly asked.

"As far as we know," Brown replied.

Sabrina ignored her protesting insides. "How did you learn of this?"

"Rather unbelievably, one of the Barrs came to me looking for help. He's not keen on kidnapping and is most unhappy with Jackie Barr."

"Jackie Barr is the ringleader?" Royal asked.

"Correct," the vicar replied. "Magnus is part of the smuggling ring, yet is rather a simple soul."

"For a smuggler," Ainsley dryly interjected.

"Most of the family is quite decent," Brown earnestly said. "Jackie's the true problem. He's frightened his family into doing his bidding. But this business with Mr. Kendrick was too much for poor Magnus. He showed up on my doorstep less than an hour ago. I would have come sooner, but it took me some time to get the story out of him."

"Where is Magnus now?" Sabrina asked.

"I brought him to the pub to speak to old Mr. Chattan. Mr. Monroe is keeping an eye on him." Brown grimaced.

"They're demanding a ransom. Magnus was to pass a note to you through a servant at Lochnagar. One of the demands is that you bring the ransom money yourself, Lady Sabrina."

"Good God," Royal said, disgusted. "Not this again."

Sabrina waved an impatient hand. "Why didn't Magnus come directly to me for help?"

"He's frightened." Brown shrugged. "And he trusts me."

She nodded. "I'll go fetch my purse."

And she'd need to get a few of the jewels she'd brought on this trip. If she and Graeme persisted in getting held up and kidnapped, she'd soon have nothing left to wear.

Royal put out a restraining hand. "Hang on. We need a plan—and help. Vicar, do you think any of the villagers would be willing to assist?"

"Possibly," Brown said. "I can't be sure."

"Blast. Because they don't trust me yet," Sabrina said.

The vicar gave a helpless shrug.

Royal grimaced. "We don't dare go charging into this situation without backup."

"We're not going to charge," Sabrina said. "I'm simply going to bring the ransom and get Graeme back."

"Sabrina, Barr hates you. There's no telling what he would do once he got you in his clutches."

"I'm afraid that's true, my lady," Brown said.

She flapped her arms. "Well, do any of you have a better idea?"

"You have to ask for help," Ainsley calmly said. "From *your* people."

"But they don't trust me."

Ainsley shook her head. "That's not clear. What they *do* know, however, is that you haven't cut and run."

Sabrina stepped on her panic. What choice was there? She had to trust that Ainsley was right.

"I need to speak to Magnus Barr," Sabrina said, heading for the door. "And then we need to muster a rescue."

The others scrambled after her into the hall.

"Royal, can you see that our horses are saddled?" Sabrina asked. "I'm going up to put on my riding boots and fetch my purse."

He nodded and strode down the hall past a startled Mrs. Wilson.

"Mrs. Wilson, please fetch your husband," Sabrina instructed. "I might need his help."

"Aye, my lady." She hurried off in Royal's wake.

"What do you wish me to do?" the vicar asked.

"Keep Magnus at the pub, please. Tie him down if you must, but don't let him leave." She then dashed for the stairs.

Ainsley caught up with her. "That was very masterful. Graeme would be proud."

"If anything happens to him . . ." Sabrina couldn't even finish the thought.

"Just get your things. I'll meet you out front in ten minutes."

Ainsley picked up her skirts and ran down the corridor toward her bedroom.

Sabrina pelted in the other direction, bursting into her room. She threw a wool pelisse over her evening gown and wrestled on her boots. Then she grabbed her reticule, along with a few bracelets and an opal necklace, and went back down the hall at a dead run.

When she reached the front door, Wilson and Ainsley were waiting for her.

"We look ridiculous," Ainsley said as they hurried to the courtyard. "A mad rescue in our evening gowns. We'll never hear the end of it from Graeme."

Sabrina flashed a wobbly smile as the groom gave her a

leg up into the saddle. The others quickly mounted, and within seconds they were pounding down the drive toward Dunlaggan.

Ten minutes later, they pulled up in front of the pub. It appeared the entire hamlet had gathered there.

"Here, my lady, let me help ye down," said the butcher.

"Thank you." She glanced around. "Quite the crowd."

"Waitin' to see what ye'll do." He leaned in to murmur. "We're all sick of the Barrs, ye ken. But some still be fashed ye might be leavin' us. Then we'd be in the lurch."

Sabrina thanked him before facing the crowd. While some of the villagers seemed wary and suspicious, most looked to be quietly anxious and waiting for a sign.

"Ah, Mrs. Ferguson," she said to the middle-aged woman who ran the small fabric and notions shop. "I've been meaning to chat with you. The draperies at Lochnagar are simply falling apart. May I come by your shop next week to discuss replacement materials?"

The woman blinked, then gave an eager nod. "Aye, my lady. I'll start pulling samples."

"Thank you." Sabrina cast a glance over the small assembly. "I intend to visit all the shops and services in Dunlaggan over the next few weeks. There is a great deal of work to be done at Lochnagar, and I'm counting on your support to accomplish it."

Without waiting for a response, she turned and strode to the pub door. Royal reached it ahead of her.

"Well done," he said.

"Money talks," Ainsley added as she followed them inside.

"Let's hope it speaks loudly to the Barr family," Sabrina replied.

At a center table sat a brawny young man holding a cloth to his face. In his plain shirt, leather jerkin, and breeches, he looked like a local crofter. Sitting with him were Chattan and Monroe. A few other villagers were scattered about the room, most scowling at the young man.

Patty came out from behind the bar with a wet cloth in her hand. "Here, Magnus. Change it out with this one."

The fellow gingerly pulled away the cloth he'd been holding and accepted the new one from her. "Thank ye, Patty. Yer a peach."

Magnus had a black eye and his nose was obviously broken. Sabrina had a good idea who'd inflicted the damage.

"I'll peach ye, ye booby." Patty glanced at Sabrina. "Her ladyship is here. Now, ye behave yerself or I'll break more than that nose, do ye hear?"

"Aye, Patty."

The young man's gaze followed the girl as she returned behind the bar.

Monroe jabbed his shoulder. "And dinna make those sheep's eyes at my daughter. Yer nae good enough for her."

"Och, Da. Leave him alone. He's had enough of a beatin' for one day," Patty replied.

"Love is in the air," Royal murmured.

"Maybe that's why he decided to throw over the evil Jackie," Ainsley replied.

"Let's find out," Sabrina said.

She walked over to the table and crossed her arms. "Magnus Barr, I presume."

The young man scrambled up and bobbed his head. "Aye, my lady. Thank ye for comin'. I'm right sorry about all this."

"As you should be. You're very lucky that Mr. Brown vouched for you, or I'd have already turned you over to the law."

Magnus breathed out a morose sigh. "I'd deserve it. Makin' homebrew is one thing, but kidnappin' and such? And my mam's been after me to quit. She dinna like duffers and free traders, ye ken."

"Your mother sounds very wise."

"She'll be givin' me a worse lickin' than this when she finds out what we done."

"Did Graeme do that to you?" Royal asked.

"Aye. Mr. Graeme got me and Dickie both. Just about broke puir Dickie's nutmegs."

Sabrina frowned. "I don't know what that means."

"Never mind," Royal hastily said. "Is my brother unharmed?"

"Oh, aye. Jackie did threaten to shoot him and dump him in the loch, but Dickie and me said nae. We couldna allow that."

Sabrina pressed a hand to her temple. "Oh, thank God."

Monroe, who'd also risen, touched her arm. "Sit ye doon, my lady."

Sabrina sank gratefully into the empty seat, mustering a shaky smile for Mr. Chattan.

The old man regarded her thoughtfully before reaching across and patting her hand. "We'll get yer man, my lady, never fear."

"We'll need Dunlaggan's help." She grimaced. "I know it's a lot to ask, especially since . . ."

"Since yer da neglected us all these years?"

She nodded.

"And are ye thinkin' of packing up and scampering back to England, or will ye be stayin' here a spell?"

"No scampering anywhere, I promise."

"Even with all the shootin' and kidnappin' and such?"

"We're hoping to put an end to all that," Royal said dryly.

"I wasna tryin' to hit ye, my lady," Magnus earnestly said. "I made sure my shots went wide."

"Ye were the one shootin' at Lady Sabrina?" Patty yelped. "Ye lumpen fool!"

"I said I made sure I missed her, ye ken!"

"The lad may not have much brain, but he's a grand shot,"

Chattan commented. "If he says he missed ye on purpose, he did."

"Why did you shoot at me, Magnus?" Sabrina asked.

"Jackie wanted to scare ye away. Ye dinna seem like the scarin' type, though."

"You're right about that. Now, can you tell me Jackie's ransom demands?"

"Aye. Yer to bring the blunt to the shed on Loch Mashie, where we've been storin' the goods. Then Jackie'll let yer man go."

"Just like that?" she skeptically asked.

"Jackie says we canna stay here anymore. But Dickie and me? Well, Dunlaggan's our home, ye ken. My mam is here, and . . ."

His gaze flitted to Patty, who commenced a vigorous polishing of the bar. Apparently, the girl had discovered a new object for her affections.

Magnus grimaced. "Jackie ain't a good man, my lady. He dinna care about anyone but himself. I'm right afeared of what he might do if he canna get his way."

Sabrina was afraid, too, for Graeme and for everyone here who'd suffered from the Clearances and the years of neglect. In his own way, her father was as much to blame as Jackie Barr for the current state of affairs.

It was up to her to fix it.

"If you help me rescue Mr. Kendrick," she said, "I promise you and Dickie can stay at Lochnagar. I'll see that your crofts are restored, and that you are able to take care of your mother."

Magnus stared down at her, clearly thunderstruck. "That . . . that would be grand, my lady. And Mr. Kendrick said ye'd be happy to go into business with us, too. We'd work as hard as can be, ye ken. I promise."

Sabrina felt her mouth sag. "Um, what business?"

"The whisky business." He gave her an encouraging

smile, which made his swollen eye all but disappear. "It's legal now, ye ken."

Royal softly laughed. "Well done, Graeme. That's brilliant."

Sabrina threw him a questioning look.

"I'll explain later." Royal pulled a chair over and sat next to Chattan. "If it's the right shed that I've got in mind, it'll be hard to get a jump on Barr. There's barely a tree for miles around."

Concerned mutterings sounded from the other tables.

After glancing around the room, Sabrina pinned Chattan with her gaze. The old man held the key. He was the closest thing Dunlaggan had to a village elder. He was also a member of her clan, and his support could mean the difference between success and failure.

Chattan—and the villagers—would have to trust her. And she would have to trust them.

"Well, sir?" she asked. "Will Dunlaggan come to my help?"

He removed the unlit pipe from his mouth. "Yer our lady, are ye not?"

She smiled. "Aye, that."

"Then just say what ye need, and ye shall have it."

The days were long this time of year. Even so, dusk had fallen by the time they were in position. That should have made things easier, but Sabrina's nerves were still taut as an overstrung harp.

"You don't have to do this," Royal said. "I'm sure Barr would take the money from me."

She shook her head. "Magnus said Jackie blames my father for everything. Humiliating me is one way for him to exact a measure of revenge."

Royal made a frustrated noise. "Graeme will kill me if anything happens to you."

"Barr won't hurt me. He just wants to embarrass me."

She sounded more confident than she felt. Pistols and criminals made for a bad combination. As Graeme said, things could quickly go sideways.

"I have to do this," she added. "Graeme needs me."

Royal's flinty gaze grew soft. "Aye, he does. All right, then. Just stick to the plan, and we should be fine."

Chattan, who was standing beside them on the hillock overlooking the shed, waved a hand. "Barr's a right bastard, but he's nae stupid. He won't hurt Musgrave's daughter. Not worth it."

Royal peered at his pocket watch in the dim twilight. "It's past time to hand over the money, so we'd best not dawdle any longer. Hopefully the others are now in place."

Their plan was simple. Sabrina, with Royal and Chattan, had boldly ridden in. Since Barr would be expecting them, there was no reason to try to mask their approach.

In fact, their obvious arrival would hopefully serve as a diversion. Wilson, Mr. Monroe, and several villagers were to row quietly across the loch under cover of the falling dusk, and wait just offshore. If Barr tried to escape or hurt someone, they would spring into action.

It sounded easy, but could go wrong in so many ways.

Sabrina smoothed the skirts of her pelisse, surreptitiously checking the inside pocket to ensure her pistol was easily accessible.

"Remember, just give him the money and get out of the way," Royal instructed. "No heroics, all right? We'll do the rest."

Good thing she'd neglected to mention that she was carrying a weapon. "You must be thinking of some other Lady Sabrina. I'm never reckless."

He snorted. "You're as bad as Graeme. No wonder you're perfect for each other."

"It's grand to have such a brave lady come home to Lochnagar," said Chattan. "Your grandda would be fair bustin' with pride, ye ken."

Since that made Sabrina feel rather misty, she simply gave him a smile.

Royal gave her a quick hug. "Off with you, lass, and be careful."

She headed down the hill, carefully picking her way over the rocky, gorse-covered ground. How absurd would it be if she tripped and sprained an ankle, like one of those silly heroines in lurid stories? Sabrina knew she was no heroine, but the current situation seemed to call for one. That meant making no careless moves, keeping her nerve, and not falling flat on her face.

The shed was just a squat, dark blot on the shoreline. A light flickered at the back window as a curtain was moved aside. Then all went dark again but for the glow from a lantern on the pier. It cast enough light for her to safely walk around to the front, where another lantern sat on a crate by the door. It illuminated the rustic porch and a boat tied close to the shoreline.

Sabrina had no idea if the villagers were already in place out on the water, safely hidden by darkness from prying eyes. If not . . .

You're a heroine, remember? Go rescue your hero.

She stepped firmly onto the porch, but stayed at the edge when the door opened. Suddenly, a bulky figure stood backlit in the doorway.

"Took ye long enough," he growled.

"Mr. Barr, I presume?"

"Jackie'll do fine. We don't hold with fancy titles in these parts, lass."

"My name is Lady Sabrina, and you *will* address me

by my proper title, especially since you are trespassing on my lands."

When she heard a familiar snort from inside, her knees wobbled with relief. Graeme was alive and apparently well enough to be amused by her answer.

Jackie strolled out. He spat a wad of chewing tobacco that landed mere inches from her boots. Royal had warned her that Barr would try to bait her.

"Yer lands? Ye never set foot on them until a few weeks ago. My family's been here for decades, ye ken. Until yer bastard of a da kicked us off."

"I regret the negative impact of the Clearances, and I will do everything I can to correct all of it. What I cannot do, however, is ignore criminal activity or allow you to terrorize the villagers or my people."

"Sabrina," Graeme called from inside, "just give him the money and let him be on his way."

Jackie's hard, intelligent gaze studied her, so she studied him back. His stance was relaxed, both hands thrust into the pockets of a rough wool coat. He didn't look nervous at all.

"Yer fella's got some sense, ye ken. Get ye in here, and let's make the deal."

"Sabrina, stay out on the porch," Graeme barked.

She mentally rolled her eyes. "Yes, Mr. Kendrick. I'm aware."

Royal had warned her about that, too. If she went inside the shed, she could be taken hostage. Keeping her distance from Barr would allow the men in the boats a clear line of fire, if necessary. Royal was also making his way around to the other side of the shed, so—

"And we can see that other fellow creepin' along the side," Jackie said, as if reading her thoughts. "I got other men in here, ye ken. Best not be tryin' to pull a fast one, lassie."

"I simply wish to pay you off and see you gone from

Lochnagar," Sabrina replied. "If you bring Mr. Kendrick out, I will do just that."

"Ye have the money?"

Sabrina pulled a wad of notes from her reticule.

"How much?"

"Fifty pounds."

Jackie sneered. "Ye'll need to do better than that."

"I also have jewelry—two gold bracelets and an opal necklace."

"Hand 'em over."

"Not until you bring Mr. Kendrick out."

Jackie suddenly peered beyond her into the gloom. "Where's Magnus, by the way? What did ye do with him?"

"Not a damn thing," said Chattan, suddenly looming out of the dark. He strolled up beside Sabrina.

For such an ancient, he was certainly spry. And very stealthy.

"Oh, hell, not ye," Jackie groaned. "Where's my cousin, ye old coot?"

"Kept him as a hostage," Chattan said. "Just to make sure ye held to yer word."

Of course, Magnus had been pathetically grateful to play the role of hostage, so as to avoid the confrontation with his cousin.

"He's useless, anyway. Yer welcome to him."

"Magnus is certainly well rid of you," Sabrina said. "Now, if you want your ransom, bring Mr. Kendrick out. This episode is growing quite tiresome."

Jackie tipped his hat in a mocking salute. "As ye say, yer ladyship. Bring him out," he called over his shoulder.

A gangly and exceedingly nervous lad led his captive out to the porch. Sabrina winced when she saw Graeme's arms so tightly lashed behind his back.

"Och, Dickie," Chattan said with disgust. "What have ye gotten yerself into?"

"I dinna ken, Mr. Chattan—"

"Shut yer trap, boy," growled Jackie. "And stay right there with that bloody great bloke."

Sabrina anxiously studied Graeme for any sign of injury. He was disheveled and grim-looking, but mostly seemed unhurt.

"Are you all right?" she asked.

"Aye, but you should *not* be here."

"Mr. Barr's instructions were very clear."

"You didn't have to follow them."

She scoffed. "I couldn't let him hurt you."

"Save yer lover's tiff for later," Jackie ordered. "Now, bring me the ransom."

"Throw it to him, lass," Graeme said.

She was about to comply when Jackie's hand emerged from his pocket. The cad pointed a pistol right at her.

Graeme cursed and lunged forward, but a man barreled out of the shed. The brute shoved Dickie aside and clamped a hand on Graeme's shoulder, restraining him.

"Stand fast, ye bastard," he barked.

Of course Jackie would have his men waiting in the shed. He was a criminal, but certainly not a stupid one.

Jackie waved the pistol at her. "Get over here."

"Do as he says, Sabrina," Graeme calmly said. "I promise it will be fine."

She flashed him a shaky smile, then inched forward. Jackie clamped his hand around her wrist and yanked. She yelped, crashing into him, but the blasted man barely moved.

"If you harm even one hair on her head, I *will* kill you." Graeme's low, lethal snarl lifted the hairs on the back of Sabrina's neck. Even Jackie looked disconcerted.

"I'll nae be hurtin' her. She's just a little insurance till we get clear of ye." He gave Sabrina a shake. "And stop wriggling aboot and open that damn purse, so I can have a look."

While she complied, Chattan strolled over to the lantern that was perched on the crate. He fetched a small spill from his pocket, thrust it into the lantern's flame, and then made a show of lighting his pipe. He'd overstuffed it, so sparks flew and the tobacco flared up.

It was the signal to the men out on the loch.

"Always knew ye were a fool, Jackie," Chattan said, puffing away.

Jackie peered into Sabrina's reticule, then gave a satisfied grunt and nodded at the man holding Graeme. "All right, Sam. Shove him down on that bench, and let's be off."

Jackie started to pull Sabrina toward the pier.

She resisted. "What are you doing?"

"Let her go," Graeme barked. "Take me instead."

"Och, I'm sick of the sight of ye, Kendrick." Jackie dragged Sabrina toward the boat. "And I'll nae be harmin' her. We'll let her off on the other side of the loch. Ye can fetch her when ye find a boat."

Graeme was on his feet. Jackie's accomplice leveled a pistol at him as he backed toward the pier.

"Stop, Graeme," Sabrina yelled. "I'll be all right."

Actually, she was no longer certain of that. Still, she couldn't allow Graeme to get shot trying to save her. With his hands tied, what could he do?

Where in God's name was Royal?

"Sabrina." Graeme's face looked pale in the light of the lantern, his expression anguished.

"I'll be all right," she repeated.

"Dickie, untie the boat," Jackie ordered.

The lad jerked forward, starting toward the pier.

"Don't do it, boy," Chattan said.

Dickie cast a panicked look at Jackie. "But—"

The old man smiled. "It'll be fine, lad. Trust me."

Dickie drew in a wavering breath and stared at his cousin. "I'll nae be goin' with ye."

Jackie snorted. "Stupid lad. Suit yerself."

Graeme moved up to stand with Dickie and Chattan, looking ready to murder Barr. Then he glanced to his left. "Finally."

A pistol fired, and Sam screamed and fell to his knees on the damp planks of the pier. Royal appeared out of the night, smoking weapon in hand.

"Goddammit," Jackie yelled. "I swear I'll shoot her."

Sabrina realized she only had one choice. She steeled herself, and then threw all her weight against her captor. Jackie cried out, wheeling an arm in a desperate bid for balance before falling off the side of the pier, taking Sabrina with him into the water.

The *freezing* water.

Unlike the Serpentine, there was no shallow bottom here. As her boots filled and her clothes weighed her down, Sabrina fought panic and struggled to reach the surface.

She broke free, gasping, hair streaming in her eyes. Flailing about, she smacked someone's face.

"Stupid cow!" yelled Jackie from right behind her.

He shoved her down, and she went under again. The water sucked her into its dark, terrifying void.

She felt more than saw a body arrowing into the loch, right next to her. A hand clamped onto the back of her collar and pulled her up to the surface. Coughing, she drew the sharp night air into her lungs. An arm snaked around her shoulders and pulled her against a broad chest.

"I've got you, love," Graeme said. "Don't struggle."

Sabrina managed to wipe her eyes, and the shoreline wavered back into view. There were other boats now beached on the sands and men running toward the pier.

"Where's . . . where's Barr?" Her teeth chattered.

"Royal's got him," Graeme said as he swam them to the shoreline.

Monroe and Wilson splashed out into the shallow water to meet them, pulling them toward the gravelly shore.

"I can't b . . . believe how deep that water is," Sabrina stuttered as she and Graeme sloshed through the last few feet. "And how cold."

"It's quite a drop-off."

"How did you get free?"

"Dickie cut me loose."

"G . . . good for Dickie."

Graeme swept her up, sodden clothing and all, and carried her to the shed.

She gazed up at him, his hair shiny and sleek against his skull. His mouth was set in a taut line, and he looked grim as death.

"Are you all right?" she asked, patting his cheek.

"I'm fine. But if we don't get you out of these wet things . . ."

She mentally grimaced. The idea of her drowning or falling ill from a dunking would naturally terrify him.

"I'm f . . . fine, too," she said. "Please don't worry."

He carried her through the front door and carefully set her down on a bench.

"Ye could've been killed, ye daft lass."

He snatched a blanket off a bed, wrapped it tightly around her, and then went to the stove to layer on peat. Within a minute, a roaring fire poured out blessed warmth into the room.

"Graeme, I didn't hit my head or inhale any water. I just need a change of clothing." She smiled up at him. "After all, you'll recall that it's not the first time I've had a dunking."

He snorted. "You *are* daft."

"As are you."

"True, that."

"You need to get out of those clothes, too," she said, eyeing his dripping greatcoat.

He shrugged out of his coat and tossed it on the floor. "Dickie," he yelled out the door, "we need some dry clothes."

The young man dashed into the shed and grimaced at Sabrina. "Sorry, my lady."

"All will be forgiven if you can find something for her to wear," said Graeme.

"And something for Mr. Kendrick," Sabrina added.

Dickie rummaged in a trunk. "We only got stockings, breeches, and shirts."

"As long as they're dry." And clean, she hoped. "Anything for Mr. Kendrick?"

"Aye. Magnus used to sleep here, too." Dickie began pulling clothes out.

Graeme eased aside the blanket and unbuttoned her pelisse. His eyebrows shot up. "Your evening gown?"

"I didn't have time to change into appropriate rescue attire."

His gaze narrowed to green slits. "You shouldn't have been rescuing at all."

"And you shouldn't have gone and gotten kidnapped."

He winced. "Good point."

"Here be some towels, sir," Dickie said.

Graeme gently wiped her face, then briskly went to work on her hair.

"I have a suggestion," Sabrina said, her voice muffled by the towel.

"Yes?"

"You stop getting kidnapped, and I'll stop falling into lakes."

He pulled back the towel, tipped up her chin, and pressed a hard kiss to her lips. His tongue dipped into her mouth, tasting her with a passion that almost knocked her flat. Sabrina clutched at his wet shirt. If she'd thought she was drowning before, she was mistaken. Because now she was drowning in Graeme—the scent, the taste, the feel of him, the emotions that poured through his desperate kiss and into her very soul.

And suddenly, she was no longer cold. In Graeme's arms, she knew she would never be cold again.

When Dickie cleared his throat, Graeme reluctantly released her.

"Yes, Dickie?"

The poor lad had blushed as red as a cherry. "Here be the clothes, sir," he said pointing to a stack on the table. "Will ye be needin' anything else?"

"No, lad. Just tell the others that we'll change and be right out."

Dickie scampered out the door.

"He seems like a nice boy for someone you kicked in the nutmegs."

Graeme choked. "Magnus told you."

"Yes."

"I take it Magnus had a change of heart when it came to Jackie." He stood her up and turned her around to unbutton her dress.

"Yes, thank goodness." She craned over her shoulder to look at him. "Apparently, I'm going into business with Magnus."

"Sorry. I had to come up with something on the fly."

"Whatever you said is fine. As long as you're safe."

"As long as *you're* safe, lass. Don't ever scare me like that again."

"I suppose you'll just have to marry me and make sure that nothing like this ever happens again."

"You know I will," he answered.

When he pressed a soft kiss to the back of her neck, she shivered.

"Still cold?"

She smiled. "The opposite."

He finally wrestled the soaked gown off then wrapped her again in the blanket.

"Knock, knock. Is it safe to come in?" Royal peered around the door, holding a bedraggled piece of fabric. "Found it."

"My reticule!" Sabrina exclaimed.

"Aye, and everything's there, money and jewelry."

"Thank you so much, Royal," she earnestly replied. "For everything."

He bowed his head. "Thank *you*, my lady, for saving my brother's life."

Graeme stripped off his shirt. "We'll just get changed and be right out, all right?"

"No rush."

"Royal?" Graeme said as his brother started to close the door.

"Yes?"

"Thank you for taking care of her."

Royal smiled. "Och, laddie, that's what Kendricks do, ye ken. We take care of one another."

"I ken," Graeme softly replied.

When the door closed, he turned back to Sabrina. "All right, my darling lassie. Let's get you warmly dressed and back home where you belong."

She went up on tiptoe to kiss him. "Where *we* belong."

His arms went around her. "Aye, that."

She nestled against him.

Home. With Graeme. Nothing had ever sounded so right.

Epilogue

Bellwood Manor, Northumberland
November 1822

Graeme studied the picture that had pride of place in the hall. Dozens of paintings hung in the long portrait gallery, but none as lovely as this one of a joyfully smiling young woman dressed in a simple, flowing gown. Sitting on a rustic bench in a garden, she held an impish-looking toddler on her lap. That imp, with her golden curls and peacock-blue eyes, had grown up to be the darling lass Graeme held in his arms.

"Your mother was a true beauty."

Sabrina leaned against his chest as she gazed up at Lady Musgrave. "Father always said she was the sweetest, most gentle-tempered woman he'd ever met." Sabrina tilted her head back to smile at Graeme. "Unlike me, the bossy sort."

Graeme turned her so he could give her a kiss.

"I'll not have you defaming my bride," he said. "She's the sweetest lassie in all of Britain."

"She's certainly the happiest." Sabrina patted his chest. "Thank you for doing so much to make Father comfortable. I think he's actually enjoying himself. He was quite approving of tonight's dinner, even with so many guests and such an elaborate meal."

The formal party was the conclusion of their official wedding celebrations. Sabrina had worried that her father would be overwhelmed, but the Kendricks had stepped up to help, coddling the old boy with unfailing kindness and patience. Rather hilariously, Musgrave had taken a particular shine to Angus. The old gents gabbed for hours, complaining about their aches and pains. Angus, healthy as a bull, had invented a host of imaginary ailments, each more inventive than the next. Since Musgrave liked nothing better than talking about his health, Grandda's strategy had worked like a charm.

In fact, the evening was going so well that Graeme and Sabrina had managed to sneak away for a bit. Sabrina had wanted to spend time with her mother, and Graeme had wanted a few stolen kisses with his bride.

"I'm hoping your da will also approve of his new son-in-law, eventually," Graeme joked.

Sabrina crinkled her nose. "He will. I promise."

"Good thing we didn't give him a choice. If I had asked for your hand first, I suspect he'd have put a bullet through my heart."

Graeme and Sabrina had tied the knot in Scotland. There'd still been a pile of problems to sort out at Lochnagar, and Sabrina had been determined to quickly fix as many as possible. That had meant a stay of several weeks. Since Ainsley and Royal had wished to return to Edinburgh, leaving Sabrina without a chaperone, there'd been only one solution: marriage. And with the deed done, any objections from her father would be forestalled.

Less than a week after Graeme had pulled Sabrina out of the loch, Reverend Brown had married them. Royal and Ainsley had served as their official witnesses, and the villagers of Dunlaggan as their unofficial ones. The villagers had insisted on throwing a grand wedding fete on the town green. The ladies of Dunlaggan had provided the food, Monroe the ale, and Magnus several casks of excellent—if illegal—whisky. Sabrina, in a pretty white gown and with a wreath of flowers in her hair, had glowed with happiness throughout the simple but heartfelt celebrations.

As for Graeme, bringing his bride back to Lochnagar had been the best moment of his life. The trials and sorrows of days gone by were now firmly in the past. Those sorrows could now rest gently in the past, never forgotten, but no longer weighing him down.

After a month, Graeme and Sabrina had returned to Edinburgh for a visit before heading to Bellwood Manor to face Sabrina's father. Musgrave had wanted a proper *ton* celebration in London, but Sabrina had insisted on the family estate in Northumberland. It had been years since she and her father had visited Bellwood, and she was determined to ensure that all was well at the old family pile. Most of the Kendricks had joined them, although Lord and Lady Arnprior had sent their regrets, since Vicky had recently given birth to a healthy baby boy and wasn't yet up to traveling.

"Speaking of shooting you," Sabrina said, "I do think Father gave you a very nice present."

"It was a grand and generous present. And very practical."

His father-in-law had gifted him with a truly splendid set of matched pistols from Manton's. Graeme had found it a surprising gift from an elderly man afraid of his own shadow, until he'd received a stern lecture from Musgrave on protecting Sabrina in *the wilds of Scotland*. Graeme had solemnly thanked his father-in-law, promising to keep Musgrave's daughter safe always.

"Although I do think Father should have given me the

pistols," Sabrina added. "I've done just as much rescuing as you have."

"I sincerely hope those days are behind us." Graeme reached into his pocket. "Speaking of presents, I've got something for you."

Sabrina wagged a finger. "Graeme Kendrick, you simply must stop giving me presents. It's getting ridiculous."

"I've hardly given you anything," he protested.

She held up her hand, which sported a band studded with diamonds and sapphires.

"Well, I can't have you running around without a wedding ring," he said. "All the fellows will think you're a spinster and try to flirt with you. Then I'd have to shoot them."

"With Father's pistols?"

"I'll only use those on smugglers."

"We don't have any smugglers. We now have a perfectly respectable distillery, and I predict it will be the best in Scotland, thanks to you."

"You mean, thanks to Magnus."

It turned out that Magnus was a veritable prodigy when it came to making Highland whisky. With Graeme managing the legalities and the setup, and Nick providing additional support, they were well on their way to establishing a bang-up distillery in Dunlaggan that would provide jobs for the villagers for years to come.

Graeme found it hilarious that he was finally able to put the skills of his misspent youth to good use.

"No, I mean thanks to you," Sabrina said. "Your work will do more to revitalize Dunlaggan than anything."

He kissed the tip of her nose. "It's a joint venture, lass. None of this would have happened without you."

"That's true. I am rather wonderful," she said with the adorably smug smile he loved so much.

"Which is why I'd like to give you this particular present."

She let out a dramatic sigh. "I suppose you'll just pester me until I let you."

"I will. Now, close your eyes and put out your hand."

When she did as instructed, Graeme opened the small velvet bag and carefully tipped the contents into her palm.

Sabrina's eyes flew open. "My mother's pearls! How did you find them?"

"Aden did most of the work. Took a bit of sleuthing, but he finally tracked them down."

Since the theft at the theater, Graeme had been determined to find the pearls. Aden had been more than ready to help, finally unearthing them in a small pawnshop. It had cost Graeme a fair sum to get them back, but the look on Sabrina's face made it all worth it.

She gave him a teary smile. "You are the most wonderful man in the world. And Father will be absolutely thrilled."

"I already told him, which is probably why he hasn't shot me yet."

She let out a watery giggle and unclasped the magnificent set of pearls she was already wearing, placing them on a nearby table.

"Love, those pearls are your wedding present from the king," Graeme pointed out.

She turned her back so he could fasten the old set around her neck. "Pish, they're not nearly as nice as Mamma's pearls. Besides, this necklace helped bring us together, so that makes it even more special."

The king's present was extravagantly expensive and truly beautiful. But to Sabrina, the sentimental value made her mother's pearls infinitely more precious.

Once Graeme had fastened the necklace, he nestled her back against him as they looked up at her mother's portrait.

"I so wish she were here to see this," Sabrina said. "I wish I could tell her about everything, especially you."

He gently tapped her breastbone, over her heart. "Och, lass, your dear ma is always with you, right here."

She twisted a bit to look at him. "The way your mother is always with you, my darling."

"Aye."

Graeme now understood that his mother had always been in his heart and in the love of his family. The unwavering loyalty and devotion of his grandfather and brothers through those reckless, difficult years had helped to bring Graeme to safe harbor with his lovely lass.

After a few quiet moments, Sabrina stirred. "I have a present for you, too."

He kissed her golden curls. "You're my present, love. Nothing can top that."

"True, but this comes close."

She slipped from his arms and retrieved a vellum packet from a chair by the table.

"What's that?" he asked.

"Open it and see."

He flipped it over and frowned. "That's the royal seal."

Sabrina twirled a finger, as if to hurry him up.

Graeme broke the seal and extracted a letter written in an elaborate hand on fine parchment. He quickly scanned it, blinked in disbelief, and then slowly read it again.

"Well?" Sabrina asked with a touch of impatience.

Stunned, he took a few moments to answer. "A knighthood? You must be joking."

"Not even a little bit. The next time we're in London, His Majesty will confer a knighthood on you for services rendered to the Crown."

"I truly don't know what to say." It was ridiculous, perhaps, certainly undeserved . . . and yet rather wonderful, for all that.

"I know you don't care about these things, but Aden and

Dominic were quite determined. And of course I thought it a splendid idea." She gave a little chuckle. "Father will like it, too. Then he can't fuss about you being a plain old Scotsman anymore."

When Graeme didn't answer, she grimaced. "Graeme, if you truly don't want it . . ."

He swept her into his arms and pressed a resounding kiss to her lips. "Of course I want it, daft lass. I'm just rather dumbstruck. It's not as if I deserve the honor."

She gave him a little shake. "Graeme Kendrick, you are the finest man I have *ever* known. No one deserves a knighthood more than you."

He had to clear his throat before answering. "Och, my brothers will have a field day, ye ken. I'll never hear the end of it."

"I told your family before dinner. They are all incredibly proud. Angus was so excited I was afraid he would ruin the surprise."

"Sir Graeme Kendrick." He let out a ghost of a laugh. "Who would have believed it?"

"Only everyone who knows you." Then she patted his chest. "Well, Sir Graeme, I suppose we'd better get back to our guests. Father will start to wonder where we are."

"We can't have dear, old da fretting about you." Graeme offered his arm. "Ready, Lady Sabrina?"

"It's Lady Kendrick, if you please. And I'm ready for anything, now that I've got you. Even a dunking in the Serpentine."

"Pulling you out of that lake was the best thing I ever did, ye ken."

Sabrina tucked herself close to his side. "I ken very well. It was the luckiest day of my life, because I met you."

"The luck was all mine, sweet lass. The luck was all mine."

Connect with Us

Visit us online at
KensingtonBooks.com
to read more from your favorite authors, see books
by series, view reading group guides, and more.

(Join us on social media)

for sneak peeks, chances to win books and prize packs,
and to share your thoughts with other readers.

facebook.com/kensingtonpublishing
twitter.com/kensingtonbooks

Tell us what you think!

To share your thoughts, submit a review,
or sign up for our eNewsletters, please visit:
KensingtonBooks.com/TellUs.

Books by Bestselling Author
Fern Michaels